Raising the Queen of Heaven

Additional works by Mr. Knape
from Preparation Press:

The Magic of Consciousness series:

Workshops

(Scheduled for publication in 2005)

Mother

(Scheduled for publication in 2006)

Daughter

(Scheduled for publication in 2006)

Father

(Scheduled for publication in 2007)

Son

(Scheduled for publication in 2007)

The Guardian Chronicles series:

The Knight of the Temple, Vol. 1

(Scheduled for publication in 2006)

The Aquarian Christ

(Scheduled for publication in 2006)

Further information on these and other works
is available at: www.preparationpress.com

Raising the Queen of Heaven

By Glen Knape

Preparation Press
Whittier, CA

Raising the Queen of Heaven
by Glen Knape

First edition, 2005

Preparing the way

Preparation Press
Whittier, California
www.preparationpress.com

Cover Art: "La Dame du Lac", by Lucette Bourdin,
http://www.lbourdin.com/

ISBN 0-9760084-0-8

Disclaimer

This is a work of nonfiction, structured as a dialogue.

All of the characters included herein are entirely fictional. They represent archetypes, not real persons, and any resemblance between them and real persons, living or deceased, is purely coincidental. The opinions expressed by these characters do not represent those of the author, the publisher, or anyone else. The location of the classes, and the classes themselves, are also wholly imaginary. No such location exists and no such classes occurred. They are all, simply and entirely, a means of posing ideas, asking and answering questions, and taking the reader through a series of inner experiences.

However, the ideas and inner experiences at the heart of the text, around which the characters, setting, and classes revolve, are entirely real.

Table of Contents

Appendix

Prelude

I was almost done preparing the tea tray when Chantel flew in and told me the students were beginning to arrive.

Like all angels, Chantel's thoughts look like waves of vibrating light and color. Hers are mostly violets, which I've always heard as a soft contralto vibrating in the center of my head. Quinn says the tele-thingy in my brain translates the light into words.

I glanced past the new dining room window treatment just as someone's shadow slid past it to our front door. I opened the door at the knock, revealing a tall, slender, junior-Aragorn beefstick, with muscular shoulders and short brown hair, in a t-shirt, blue Levis, and a brick-red aura that sounded a bit like the chorus from Quinn's favorite opera.[1] He grinned down at me, offered his hand, and said, "Hi! I'm John. You must be Ellora?"

I smiled back, nodded, retrieved my hand, and said, "Quinn will be right out. The class is meeting in the library."

Chantel flew back out to keep watch, and I led John down the hall, through Quinn's newly-cleaned home office —scooping up a copy of Plato's *Dialogues* from the "refile" spot as we passed— to the library. John paused at the threshold, gaped up at the ceiling, and said, "Wow!"

The library was a two-story ad-on whose walls were packed with bookshelves, and sprinkled with shaman's masks and odd bits of old magical tools. Straight ahead, a cast-iron stairway spiraled up to the fiction section in

---

[1] Quinn: *The Ride of the Valkyries*, by Wagner

1

the loft. John headed for one of the white plastic chairs that encircled the center of the room, and I refiled the Dialogues in the western philosophy section and returned to the kitchen.

I placed Ginger Twist and Green Tea on the tray, packets of stevia in the sugar bowl, soymilk in the creamer, and carried the service into the library. I felt something's gaze on me, and glanced up to the rafters. There I spotted Maxwell's eyes, twin stars glowering from the shadows. Quinn says air elementals are really flighty, and I'd no idea how he'd managed to befriend Max, but he was always around somewhere.

John was standing in front of the gun case, admiring the swords, and blocking the credenza below it. I said, "Excuse me."

His aura swirled, and snapped to a stop in the shape of a ghostly khaki uniform. John said, "Yes mam!" as he stepped back, and I set the tray on the credenza, next to the coffee makers, bottled waters, and ceramic mugs.

John reached for the coffee, and I checked the dry-erase board next to Quinn's chair and the tape recorder on the side-table next to my chair, turned on the fans with the remote, and on my way back to the kitchen checked that the 'puters were off and the phones were on silent answer.

There was a muffled, "Yip!" from the garage, and I walked through the kitchen and out to that tool-filled workspace. There I found Guido sitting on his haunches, making sad-puppy eyes at me and radiating muddled yellow-orange and pink. He was a six-month old mutt — his license said Cocker Spaniel–Pit Bull— that we'd rescued from the pound. He has the Cocker coloring and playfulness, and the Bull build and tenacity. The wall fan was keeping him cool enough, he had his doggy pillow, plenty of water and I'd fed him, but he was lonely and wanted to play. I scratched behind his ears, radiated cool–blue light into his aura, and told him he was a good dog and that I'd be back as soon as I could. His swirling aura started to slow, clear, and quiet, and then the doorbell rang.

The rest of the students arrived by ones and twos over the next fifteen or twenty minutes. I escorted each of them into the library and made sure they had everything they needed. They'd been chatting together softly for a couple minutes when a long "OM" sounded faintly from the meditation room, and a few moments later Quinn joined us.

He wasn't bad looking for an old man—fiftyish, slender, with khaki pants and an earth-tone plaid short-sleeve, a real goatee —not one of those angsty wanna-beards— and graying hair that he combed back. He was fashion challenged when I found him, but we'd done some shopping since then. His aura blazed around his head in a bright indigo corona, sounding a chorus of silent om's into the ether, and I considered matching accessories. Quinn smiled, said a few words of greeting, and sat in his chair with his back to a wall of books.

When everyone had quieted, he nodded to me, and I turned on the recorder.

✦

Quinn: "We'll begin with a meditation."

(A blue-white line of light shot upward from the center of Quinn's head, blue-white lines shot out to each of the students —whose auras rang like mistuned bells— and from them went up and out of my sight.)

Quinn: "Sit comfortably with your back straight, your feet flat on the floor and your arms on the armrests or in your lap.

"Close your eyes and try to sense where you live inside

of your body, where you, the conscious thinking 'I' reside within your physical form. (pause)

"Point to that place.

"Take a deep breath, and open your eyes.

(Everyone opened their eyes, and gazed expectantly at Quinn)

Quinn: "The place where you pointed is where you, the consciousness indwelling your body, live now. You have not always resided there, nor will you always do so. As you progress on the spiritual path, your home in your body will change in reflection of that growth. Eventually you will be able to move your place of residence at will, by changing your state of awareness or consciousness.

"Now, in order to understand where we are, the place where we reside as a consciousness, we have to give that place a context. We need to understand both where we have been and where we are going. This is true of individuals, groups, and of humanity as a whole.

"In this course, we are going to explore where humanity has been during the last four ages —Gemini, Taurus, Aries, and Pisces— so that we can understand where we are now, and where we are going in the Age of Aquarius. In the process, we will be taking our next step, individually and as a group, thereby helping humanity take its next step as a kingdom within the One Life.

"Thus, in a sense, this course is about movement, the magical motion of consciousness which creates everything that is.

"Are there any questions so far?"

(Everyone shook their head or said no.)

Quinn: "Well then, since we don't all know each other yet, let's go around the room and introduce ourselves, including our names and spiritual backgrounds. Just to start things off, I'll begin.

Dramatis Personae

Quinn: "As you all know, I'm Quinn MacAndrews. Spiritually, I was raised a potato-salad Christian...Yes Wil?"

Wil: "Potato salad?"

(Quinn grinned) "They were more concerned with social activities than doctrine."

Wil: "Ah."

Quinn: "I've been studying the Wisdom since the mid '70's, and teaching since the mid '80's. Among other things, I'm a Freemason —in a Lodge that recognizes and performs the inner work of the craft— and a practitioner of the Magic of Consciousness."

(Quinn turned to his left) "Thea?"

(To outer sight, Thea was a plain, slightly matronly woman who would have been nearly invisible in any mall in North America. But inner vision revealed a wide-open heart, infusing the room with pure, yellow light.)

Thea: "My name is Thea Laine, I'm a non-practicing Catholic, a nurse, and mother of five children. I've been studying the Wisdom for five years, have taken *The Nature of The Soul* course twice so far, and I'm just so happy to be here and working with you all!"

Quinn: "Thank you, Thea. Tess?"

(Tess appeared to be somewhere in her late 20's, a couple inches taller than me, maybe five foot two, a natural strawberry blond with wavy hair, boyishly slender —a real hottie. She had one of the overall clearest auras in the room— azure swirled around her waist and heart, and yellow at her throat shaded into amber around her forehead.)

Tess: "Hi! I'm Tess Slany. I'm an acupuncturist, I don't have any formal religious training but I've studied on my own a lot, including *The Nature of The Soul*, and I do a lot of charity work setting up free clinics in distressed communities."

Quinn: "Thank you, Tess. John?"

(John's aura was infused with brickish red that darkened to near black at his waist but clarified to burgundy around his neck and brow.)

John: "I'm John Giles. I was in the army up until last year. Since then I've done a lot of reading, on a variety of spiritual subjects. I heard about this class at a Full Moon meeting, applied for it, and here I am."

Quinn: "Thank you, John. Ema?"

(Ema was a large, grandmotherly woman. Her harsh Nordic features were softened by age and smile lines, she wore loose pants and a white blouse, and her short, gray-white hair was brushed away from her face. An energy vortex behind her lower back sucked in dark muddy energy, swirled it around inside her belly, and spat out clean, clear golden light from an out-vortex just above her waist.)

Ema: "My name is Ema Gudrun. I was raised Lutheran, on the family farm in Minnesota. My husband Bill was a Sergeant in the Army, and I was a secretary. We raised our children at bases the world over, but are retired now. We come here to be with our grandchildren, and I study the Wisdom for three years now."

Quinn: "Thank you, Ema. Colette?"

(Colette was maybe ten years older than me, about twenty-two, five foot four with black hair gelled into a rumpled helmet, and Asianly features. Her aura swirled with vital energy, mostly chestnut brown, but with flashes of lemon near her waist and hints of saffron by her throat.)

6

Prelude

Colette: "I'm Colette Taji Averill. I didn't have any early religious training. I've been attending a Science of Mind church, but it feels like something's missing. This is my first class in this... Wisdom stuff."

Quinn: "Thank you Colette. El?"

Me: "Well... I'm Ellora Porter. My mom was afraid of spiritual stuff, and kept me away from it. But after she died, my grandparents put me in a Christian boarding school. The teachers power-freaked and tried to do a Father Damien[2] on me, so I got gone and found dad. He's helping me understand a lot of things —etheric vision, angels, magic, meditation and stuff."

(Rosy light infused Quinn's lower aura when I said "dad", publicly acknowledging the relationship for the first time. Some of the other's raised their hands, but Quinn waved them off.)

Quinn: "Ummm... Thank you El. Ed?"

(Icky gray smog blanketed his lower body, fading over his chest where golden flashes glowed like fireflies in a foggy night. Further up, the smog cleared and the flashes became sparks at his throat. He was the most nerdishly suppressed of the group, and wore a pale-pinkish dress shirt with three pens in the pocket, matching slacks, and black-framed glasses.)

Ed: "Hi! I'm Ed Mooney. I was an investment banker, but was thrust out during the hi-tech madness —I kept asking how and when all those IPO's were going to show a profit. I'm an Episcopalian because I like the ritual, but I find the theology limited. I went looking for something more inclusive and wound up here."

Quinn: "Thank you Ed. Jeff?"

(Jeff looked the weirdest to outer sight. He had long

---

[2] El: The fictional character, Father Damien Karras, the first priest in the 1970 movie "The Exorcist."

blond hair that hung past his shoulders, a graying beard tied into a pony tail —with crystals and beads woven in— patched and faded cut-off jeans, and a tie-dye t-shirt with a weird symbol printed on it.[3] His aura had bright orange around his throat, darkened below to smog-brown at his waist, with firefly flashes of apricot.)

Jeff: "My name is Jeff Carver. I'm an artist, mostly wood sculpture in a very nativistic, primitive style. I was raised Four Square Gospel, but did the hippie thing in college and got into eastern stuff—Buddhism, Hinduism and like that. After college I moved into a commune, did the ashram scene in India, hiked the Himal, and eventually wound up back here pretty much burnt out on all of it. Last few years I've gotten into nature spirits, devas, and the Great Mother."

Quinn: "Thank you Jeff. Terry?"

(Avocado-green pulsed out Terry's waist, cascaded up to the throat, and pulsed out from there as a bright lime green that reached up toward Terry's forehead.)

Terry: "Hello everyone! I'm Terry List. I'm an Electronics Engineer, currently unemployed by the dot bomb. I was raised Christian, but we didn't attend church much, mostly just Christmas and Easter. I really wasn't interested until college, when the *Celestine Prophecy* came out. That led to studies of telepathy, distant viewing, Lazarus, and now this class."

Quinn: "Thank you Terry. Bhikku?"

(Bhikku was darkly handsome, with a pale violet aura centered over his heart, thickening to plum elsewhere, and a hint of bright lilac fluttering like a butterfly atop his head.)

---

[3] Quinn: It was the Tibetan symbol for "Aum". Jeff looks like a hippie version of Captain Jack Sparrow (Johnny Depp's character in *Pirates of the Caribbean*).

Bhikku: "My name is Bhikku Anand. My family is traditional Hindu, but mostly for the social life. My parents wanted me to major in electronics at U.S.C. like my cousins, but I transferred to religious studies my first year. These days I'd say I'm spiritual but not religious. I attended Quinn's lecture at the Church of Truth, applied to this class, and now I am here."

Quinn: "Thank you Bhikku. Wil?"

(Wil had a rosy throat, a band of maroon around his waist, and flashes of green at his forehead.)

Wil: "I'm Wilber Abbot or Wil. I was a Marine during the late 60's, discovered the Bailey books and Theosophy during college, and have studied that for many years. A couple years ago I found the works of Lucille Cedercrans, and read *The Nature of the Soul*. I serve on the board of directors of several spiritual groups, and have lectured all over the U.S. and in Europe."

Quinn: "Thank you Wil. Celine?"

(Indigo-white cascaded into the top of her head from out of my *sight*, flowing into a blue-white point in the center of her head, out through a vortex in her brow, and radiating teal and turquoise into the room. She was as thin as one of Brian Froud's Faeries, and waves of color flowed out and back from her brow and heart in great, wing-like fans of light.)

Celine: "Hello everyone! My name is Celine Garner. I didn't have any religious training until college, when I joined the local Theosophical Lodge. I learned about the Bailey works there, and became an astrologer and a co-mason. I heard about *The Nature of the Soul* from *The New Age Professional*, and moved out here to study it. Since then, I've taken *Nature of the Soul*, *Creative Thinking*, *The Soul and Its Instrument*, and *Practitioner Training*, and applied to this class as soon as it opened."

Quinn: "Thank you Celine. Yes Wil?"

Wil: "The New Age Professional?"

Quinn: "A magazine an associate of mine used to publish.

"Colette?"

Colette: "Celine, what's co-masonry?"

Quinn: "Briefly please."

Celine: "Well, it's a modern expression of the ancient mysteries, the same as Freemasonry, but we don't distinguish between genders and most of our members have some sort of esoteric background."

Quinn: "Which brings us to our present subject...

Prelude

Quinn: "The ancient mysteries are teachings that present spiritual Truth in symbolic ritual and allegorical tales. Those teachings have always been available to humanity, through popular myth, public rites, and hidden rituals.[4]

"Each version of the public myths and rites was designed for a particular people, in a specific time and place. The myths interpreted the secret rituals —which were hidden from all but their initiates— into those symbols which the people could best appreciate.

"Each version of the hidden rituals was also designed for a particular time and place. The hidden rituals interpreted the Path of spiritual growth and development into a symbolic experience, and started seekers on the quest of that Path.

"There was never, nor could there be, a single 'correct' interpretation of the Spiritual Path. It was, is, and must be, re-interpreted in every time and place, by every people, and by every group and individual who walks it.

"However, during the last age this basic truth was forgotten by many. Religious intolerance in the West drove the mysteries underground. The path of initiation became furtive and secret, hidden from everyone but the elect. Thus hidden, the fragments of mysteries that remained were gradually colored with the patriarchal views of the times.

---

[4] Many historians apply the term "ancient mysteries" to the ritual rites that appeared in Greece and Rome. However, its use here is somewhat different.

11

"The resulting over-emphasis on The Divine Father and 'His' Son obscured the reality of The Divine Mother and 'Her' Daughter, formerly symbolized in the more balanced myths, rites, and rituals of the ancient mysteries.

"Both the Divine Mother and the Divine Daughter were veiled, diminished, and distorted.

"In Raising the Queen of Heaven we will explore the place of the Great Goddess in the path of spiritual growth and development. The course will reveal the balanced relationship we must have with the Tetrad of Divine Mother, Daughter, Father, and Son if we are to discover our true identity and take up our purpose, place and function within the One Life.

Summary

Quinn: "Now, each of the lessons in this course will consist of three sections:

"The first section will be a meditation exercise that aligns us with the abstract Truth overshadowing the course.

"The second section will focus on the myths that help us understand the hidden rituals, secret initiations, and public myths of the path of spiritual growth and development.

"The third section will be an inner spiritual journey —a quest through our creative imagination— that takes us through the course the consciousness follows as it moves between the Aspects of Divinity.

"If we are able to realize enough of the Truth overshadowing this course, then by the time we finish it we will, by our creative inner action, have helped raise the Queen of Heaven to Her rightful position, helped restore right relationship between the Divine Feminine and Masculine, and helped rejoin that which was sundered at creation.

Closing Ritual

Quinn: "Having said all that, it's time to close this opening lesson. Now some of you have a lot of experience with this sort of thing, and some less, so everyone please follow along as best you can.

"Close your eyes, and sit up straight, with your hands in your lap or resting on the arms of the chair, and your feet flat on the floor.

"Beginning with your toes, relax your physical body. You may imagine the muscles relaxing, simply command them to relax, or feel a tingling warmth, or imagine a golden light —whatever works for you.

Continue up from your toes to your feet... lower legs... thighs... abdomen... lower back... waist —paying particular attention to the diaphragm... upper back... chest... fingers... hands... forearms... upper arms... shoulders... neck and throat —paying particular attention to the vocal cords and base of the tongue... muscles of the jaw... scalp... and behind the eyes.

"Recognize that, having impressed the mind, the ideas, concepts, and thought-forms overshadowing this course will gradually move through the emotions to emerge in the brain awareness as conscious realization and new behavior in the world of affairs...

"Maintaining the receptivity to those ideas and concepts, take a deep breath, slowly relax the attention, and open your eyes.

"Any questions?...

"OK, that's all for today."

Lesson 1

Discovering the Inner Vision

The New Path of Initiation

The indigo stone on Quinn's bolo matched his halo, almost as if he'd done it on purpose. Quinn picked up his Rosicrucian mug, sipped his tea, and said, "Good evening everyone."

He acknowledged their replies with nods, and asked, "Jeff, how's the show doing?"

Jeff replied, "Pretty good, considering the market these days. I've sold six pieces already."

"Including that chair thing?"

"Recline of the West'? Yeah, to a couple from Claremont."

"Great!

Quinn glanced around, and said, "Well, everyone's here. Let's get started."

I turned on the recorder.

Opening Alignment

Quinn: "Close your eyes, and sit up straight, with your hands in your lap or resting on the arms of the chair, and your feet flat on the floor.

"Beginning with your toes, relax your physical body. You may imagine the muscles relaxing, simply command them to relax, or feel a tingling warmth, or imagine a golden light —whatever works for you.

"Continue up from your toes to your feet... lower legs... thighs... abdomen... lower back... waist —paying particular attention to the diaphragm... upper back... chest... fingers... hands... forearms... upper arms... shoulders... neck and throat —paying particular attention to the vocal cords and base of the tongue... muscles of the jaw... scalp... and behind the eyes.

"Become receptive to that truth or wisdom overshadowing this evening's lesson...

"Maintaining that receptivity, take a deep breath, and open your eyes."

A Coup in Heaven

Quinn: "Has everyone been studying their preparatory reading, including their myth tale?"

(Everyone nodded or murmured yes. Quinn took a sip of his tea, and then began.)

Quinn: "OK. In this first lesson we're going to cover the basic structure of divinity.

"Now, it's been said that there is only One God out of whom all things flow and within whom all exists. This is quite correct.

"Yes Jeff?"

Jeff: "Is that one-being male or female?"

Quinn: "It's more like Yin and Yang, but we'll get to that in a minute."

Quinn: "This single Being has been described as 'the One about whom naught may be said'. We cannot really say anything about the One Divine Being, for that Being exists beyond any *thing* that we can recognize or identify.

"Now, although this no thing cannot be recognized or described, it can be represented by a symbol such as the empty circle or zero.

(Quinn stood up and drew a large red circle on the

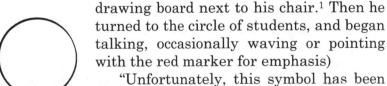

drawing board next to his chair.[1] Then he turned to the circle of students, and began talking, occasionally waving or pointing with the red marker for emphasis)

"Unfortunately, this symbol has been misinterpreted and distorted from the

---

[1] Quinn: An easel holding a pad of poster-sized sheets of white paper.

representation of no thing into the symbol of 'nothing'. The result is the illusion that all things are separate—that the relationships between things cannot be counted and are not real or important. This illusion deforms our mathematical system and is impressed on our children along with basic arithmetic. Now this last point is very, very important, for how can our children value relationships when they're taught that relationships don't count?

"Thea?"

Thea: "That relationships don't count?"

Quinn: "How much is one plus one?"

Thea: "Two."

Quinn: "What about the relationships between those two, such as between two people?

"In a mundane, practical sense, the zero is a placeholder in numerical calculations.[2] When used in this fashion, the relationships between people, between people and the world around them, are not and cannot be counted. They aren't 'real'.

"However, in the higher sense, the zero symbolizes that no thing, which is everything, before it is anything. In other words, it represents the One Divine Source out of which all comes and through which everything is related.

Wil: "The zero represents the One about whom naught may be said?"

Quinn: "What does 'naught' mean?"

Wil: "Naught? 'Nothing' or—"

Quinn: "Zero. Precisely.

"Now, the primary difficulty with the concept that the zero represents nothing is that it veils the reality that everything is part of one thing.

"When the zero represents nothing, arithmetic as-

---

[2] Quinn: See the Addendum to Lesson 1

sumes that all things are isolated, and that there are no relationships between them that can be counted. Thus, 'one plus one equals two'.

"This is the mathematical basis of the delusion of separation. Children taught this system of arithmetic automatically learn that everything and everyone is separate, and that what affects one person or thing has no necessary relationship to or effect on any other person or thing. It teaches them that whatever they do to another person —an animal, a plant, a rock, to anything— has no relationship to and thus does not affect them. This is a complete denial of the One Life.

"When the zero represents 'everything before it is any thing,' arithmetic assumes that all things are related and that those relationships must be counted. Thus, 'one plus one equals three' (the two things and the relationship between them).

"This is the foundation of a correct system of mathematics. Children taught this system automatically learn that everything is an interconnected part of a One Life, and that whatever affects one person or thing automatically affects everyone and everything.

"When we were taught the separative system of arithmetic as children, we learned the delusion of separation along with it, and now find it very difficult to recognize the reality of relationships as adults. This recognition is made even harder by the nature of the One Life.

"As indicated earlier, the One Divine Source of everything is so far above us that there is nothing we can know or say about it.

"It has no purpose that our self or Soul can identify.

"It has no consciousness for our Soul to relate with.

"It has no thoughts or ideas for our minds to think about.

"It has no emotions for us to feel.

"It has no physical-dense forms for us to see, hear, touch, smell, or taste."

Jeff: "What about gender?"

Quinn: "Gender or sex is a product of polarity, which we'll get to in a moment, but in any case the One does not have it.

"Without any thing for us to comprehend, our human consciousness, mind, emotions, and brain are simply not capable of perceiving or interpreting that One Divine Source.

"However, it is the ultimate source of everything. Thus, every thing that exists emanates from this no thing, and we can, of course, perceive and know some of the expressions of that no thing...

(Quinn nodded to Jeff.)

"which brings us to polarity.

"The first of these perceivable expressions is a Trinity, the Three Aspects of Divinity. This Trinity is sometimes symbolized by a circle with a dot at the center.

(Quinn stepped back to the board and drew a red dot in the middle of the large zero. Then he turned, and faced the circle of students again)

"Over the last few thousand years, the patriarchal bias of western culture has severely distorted our concept of the Trinity, and even this distorted view of the Trinity is itself seldom presented accurately or clearly. As a result, the concept of the Trinity has obscured rather than revealed the true nature of the Three Aspects of Divinity.

"The actual Trinity is perhaps best illustrated by an electro-magnet.

(Quinn returned to the board and drew the following

next to the circle-dot.)

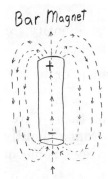

Bar Magnet

"Like the bar magnet, the Trinity has a positive pole, a negative pole, and a magnetic field of relationship between the two poles. These three things —Positive Pole, Negative Pole, and Magnetic Field— are actually One Thing, the first expression of that no thing from which all comes. These Three Aspects of Divinity function so much like an electromagnet that we may apply the scientific 'laws' of electromagnets to them:

"If you have one pole, you must have two poles.

"The two poles must always be equal in strength.

"If you have two poles, you must have a magnetic field.

"The strength of the magnetic field is determined by the strength of the poles and their distance from each other—the closer the poles, the more powerful the magnetic field.[3]

"Yes Terry?"

Terry: "Is this the Christian Trinity —what it is and how it actually works?"

Quinn: "Actually, it's more the other way around. The Christian Trinity is an interpretation of the actual Trinity, one of many such interpretations. But we'll get to that shortly.

"To continue...each of the Three Aspects of Divinity has its peculiar divine characteristics or energies. These characteristics include:

---

[3] Quinn: In the case of the Trinity, we might add, "the more powerful the magnetic field, the closer the poles."

"The Positive Pole is the source of purpose, power, and will, or Divine Intent.

"The Magnetic Field is consciousness, identity, or awareness.

"The Negative Pole is Divine Intelligence, or Intelligent Activity.

"There are many names and terms for these Three Aspects of Divinity, each describing them from a slightly different —but no less valid— point of view. Some of these terms are:

"First Aspect, Second Aspect, Third Aspect.

"Positive Pole, Magnetic Field, Negative Pole.

"Spirit, Consciousness, Matter.

"Father Aspect, Daughter-Son Aspect, Mother Aspect.

"God, Christ, Holy Spirit.

"YHWH, Adon, Asherah.

"First Logos, Second Logos, Third Logos.

"Divine Will, Divine Love-Wisdom, Divine Intelligence.

"Purpose, Evolution, Activity.

"Monad, Soul, Man.

"Power, Light, Form.

"Cause, Meaning, Effect.

"These Three Aspects, expressing at different levels and in different relationships, make up everything that is. Or, to put it the other way around, in order to exist, everything that exists must consist of a formulation of these Three.

"Yes Terry?"

Terry: "What do you mean they 'can't exist'?"

Quinn: "I mean that's the way creation works. In order to come into existence, anything and everything has to include all Three Aspects. The precise formulation will differ in each thing, but all Three must be there. Otherwise, it simply could not exist.

"Tess?"

Tess: "What about the Soul?"

Quinn: "The Magnetic Field is emphasized, but all Three are part of it."

Wil: "Spirit?"

Quinn: "The Positive Pole is emphasized."

Thea: "A thought or idea?"

Quinn: "The Negative Pole.

"Now wait. We could play 'what about' all evening, but we need to move on and add to the context of all this.

"Now, unlike the One Divine Essence out of which all comes, the Three Aspects can be known and experienced —through the mystical and magical process of at-one-ment. At the beginning of the inner process of union, we are receptive to the Trinity but unable to experience them directly. This forces us to rely on allegorical descriptions of them. These allegories or symbolic tales represent the divine with forms that are familiar to our daily experience and thus within the scope of our understanding.

"One of the traditional allegories, used in many ancient myths, is that of a Divine Family, which typically consists of:

"The Father Aspect or Positive Pole.

"The Mother Aspect or Negative Pole.

"The Child Aspect or Magnetic Field —the Divine Son and Daughter.

"Yes, Ellora?"

Me: "What's the Divine 'Daughter'?"

Quinn: "The inner polarity of the Soul, but we'll get to that shortly.

"The Divine Family was often used in the allegories of the Divine Marriage —symbolizing the union of the two poles— and the death of the Corn King —representing the death and resurrection of the Soul. This dual myth cycle illustrated the interaction of the Three Aspects in symbols that were familiar to the people of ancient cultures.

"Now, as our capacity for understanding increases, we learn to approach and at-one with the divine directly, through inner experience of them, via the cyclic process of aspiration, contemplation, and embodiment."

Wil: "You mean meditation?"

Quinn: "Yes, but a type of meditation that includes our entire being—physical, emotional, mental, Soul, and Spirit.

"Celine?"

Celine: "We use the Three Aspects within us to contact the Three Aspects outside of us?"

Quinn: "Well, yes, but it's not really a matter of inside or outside it's really all One sort of pretending to be many.

"Now, this three-fold process of union or at-one-ment is, in essence, the attraction —by the magnetic field— of the two poles toward each other. It is the process by which the Three again become One.

"Thus, the One Essence becomes Three, the Three become everything, everything becomes Three, and the Three again become One. This is the cycle of creation."

Thea: "Oh!"

Quinn: "Yes, Thea?"

Thea: "You mean that we, in meditation, reunite the

Three?"

Quinn: "Beginning with ourselves —that formulation of the Three which is who and what we are— yes. You see, having been born of the Three, human beings inherit the divine nature of the Trinity. Thus, every human being consists of a formulation of:

"Spirit —the Father Aspect— or Divine Purpose, Power, and Will

"Soul —the Child Aspect— identity, consciousness, or relationship

"Substance —the Mother Aspect— or energy, force, and appearance

"Because we are a formulation of the Three, we are not only capable of participating in the creative process, but we have a role in it. However, since the universal creative process includes all Three Aspects, if our creative efforts are to be successful they cannot exclude any portion of the Trinity.

"Yes, Celine?"

Celine: "How do you 'exclude' an Aspect of Divinity?"

Quinn: "Well, the usual method is polarization."

Me: "Polar what?"

Quinn: "Polarization. That's when a person or thing becomes so attached to and identified with a magnetic pole that they take on part of the characteristics of that pole.

"Bhikku?"

Bhikku: "So polarization is a way of becoming divine?"

Quinn: "Well, yes, but as with most things we have a tendency to go overboard with it. When the self or Soul identifies with one of the Divine Poles, we tend to become so fixated on the forms of that Pole that we exclude or even reject and attack the other Pole. This is seen, for instance, in those religions that address their prayers and aspirations to the Divine Father, but not to the Divine Mother.

"Yes, Jeff?"

Jeff: "Like with Christianity?"

Quinn: "Let's not get specific yet. We'll do that when we look at various myth tales.

"Now, the forms we can become attached to include:

"Mental forms —including thoughts, theological concepts, and philosophical ideas of the Divine.

"Astral or emotional forms —including visions, sounds, and other emotional feelings of the Divine.

"Physical-dense forms —including books, rituals, songs, objects, places, structures, etc.

"Yes, Bhikku?"

Bhikku: "So the goal is to free ourselves from attachment to all form?"

Quinn: "Um… Not really. Imagine, for instance, that you were a cosmonaut aboard the Mir space station (laughter and groans)… There was a breakdown and you had to go outside the station to fix it. Of course, before stepping out the airlock, you snapped a safety line to the station. But suppose when you stepped out of the station you slipped, your magnetic boots lost their grip, your safety line broke, and you floated away from the station. There you'd be, free of any and all attachment, and utterly and completely unable to do anything.

"The belief that form is bad, that the goal is to leave substance behind, is a primary example of polarization. Actually, substance is a part of who and what we are, and we could not move, we could not grow, we would not *be* without it.

"It would be much more correct to state that we have

to become fixated on the right forms at the right time.

"Yes, Jeff?"

Jeff: "Fixated?"

Quinn: "When consciousness becomes focused on, identified with, and thus attached to a form. That's how the consciousness moves.

"Ema?"

Ema: "Like inch worm, stretching, grasping, and pulling self along."

(Grins and nods)

Quinn: "Yes, very much like.

"Now, that movement of the consciousness produces experience, and the experience produces growth of the consciousness. This is a natural and normal part of the spiritual path, we all do it, and when we do it consciously, in full waking awareness of what we are doing, we become truly creative. In a sense, it's the movement of the consciousness which creates everything. It's a creative process or magical motion.

"Yes Jeff?"

Jeff: "But how does the motion of consciousness create things? It's just, well, awareness isn't it?"

Quinn: "Ahh...Now that would take a course in itself. Let's see... Didn't you do the 'magic bus' thing in the late '70's?"

Jeff: "Yeah... rebuilt a '53 Ford school bus and took it cross-country. Lived in it for a couple years."

Quinn: "OK, what would happen if one of the battery cables came loose, and then you tried to start it?"

Jeff: "Well, nothing."

Quinn: "Why?"

Jeff: "You have to have a complete circuit."

Quinn: "Exactly!

"You see, humanity as a Kingdom, and every individual human being as a member of that Kingdom, is born of the relationship between the Two Poles of Divinity. We are that relationship, that connection. Thus, when we relate one thing with another in our consciousness, we create a circuit between them.

"Terry?"

Terry: "Along which energy can flow!"

Quinn: "Along which energy must flow.

"Since we are born of the two Divine Parents, we inherit their Divine characteristics, the Purpose, Power, and Will of the Father, and the Intelligent Activity of the Mother. Thus, when we create a relationship between two things, by relating them in our consciousness, power must flow from one to the other, resulting in intelligent, creative activity.

Jeff: "So when we become 'fixated' on a form..."

Quinn: "Our fixation results in development of that form.

"Now, originally, humanity existed in a state of undifferentiated at-one-ment. However, so long as we remained in that state, we were unable to help unify the Three Aspects of Divinity. We lacked the ability to focus on each of the Three Aspects in turn, and work the creative process that transforms the Three into One.

"Yes, El?"

Me: "Undifferentiated at-one-ment?"

Quinn: "Ummm... Imagine you're at the beach, facing the ocean, and holding a handful of sand in front of your face.

"Now, because of the way our eyes work, you can either focus on the entire scene, the grand vista in front of you, or you can look at the sand in your hand and see the individual grains.

"Well, you could. I'd have to find my reading glasses. (Laughter) But you can't do both at once.

"Now, the ability of the consciousness to identify

with and as something works the same way; it can identify with and as a big thing, or with and as a small thing, but has a very difficult time doing both at once. Undifferentiated at-one-ment is that state of consciousness in which you are identified with and as everything —with the grand vista of life— but are unable to focus on or identify with any one thing. A sort of farsighted identity.

Terry: "So most people today are nearsighted?"

Quinn: "Yes, in their consciousness. But remember that in this context far and near sightedness are an analogy for a natural process, for different states of consciousness or identity that we all pass through.

"Now, the method of developing our ability to focus on each of the Three is polarization, or the fixation on the forms of one of the Divine Poles to the exclusion of the other."

Terry: "But, that's a contradiction!"

Quinn: "It looks like one, yes. Since the polarized fixation on a single Pole makes it impossible to unite the Two Poles, one cannot bring the Poles together so long as one's relationship with them is out of balance.

"However, over the ages, polarization brought evolutionary developments that will eventually make at-one-ment possible.

"For instance, the religious expressions of polarization take the forms of Matriarchy and Patriarchy, each of which has a different effect on the growth and development of humanity.

Matriarchy

"Polarization with or on the Negative Pole produces matriarchal spiritual systems. Under this polarization, all Three Aspects —Divine Will, Consciousness, and Intelligence— are interpreted from the perspective of the

Mother. This imbalanced perspective distorts our perception and expression of each of the Aspects.

"Take, for instance, the Divine Will of the First Aspect. When the Poles are in right relationship, the Positive Pole transmits Divine Intent to the Negative Pole via the external Magnetic Field. Or, in symbolic familial terms, the Father transmits Divine Will to the Mother via the Son.

"However, when the Mother is over-emphasized, Substance appears to be the source of motivation. One fails to see the Divine Intent of the Father, and perceives the cycles of nature as the prime cause, rather than part of the interaction of the Three.

"A similar problem occurs with the Second Aspect or Consciousness. Since everything that exists, in order to exist, must be a trinity, the consciousness or Soul is, in itself, a trinity. These three attributes of the Soul are reflections of the Three Aspects, and can be expressed as three statements of identity:

"The positive pole of the Soul, or Divine Son, as, 'I will to be'.

"The magnetic field of the Soul, or pure identity, as, 'I exist'.

"The negative pole of the Soul, or Divine Daughter, as, 'I create'.

"Yes, El?"

Me: "The Daughter is the negative pole of the Soul?"

Quinn: "Well, that's one way of putting it. But keep in mind that by 'positive' and 'negative' we mean polarity and not 'good' or 'bad'."

Me: "Why have the male 'positive' and the female 'negative'? Why not the other way around?"

Quinn: "Do you mean why do we call positive 'positive' and negative 'negative', or why do we associate the male aspect with one pole and the female aspect with the other, irrespective of what the poles are called?"

Me: "Umm... Both."

Quinn: "Well, I don't know who labeled the magnetic poles 'positive' and 'negative' or why. My guess would be that it was a fairly arbitrary decision by a natural philosopher back in the 18th or early 19th century. However, since you ask, how about we make finding out your science homework for this week?"

Me: "Oh! Daaad!"

Quinn: "As for why we associate the output end of the magnetic field with the Male Aspect, and the input end with the Female Aspect; well, it's a fairly obvious physical analogy that has nothing to do with what those ends or poles are called."

Me: "Oh. But, why is the Daughter the..?"

Quinn: "The negative pole of the Soul?"

Me: "Yes, that."

Quinn: "It's a continuation of the analogy.

"Since the magnetic field as a whole is born of the relationship between the two poles, we refer to it as the Divine Child, but, it has two portions—

"There is an external portion in which the energy moves from the positive pole to the negative. Since the external portion moves from the Positive Pole to the Negative, carrying the Will of the 'Father' to the 'Mother', it is most properly symbolized in gender terms as the Divine Son.

"And then there is the inner portion, in which the energy moves from the negative pole to the positive. Since the internal portion moves from the Negative Pole to the Positive, carrying the Intelligent Activity of the 'Mother' to the 'Father', it is most properly symbolized in gender terms as the Divine Daughter. But we'll get into that more shortly.

"Now, to continue...

"In Matriarchal systems, the Divine Daughter is overemphasized along with the Mother, and the feminine aspect of the Soul, 'I create', becomes predominant. 'I will to be' and 'I exist' are suppressed, and with them the individual sense of self.

"Yes, Terry."

Terry: "So you wind up with a far-sighted culture?"

Quinn: "From our current perspective, yes. But what they're really doing is focusing on a narrow point within a larger system. So it's more 'middle-distance' vision.

"Now, the evolutionary result of this was the development of group identities built around shared forms — those they all focused on, created, and identified with— such as ties of blood, religion, nationality, etc., with relatively little individual self-awareness. At the time, this was a necessary development, for it enabled the progression from identification with the species —such as, 'I am a human being'— to identification with a group within humanity —such as, I am a 'Babylonian'.[4]

"The emphasis on an immanent Mother Goddess — experienced in the cycles of nature— and identification with one's forms emphasized the intelligent form-building activity of Substance. Over many centuries, this produced ever-more-complex group forms, including all the basic structures of civilization —such as centralized government, writing, systems of weights and meas-

---

[4] Quinn: The various levels of self-awareness are illustrated by the "mirror test". For instance, if one has a lonely parakeet companion, one need merely place a mirror in their cage. The parakeet is aware as and of its species, and thus can recognize a member of that species when it sees one. However, it does not have the ability to recognize it's self, sees only "a" parakeet when it looks in a mirror, and thus will no longer feel lonely.

urement, etc.

Jeff: "So we're supposed to identify with forms?"

Quinn: "Yes, but the right forms at the right time. We'll get into the details of that in a later lesson."

"Now, once humanity had built and identified with the forms of civilizations, it was time to narrow our identity still further, and achieve individuality. This was accomplished by switching the polarization from the Negative to the Positive Pole, and worshiping a transcendent Male deity.

Patriarchy

"Polarization with the Positive Pole is expressed as Patriarchy. Under this polarization, all Three Aspects —Divine Will, Consciousness, and Intelligence— are interpreted from the perspective of the Father. This imbalanced perspective produces a number of distortions.

"When the poles are in right relationship, the Positive Pole transmits Divine Intent to the Negative Pole via the external Magnetic Field, the Negative Pole responds with creative activity, and transmits that activity to the Positive Pole via the internal Magnetic Field. Or, in symbolic familial terms, the Father transmits Divine Will to the Mother via the Son, and the Mother responds by transmitting Her intelligent activity to the Father via the Daughter. The Father responds in turn, repeating the cycle. This is the creative process by which everything that is comes into being.

"Colette?"

Colette: "Which came first?"

Quinn: "The Father or the Mother?"

Colette: "The movement between them."

Quinn: "Ah. There was no 'first' in that sense. All Four, the Mother, Daughter, Father, Son came into being and began functioning simultaneously. When we enter the process consciously, where we enter depends on what's going on and what we're trying to accomplish at that moment. But we'll get to that when we discuss the details of the creative process.

"Now, when the Father is over-emphasized:

"The Daughter is forgotten, ignored, and/or demonized.

"The goal of the Son appears to be union with the Father.

"The Mother seems to oppose this union, and is demonized for that apparent opposition.

"The Divine Purpose appears to be the abandonment of Substance and at-one-ment with the Father/Son. However, as we have seen, this polarized union is not possible.

"In Patriarchal systems, the Divine Son or consciousness is overemphasized along with the Father, and 'I Will to be' and 'I exist' become predominant. The feminine aspect of the Soul, 'I create', is suppressed, and with it the Daughter's function of relating Substance to Spirit.

"The evolutionary result was the development of individual identities internally isolated from their group life. This was a necessary development at the time, for it continued the progression of identification from species and physical group, to the individual self.[5]

"Yes, Bhikku?"

Bhikku: "You mean that individuality came after group awareness and was necessary?"

Quinn: "Hmmm...Have you ever known anyone who owned a parakeet. A single parakeet?"

---

[5] Individuality brings the ability to look into a mirror and see, not only one's species, but one's individual self.

Bhikku: "Ah... yes."

Quinn: "Was there a mirror in its cage?"

Bhikku: "I don't..."

Quinn: "Ema?"

Ema: "My sister keeps a parakeet, with a mirror so it won't be lonely."

Quinn: "Aha! Now, why would a mirror keep the parakeet from being lonely? What does it see when it looks in the mirror?"

Ema: "A parakeet."

Quinn: "Exactly! It sees *a* parakeet. Now, Bhikku, when you look in a mirror, do you see a human being?"

Bhikku: "Yes."

Quinn: "What else?"

Bhikku: "Me. I see myself."

Quinn: "Exactly! So, when an animal looks into a mirror it sees a member of its species, but when a human being looks into a mirror we see both a member of our species and ourself.

Ema: "What about dogs? My Georgie sees himself."

Thea: "Really? I'd have thought you were a cat person."

Ema: "I have cats too. They see cats. Georgie sees himself."

Quinn: "That is one of the services humanity is performing for the Animal Kingdom. By identifying and relating with our pets as individuals, we are developing their individuality. We give them names, call them by those names, treat them as members of our family, train, pamper, and work them. It has been an intensive learning experience for dogs, especially. We've been working with dogs for at least 10,000 years now, and many of them have developed individual self-awareness as a result. Thus, when they look in a mirror they 'see' themselves.

"Terry?"

Terry: "So, they'd pass the 'mirror test'?"

Quinn: "Um... Technically, no. The protocols of the actual, scientific, 'mirror test' are very specific. First, you acquaint the subject with a mirror. Then, while the subject is unconscious, you apply an odorless dye to the head of the subject, where they cannot see it except by looking in the mirror. Then you observe their behavior, if, when they look in the mirror, they touch the dyed spot, then they've passed the test.

Terry: "Oh! They have to demonstrate that they recognize the connection; the dyed spot on the image in the mirror means that there's a dyed spot on their own head."

Quinn: "Yes."

Tess: "But, that's not fair! You have to have hands or something!"

Quinn: "That's true. Under the present protocols, Dolphins can't pass the test, no matter how self-aware they may be, because they have flippers instead of hands."

Thea: "It's an anthrocentric test!"

Me: "Anthrowhat?

Quinn: "Anthro is Latin for 'man'. Thea is having us on with a little P.C. humor, but she's not far off.

"Actually, elephants can take the test. The results have been inconclusive, but at least they have the ability to touch their faces with their trunks. Adult chimpanzees have done very well, orangutans less so, and gorilla's not well at all.

"Now any animal —parakeet, cat, whatever— is aware of its species and can recognize a member of its species when it sees one. This is an early form of group or species awareness which precedes individuality and which the members of every species must have if that species is to survive.

"Thus, a human being is aware of their self as both a member of a species and as an individual. We have developed sufficient individual consciousness that we can recognize ourself when we see ourself. There are, of course, stages of awareness and types of recognition beyond individuality, but we will get to that in a later lesson.

"Now, where were we?

Me: "Patriarchal systems."

"Ah, yes. Thank you.

"The emphasis on a transcendent Father God — residing in Heaven— and the demonization of Substance, produced an overemphasis on the distant Father. By aspiring to the overshadowing Father and rejecting the Mother, human beings developed the ability to transcend form by identifying with the Father.

"Unfortunately, the rejection of the Mother meant that their relationship with the Father must remain an abstract potential. It cannot manifest in time and space so long as the seeker maintains a misrelationship with the Mother —since She is the vehicle of appearance.

"The evolutionary result was the individual ability to contact the Father and the Son, and the inability to express that contact in a practical way in the everyday world of affairs.

The New Path

"Thus, patriarchy and matriarchy were expressions of and methods whereby humanity evolved. Both were appropriate to their time, but their work is done. Humanity is now ready to merge the two into The New Path of Initiation that will take us to our next stage of spiritual growth and development. But what is that new path?

"Given the above, in order to be effective, this new method must include:

"An allegory or myth tale, appropriate to these

times, that symbolically describes:

"The One no thing that is everything before there is anything.

"The Three Aspects or Trinity in right relationship with the One, each other, and the many.

"The quest of the many for at-one-ment with the Trinity, and union of the Trinity with the One.

"An inner ritual or meditation process that incorporates:

"The creative process.

"At-one-ment of the many with the Trinity.

"Union of the Trinity with the One.

"A system of rituals or outer exercises that both portray the allegory and move the inner work into outer expression.

"Bhikku?"

Bhikku: "Is there such a thing?"

Quinn: "Well... Yes and no. It exists as an abstraction, as a formulation of Truth into idea and thought, but it still has to be brought into appearance. And that's what we're doing in this class.

Celine: "We're creating a form of appearance for the new path?"

Quinn: "We're helping to, yes. But humanity is only in the beginning —you could say we're at the foot of the mount of initiation, and have only begun to build a new path up its slopes.

"Now, we have to begin somewhere, and the best place may be on the foundation of the old path, the ancient mysteries. The old myths of Divine Marriage and Sacrifice preserve symbols of the path of union, as that

38

path was worked in past ages. Thus, by studying the symbolic meaning of the ancient myths, we discover—

"How those traditions walked and worked the path of union, and

"How we can journey along the path ourselves.

"We will begin exploring those ancient allegories in lesson three, with the myths of Gemini. But before we begin our myth tales, we must first examine the fate of the Great Goddess, and why She must be restored to Her place in the path of spiritual growth and development.

"Any questions? OK, that concludes our lesson for today. As usual, we'll close with an inner exercise."

Relaxation

"Having established where we dwell within the body, we will begin a series of exercises that take us through the path of spiritual growth and development.

"The first part of that inner work necessarily focuses on the physical-dense body of appearance. So long as tension is held anywhere within the physical body, that body will resist movement or change. Thus, we will begin by relaxing the physical-dense instrument.

"Sit comfortably with your back straight, your feet flat on the floor and your arms on the chairs armrests or in your lap (not crossed).

"Close your eyes and relax your physical body, beginning with your toes and moving upward to your head. You may command each portion to relax, imagine a relaxing warmth or tingling sensation, or use whatever other method works for you.

"Include every portion of your body and pay special attention to the muscles of your diaphragm, throat, tongue, jaw, and behind the eyes. Complete the relaxation with your consciousness focused in your head, and endeavor to remain there... (For three minutes.)

(At the end of three minutes...) "Take a deep breath, open your eyes, and return your awareness to your surroundings.

"Practice this technique once a day, every day, for at least one lunar cycle —from New Moon to New Moon. Continue to include it at the beginning of your daily inner work until physical relaxation becomes automatic.

Lesson 1

"That concludes this evening's lesson. Please feel free to call me if you have any questions. See you all next week!"

Raising the Queen of Heaven

Lesson 2

Recovering the Goddess

The Fall of the Queen of Heaven

Quinn said, "Good evening everyone." And the class replied with ragged but hearty "Good evenings!"

Quinn asked, "Has anyone heard from Ed?"

I replied, "He's having car trouble, and will get here if he can."

Quinn said, "Ah. Well, we'll start, as usual, with an opening exercise."

I turned on the recorder.

Opening Alignment

Quinn: "Close your eyes, and sit up straight, with your hands in your lap or resting on the arms of the chair, and your feet flat on the floor.

"Beginning with your toes, relax your physical body. You may imagine the muscles relaxing, simply command them to relax, or feel a tingling warmth, or imagine a golden light —whatever works for you.

"Continue up from your toes to your feet... lower legs... thighs...abdomen... lower back... waist —paying particular attention to the diaphragm... upper back... chest... fingers... hands... forearms... upper arms... shoulders... neck and throat —paying particular attention to the vocal cords and base of the tongue... muscles of the jaw... scalp... and behind the eyes.

"Become receptive to that truth or wisdom overshadowing this evening's lesson...

"Maintaining that receptivity, take a deep breath, and open your eyes."

A Coup in Heaven

Quinn: "The religion of the Queen of Heaven was overthrown in a series of violent coups. This change took thousands of years, and transformed the emphasis of our spiritual traditions from matriarchal polytheism to patriarchal monotheism. One of the best-known examples of this process was the struggle for the Temple of Jerusalem, at the end of which our Divine Mother was thrown out of Her home and turned into a whore.

(Wil raised his hand.)

"Just a moment.

"Now, I am not trying to be inflammatory. This description is quite correct. The prophets of YHWH called the Queen of Heaven a whore, expelled Her from the Temple in Jerusalem, burned Her symbols, and established a patriarchal monopoly. The results of this violent struggle are still resounding."

"Yes, Colette?"

Colette: "YHWH?"

Quinn: "It's a common name of the God of the Old Testament, only we don't really know what the vowels are since the Jews wrote without them."

Colette: "Without vowels?"

Quinn: "Yes. Look, suppose I write this on the board...

(Quinn wrote "Cltt" on the board with a black marker.)

"What is that?"

Colette: "Oh. It's my name."

Quinn: "Right, with the vowels left out. The ancient Hebrews wrote everything that way, without vowels. Now, with most Hebrew words they know what the vowels are, so even today someone who reads Hebrew sim-

45

ply inserts the vowels without thinking about it. However, the name of God was sacred, never to be spoken, and so the vowels have been forgotten.

"It's as if we didn't know what the vowels of your name were, and had to guess. It could be anything from Calotta to Culittee.

"The most popular spelling of YHWH is Yahweh, but that's only a guess."

Jeff: "What about 'Jehovah'?"

Quinn: "Same thing. It's YHWH with the Hebrew 'Y' sound pronounced more like and spelled with a 'J', the 'W' as a 'V', and with different vowels."

Wil: "So, which is right, 'Y' or 'J'?"

Quinn: "Well, technically neither. It's not an English word and neither sound is quite right.

"Now, to continue, the ancient Judeans were originally a matriarchal culture, and did not become patriarchal until the time of the prophets.[1] At that time, Judean prophets and priests who were fixated on the Positive Pole of Divinity gradually gained control over both the Temple and the religious practices in the countryside.

"The remnants of early Judean matriarchy are still seen in the Jewish custom of matrilineal descent —i.e., one must have a Hebrew mother in order to be born a Hebrew.

"Tess?"

Tess: "Not all of us."

Quinn: "Yes, but some still follow the old custom.

"Now, Judean patriarchy arose with the monotheistic cult of YHWH, which —officially, at least— rejected almost all of the matriarchal aspects of their culture and religion, including worship of the Great Goddess.

---

[1] Approx. 1025 – 586 B.C.E., during the Age of Aries.

"We know about the fate of the Goddess from hints in the Bible, archeological discoveries, and from regional religious tales —Babylonian, Canaanite, Egyptian, Sumerian, and Phoenician— that influenced the Judean beliefs.

"According to biblical scripture, the Temple of Solomon was built with the aid of King Hiram of Tyre. Tyre was a small but wealthy nation of Phoenician sea traders located to the north of Israel. King Hiram's aid is said to have included—

"Cedar from the forests of Lebanon—used in the Temple beams and furnishings.

"Woodsmen to cut and carpenters to shape the cedar.

"Stone masons to cut and shape the stone of the Temple.

"Smiths who made the implements, vessels, altar, etc.

"King Solomon provided the purpose, unskilled Judean labor, a building site, and wages for the workers.

"All of this makes King Hiram's crucial supportive role quite odd, as there is no indication that he or any of his people worshipped YHWH. Quite the contrary, like all Phoenician cities, Tyre had its own 'ba'alat'—female goddess—who had a male consort or 'ba'al.' Thus, in patriarchal terms, King Hiram of Tyre, his woodsmen, and his masons were all matriarchal 'heathens'.

"This was not as unlikely as it sounds, for the Bible indicates that the Judeans followed much the same custom. At that time, the name of the Judean ba'alat was 'Ashe'rah'. When Asherah first appears in the Bible, she is already being transformed from a dominant female ba'alat with a male consort, into a subsidiary female deity who is the consort of a male ba'al. However, at that time the priests did not agree on the identity of the ba'al.

"There appears to have been a power struggle between the priests of an unnamed northern ba'al and those of YHWH, with Asherah as part of the prize. At the time, Israel and Judea were two separate nations, with Israel to the north and Judea to the south. The Israelis supported the ba'al, while the Judeans supported YHWH. The Judeans 'won' the struggle, and killed off the Israeli priests of ba'al. In the end, even the name of the Israeli ba'al was lost.

"Yes, Wil?"

Wil: "This is what you meant by a 'coup'?"

Quinn: "Yes. It was a change in our relationship with the Divine, expressed in our religious and spiritual myths and practices. The actual nature of the Poles did not change.

"Now, Asherah was a very popular goddess in both Israel and Judah, with altars in many high places. In Israel, she was worshipped alongside the ba'al, but in Judah —including the Temple of Solomon— she was worshiped alongside YHWH.

"This began to change with the advent of extreme patriarchy, and the rejection of all gods but YHWH.[2] Over a long campaign —lasting about 400 years— the prophets demonized Asherah, threw Her out of the Temple, and instituted the exclusive worship of YHWH.

"Now, I've started with this example both because these events had a profound effect on our own culture, and because it's fairly typical behavior.

"When patriarchy dominates matriarchy, it usually

-----

[2] 2 Kings 21, 2, 2 Kings 23, 1 – 3, & 1 Kings 18, 19-40 Please note that the worship of other gods was restricted, but that their existence was not denied.

does a number of things to the Goddess, including:

"The male gods 'rape' the goddess —symbolically stealing the power of the goddess and establishing the preeminence of the god.

"Turn the goddess into a lesser being, such as a queen, princess, or heroine.

"Turn the goddess into an evil or demonic lesser being.

"Transform the goddess from the dominant divinity into a subsidiary divinity, dependent on the god.

"Transfer characteristics and powers from the goddess to a god.

"These are often done in combination, as when the Greek Zeus —among others— raped various heroines.

"Now, the patriarchal Judean priests and prophets were more prudish than the Greeks, and were striving against a goddess —Asherah— whose rites included sexual passion.

"Yes, Jeff?"

Jeff: "Are sexual rites OK, then?"

Quinn: "Um... That would be a whole course in itself. Let's just say, for now, that it depends on the context, but that it's usually not a good idea for modern humanity.

Colette: "Why not?"

Quinn: "Oh, gosh. That gets into all kinds of things. Look, if you really need to know we can do a course on it, but let's stay on topic and move on for now.

"Let me see... The reaction of the Judean priests included:

"Demonizing the goddess.

"Removing all hint of sex from their public rites.

"Transferring the entire creative process, including the angelic builders or 'hosts of heaven' from the goddess to YHWH.

"And, turning the joyful act of sexual passion into a solemn duty, commanded by YHWH.

Wil: "Solemnization."
Quinn: "Via consummation? Yes."
Me: "Solumwhat?"
Quinn: "S o l e m n i z a t i o n. Umm. Traditionally, the marriage ritual was not considered complete until the newlywed couple had sexual relations."
Me: "They weren't really married until they did it?"
Quinn: "Yes."
Me: "Yuck!"
Quinn: "Wait a few years."

"Now, of course, none of this changed how the universe actually works. It only distorted the symbols that represent the cosmos. Unfortunately, the more imbalanced and distorted the symbols, the less effective they are and the more difficult it is to use them to achieve union.

"As I mentioned, in Judea and Israel the process of patriarchal crystallization lasted hundreds of years, and began with the advancement of YHWH to primacy. However, the Judean priests were never able to eliminate all the remnants of the Goddess.

"Those who built Christianity on the Jewish foundation dealt with the remnants of the Goddess by continuing the process of distortion, and by adding mistranslation.

"A prime example of mistranslation is the Christian Trinity, the 'Father, Son, and Holy Spirit'. All three aspects of this trinity are often considered masculine. However this is not correct.

"'Holy Spirit' is a translation of 'Espiritu Sanctu', a masculine Latin pronoun. However, 'Espiritu Sanctu' is a translation of the Hebrew 'Shekinah', which is a feminine pronoun. In Jewish tradition, the Shekinah—or 'presence'—was the cloud that appeared between the wings of the Cherubim on the lid of the Ark of the Covenant. This cloud was the diminished representation of the Goddess. Thus, the Holy Spirit is the Great Goddess, hidden behind a masculine shroud.

"As we have already discussed, the 'Divine Son' is one pole of the Divine Child, Its other pole being the 'Divine Daughter'.

"Unfortunately, the followers of YHWH failed to understand the nature of polarity. Yes, there is only One God, but It is not patriarchal YHWH. As mentioned earlier, the One God is so far above us that there is nothing about that Being that we can know. It exists above polarity, and thus cannot be represented as male or female, and It does not have a name!

"YHWH and Asherah, the Father and the Mother, are symbols of the two poles of the Trinity, the first expression of the One God.

"These Three Aspects, that are One, produce everything that is via the magnetic field of relationship between them. Everything that is, in order to exist, must consist of these Three, in a formulation unique to that thing.

"Everything has a positive pole —spark of Spirit— a negative pole —Substance— and the magnetic field between them —Consciousness.

"These two Divine Poles are always in balance. As in an electromagnet, the strength of one pole must be equal to the other. Thus, by cutting themselves off from the negative pole, patriarchists limit their access to the positive. By rejecting Asherah, they distanced themselves from YHWH.

"The result is the situation we have today, in which, for thousands of years, the primary goal of the spiritual quest was to escape. Matter, the body of the Divine Mother, was viewed as the enemy of the spiritual quest, and those on the path sought to escape Her and achieve union with the Father.

"However, the planet has moved into a new age, and humanity has moved past the need for this type of polarization. But, we continue to use the old, polarized forms —patriarchal and matriarchal— out of habit and the absence of a clear alternative. A prime modern example of this persistence is the concept of the 'rapture' in which thousands of followers of the Divine Son hope to escape the material world and go to the Father. This is based on a complete, utter rejection of Substance, the Mother Aspect of Divinity, and is a severe distortion of the way Divine Union works!

"John?"

John: "There's no such thing as the Rapture?"

Quinn: "The term itself does not even appear in the Christian scripture, and the whole concept is a misunderstanding, a delusion based on feelings of fear and inadequacy. But, let's not go there. It's a huge bypath, it would sound critical, and you can't cure insecurity with criticism."

Terry: "How..."

Quinn: "Tess?"

Tess: "Hm? Oh, with love, always with love."

Quinn: "Yes. You become a beacon, shining the light of Divine Love into 'all the dark and lonely places where men must walk'.[3]

"Now, in order to understand this patriarchal distor-

---

[3] Quinn: I was paraphrasing an ancient Egyptian blessing.

tion more clearly, we need to explore the nature of the Great Goddess.

The Nature of the Goddess

Quinn: "If everything that exists, in order to exist, must be three things, then the Goddess Herself must be a trinity. There are abundant symbols of this fact, and one of the most common is the three-fold goddess, or Crone, Mother, and Virgin.

"Other trinities of the Goddess include:

"Energy	Force	Substance
"Potential	Activity	Appearance
"Wisdom	Strength	Beauty

"These trinities include the four elements of:

"Fire	Water	Earth

"or esoteric:

"Color	Vibration	Light

"With Air, or Esoteric Sound, as the One Substance from which the other three emanate —making four elements in all, or a tetrad.

"Yes, Tess?"

Tess: "Tetrad?"

Quinn: "Its Latin, means 'rule by four'."

Tess: (Flushing) "Oh! Of course."

"Now, the Goddess is Substance, the stuff out of which all things are made. That Substance exists in three conditions. These conditions may be compared to a huge boulder balanced on the edge of a cliff.

"One time when my brothers and I were boys the family visited the Craters of the Moon National Monument. While there, we stopped for lunch at a scenic picnic spot, and after we ate, we boys checked out a trail. A ways up the trail, we discovered a huge balancing boulder, about, oh... half the size of this room. Now, one of us suggested to the others that we'd never be able to push it over the edge. So, of course we had to try.

"We checked to be sure no one was under it, and then tried to push the boulder over the cliff, rocking it back and forth, back and forth...

"Now, so long as the boulder was balanced on the edge of the cliff, it had kinetic energy, the energy of its position at the top of a gravity-well. However, that energy is just potential. It is not actually doing anything and is not yet capable of doing anything.

"If we had managed to push the boulder over the cliff, then that potential would become activity and the energy would become force as the bolder rushed toward the ground.

"The moment the boulder struck the ground, the activity would have become appearance and the force would become substance as it took on shape and form."

Me: "So, you didn't push it over?"

Quinn: (Grinning) "No."

"This demonstrates the basic principle that the Mother cannot do anything on her own. Without an external motivation —a push— the bolder will remain balanced on the edge of the cliff, substance will continue in its present condition, and nothing will change.

"That external motivation is a focus of Will or Intent, conveyed to the Mother —as potential— from the Father by the Son.

"The Mother responds with the intelligent activity— or force— that produces a new form or appearance.

"The Daughter then conveys the results of the creative activity to the Father, and the cycle repeats."

Wil: "So the creative process begins with the Father?"

Quinn: "No, it doesn't have a beginning. The complete cycle is always taking place. There's always movement from one pole to the other. When we view it from our current linear perspective, we see a sequential cycle. But that sequence, where the cycle 'starts', is fairly arbitrary, a matter of orientation."

Colette: "Orientation?"

Quinn: "That gets back to polarity. Those who are fixated on the Positive Pole, the Father, will see the cycle beginning there. Those who are fixated on the Negative Pole, the Mother, will begin there. The cycle doesn't really 'begin' anywhere. Not in that sense.

"Now, when the Three Aspects are held in right relationship, this creative process gradually refines Substance, slowly transforming matter into light.

"As the forms are lifted up in frequency via transformation, the consciousness trapped within those forms —through identification with them— is liberated.

"Bhikku?"

Bhikku: "I thought you said liberation was a trap?"

Quinn: "The Mir thing?"

Bhikku: "Yeah."

Quinn: "That was about 'complete detachment' from all form.

"Remember, I said one had to become 'attached' to the 'right' forms at the right time?"

Bhikku: "Yeah."

Quinn: "Well, the result of that attachment is liberation from form."

Terry: "But that's a contradiction!"

Quinn: "How do you sail against the wind?"

Terry: "Tacking?"

Quinn: "Right. You have the wind blow you back and forth, back and forth, all the while inching toward your destination."

Celine: "So, the magical process is the 'tacking'."

Quinn: "In that analogy, yes.

"Once we recognize that Substance is Divine, we can work with it, we can 'tack' back and forth, back and forth —from the physical-dense realm, through subtle substance, astral force, and mental energy, to Spirit and back. In the process, refining the gross matter in which we are trapped, transmuting dense form into light."

Bhikku: "But, how does that... transformation into light liberate the self?"

Quinn: (Turning to pick up his tea mug, and then turning back to Bhikku) "In order to make this tea we had to move liquid from one place to another, doing something different with it in each one. Well, actually, El did, but you get the point. Without the containers, it would be practically impossible to make tea. With them, it's fairly easy. However, once all the elements have been brought together — the herbs, minerals, water, and fire— in the proper sequence and equation, the tea is ready... (Quinn took a long sip from the mug, emptying it) ...and then you are done with the container.

"The tea needs to move on. The container has served its purpose and the longer it holds on to the tea the longer it delays the fulfillment of its purpose.

"Now in our case, we have become so identified with our 'container' that we resist moving on. We have identified our selves with the name, gender, nationality, likes and dislikes, beliefs, appetites, desires, thoughts, and feelings of our bodies, and every such identification, every 'I am' —tall, short, thin, fat, male, female, whatever— traps some fragment of our self in that form. However, when that form is transformed into light, it leaves nothing, no form, for that fragment of self to hang on to."

Bhikku: "So, the self is liberated."

Quinn: "Yes.

"Now, without this transmutation of the form, some portion of the self remains trapped within it, and the consciousness cannot make its way home.

"We see the working of this cyclic activity of consciousness on a grand scale in the motion of the Wheel of Heaven through the twelve signs of the Zodiac. As this Wheel turns, our solar system, planet, and humanity, move through a great cycle of ascent and descent, from one Pole to the other and back.

"While our recorded history does not go back far enough to trace a complete heavenly cycle, we do have records of the passage through four of the twelve signs of the Zodiac, and into the beginning of a fifth. In a way, these five constitute a complete mini or sub-cycle within that of the Zodiac, a period in which our consciousness has moved from a balanced recognition of the Two Poles, toward identification with the Negative Pole, to Aspiration to the Positive, and back toward reunion of the Two."

Terry: "A complete tack, back and forth?"

Quinn: "Well, yes, although we've probably stretched that analogy far enough.

"Now this cyclic motion of the consciousness, through these four signs and into the fifth, shaped the Spiritual Paths of each of those five Ages. Those five are:

"The age of Gemini, which lasted...

(Quinn glanced at a list of the ages and their dates.)

"...from around 6900 BC to 4700 BC. This age was the high-point in a sub-cycle within the heavenly cycle, when the Self or Soul of humanity recognized the Poles as Divine Twins, a duality separated by the balance of Life and Death.

"Celine?"

Celine: "This doesn't sound like astrology..."

Quinn: "Well, it isn't, not the kind you're familiar with. Remember, we're looking at a complete cycle — Mother, Daughter, Father, Son. This is as true in the greater life as it is here, so the flow isn't one way, from a sign or planet to earth. It's a complete circuit. In this context the signs are more of a celestial clock or signpost that enables us to track the motion."

Wil: "Is this 'spiritual astrology'?"

Quinn: "Oh, that would be a long discussion, and I'm not really qualified... I suppose it depends what is meant by the term. Basically, you can look at astrology from the perspective of any of the Three Aspects.

"The 'Substance' perspective would focus on the effects of the energies and forces of the heavenly bodies.

"The 'Soul' perspective would focus on relating the poles of the terrestrial and heavenly.

"The 'Spiritual' would focus on identifying with and as the life at the heart of the planets and signs.

Jeff: "You can do that?"

Quinn: "Me? No, no that sort of work is done by group workers with that particular task. But they work the same creative process, relating the Poles. Remember, that's what the Child Aspect does. We relate things, one to another, and thus bring about the interactive motion of Intent and Substance."

Wil: "So how does—"

Quinn: "Hold on. That would take a whole course in itself, a long one, and it's not really my field. Let's move on.

"Ummm... Where were we?"

Celine: "Taurus. You were listing ages."

Quinn: "Ah! The age of Taurus, which lasted from... (another glance at the notes)

"...around 4700 BC to 2500 BC. This age was the descent phase of the sub-cycle, when the attention of the Soul or Divine Son turned from the Positive Pole or Divine Father toward the Negative Pole or Divine Mother.

"The age of Aries, which lasted from around 2500 BC to 300 BC. This age was the 'low-point' of the sub-cycle, when the Soul of Humanity moved into and identified with the Negative Pole or Divine Mother.

"The age of Pisces, which lasted from around 300 BC to 1945 AD. This age was the ascent phase of the sub-cycle, when the attention of the Soul or Divine Daughter turned from the Negative Pole or Divine Mother toward the Positive Pole or Divine Father.

"The age of Aquarius, which began around 1945 A.D. This age is another 'high-point' within a sub-cycle; an age of synthesis in which the Divine Daughter-Son recognizes the Divine Mother and Father, and reunites them via the magical activity of consciousness.

"Thus, we see that the transformations of the Ancient Mysteries over the last nine thousand years have all been part of the cyclic motion of human consciousness through the great Wheel of Heaven. Each change of emphasis had its purpose and function in our spiritual growth and development, and all create the foundation for the developing Mysteries of this new Aquarian Age.

"Thea?"

Thea: "You mean, all that, that change from balance to matriarchy to patriarchy, it all had a purpose. It was supposed to happen?"

Quinn: "Well, if you mean the physical events, no. The actual physical activity and forms, the history, is not the goal of all this, but an effect of the process. We have free will and choose how we respond to the opportunities for growth. But the process itself, yes, that has always happened, and it continues today. Part of our goal in this course is to become aware of that magical creative process, so that we can participate in and contribute to it consciously."

Thea: "How do we do that?"

Quinn: "That?"

Thea: "You know. How do we, down here, participate in that process?"

Quinn: "That's a very good question. How do we, as incarnate human beings, manifest Divine Intent, transmute form into light, make our way home, and achieve union of the Divine?

"Well, fortunately, we don't have to invent the answers, but only seek them out.

"In ancient times, aspirants to the path of union had only to gain admittance to one of the centers of the Ancient Mysteries. There, the path of at-one-ment was preserved in their symbols, taught in their outer rituals, and experienced in their inner rites. Certainly those mysteries were colored by the age in which they were cast, but the essence was there and could be found by the earnest seeker.

"While the rituals and rites of most of those mystery centers have long been lost to us, their essence is preserved in the symbols of their myths. This is because the mystery schools used:

"Inner experiences to begin the path of union,

"Outer rituals to prepare candidates for the inner experiences, and

"Myths to impress the symbols of the mysteries and the process of union on the public, without giving away the secrets of initiation.

"As a result, the process of union is preserved in those mystery tales that tell the story of the Divine Family. All we need to do is:

"Collect the remnants of allegorical mystery tales.

"Translate the ancient family allegories into modern

symbols.

"Convert the modern symbols into outer and inner rituals, or a Ceremony of Life.

"We will then have restored the path of union, giving it a form of expression appropriate to our times.

Thea: "So we're going to reverse engineer the path?"

Quinn: "Yes."

Me: "'Reverse engineer?'"

Quinn: "Well, normally you begin an engineering project by creating the specifications for the product — the precise description of what it does and how it works— then you draw up the plan, and build the product from the plans. Reverse engineering is when you start with a finished product, take it apart, and then create the specifications for that product."

Thea: "Yeah. Compaq reverse engineered the first PC Clone. It was the only way they could do it without violating IBM's patents."

Quinn: "Yes, and that's what we'll be doing with the myths, reverse engineering them to arrive back at the original 'specifications', the complete and balanced Path.

"Now, collecting all the appropriate myths would be a daunting task, and it's not necessary to our purpose. We need only use a representative sample. Thus, I've chosen to begin our search in the well-studied regions of the Middle East and Mediterranean.

"Yes, Terry?"

Terry: "That's why you assigned the myths?"

Quinn: "Partly, yes. We'll be moving roughly chronologically through the ages, studying representative samples of the mysteries, and experiencing their collective essence via an inner journey.

"Now, having decided which myths to examine, the next step is to figure out how to decipher the symbols of those myths.

The Symbols of Polarity

"As mentioned earlier, many of these ancient myths portray the relationships between the Three Aspects as familial ties. This includes:

"The Positive Pole is often portrayed as a Father or King.

"The Negative Pole is often portrayed as a Mother or Queen.

"The portion of the Magnetic field that relates the Negative Pole to the Positive Pole is often portrayed as a Daughter or Princess, while that portion which relates the Positive Pole to the Negative Pole is often portrayed as a Son or Prince.

"This is the basic Trinity of Father, Mother and Child —or the Tetrarchy of Mother, Daughter, Father, and Son— that we have already discussed. However, in addition to these relationships, the myths often include:

"The Sister/Brother relationships can be either vertical —between the Positive and Negative Poles— or horizontal —between the internal Daughter and external Son poles of the magnetic field. In either case, it indicates an immature —non-fruitful— relationship.

"Yes Jeff?"

"How can a magnetic field be separate from itself, and what happens when they come back together?"

Quinn: "Ah. Well... that gets into the whole question of identity and the magic of consciousness, and we'll get into that in the next course. However, in the meantime, the answer to the first part is in the basic nature of the magnetic field. Since it is born of the relationship between the two poles, its basic function is to relate.

(Quinn turned back to the drawing board and drew the following, representing the inner magnetic field or Daughter.)

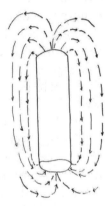

"Again, the Divine Daughter relates the Negative Pole or Divine Intelligence to the Positive Pole...

(He then drew the following, representing the outer magnetic field or Son.)

"...while the Divine Son relates the Positive Pole or Divine Will to the Negative Pole. Thus, the Daughter is responsible for the upward motion or aspiration to the Father, while the Son is responsible for the downward motion or ceremonial magic that brings Divine Will into Form. However, in order to move from one pole to the other the self or Soul must be able to identify with one of the poles, achieve union with it, and then detach from that union and move on. Only when the self can do both do you have a complete magnetic field and flow of consciousness.

(Quinn drew a complete magnetic field, representing the combined Daughter–Son)

"The poles of the Soul, the Daughter and Son, are kept apart by an inability to detach from identification with the form.

"Wife/Husband relationships indicate a mature, creative pairing of two of the Three Aspects, including:

"Negative Pole mated with the

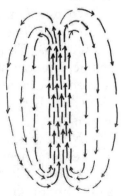

Positive Pole.

"Internal Magnetic Field mated with the Positive Pole.

"External Magnetic Field mated with the Negative Pole.

"As we will see, when these polar relationships are symbolized as family ties, the results can be quite uncomfortable to literal-minded modern students.

"These uncomfortable relationships occur when the direction of the flow —of either Divine Intent from the Father to the Mother, or of Creative Intelligence from the Mother to the Father— is symbolized by sexual activity."

Wil: "Sex! But that's—"

Quinn: "Oh, come on Wil. You're more sophisticated than that. They were simply using the symbols they had. Most of the members of those societies would no more have done that sort of thing than we would.

"Terry?"

Terry: "So, it really had nothing to do with sex? They were just using sexual relations to represent the motion of consciousness?"

Quinn: "Ummm...Not quite."

Celine: "The symbol is the thing."

Quinn: "That's right. In the old systems of ritual magic, the symbol was the thing it symbolized, thus, the ancient rituals of Divine Marriage and the Sacrifice of the Corn King. But we'll get to that as we discuss the myths.

"Now, where were we?"

Terry: "Direction of flow."

Quinn: "Ah. OK. Now, we have the consciousness or self, the magnetic field along which the flow occurs. Now, as this flow moves, it carries the characteristic of each Aspect, from one to the other.

"For instance, the Divine Intelligence of the Mother always flows from:

"Mother to Daughter, or Negative Pole to internal magnetic field.

"Daughter to Father, or internal magnetic field to positive pole,

"The Divine Intent of the Father always flows from:

"Father to Son, or Positive Pole to external magnetic field.

"Son to Mother, or external magnetic field to Negative Pole.

"This flow is a natural and normal part of the magical activity of the consciousness. In ancient Mesopotamia, Greece, Egypt, and Israel, they used familiar images in popular tales to portray this process of creation, liberation, and union. Generally speaking, in those myth tales:

"The creative process became sexual relations.

"The 'fall of the Soul' into Substance became birth and death.

"Liberation from the form became resurrection.

"In our modern times, we can portray this cyclic activity using other symbols, such as polarity and magnetism. The new symbols do not detract from the old — although our literal-mindedness might— but add to the wealth of symbols and thus to the potential for understanding.

"Now, in the following lessons we will use the above as a template, or a starting point for translating the ancient symbols, as we proceed through our myths. Please keep in mind that this template is a general guideline. It does not apply in all cases —by any means— but it will help us understand what the characters in an allegory represent.

"The next step in our quest will be to begin exploring how each astrological age has affected the spiritual path, starting with the myths of Gemini.

"That concludes this evening's lesson. We will close, as usual, with an inner ritual."

Right Relationship

Quinn: "As mentioned earlier, during the past age, the polarization on the positive pole created a misrelationship with the Mother Aspect or Substance. This misrelationship includes the substantial forms of our own persona—that portion of the Divine Mother with which we have the most intimate relationship. In order to relate properly with both Divine Parents, we must right our relationship with that substance which we inhabit.

"Since everything that exists, in order to exist, must be a formulation of three things —a positive pole, a negative pole, and the magnetic field of relationship between them— every human persona must also be a trinity. These three aspects of the human persona are sometimes symbolized by the trinity of Virgin, Mother, and Crone:

"In this context, the Virgin represents the negative pole of human substance, the physical-etheric body. This body interpenetrates the physical-dense form, and extends outward from it several inches. The bio-electric field of the physical-dense body is actually the densest portion of the physical-etheric. The substance of the physical-etheric body molds and shapes the form of the physical-dense body of appearance, and is itself molded and shaped by the more subtle substance of the Mother.

"The Mother represents the magnetic field of human force, the astral or emotional body. This body interpenetrates the physical-dense and physical-etheric forms, and extends outward from them up to eighteen inches or more, forming an ovoid body. The substance of the astral/emotional plane is the source of the images, sounds, and other sensations of our dream life. The astral body molds and shapes the physical-etheric, and is itself molded and shaped by the more subtle substance of the Crone.

"The Crone represents the positive pole of human energy, the mental body. When fully developed, the mental body receives ideas from the Overshadowing Self or Soul, translates them into thought-forms — organized patterns of mental substance— and passes those thought-forms on to the receptive Mother. The substance of the mental body holds and shapes the physical-etheric, and is itself molded and shaped by the more subtle substance of the Overshadowing Soul.

"It has traditionally been said that each of these bodies is positive or causative to the one below it in frequency —the Mental being causative to the Astral, the Astral causative to the Physical-Etheric, and the Physical-Etheric causative to the physical-dense. However, this is another example of overemphasis on the Positive Pole, and thus is only partly correct.

"As in our electromagnet analogy, the poles are equally causative to each other. In order to be fully effective, any spiritual path must recognize this mutual causality, both in the Aspects of Divinity and in the reflections or fragments of those Aspects within human beings. This has not been and cannot be the case in any system that emphasizes one pole over another.

Calming Your Emotions

"Having released the tensions in the physical-dense body in the previous exercise, our next step is to calm and purify the astral/emotional body. This body is intimately related with the power of our sensations, and both affects and is affected by those sensations. Thus, we can use our creative imagination to formulate visual, auditory, olfactory, and tactile experiences that calm and purify our emotions.

"An astral body that is bursting with active emotions, of any kind, whether so-called good or bad:

"Is unable to accurately receive a thought from the mind and pass it on to the physical-etheric. Rather, it distorts and misinterprets that thought.

"Is unable to accurately receive an intelligent activity from the physical-etheric and relate it to the mental body. Rather, it distorts and misinterprets that activity.

"Can devote only a fragment of its force to the downward transmission of a thought, or the upward transmission of an intelligent activity. So long as that force is trapped in emotional feelings, it is not available for its true purpose, relating the two poles of the persona.

"Thus, calming and purifying the astral body is a necessary part of the spiritual path. Only then can this portion of our Mother Aspect perform its function in the One Life. The following visualization exercise is designed to begin this process of bringing the astral/emotional body into harmony with the other bodies, and with its higher purpose and function.

"Is everyone ready?

"OK. Sit up straight, and relax your physical body, bringing your consciousness to a point of focus within your head.

"Calm your emotions by picturing them as a perfectly calm, clear pool of water in a forest glade. Listen to the happy chirping of birds in the trees.

"Smell the perfume of the wildflowers midst the grass of the glade.

"Gaze into the mirror-smooth pool and see the reflection of the deep-blue sky.

"Hold this image for at least three minutes, then take a deep breath, open your eyes, and return your awareness to your surroundings.

"I will email a copy of this technique to each of you tomorrow. Practice it once a day, every day, for at least one lunar cycle —from New Moon to New Moon. Continue to include it at the beginning of your daily inner work until emotional relaxation becomes automatic.

"That's it for tonight. See you all next week."

Section One

The Cycle of Life and Death

The Age of Gemini

The "girls" were twittering like starlings over Tess's news when Quinn walked in. He moved to his usual spot, and the women darted to their seats. When everyone had quieted, Quinn turned to Tess and said, "Congratulations! Have you set a date?"

Tess replied, "Next spring sometime. We haven't even started looking at places yet."

Quinn nodded, and said, "Well, Mark is a lucky man."

Tess replied, "Thank you."

Quinn gazed around at the room, and said, "Now, if everyone will please turn their attention to the matter at hand. We'll begin, as usual, with an opening exercise. ..."

I turned on the recorder.

Opening Alignment

Quinn: "Close your eyes, and sit up straight, with your hands in your lap or resting on the arms of the chair, and your feet flat on the floor.

"Beginning with your toes, relax your physical body. Continue up from your toes to your feet... lower legs... thighs... abdomen... lower back... waist —paying particular attention to the diaphragm— upper back... chest... fingers... hands... forearms... upper arms... shoulders... neck and throat —paying particular attention to the vocal cords and base of the tongue— muscles of the jaw... scalp... and behind the eyes.

"Calm your emotions.

"Bring your consciousness to a point of focus within your heart center, a tiny golden sun approximately three inches behind the spine and between the shoulder blades. If it helps, you may imagine yourself to be a tiny figure standing within that small golden sun.

"Now, from that tiny golden sun, turn your attention upward to that wisdom or truth overshadowing this evening's lesson, and become receptive to it by silently sounding the OM. (pause)

"Maintaining that receptivity, take a deep breath, and open your eyes."

The Divine Twins

Quinn: "As mentioned in our earlier lessons, the inner path of spiritual growth and development remained basically the same throughout human history."

Wil: "What about the intellect? They didn't have that in Atlantis, or the astral earlier."

Quinn: "They existed in potential, in both humanity and in the Path."

Jeff: "Atlantis?"

Quinn: "Well, in this context, it refers to that stage of the evolution of human consciousness in which we had developed a form much like this one, as far as the physical-dense and etheric bodies were concerned, but were developing the astral-emotional body, and had not yet developed the intellect or concrete rational mind. The spiritual disciplines of the time focused on cleansing or purifying the lower emotions and developing the mystical awareness of union."

Celine: "Via the heart center?"

Quinn: "Via the heart-center-to-crown center alignment. But, we'll get to centers later.

"Now, since the spiritual path is an entirely subjective activity of the consciousness, it has always been presented to incarnate humanity via symbol —to those who are consciously walking the path via the symbolic rites of secret initiations, and to the unconscious populace via public myths that translated the rites into symbolic stories.

"Each of the four astrological ages for which we have representative myths —Gemini, Taurus, Aries, and Pisces— altered the motion of human consciousness, focusing our attention on a particular portion of the Tetrad —

the Divine Mother, Daughter, Father, and Son. This focus produced a particular emphasis within the rites and myths of each age. The hidden rites and public myths were adapted *to* the people, and *by* the age in which they were recreated and retold. This in turn transformed the experience of the path, producing different effects on the body, emotions, mind, and consciousness of those who walked it.

"Celine?"

Celine: "So, the motion of the stars during an Age affected the motion of human consciousness during that Age?"

Quinn: "Basically, yes. Each age added its own peculiar motion, changed the subtle conditions in which humanity dwelt, the way humanity experienced and perceived life. And this was in turn reflected in the mysteries and their myths.

"Now in total, the changes of the last four epochs give us a snapshot of a complete cycle of the consciousness, moving from a 'high-point' of union in Gemini, to a descent toward Substance in Taurus, and a low point of embodiment in Substance in Aries, and an ascent toward Spirit in Pisces, followed by a movement into a new highpoint —and the synthesis of all that came before— in Aquarius.

Tess: "Tacking!"

Quinn: "Well, yes. We could describe the four as one 'back-and-forth' within the greater Zodiacal cycle.

"Now, we will be examining myths formed during and thus carrying the frequency of each of these ages, in a roughly linear progression, in the four sections of the course. For instance, this first section focuses on the myths of Gemini, and the way the path was interpreted during that age."

Celine: "But how…"

Quinn: "Yes?"

Celine: "Are any old enough?"

Quinn: "Well, it's difficult, but possible. One reason for starting as recent as Gemini is that the further back you go, the harder it becomes to reconstruct the myths. But hold on. We'll get to that in a moment.

"Our purpose is to experience and thus understand the progression of the path through these ages, and on that foundation, to begin walking the path in this new age.

"Tess?"

Tess: "Let's see... You're saying that everything that exists is a product of the polar relationship between the Positive and Negative Poles of Divinity, and that each of these ages expressed that polar relationship differently, so that by studying those similarities and differences we can reverse engineer the path and create a complete picture?"

Quinn: "Basically, yes.

"Now, creation cannot occur until the Divine Child at-one's with the Divine Father, conveys the Divine Intent of the Father to the Mother as the Son, at-one's with the Mother —thereby impregnating the Mother with that Intent and producing a new activity of Substance— and ascends with that intelligent response of Substance, that Wisdom, toward the Divine Father as the Daughter.

"Each of these phases is going on constantly, in the cycles of a meditation, of a day, a lunar month, a year, an incarnation, an astrological age, and in a series of such ages. Every astrological age emphasizes some portion of this creative process, and that emphasis is expressed in the hidden rituals and public myths of that age. Which leads us to our first age, that of Gemini.

"The age of Gemini was a high-point in a sub-cycle within the twelve-age heavenly cycle.

"Colette?"

Colette: "I didn't get that."

Quinn: "That?"

Colette: "About the cycles and sub-cycles."

Quinn: "Oh... Well... it's like the four seasons. Every year has a life cycle, a beginning, middle, and an end. But we divide the year up several ways, including twelve months and four seasons —Winter, Spring, Summer, and Fall. Each season also has a life cycle, a beginning, middle, and an end. So you have the cycle of the year, and within that you have the cycle of the seasons.

"This is like that. You have the twelve signs of the Zodiac, and you have smaller cycles within that.

"Jeff?"

Jeff: "Is it a kind of Quaternary?"

Quinn: "Um... I wouldn't use that term in this context. "Celine?"

Celine: "A Quaternary is one of three groups of signs —cardinal, fixed, or mutable— related by type and by placement on the Zodiac. By type, in that each of the signs in a Quaternary has similar characteristics —for instance, the Mutable Quaternary includes Gemini, Virgo, Saj, and Pisces, which are all very adaptable and changeable. By placement, in that if you take a chart of the zodiac, and draw lines between the signs of a Quaternary, you will draw a square bisected by an equal-armed cross."

Quinn: "Thank you Celine.

"Here, of course, we're talking about a sequence of five ages —Gemini, Taurus, Aries, Pisces, and Aquarius— so it's really quite different.

"Umm..."

Me: "'Gemini was a high point'..."

Quinn: "Right... The Daughter had united the Mother with the Father, giving birth to the Divine Twins, equal

76

but separated by Life and Death. Thus, in the myths of Gemini the Poles represent life and death, day and night, light and darkness, yang and yin, male and female —all characteristics or expressions of the Divine Polarity.

"In the following lesson we'll examine how the myths of Gemini convey this via symbol."

Lesson 3

Twin Flames of Heaven

The Myth of Pollux and Helen

Quinn: "Now, you will have noticed that I have not assigned anyone a myth from the Age of Gemini. The reason of this is quite simple. We don't have any.

"Yes, Terry?"

Terry: "What about Castor and Pollux?"

Quinn: "Good question. Celine?"

Celine: (Surprised) "Oh... Well... Umm... According to the myth, Castor and Pollux were twins who were rewarded by Zeus, for the intensity of their brotherly love, by being set into the heavens as the sign of Gemini or 'The Twins'."

Quinn: "And how old is their myth?"

Celine: "Well, they're Greco-Roman, were Argonauts, and appear in the Illiad... probably late Aries, early Pisces."

Quinn: "So, while the myth of Castor and Pollux may be descended or derived from a Gemini-*era* myth, it's from about four thousand years later?"

Celine: "Oh, at least."

Quinn: "Of course, we do have other myths *about* Gemini, including Egyptian, Babylonian, Indian, and Chinese. However, none of them are old enough either. They can't be.

"As I mentioned earlier, the astrological age of Gemini lasted from around 6900 BC to 4700 BC. Now, the earliest forms of writing did not appear until around 3000 BC..."

Wil: "The cuneiform inscriptions of ancient Mesopotamia."

Quinn: "Well... yes, but some recent evidence suggests that proto Egyptian hieroglyphics may have begun a bit earlier.

"Now, it took hundreds of years for those first primitive pictographs to develop into true writing. Thus, there is a span of about two thousand years between the end of Gemini and the possibility of writing down the myths of that Age.

"So, you see, I couldn't assign a myth *from* the age of Gemini because we don't have any."

John: "So, you're going to backward engineer them?"

Quinn: "'Reverse engineer'. We're going to look at the common characteristics of what we do have, in the myths *about* Gemini from Rome, Greece, Egypt, Mesopotamia, India, and China, and apply the guidelines and template discussed last week.

"Now, since it would be unfair to assign anyone more than one myth, I'll tell a short, digest version of each of these Gemini myths, beginning with the familiar Greco-Roman version."

Gemini

Greco-Roman

Quinn: "While a number of twins were associated with Gemini, including Romulus and Remus, the legendary cofounders of Rome, the most popular in our culture are Castor and Pollux, who were collectively known as the Dioscuri. Now, there are a number of versions of their myth, but an outline of the best-known version might sound something like this:

"The god Zeus was such a notorious philanderer that

all women knew it, both divine and mortal. So, in a vain attempt to hide his escapades from his wife, and in order to sneak up on unsuspecting mortal women, he adopted various disguises.

"Well, Zeus became enamored with Queen Leda of Sparta, disguised himself as a swan, and lay with her. Leda became pregnant, bore two eggs, and from each egg hatched twins. From one egg emerged Castor and Clytemnestra, the mortal children of Leda and her husband Tyndareus, the King of Sparta. From the other egg emerged Pollux and Helen, the immortal children of Leda and Zeus.

"Castor and Pollux were both raised in Sparta, where they became quite close. Educated by the centaur Chiron, they became noted horsemen, and each rode a snow-white mount, carried a spear, and bore a star on his brow.

"As members of the Argonauts, they participated in the quest for the Golden Fleece. During a storm, they called on Zeus for aid. Two flames descended from heaven and hovered over their heads, and the storm ended.

"When Paris abducted their sister Helen, they fought in the Trojan War to return her to her husband Menelaus.

"They fell in love with Hilaeira and Phoebe, who were already engaged to the twin's cousins. Taking after their father Zeus, the boys abducted the girls, but the girl's fiancé's caught them and Castor was killed in the ensuing fight.

"Shattered by grief, and weeping over the body of his mortal brother, Pollux begged his father Zeus to restore Castor to life by giving Castor his own, Pollux's, immortality.

"Greatly moved by this unprecedented height of

brotherly love, Zeus divided Castor's immortality between the brothers. Ever since, the twins have spent
half their time in the Underworld and the rest on Mount
Olympus with the gods."

✦

"Now, their myth symbolizes the dual day and
night, life and death, morning and evening character of
the twins. They were believed to come to the aid of
mariners in distress, and they were associated with
healing and with what later became known as St.
Elmo's fire, a favorable omen when it appeared in two
flames, unlucky as one.

(Bhikku raised his hand.)

Quinn: "Wait. Let's get through the myths first."

✦

Egyptian

Quinn: "We don't really have a complete narrative of
the Egyptian myths related to Gemini, just scraps from
a variety of periods and perspectives. However, a very
basic outline might go something like this...

"Before there was anything else there was Atum.[1]
Atum masturbated into his hand, and from that seed
made the one-souled twins —the sister/wife Tefnut and
brother/husband Shu.

"Now, Tefnut was the lion-headed goddess of mois-
ture and the Sun's heat, whilst Shu was the lion-headed
god of air.

"Shu knew Tefnut, and she bore Geb and Nuit, the
earth and the sky. And thus the sky was divided from
the earth, giving the creatures thereof a place to dwell.

---

[1] Quinn: Atum is sometimes identified with Amun-Ra, or Amun-Ra
with Atum, depending on the perspective.

"Geb in turn knew Nuit, and then Shu, jealous of his children, thrust them apart, dividing the sky from the earth.

"In time, Nuit bore the sun, the stars, the planets, and the gods Osiris, Isis, Set, and Nephthys.

"Osiris knew Isis in the womb, and so was born Horus the elder. And later Isis knew the restored Osiris, and so was born Horus the younger."

✦

Wil: "That's way oversimplified, and you didn't—"

Quinn: "It's the 'Reader's Digest'® version. But this bare outline of an Egyptian creation story is of particular interest to us, because it shows how each level includes a reflection of the original polarity. First there was the One, Atum, who existed before all and from which all comes.

"Then Shu and Tefnut —the twins of the solar system— are born from Atum.

"Geb and Nuit—the twins of the earth —are born of Shu and Tefnut.

"Osiris and Isis —the Twins of human Spirit and Substance— are born of Geb and Nuit.

"Horus the elder and Horus the younger —the descending and rising poles of the human Soul— are born of Osiris and Isis.

Wil: "What do you mean 'one-souled'?"

Quinn: "Hmmm?"

Wil: "You called Shu and Tefnut 'one-souled twins'."

Quinn: "Oh! Well, the Egyptians apparently believed that Shu and Tefnut were a single soul in two bodies, what we might call a 'twin soul'.

"Yes, Tess?"

Tess: "Is that like a soul mate or a twin flame?"

Quinn: "Ummm... I'd rather not go into those terms

right now. There are so many different interpretations, there's too much romantic stuff attached to them, and 'twin soul' as we're using it here has nothing to do with romance. It's, well, basically it's the polarity of the Soul, the inner and outer Daughter-Son polarity.

"Yes, Celine?"

Celine: "The Egyptian system portrays all these twins creating things —plants, animals, people— by having sex. Do twin souls have anything to do with sex magic?"

Quinn: "Well... yes and no. Keep in mind that we're talking about the Daughter-Son polarity. The interaction of that polarity is a major part of the creative process, the part for which we, as human beings, as Souls, are responsible. Performing that process consciously is what true 'magic' is, and one of the physical-dense expressions of the creative process is sex, so, in a way, yes.

"However, as I mentioned earlier, in the myths sex is used as a symbol for the creative process. So when the twins are mentioned as engaged in sex, what it really means is that they're working the magical process. It does *not* necessarily mean that physical relations took place between these aspects of divinity.

"Now, we'll focus on the magical activity of consciousness in the next course."

Wil: "What about Tantra?"

Quinn: "We can cover that in the next course as well. But for now, let's move on.

"Now as we've seen, the Egyptian system has several sets of twins, including Tefnut and Shu, and Isis and Osiris. We'll examine the latter at length in a following lesson, but for now it's interesting to note that Osiris, like Castor, is killed by a close relative, resurrected, and set on an eternal journey between heaven and the underworld."

✦

Lesson 3

Mesopotamian

Quinn: "Despite the fact that the oldest known written epic comes from Mesopotamia,[2] I wasn't able to find very much about their myths of Gemini. The Sumerians and the Babylonians called the stars of Gemini the 'Great Twins' and the 'Little Twins', which suggests a relationship with the two sets of twins in the Greco-Roman tradition.

"However, the translation 'Great Twins' and 'Little Twins' is deceptive.[3] A more literal translation of 'Great Twins' might be 'the two brothers or sisters at the bottom or end of the constellation'."

Celine: "The bottom?"

Quinn: "Yes, that's where the confusion comes in. The 'Great Twins' were not Pollux and Helen, but two lesser 'gods'.[4]

"These lesser gods or 'Great Twins' were believed to guard the entrance to the underworld, and to dismember the dead as they entered. This is particularly interesting in light of the dismemberment suffered by Osiris.

---

[2] Quinn: The ancient Epic of Gilgamesh, which dates to around 2000 BCE. Some have tried to identify its chief characters with Gemini. However, while Gilgamesh and Enkidu had many adventures together and became very close, they clearly were not twins or even related.

The two great Indian epics, the Mahabharata and the Ramayana, have been dated at between 1000-800 BCE, while the Greek epics, The Iliad and The Odyssey, have been dated at between 900-700 BCE.

[3] "'Great Twins' is a translation of 'Mash Tab Ba Gal Gal', while 'Little Twins' comes from 'Mash Tab Tur Tur'. They don't seem to have had a word for 'twin'. Apparently 'Mash' means 'a relative, either a sister or a brother'. 'Taba' indicates 'two' or 'double'. 'Gal' means 'end' or 'bottom', and repeating a word indicates plurality.

[4] Named Lugalgirra' and Meslamtaea. The 'Little Twins' were named Lal and Nin Ezen Gu.

However, it also suggests that they're not a cognate of the immortal twins, as those are lords of light and givers of life.

"Yes, El?"

Me: "Cognate?"

Quinn: "Oh... well... the word means that something is related to or shares the same source as another thing. If, for instance, one finds three mythological heroes who experienced the same, basic, adventures, one might propose that they are cognate, or related. The question then becomes, 'how are they related?' And the answer to that depends as much on the orientation of the one asking the question as it does on the actual evidence.

"Anthropologists, for instance, might look at trade routes, adopted and similar words, etc., while those with a psycho-spiritual orientation might look at the similarities as expressions of patterns common to everyone's psyche.

"Does that make sense?"

(I nodded yes.)

"What we're doing here appears similar in some ways to both of those, but has a very different perspective and purpose. We're approaching the myths as expressions of the path of spiritual growth and development, the motion of consciousness which is reinterpreted in each epoch and culture as hidden mysteries and public myths.

"Yes, Thea?"

Thea: "How does that differ from the psycho-spiritual?"

Quinn: "Well... from our perspective, they're looking at the motion of forms; mental ideas and astral feelings, but still forms. We're looking at or for the motion of consciousness that creates and moves those forms. It's rather like, well, using the tides to follow the moon."

Terry: "You mean, if the moon were, say, hidden by clouds, we could still find it by its gravitational effects?"

Quinn: "Yes. Because consciousness is the magnetic field, it is both radiatory and magnetic; the descending Son 'pushes' on substance, while the ascending Daughter 'pulls' on it. Thus, we can follow its motion by following the effects of that motion, its 'tides'.

"Now, the Great Twins were also used to guard the doorways of homes and to protect the sick from demons. Thus they, like Castor and Pollux, were associated with healing. However, they weren't Castor and Pollux.[5]

"Now this suggests that the Little Twins are cognate with the immortal twins Pollux and Helen, and with Isis and Osiris. And that the Great Twins are the cognates of the mortal twins Castor and Clytemnestra, and with Set and Nephthys."

Celine: "So, we have two sets of twins again."

Quinn: "Yes."

"Now, in regards to the function of the mortal twins in the creative process, it is interesting that in ancient Sumeria the Great Twins were associated with building. The name of the month when the sun was in Gemini — May-June— meant "Bricks", and thus a pile of bricks was one of their symbols. This building symbolism appears in the myths of other Gemini Twins, such as Romulus and Remus, the founders of Rome, and makes a great deal of sense when one considers that the earliest known cities appeared during the age of Gemini. It is particularly interesting when we consider that the mortal persona, the mental, emotional, and physical instrument, is the house or temple of the immortal Soul during the incarnation process, and that it is the function of this instrument to

---

[5] The 'Tur' in Mash Tab Ba Tur Tur (the Little Twins) is cognate with 'al Dhira', which is Arabic for Pollux (the star).

build the forms of the Divine Plan."

Indian

Quinn: "Moving further east we come to the Hindu Pantheon, which includes a number of twins. However, the most pertinent are the Aquini, Ashwins, or Asvins, the 'Twin Horsemen of the Dawn', the sons of Saranyu (the goddess of dawn) and Surya (the sun god and husband/son of Saranyu). It has been suggested that their myth dates back to 4,000 BCE, which would still place them seven hundred years into Taurus, well short of the age of Gemini.

"Archeological evidence suggests that the 4,000 BCE date is barely possible for horsemen. Wear marks on 6,000 year old horse teeth, from the Ukrainian steppes, suggests that horses were wearing bits by then. However, I have not found anything that would enable us to push the concept of the twins as horsemen all the way back to Gemini.

"This is a problem for both the Dioscuri —Castor and Pollux— and the Asvins, for there doesn't appear to be any evidence to support the idea that horses were either ridden or pulled chariots during the age of Gemini. Thus, the horseman motif is probably not part of the original Gemini myth.

"However, there are versions of the myth in which the steeds that pull or carry the Asvins are birds. It's possible that this is the earlier symbol, that their steeds were originally birds and were transformed into horses when humanity began using horses as steeds. If so, then we have another connection between the Asvins and our earlier twin myths, for the Mesopotamian Twins were winged —as were Isis and Nephthys— and one of the parents of the Dioscuri (Zeus) was disguised as a bird.

"One remaining problem we have in comparing the Asvins to the Dioscuri is that there are four Dioscuri but only two Asvins. Or are there? In some versions of the Asvins' myth their mother disguised herself as a horse, had sex with their father, and then gave birth to the Asvins. Now, since the Asvins are depicted as riding white horses, it may be possible that those horses are, in fact, their siblings.

"If that's the case, and those horses were originally birds, then their mother —originally symbolically represented as a bird— would have given birth to four children, two in human form and two in bird form. The two human-form children represented the polarity of the consciousness that was carried from darkness to light and from light to darkness. The bird-form twins represented the polarity of the persona instrument that carried the consciousness. Thus, you have the immortal Sister-Brother twins of the Soul, and the mortal sister-brother twins of the persona.

"This series of assumptions is supported by the myth of Leda and the Swan —Zeus. You will recall that I described how in the later patriarchal systems the male gods often took over the functions and symbols of the female gods, took their power via rape, and demoted the goddess to a lesser being. Queen Leda, the mother of Castor and Pollux, is an excellent example of this process. It appears that Leda was originally the moon goddess Lat —the giver of milk— and that she was also Letto, the mother of both the World Egg and the Sun. Thus, originally Leda was the 'swan'. Zeus was merely a later, patriarchal usurper of that symbol.

"Thus, the joining of the Divine Mother and Father gave birth to two sets of sacred twins, the Soul and its vehicle the persona, who journey together from earth to heaven, darkness to light, night to dawn. Moving back and forth between their Divine Parents, carrying the message of one to the other, ever relating their parents one to the other and seeking to heal the division, to re-unite the Sister–Brother poles of the Soul and thereby the Mother-Father poles of Divinity.

"This is the work of the Divine Twins. This is who we are, why we are here, and how we perform the magic of consciousness.

"This is supported by the very different Chinese approach to this duality."

✦

Chinese

"The ancient Chinese perspective was somewhat different, but supported these conclusions. They represented the duality of nature as 'Yin' and 'Yang', a relatively recent concept from the Han Dynasty —206 BCE to 220 AD.

"In this system 'Yin' represents the Feminine Aspect, the moon, passivity, shade, or the dark side of a mountain. 'Yang' represents the Masculine Aspect, the sun, light, heaven, the active principle, or the bright side of a mountain. Thus we see again the duality of female and male, light and darkness. But what about the two sets of twins, the tetrad?

"The tetrad is represented by four of the five Chinese elements. Water and metal are Yin or feminine, while wood and fire are Yang or masculine. The fifth element, earth, assists both poles and therefore represents a union of the Divine Feminine and Masculine.

"The poles of Yin and Yang are in a constant state of flux, constantly seeking balance, which echoes the journey of the Divine Twins between light and darkness."

✦

"Now all of this suggests that the Greco-Roman Dioscuri, the Egyptian Isis–Osiris–Nephthys–Set, Mesopotamian Great and Little Twins, the Indian Asvins, and Chinese Yin and Yang are all cognates of the Tetrad of Divine Twins.

"Thus, when the energy and motion of Gemini was in the ascendant:

"The emphasis and goal of the Mysteries was on balancing the pairs of opposites,

"The Divine Feminine and Masculine were equally recognized and valued, and

"The myth tales emphasized the cyclic journey of the consciousness.

"What happened? How did we get from that point of balance to where we are today?

"The Wheel of Heaven turned, and we moved on to the next stage of our great journey, the Age of Taurus."

Focusing Your Mind

Quinn: "Having calmed the astral/emotional body, our next step is to focus the mental body. This body is intimately related with the ability to direct the attention of the incarnate consciousness. The mind acts as a lens to focus the astral force —upward to the Divine Mother, Child, or Father, or downward into the three worlds of the Virgin, Mother, and Crone. This creative magic is performed by the consciousness in cyclic relationship with the Two Poles.

"The Divine Son relates the Purpose, Power, and Will of the Divine Father to the Divine Mother. When the Divine Mother responds, the Divine Daughter relates the Mother's Intelligent Activity to the Divine Father. The Father responds, and the cycle continues.

"Thus, the creative process is an activity of the consciousness or Soul, which, being born of the relationship between the Two, inherits the divine ability to relate.

"A mental body that is unable to focus and maintain a thought cannot perform its dual function in this process.

"A mental body that is directed or controlled by emotional feelings will not be able to detach from those feelings and focus on the overshadowing Idea of Divinity — Mother, Child, or Father. Thus, the mental body will perceive only a vague shadow of the overshadowing Truth.

"An inflexible mental body that cannot formulate new thought will be unable to focus the descending Divine Energy in a new direction. Thus, that vague realization of truth will be misdirected into an old form, instead of into a new creation.

"Thus, focusing the mental body is a necessary part of the spiritual path. Only then can this portion of our

Mother Aspect perform its function in the One Life. The following exercise is designed to begin this process of bringing the mental body into right relationship with the other bodies, and with its higher purpose and function."

✦

Sit in a comfortable chair, and relax your physical body, bringing your consciousness to a point of focus within your head.

Calm your emotions.

Focus on the image of a circle with a dot at its center, without thinking about it, or anything else, for one minute.

Focus on the image of an equal armed cross, without thinking about it or anything else, for one minute.

Take a deep breath, open your eyes, and return your awareness to your surroundings.

✦

Practice this technique once a day, every day, for at least one lunar cycle (from New Moon to New Moon). Continue to include it at the beginning of your daily inner work until focusing the mind becomes automatic.

Raising the Queen of Heaven

Section Two

The Son Descending

The Age of Taurus

John arrived a bit early, as usual, and I had him fetch an ottoman from the living room. I was showing him where to put it when Guido's barks announced Tess's arrival. Her crutches were plunk, plunk, plunking across the porch as I reached the door. When I opened it, her backpack was slipping from her shoulder, so I dashed out and grabbed it.

A startled hummingbird chirped as it fled, and I led Tess back to the Library. Quinn had mentioned an accident, and each of the others asked about her bandage-swathed foot as they arrived, but the group vagued up in front of me. From the bits I heard, she'd had an accident with a wine glass during a cuddle-monkey clutch.

The group quieted when Quinn arrived. He voiced a cheerful, "Good evening!" and the group echoed him. Quinn sipped from a mug —the big one with the profile of a moose— and turned to Tess.

He nodded to her foot, and asked, "What's the prognosis?"

Tess replied, "Thanks for the card. I'll be fully mobile soon."

"You're welcome."

Quinn turned to Ed, and said, "Welcome back. How's the new car?"

Grinning broadly, Ed replied, "A white Ford Taurus, 22,000 miles, lots of features, runs great."

"Good. Glad you're happy with it.

"Is everyone ready?... We'll start in the usual fashion,

with an opening ritual."
    I turned on the recorder.

Opening Alignment

Quinn: "Close your eyes, and sit up straight, with your hands in your lap or resting on the arms of the chair, and your feet flat on the floor.

"Relax your physical body.

"Calm your emotions.

"Bring your consciousness to a point of focus within the ajna center, a tiny golden sun approximately three inches in front of the forehead and between the eyes. There integrate your three-fold persona, body, emotions, and mind, into a single unit.

"Now from that tiny golden sun, turn your attention upward to that wisdom or truth overshadowing this evening's lesson, and become receptive to it by silently sounding the OM.

"Maintaining that focus of receptivity in the ajna, take a deep breath, and open your eyes."

The Myths of Taurus

Quinn: "Our next myths originated during the Age of Taurus, when the attention of the Soul or Divine Son turned from the Divine Twins toward the Negative Pole or Divine Mother. This downward motion of the consciousness focused its attention on, and increased its identification with form.

"Bhikku?"

Bhikku: "So... in Taurus the devotee was devoted to the mother?"

Quinn: "Well... I wouldn't put it quite that way. The devotional energy that we're familiar with, and the thoughts, feelings, and outer forms of devotion, are mostly Piscean. It would be more accurate to say that the emphasis during Taurus was on the downward motion of the Son toward the Mother, and thus the attention of the consciousness was focused on the form, and the self tended to identify with the form."

Bhikku: "So we were more identified with the form?"

Quinn: "No, actually we were less."

Bhikku: "Less!

Wil: "How?"

Quinn: "Well, it was earlier in the process of identification with and as form."

Bhikku: "So we're more materialistic now!

Quinn: "In that sense, yes. But remember, the Poles *must* be equal. The more attention you focus on, the more energy you put into one Pole, the more you put into the other Pole. The two remain balanced. You can't strengthen one without automatically strengthening the other."

Celine: "So when we focus on the Mother, we also

feed the Father, and when we focus on the Father, we also feed the Mother."

Quinn: "Automatically, yes."

Jeff: "Then how do you escape?"

Quinn: "Escape?"

Jeff: "You know, the 'wheel or rebirth' or whatever."

Quinn: "Ah. Does everyone know what Jeff means?"

(Everyone nodded.)

"Well, it's good to see ideas moving out there. Back when I started, the idea that the Soul incarnates in Substance, identifies with form, loses its self-awareness, and is thus trapped on the Wheel of Rebirth, wasn't so well known.

"Now, the way to escape the Wheel is to step off it. This is accomplished using the same method of detachment we discussed earlier. Which was?"

(Quinn glanced around the group.)

Quinn: "Celine?"

Celine: "By identifying with something else?"

Quinn: "Yes! You step off the Wheel by identifying with and as the consciousness, taking conscious control of the motion of consciousness, and then using the motion of consciousness to control the motion of substance."

Celine: "The 'magic' of consciousness?"

Quinn: "Yes."

Terry: "Which we're sort of 'reverse engineering'."

Quinn: "Well... sort of. We're recovering a complete outline of the path, and once we have it, we'll use the magic of consciousness to walk it.

"Bhikku?"

Bhikku: "So this course is about *finding* the way, and the next one will be about *walking* the way?"

Quinn: "Sort of. Both courses cover both —we're walking the way in 'Raising' via the inner rituals— but the emphasis is different from one course to the other.

"Now, where were we?"

Me: "The downward motion of the Son toward the Mother in Taurus."

Quinn: "Ah... Now, under Aries and Pisces, the role of the Mother was warped, rejected, and obscured. Of course, when Substance was rejected, the crucial role of the Mother in leading the Soul to liberation was all but forgotten. Fortunately, the Mother's essential role in both liberation and union was illustrated in a number of surviving allegories.

"These allegories include the myths of Inanna and Dumuzi, Ishtar and Tammuz, Aphrodite and Adonis, Isis and Osiris, Eve and Adam, Sarai and Avram, Baal and Anath, Joshua and Miriam, and Matronit and YHWH.

"The consequences of a misrelationship between the Divine Poles are illustrated in other myths, such as those of Moses and Zipporah, Demeter and Persephone, and Orpheus and Eurydice.

"We will examine each of these myths in our quest, roughly following a progression from the oldest and more matriarchal allegories, to the newer and more patriarchal myths, and then begin the move towards balance and union. In the process we will follow the motion of the consciousness from Gemini through Taurus, Aries, and Pisces, and into Aquarius.

"Now, our next step in this journey takes us to our first Taurus myth, Ishtar and Tammuz."

Lesson 4

Falling from the Tree of Life

The Myth of Ishtar and Tammuz

Quinn: "Our journey through Taurus begins with Ishtar and Tammuz, a Babylonian myth that grew out of the Sumerian Inanna and Dumuzi, and was later translated by the Greeks into the myth of Aphrodite and Adonis.

"The earliest known fragments of this myth, written in more Matriarchal times,[1] have the goddess sending her consort to the underworld in her place, and abandoning him there. This hints at the type of distortions resulting from overemphasizing either polarity.

"I understand from Colette, that in her version of the myth, she begins with the Greek version, and combines it with the earlier Babylonian and Sumerian versions, giving us a symbolically complete myth. For simplicity's sake, she's combined the names of Dumuzi, Tammuz, and Adonis into Tammuz, and those of Inanna, Ishtar, and Aphrodite into Ishtar.

"Colette?"

The Myth

The Birth of Tammuz[2]

Colette: "Umm... Well, the myth begins when queen Cenchreis, the wife of king Theias of Syria, brags that

---

[1] Quinn: During the Age of Taurus.
[2] Quinn: Originally the birth of "Adonis."

her daughter Myrrha is even more beautiful than Ishtar[3] —the goddess of springtime and love. Angered at this supposed slight, Ishtar fills princess Myrrha with lust for her father, king Theias.

"Dismayed by her incestuous passion, Myrrha wants to hang herself, but her nurse convinces her to satisfy her desires. With the nurse's help, Myrrha tricks her father, and spends twelve nights with him. On the twelfth night, king Theias uncovers the trick, and pursues his daughter with a knife, intending to kill her.

"Myrrha flees into a forest, and hides in shame. Ishtar finds the princess in the forest, takes pity on her, and transforms her into a Myrrh tree. Ten months later, the tree splits open and the infant Tammuz emerges. Smitten by his beauty, Ishtar hides him in a chest, and gives the chest to Persephone —the goddess of the underworld and the wife of Hades— for safekeeping.

"Curious about the treasure she is guarding, Persephone peeks inside the chest. She is smitten by Tammuz in turn, and refuses to return him to Ishtar.

"Zeus is called in to arbitrate their argument, and rules that Tammuz should spend one-third of the year with Ishtar, one-third with Persephone, and one-third wherever he wishes. Given that choice, Tammuz always spends two-thirds of the year with Ishtar and only one-third with Persephone."

The Marriage of Ishtar and Tammuz

"Anticipating a visit by her would-be lover, the goddess Ishtar bathes. Tended by her handmaidens, she cleanses and clothes herself in preparation for the sacred rite of renewal.

"When all is ready, the procession of Tammuz ap-

---

[3] Quinn: Originally "Aphrodite."

pears at the door, and is admitted to the throne room of her temple. He approaches, kneels, and offers her seven courting gifts, including fine jewelry and clothing. His servants follow, carrying baskets of fruits and vegetables that they lay at her feet. Ishtar accepts his gifts, and selects Tammuz as her mate.

"As the priestesses sing hymns of love, the goddess rises, takes Tammuz by the hand, and leads him to the privacy of her bedchamber. There, they lay on the sacred bed of woven rushes, and renew the life of the land with their love.

"When they finally rise, they return to the great hall, where they feast at a great banquet celebrating the renewal of life and the elevation of Tammuz to the god of fertility.

"Shortly thereafter, Tammuz angers Artemis (the goddess of the hunt) and he is gored to death during a bore hunt."

The Descent of Ishtar

"When Tammuz is killed, Ishtar decides to descend into the underworld and search for him. In order to reach the underworld she must pass through seven gates. When she reaches the first, she finds it closed. Raising her kappu-toy—a whipping top—she threatens to smash the gate and raise the dead unless she is allowed to pass.

"The gatekeeper opens the gate and escorts her through. However, she must submit to the rites of Ereshkigal, the queen of the Underworld. Thus, she is stripped of a piece of jewelry or clothing —one of the courting gifts from Tammuz— at each gate. In order, these items include:

"Her crown.

"Her earrings.

"Her necklace.

"Her breast pins.

"Her belt of birth stones.

"Her wrist and ankle bangles.

"Her garment.

"The goddess is reluctant to give up the gifts, but is determined to achieve the resurrection of Tammuz.

"She appears naked before Ereshkigal, and sprinkles Tammuz with her tears, the water of life. Ishtar slowly rises back through the portals of darkness, regaining her attire at each gate, until she glows again as the Queen of Heaven."

The Characters

Quinn: "Thank you Colette. Very well done."

"Now, in order to understand this myth, we need to know something about both the characters and the symbols that appear in it."

(Quinn stood and stepped up to the drawing board.)

Quinn: "Let's start with the characters. What were their names? Anyone"

"Terry?"

Terry: "Ishtar, Tammuz, Persephone…"

(Quinn wrote the names on the board.)

Quinn: "Celine?"

Celine: "Artemis, Persephone…"

Quinn: "Bhikku?"

Bhikku: "Myrrha"

Quinn: "Anyone else? Ema?"

Ema: "Theias"

Quinn: "Ok. Now, although his name did not appear

in Colette's version of the myth, I suggest we begin with Adonis, and continue alphabetically.

"His name originated in the Semitic title Adon, meaning 'Lord' which was used by devotees of Tammuz when they addressed him. For instance, where a Christian would say 'Lord Jesus', a Semite might have said 'Adon Tammuz'.

"Now, what is the relationship between Tammuz and Ishtar? Anyone?

Thea: "They're married."

Quinn: "Yes. In the myth, Tammuz was a shepherd who became a demigod when Ishtar gave him power over the fertility of plants and animals. This power was transferred through the 'Divine Marriage' between Adonis/Tammuz —symbolically the incarnating Soul— and Ishtar —the Great Goddess.

"Now in this context marriage is a symbol of union or at-one-ment. When the Soul first 'marries' the Mother, or incarnates in Substance, it identifies with the form and becomes trapped in its cyclic motion. This cyclic motion of the form is the 'wheel of rebirth', leading to birth, maturity, decline, and the death of the Soul in the Form. The Soul must eventually be rescued from that cyclic process by the creative intervention of Substance itself."

Thea: "So the Divine Marriage symbolizes the union of the Divine Mother and Father?"

Quinn: "It symbolizes both the magic of consciousness which brings about that union, and the union itself.

"Tess?"

Tess: "What about regular marriage?"

Quinn: "Well... Basically, it's part of the process of union, in which we experience and learn to unite the two aspects of ourselves."

Ed: "What about gay relationships?"

Quinn: "Mmm... Ed, it's the nature of love —not just the emotion, but the energy, force, and physical activity— to relate and unify. When two people love each other physically, then that activity unites their physical bodies. When they love each other emotionally, then that force unites their emotional bodies. When they love each other mentally, then that energy unites their mental bodies. When all three are united, then you have a complete union of the persona —the two persons become one.

"Now the polarity of that union, and thus the way the energy, force, and substance of the personas interact, is necessarily different in female–male, female–female, and male–male unions. We don't really have time tonight for me to go into details, but the point to keep in mind is that all of these pairings, of whatever sort, are preparatory, they are not the goal."

Wil: "But aren't gay relationships—"

Quinn: "You're still focusing on the outer form. The outer form is not the goal; it's a reflection of a reflection. It's not even...

"Look, the physical, emotional, and mental bodies, whose characteristics make up what we define as women and men, are all aspects of Substance, the Divine Mother. The self or Soul incarnate in that body is neither male *nor* female.

Thea: "The 'divine hermaphrodite'."

Quinn: "Only if we remember that, when we're talking about the self or Soul, the sexes are symbols of polarity. In that context, the hermaphrodite represents the union of the two poles of the Soul."

Me: "Hermafrowdyte?"

Quinn: "H e r m a p h r o d i t e. The term is formed by combining the names of the male god Hermes and the female god Aphrodite. It represents the union of male and female in a single body.

"Now, as we've discussed, the goal, the purpose of humanity is to re-unite the Divine Mother and Father. This union is brought about by the Divine Daughter and Son —the polarity of consciousness— via that magical activity symbolized by the Divine Marriage.

"Thus, our task is to unite our self, our Daughter-Son polarity, so that we can, via the magic of consciousness, help re-unite our Divine Parents.

"Yes, El?"

Me: "Um... Well, what about when one of our, well, real, you know, physical parents, is not, like, there?"

Quinn: "Oh... Well, please keep in mind that we're working with analogies here. We did not divide the One into the Many, so in that sense we do not bear the karmic responsibility for that division. It's simply that, because of the position, the nature of Soul, only the Soul *can* re-unite the Two Poles of Divinity. However, we can't extend that analogy to suggest that children are responsible for keeping parents together, for splitting them apart, or for re-uniting them, and you know that's not what happened with...

"Look, we'll talk about this more, again, after class. OK?"

Me: "Yeah."

Quinn: "OK. Now this magical motion of consciousness was a common theme in many of the ancient myths. For instance, in *The Golden Bough*, Sir James Frazer discussed the myths of the dying and rising gods, including Adonis, Attis, and Osiris among others. These gods —often symbolically a shepherd— supposedly died and were reborn every year, representing the annual cycle of nature.

"However, from our present perspective, it's not a

cycle of 'death and rebirth', but of the descent of the Son into form, and the ascent of the Daughter to spirit. This becomes clear when one realizes that the myth represents the spiritual path, and that the characters represent aspects of divinity —including that fragment which is our self.

"Now, it's really rather difficult to understand either the myths or the mysteries until one realizes what their symbols represent. This understanding comes through inner realization, which can only be achieved by *becoming* the path.

"Is that clear?"

(Everyone nodded or murmured yes, although Bhikku looked a bit unsure.)

"Now the next character would be Aphrodite. She was an ancient Mother Goddess of the eastern Mediterranean who was adopted by the Greeks. The myth of Adonis was originally central to her own, but the patriarchal Greeks dropped it, possibly due to discomfort with the sexuality. When she does appear in the myth, she is symbolically an aspect of the Goddess.

"Let me see... Who's next..."

Colette: "Artemis."

Quinn. "Thank you.

"Artemis was a complex moon goddess, a virgin who promoted promiscuity and ruled reproduction, a goddess of the hunt who protected animals; she was the moon and a tree. Here, she is symbolically another aspect of the Goddess.

"Ereshkigal or Persephone, the queen of the Underworld, may be considered another form of the Great Mother. She originally ruled alone, but gave up a portion of her rule to Nergal, her consort. She may represent the crone aspect of Ishtar.

"Inanna was a precursor of the Sumerian Ishtar and

the Greek Aphrodite. In her myth, Inanna was killed by her sister, Ereshkigal, and her body hung up to rot. She was restored to life, a reluctant Dumuzi was killed in her place and later also rescued.

"Ishtar was the Queen of Heaven, one of a number of Goddesses with that title, which brings into question our tendency to assume that a Goddess ruled the Earth while a male God ruled the sky."

Wil: "The positive pole is above, while the negative is below."

Quinn: "That depends what you mean. 'Above' and 'below', or 'higher' and 'lower' are correct when they refer to frequency, but not when they refer to, say... physical location. The Earth, the Sun, the Moon, the stars, those are all physical things made of substance. Substance is the Divine Mother, so you can't say that the physical sky is the proper place of the Divine Father.

"However, you can't say that the Earth is the proper place of the Divine Mother either. Remember, the rule of three applies to everything. Thus, in order for those negative poles to exist, there must be a positive pole, and a magnetic field between them."

Thea: "So the Earth has a positive pole, or Father, and the Sun has a negative pole, or Mother?"

Quinn: "Yes. And in that sense, one can speak of the Father Earth and the Mother Sky.

"Now getting back to Ishtar, we find the rule of three working here as well. She was, as the Great Goddess often was, a triple goddess —in her case of love, procreation, and war.

"As the eternal-virgin warrior, she was shown armed with a bow and quiver, warring with any and all who tried to take her essence.

"As the capricious procreator, she constantly plotted

to find new lovers. Modern, mostly-male interpreters have tended to interpret these activities as those of a wanton whore, but they were doubtless viewed very differently by her devotees.

"She was also the wise old judge and counselor, or in modern terms, the Crone.

"Thus, Ishtar is the Mother, moving in the eternal cycle of life.

"Myrrha, the mother of Adonis, was a personified tree spirit. Here, she represents the Daughter or inner magnetic field.

"Tammuz, the husband and brother of Ishtar, was a shepherd who became a demigod when Ishtar gave him power over the fertility of plants and animals. As a symbol of the Soul, his myth represented the death and resurrection cycle. Other allegorical divine shepherds included Adonis, Christ, Dumuzi, Hermes, Krishna, Osiris, and Pan.

"Theias, the father of Myrrha, was king of Syria and father of Adonis. Here, symbolically an aspect of the Father."

The Symbols

Quinn: (Stepping up to the board again) "There are a number of significant symbols in this myth, including, for instance, the fact that Adonis, or 'Tammuz' as we are calling him, is the product of daughter-father incest. Now, what else appears significant?

"Ema?"

Ema: "Tammuz born by a Tree."

Quinn: (Writing "T a m m u z T r e e" on the board) "Very good. This is a new symbol, one we didn't see in our outlines of Gemini myths.

"Yes, Thea?"

Thea: "Tammuz is hidden or entombed in a chest."

Quinn: (Continuing to write each point) "E n t o m b e d C h e s t.

"OK...Another new symbol. Anything... Tess?"

Tess: "Ishtar and Tammuz are sister/brother, wife/husband."

Quinn: "S i s t e r – B r o t h e r. Yes. A partial repeat of the Sister–Brother symbol, but without the 'twin' relationship.

"John?"

John: "Well, Ishtar rescues Tammuz from Hell."

Quinn: "I s h t a r R e s c u e s... Thank you John.

"Yes El?"

Me: "Ishtar carries a sacred top."

Quinn: "S a c r e d t o p...OK, another new symbol.

"What else?"

Terry: "Ishtar passes through seven gates during her descent into Hell"

Quinn: "S e v e n G a t e s...More new symbols.

"Anything else?"

Jeff: "Ishtar relinquishes a portion of her raiment at each gate."

Quinn: "R a i m e n t...New symbols again.

Me: "Raiment?"

Quinn: "Something she wore, like jewelry or clothing.

"OK. Anything else?

Celine: Ishtar is raised by the Water of Life.

Quinn: "W a t e r o f L i f e...

"OK... This first Taurus myth included a couple of the Gemini symbols, from a slightly different perspective, and added a bunch of new ones. Now, we don't have time to look at all of them this evening, so we'll hold off on some of them until we get to later myths with identical or similar symbols. At this point, we'll look at family relationships as symbols of polarity."

Daughter—Father Incest

Quinn: "As I mentioned earlier, our tendency to take myths literally can create problems with some of the ancient symbols. Thus, it may be easier to work with these metaphors if we remind ourselves that the family relationships symbolize impersonal polarities.

"Tess?"

Tess: "Why do some people insist on taking metaphors literally?"

Quinn: "Well... it's a by-product of the first stage of the path, when the heart center first begins to open, and one experiences that rush of blissful joy. It's a mystical awakening to the greater life, but it occurs when we're still very form oriented, and when our predominant centers are the solar plexus and the throat. The result is that we associate that mystical rush with a familiar outer form.

"Now we'll go into the centers more later, but at that point on the path the emotional energy of the solar plexus center dominates the intellect of the throat center, producing a very rigid, unimaginative mind. As a result of the combination of form identification and a rigid mind, one simply interprets abstract metaphors as literal truth.

"That's how the instrument works at that point. It's a normal, temporary condition, one we all pass through as we walk the path.

"Colette?"

Colette: "How long does that stage last?"

Quinn: "Oh... not very. By that point one's already over the long-slow stuff, and is almost ready to begin walking the path consciously. Maybe only a couple incarnations."

Colette: "Incarnations!"

Quinn: "That's only a long time from the persona perspective. It's not very long to the Soul, which doesn't experience time like the persona anyway. Just consider how many incarnations the Soul had to spend mucking around on the earth in the 'animal man' stage.

"Now, getting back to our present metaphors. As you will recall:

"The 'Divine Mother' is the Negative Pole.

"The 'Divine Daughter' is the inner stream of the magnetic field, which flows from the Negative Pole to the Positive.

"The 'Divine Father' is the Positive Pole.

"The 'Divine Son' is the outer portion of the magnetic field, which flows from the Positive Pole to the Negative.

"Thus, if Aphrodite is the Divine Mother or Negative Pole, Myrrha is the Divine Daughter or inner magnetic field, and king Theias is the Divine Father or Positive Pole, then together the three represent half a circuit of the creative cycle:

"The upward motion from the Negative Pole — Aphrodite—

through the central Magnetic Field —Myrrha—

to the Positive Pole —Theias.

"This is confirmed by the next development in the myth, the birth of Tammuz, the Divine Son, who is immediately found and placed under the protection of Aphrodite, the Divine Mother. This represents:

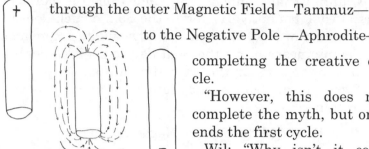

"The movement from the Positive Pole —Theias—

through the outer Magnetic Field —Tammuz—

to the Negative Pole —Aphrodite—

completing the creative cycle.

"However, this does not complete the myth, but only ends the first cycle.

Wil: "Why isn't it complete?"

Quinn: "Well, symbolically, because the Daughter has not yet 'married' the Father, and the Son has not yet 'married' the Mother. Marriage, remember, is the symbol of a mature relationship.

"However, in actuality, the creative cycle is not complete because the Daughter–Son has not yet united the Mother–Father.

"Now, the next cycle begins when Tammuz, the Soul, is hidden in a chest and sent to the Underworld. To understand this episode, we have to understand both the symbolism of the chest and of Hell."

The Chest

"The chest represents a container of the self or Soul, and is not the only such box we'll encounter in our quest. In general terms, that container represents the persona, which consists of:

"The mental body.

"The emotional body.

"The physical-etheric or energy body.

"The physical-dense body.

"The Soul, of course, is trapped within the persona

throughout the incarnation process. The incarnation process is a cyclic motion from the highest level of persona development —the mental or emotional bodies— down into physical-dense incarnation, and back up again.

"Aphrodite's symbolic chest could represent any or all of these bodies. However, the fact that Tammuz — the Son— is taken to the underworld in that chest, is an important clue. This indicates that the chest is the body in which the Soul dwells when it's in the Underworld.

"Once we know which of the bodies the Soul dwells in when it's in the Underworld, we'll know exactly what the chest represents in this myth. Of course, in order to know that, we have to know what and where the Underworld is according to the myth. The answer to this question is provided by Ishtar's journey to the Underworld, in which she descends through seven gates or portals."

The Seven Gates

"As you all know, the universe in which we live consists of seven levels or planes. Each plane consists of substance vibrating in a particular frequency range.

(Quinn stood, drew a tall rectangle on the board with six horizontal lines through it as follows:)

The Seven Planes

1 Logoic Plane

2 Monadic Plane

3 Atmic Plane

4 Buddhic plane

5 Mental plane

6 Emotional or Astral plane

7 Physical Plane

"These planes may be compared to a musical keyboard with seven octaves of seven notes each. The higher notes vibrate at a more rapid rate, while the lower notes vibrate at a slower rate.

"Yes Terry?"

Terry: "Isn't an octave eight notes?"

Quinn: "Well, let's count them ...

115

(Quinn chanted) "do re mi fa sol la ti do.

"OK, that's what, seven individual notes, with the eighth a repeat of the first, on a higher octave, right?

Terry: "Well, yeah..."

Quinn: "OK, so we have these seven vibratory levels of substance, each consisting of seven subsidiary levels.

"Now, how one counts these seven planes depends on one's orientation. Positive Pole oriented systems usually start at the top and work down, with the lowest frequency being the seventh. Negative Pole oriented systems usually start at the bottom and work up, with the highest frequency being the seventh.

"Both are rather arbitrary choices, and neither system is more correct than the other. I'm using the top-down numbering because that's what I was taught. However, since we're more familiar with the lower planes, we'll begin our discussions with them.

"Since all of you are more or less familiar with the seven planes, we need not discuss it in detail in class. However, I have prepared a brief handout for you to study during the week.

(I handed out copies of the paper)[4]

Quinn: "Now, the descent of Ishtar represents the descent of the Divine Mother, downward in frequency through the seven planes, until She reaches the densest layer.

"The mental, astral, physical-etheric, and physical-dense planes are often portrayed as the Underworld or Hades in myth, especially when the myth illustrates the death of the Soul (or of true self awareness) through incarnation in and identification with form.

"This means that the Chest in which Tammuz is hidden is the human persona, consisting of the mental,

---

[4] Quinn: See the Addendum to Lesson 4, in the Appendix.

astral-emotional, and physical-etheric vehicles, all of which are reflected in the physical-dense body.

"Yes?"

Colette: "Well, I've read that the Underworld represents the unconscious."

Quinn: "From a psycho-spiritual viewpoint it probably does. I'm not saying that's wrong —that's not my field and I'm not qualified to comment. The mythological archetypes are probably very helpful tools for understanding our psychological processes.

"But keep in mind that we're looking at these myths from the perspective of the motion of consciousness. From that perspective, those archetypes are themselves reflections or precipitations of the creative activity of consciousness."

Thea: "Joseph Campbell wrote a lot about the psycho-spirituality of myths."

Quinn: "Yes and a lot of people have been inspired by that. But remember our basic premise. There is one path of spiritual growth and development, which we are all walking, each in our own way. That spiritual path is re-interpreted in every time and place as secret rituals, and those hidden rituals are in turn interpreted into popular myths. Thus, from our present perspective, the myths are interpretations of interpretations of the spiritual path, the motion of the Soul that brings about re-union of the Divine."

Her Raiment

"Now, to continue... Ishtar's ritual removal of a portion of her raiment at each gate reinforces the identification of the seven portals with the seven planes.

"Her raiment —jewelry and clothing— are all engagement gifts from her brother/husband, Tammuz. As explained earlier, forms are created by the relationship of the Soul —here Tammuz— with Substance —Ishtar. Thus, the marriage or at-one-ment of Ishtar and Tammuz created all the organized patterns of substance —or forms— on each of the seven planes.

"In this context, each item of Ishtar's raiment represents the formulated Substance of one of the seven planes. As she passes below the frequency of that plane, she must surrender the item representing the formulated substance of that plane.

"When she has removed all of her raiment, she is left with nothing but the physical-dense form. Ishtar has descended to Hell, and there she finds Tammuz.

Tammuz in the Underworld

"The Marriage of Tammuz to Ishtar represents the union of the Soul or Son with Substance or the Mother. However, the fact that the Soul must return to the Underworld —to physical-dense incarnation once every cycle indicates that the Soul is trapped in identification with and as its form.

"This lower cycle of form, down into and out of the physical-dense, is the Wheel of Rebirth. This cycle of substance is represented by Tammuz's role as the Lord of plants, and of the fertility of plants and animals. He is lord of the natural cycles of the form because he has so identified with them that he has become them.

"Since Tammuz is identified with the cycles of form, he is not in control of those cycles but is controlled by them. This is represented in the myth by his regular 'death', and from a persona perspective, Tammuz/Adonis dies yearly in the fall, and rises again in the spring.

"From a Soul perspective, Tammuz/Adonis dies once, when caught on the Wheel of Rebirth, and is finally raised and liberated by Ishtar/Aphrodite.

"If we look at this from the perspective of polarity,

we find the following:

"Tammuz/Adonis identifies with the Negative Pole, and falls into the polarity of Substance.

"Caught in the polarity of Substance, Tammuz/Adonis moves from: energy/potential —the mental plane—

"through force/activity —the emotional plane—

"into substance/appearance —the physical-dense plane.

"This cycle of movement between the three lower worlds continues until Tammuz/Adonis is killed by Ishtar/Aphrodite. This 'death' is a symbolic representation of the process whereby the Goddess uses the cyclic motion of Substance to free the Soul from identification with matter."

Wil: "The goddess of the Underworld kills him."

Quinn: "Ah... Technically, she receives him. From this perspective, Ishtar/Aphrodite kills him when she sends, takes, or allows Tammuz/Adonis to be taken to the Underworld.

"Yes?"

Bhikku: "But why 'kill' him in the first place. Why is the death of the self necessary?"

Quinn: "Tough love.

"The One Life allows us to fall to the lowest levels of existence so that we may, when we have had enough of that death, find our way back to our Self. And it is by doing that, by reuniting that lost fragment of our self with that portion that remained at-one with the One, that we learn the process of re-union. Having learned that process, we can then apply it to re-uniting the Divine Mother–Father.

"Ed?"

Ed: "About tough love... where do A.A. and other twelve-step programs fit in this?"

Quinn: "Oh... Well, I'm hardly an expert on that, just an interested observer.

"I'd say that the problem there is the same with all forms. It's simply more, well... dramatic with some things, like alcohol or behaviors like gambling. As we identify with a form, we take on the motions of that form. It controls our behavior. The only way to get out of the trap of the form is to identify with and become fixated on the Soul, and consciously take up the motions of the Soul."

Ed: "But why do twelve-step programs work?"

Quinn: "Well, because you're fixating on a new form, you're doing it as part of a group, and you're calling on the help of a power above and beyond yourself to sort of kick-start the new motion and keep it going. Remember what I said about Divine Will and its affect on Substance?

Ed: "It gets things moving?"

Quinn: "Yes. One could say that twelve-step programs are a basic introduction to the creative process. You identify a condition that needs transforming, invoke the solution, and call on the higher power to kick-start that solution. That's a big part of the spiritual path, how it has always worked, and a lot of people go on from such programs to consciously pursue the path.

"Now, let's see..."

Me: "Ishtar."

Quinn: "So... Ishtar/Aphrodite leads Tammuz/Adonis from Hell into the Light—liberated from the lower polarity of Substance, the Goddess leads the Daughter or Soul back into its own place, the magnetic field between the two great poles of the Divine Father and Mother.

120

"Having achieved liberation from form, with the aid of both Divine Parents, the Daughter/Son is now able to help unite the Two Poles of Divinity, bringing about the at-one-ment or completion of the One Life

✦

Quinn: "Any questions?

"OK. We'll explore the process of union further in the next chapter, the Myth of Isis and Osiris. But first, we'll do our usual closing.

The Journey

Quinn: "Having relaxed the physical body, calmed the emotions, and focused the mind, the next step in the quest for at-one-ment is to transmute our relationship with our physical-dense body.

"This body is the creative instrument through which our portion of the Divine Mother (our mental, emotional, and physical-etheric activity) is made manifest. To the extent that we reject this body (as being ugly, awkward, fat, skinny, weak, sickly, etc.), we reject that portion of the Temple that enables us to work in the world of affairs.

"Thus, right-relationship with the physical-dense body is essential to the process of Divine Union. While that body is not itself a Divine Principle, it is a reflection of that which is Divine.

✦

Sit in a comfortable chair, and relax your physical body, bringing your consciousness to that point where you dwell. As a point of light within that place:

Calm your emotions.

Clarify your mind.

Identify as the Soul, and audibly state the following seed-thought:

"I am the Daughter of the Great Goddess, inhabiting this body for a time in order to grow into a likeness of the Mother."

Hold that thought for at least three minutes, without repeating it or thinking about it.

Then, irrespective of where you dwell in the body, focus your attention on a point between your shoulder blades, and about three inches behind your spine. There, imagine a tiny blue-white sun, radiating golden light into your environment.

This is the Heart Center or Chakra, a focused vortex or organ of energy, the energy of unconditional love. We will examine this center more closely below. In the meantime:

Create a tiny image of yourself within that blue-white sun, including all the details of your face, hair, etc. When this image is complete, move your identity or self awareness into it, taking up residence in the Heart Center.

This may be difficult at first, requiring repeated practice until it becomes automatic. In the meantime, do as much as you can and then continue with the technique.

Having moved your identity into the Heart Center (to the extent that you can), contemplate the following seed-thought for a few seconds:

"I am the Daughter of God, born in the Cave of the Heart to know and experience love."

Radiate love to your body, your environment, your friends and family, and to all human beings everywhere.

Take a deep breath, relax the focus, and return to your normal awareness.

✦

"Practice this technique once a day, every day, for at least one lunar cycle (from New Moon to New Moon). Continue practicing this technique until the move into the Heart Center becomes automatic.

Raising the Queen of Heaven

Lesson 5

Sailing Down the River of Life

The Myth of Isis and Osiris

Quinn said, "Good evening."

The group replied with the usual murmurs and "Good evenings!" as Quinn sipped from his "dove" mug —a white coffee cup with a bird and his name glazed onto it— and turned to Tess.

He asked, "How's your foot?"

Tess replied, "Much better! I went to the Lake Shrine yesterday and hobbled around for a bit."

"Great!"

Quinn turned to Wil, and asked, "How long will you be gone?"

"A couple weeks, Scotland, England, to Norway."

"Say 'hello' to Torvald for me. I'll email the transcripts of the lessons."

Quinn gazed over the group, and said, "Is everyone ready?... We'll start in the usual fashion, with an opening ritual."

I turned on the recorder.

Opening Alignment

Quinn: "Close your eyes, and sit up straight.

"Relax your physical body.

"Calm your emotions.

"Bring your consciousness to a point of focus within the ajna center, and there integrate your three-fold persona, body, emotions, and mind, into a single unit. (Pause)

"From that tiny golden sun, turn your attention upward to that wisdom or truth overshadowing this evening's lesson, and become receptive to it by silently sounding the OM. (Pause)

"Maintaining that focus of receptivity in the ajna, take a deep breath, and open your eyes."

Isis and Osiris

Quinn: "Isis and Osiris were complex Egyptian deities, part of a living religion from the early centuries of the Age of Taurus, through the Age of Aries, and well into that of Pisces. Those millennia saw a great deal of change in the beliefs and practices surrounding them. While often slow and gradual, the changes were very significant over time.

"Those changes included combining Isis and Osiris with lesser deities, and taking on new attributes and characteristics. This added to their complexity, and complicates the process of interpreting their myth.

"The most familiar version of their myth, by the Greek writer Plutarch,[1] is comparatively recent. Plutarch wrote long after the pyramid era, he mixed in a number of Greek names, and his version omits several important events and misinterprets others.

"The pedigree of this divine couple is a bit confused, perhaps by priests of Heliopolis who wished to incorporate Isis and Osiris into their own pantheon in a subordinate role.

"El?"

Me: "Pedigree?"

Quinn: "Oh... That would be the list of ancestors of a person or animal."

Me: "Like a family tree?"

Quinn: "Sort of, only an animal's pedigree would be, well...like a certificate of good breeding."

Me: "So Guido doesn't have one?"

Quinn: "A Cocker-bull from the pound? No, how

---

[1] Quinn: A.D. 45-126

could he? We don't know who his parents were.

"Now, we'll untangle some of the mess around Isis and Osiris this evening, but our focus will remain on the core of their myth, and its similarities to our previous myths.

"Thea will be telling it for us, and I understand that her version begins with creation.

"Thea?"

The Myth

Thea: "Thank you…

"In the beginning was the Hidden One, Amun, whose form cannot be known even by the gods.

"Amun cast forth his seed, and the gods were born. The first of the gods were Shu and Tefnut. From them descended Geb and Nut, and from them Isis and Osiris.

"Isis and Osiris knew each other in the darkness of the womb of Nut, and from this union came the elder Horus.

"After the union, Osiris was born in the western desert of Egypt, at the entrance to the Underworld.

"Following the birth of Isis and Osiris, Osiris inherited the throne of Egypt. Osiris taught the Egyptians how to cultivate the earth, and traveled the world civilizing the peoples. He brought them to his ways peacefully, by his charm, persuasion, music, and song.

"While Osiris was away, his brother Seth, with seventy-two friends, plotted to usurp the rule of Egypt. When Osiris returned, they tricked him into a chest. Seth sealed the chest with lead, threw it into the Nile, and it floated downstream to the Mediterranean.

"Eventually, the chest washed-up on the shore of Lebanon, at Byblos, and a tamarisk tree[2] grew under

---

[2] Quinn: Some versions say "heather".

and around it, raising the box high above the ground. The king of Byblos so admired the great tree that he had it cut down, and turned the portion that contained the chest into the central column of his palace.[3] There, Osiris rested, all unknown, at the top of the column supporting the roof.

"After long search, Isis learned these facts through divine inspiration, journeyed to Byblos, and sat down by a spring weeping, speaking to no one. The maidservants of Astarte, the queen of Byblos, found her there. Isis was kind to them. She showed them new ways to plait their hair, and imparted in them a wondrous fragrance.

"When the queen saw her maidservants, with their plaited hair and wondrous fragrance, she longed for the same and sent for the mysterious stranger. Isis and queen Astarte became so intimate that the queen made Isis the nursemaid of her newborn son.

"Isis nursed the babe with her finger, and at night bathed him in fire to burn away the mortal portions of his form. While the infant prince bathed, Isis turned into a swallow and flew around the pillar wailing her lament.

"The queen had been watching. When she saw her babe afire she cried out, and the fire went out, dooming the prince to mortality. Isis resumed her true form, and requested the pillar. Removing the chest, she cried out so loudly in grief that the infant prince died.

"Isis left with the chest, and opened it when she reached a remote and private place; however, the queen's older son had followed her, and snuck up behind as she wept over and caressed the face of Osiris. Hearing him, Isis whirled around and finding the boy gazing at the dead face of her beloved, glared at him in such

---

[3] Quinn: Other versions say "house" or "temple."

anger that the boy fell dead of fright.

"Then Isis set sail, and returned up the Nile with Osiris. Seth heard of their return, discovered the chest, stole it, cut Osiris' body into fourteen parts, and scattered the parts along the Nile.

"Isis searched for the parts, found them, reassembled the body of Osiris, and attempted to raise it. She failed, and her sister Nephthys tried. Nephthys failed, and their nephew Thoth tried, using a special grip. The third attempt worked, and Osiris rose up to heaven."

✦

Quinn: "Thank you, Thea.

"The myth continues from there, telling of the birth and growth of the younger Horus, and his struggles against Seth for the throne of Egypt. However, Thea has given us plenty to consider.

"This myth has a number of symbols that are obviously similar to those of our previous myth. These similarities include:

"The dual relationship of the female and male protagonists (sister-brother and wife-husband).

"The death of the male protagonist.

"The internment of the male protagonist in a chest or box.

"The rescue of the male protagonist by the female protagonist.

"The general similarities are quite striking. This is because the two myths are actually the same tale of the death of the self or Soul through its descent into form. The differences are due to time, place, and culture, not the underlying reality.

"The fact that it's the same story, told from a different perspective, will become more apparent as we explore the symbolism of the myth of Isis and Osiris. As before, we'll begin with the characters."

The Characters

(Quinn stood, stepped up to the blank board, and began writing names.)

Quinn: "Let's see, we have Amun, Isis, Osiris, Seth, Nephthys, Astarte... who else?

John: "Horus"

Me: "The two Princes of Byblos"

Celine: "Thoth"

Wil: "Geb and Nut, Shu and Tefnut"

Quinn: "That all?"

Amun

Quinn: "Well, taking them alphabetically again, we have Amun, also known as or conflated with Atum and Re, the invisible, Hidden One, whose form cannot be known —even by the gods. Amun is the primal deity, the creator of the gods and the universe.

"In the myth of Isis and Osiris, Amun represents the One no thing from which everything emerges —including the gods themselves."

Astarte

Quinn: "Astarte[4] is the queen of Byblos, and it appears that Isis had to disguise herself in order to act as the nurse to Astarte's son. However, this is a double veil. Queen Astarte is actually the goddess Astarte.

"As we've discussed, the goddesses and gods, queens and kings, princesses and princes in these myths are often symbols for aspects and attributes of divinity.

---

[4] Quinn: a.k.a. Athenais, Saosis, & Nemanus

Those symbols are related to each other in several ways.

"For instance, different characters may represent the same divine aspect or attribute. Thus, Asherah, Astarte, Demeter, Eve, Ishtar, Isis, Mary, Matronit, Sarah, and Zipporah may all be symbols of the Great Goddess or Negative Pole of Divinity. Since they represent that same Aspect, they share some characteristics. However, since each is an interpretation of the Goddess, from a different perspective, some of their characteristics are different.

"Also, characters may be conflated or combined. Thus, Asherah, Astoreth, Astarte, and Ishtar may, to some extent, be recognized by their worshipers as different names of the same goddess. This is said by some to have led to a blending of their myths, attributes, and ritual practices.

"A single Divine Aspect may be split into multiple characters, each representing different attributes of the original. Thus, the Great Goddess can be represented by both Ishtar —the goddess of life and light— and Ereshkigal —the goddess of death and darkness. In the myth of Isis and Osiris, Isis and Astarte —like Ishtar and Ereshkigal— represent two poles of the Great Goddess.

"In the Isis myth, Astarte —the evening star who descended to the Underworld to rescue her lover— represents Nephthys, the sister of Isis and lover of Osiris whose name means 'the lady of the mansion'. In this case, the 'mansion' is the palace of Byblos whose central pillar contains Osiris."

Celine: "Wait... Astarte is Nephthys?"

Quinn: "Remember the rule of three. In this context, Astarte and Nephthys, and earlier Ereshkigal, represent the negative pole of the Negative Pole.

"Traditionally, for instance, it was Nephthys who escorted Osiris to the Underworld and cried for him as her departed brother.

"Now, who's next..."

Me: "Geb and Nut."

Geb and Nut

Quinn: "Ah. From our perspective, this is a secondary, Solar, polarity that's a reflection of the Cosmic polarity of Shu and Tefnut. The Solar System is the physical-dense body of appearance for this polarity. This polarity is far above and beyond ordinary human awareness, and only those who have achieved union with their Spiritual Soul can be aware of its life and affairs."

Wil: "What about 'cosmic consciousness'?"

Quinn: "Ummm... It's been oh... over twenty-five years since I last read it, but as I recall the popularity of that term goes back to a book of that name by..."

Jeff: "Maurice Bucke."

Quinn: "Yes, thank you.

"Now, first, that book was written at the end of the 19th century, maybe two decades before the discovery that our solar system is located in a 'Galaxy', that is located in a 'Universe'. Thus, terms like Galaxy, Universe, and 'Cosmos' did not have the same meaning then that they do now."

Terry: "We didn't know the difference?"

Quinn: "We literally couldn't 'see' the difference, or our telescopes couldn't. Not until, what... I think it was the Palomar Observatory, came online with its huge telescope.[5]

---

[5] Quinn: Actually, it was two telescopes, both operated by the Palomar Observatory (on Mount Wilson, north of Sand Diego, California). The first, with a 60-inch "lens," was completed in 1908 and enabled astronomers to measure our "galaxy". The second, with a 100-inch "lens," was completed in 1917 and enabled astronomers to discover galaxies outside our Milky Way, thus proving that our galaxy exists in a larger "universe".

"Now, second, when you place that term in the modern context, it's a misnomer. 'Cosmic' consciousness refers to a mystical experience of awareness far beyond the normal, an experience of the at-one-ment of the Soul with the greater life of which it is a part. But that union is planetary, not 'cosmic'. Keep in mind that the goal of our planetary life is at-one-ment with the Solar life, and that that of the Solar is re-union with the larger life of which *it* is a part. The human soul is simply not capable, at our level of development, of functioning at the truly 'cosmic' level.

"So, in our current context, Geb and Nut represent the polarity of the Solar life."

Horus

Quinn: "Now Horus was the son of Isis and Osiris. He was known as the uniter —of upper and lower Egypt, or of the Two Poles."

"Ed?"

Ed: "I thought that was the 'Scorpion King', the real one."

Thea: "Didn't the history channel have something on that?"

Quinn: "Keep in mind that we're focusing on the motion of consciousness, and the ways that motion is reflected in rituals and myths. There probably was an actual, historical King who united upper and lower Egypt, but that does not detract from the symbolism. It merely indicates that there was some back and forth flow between subjective myth and outer reality, and we already knew that.

"So, after the union of upper and lower Egypt, the Kings and Pharaohs of Egypt were considered manifestations of the 'living Horus'.

"There were two Horuses, an elder and a younger,

representing the outer and inner magnetic field.

"The Elder Horus is less well known, which seems odd, since he represents the external magnetic field that relates the Divine Intent of Osiris with the Creative Intelligence of Isis. However, it makes sense when you keep in mind that what we have is a later version of the Myth, with greater emphasis on the Feminine Aspect or Isis, and the child born of Isis.

"Now, the elder Horus becomes Osiris when Osiris dies and descends to Byblos.

"The Younger Horus is by far the better known. He represents the internal magnetic field that relates the Creative Activity of Isis with Osiris.

"The birth of the second Horus was secret, as Seth would have murdered a rightful heir to the stolen throne, and like Tammuz in Babylon and Moses in Judea, Horus was hidden in the papyrus rushes of the Nile. Egyptian royal architecture used columns shaped like papyrus reeds, which is quite interesting given the meaning associated with those reeds and columns. But we'll explore that in the Myth of Zipporah and Moses.

"The younger Horus becomes Osiris when he is raised from death into at-one-ment with the Father.

"Colette?"

Colette: "I don't..."

Quinn: "Remember the cyclic motion of consciousness, downward to Substance and upward to Spirit. A living Egyptian pharaoh was considered an embodiment of Horus, the *Son* of Isis and Osiris. But a pharaoh became Osiris when he died."

Celine: "So the 'death' represents the upward motion?"

Quinn: "Out of the underworld, yes."

Wil: "But the Egyptians had an underworld! Navigating it was a big part of their mythos!"

Quinn: "This is where we have to be careful not to confuse symbol with outer reality. Osiris, the sun, rose up into the sky and then descended where?"

Wil: "Into the earth."

Quinn: "Which is what? What is the earth?"

Ema: "The Mother!"

Quinn: "Yes. So Osiris sails the river between Substance and Spirit, death and life.

"Now the origin of Horus in the union of Isis and Osiris, and his identification as Osiris or interaction with Isis, depends on that motion of the magnetic field. This motion gives us a cyclic movement from Osiris to Isis to Osiris that is central to our interpretation of the myth."

Celine: "The motion being the dual aspects of Horus?"

Quinn: "Yes. The flexibility of identity demonstrated by Horus is typical of the Second Aspect. Born of the relationship between Spirit and Substance, it can identify as either Substance —'I create', itself —'I am', or Spirit —'I will to be'. Thus, the Second Aspect can identify as, and symbolically take on the likeness of, any of the Three Aspects.

"Any questions about that?"

Isis

"OK. Isis is the goddess of life and rebirth, the Sister/Wife of Osiris, Mother of Horus, and the positive pole of the planetary Mother. Since everything that exists must have its poles, the planetary Negative Pole or Divine Mother is, in itself, a polarity. From our present perspective, in the Egyptian system the positive pole of the Mother is Isis, while the negative pole of the Mother is Nephthys, the sister of Isis.

"Isis raises the second Horus in secret, preparing

him to avenge his father and recapture the throne of Egypt."

Tess: "So that's the upward motion?"

Quinn: "Yes."

"She's often depicted wearing a horn-shaped crown — like those of a cow— with a lunar or solar disc between the horns. This horn-shaped crown links her to the Age of Taurus, and the identification of the Soul with and ascent from the Form.

"Bhikku?"

Bhikku: "Why ascent from Form?"

Quinn: "That's when she frees the body of Osiris from the tree and begins the journey back up the Nile. But we'll get to that in a few moments.

"So, Isis, Osiris, and Horus together represent the Egyptian version of the Trinity, again in classic familial symbols. When Isis and Osiris know each other in the womb, and thus conceive the elder Horus, we have the Divine Poles, conceiving the Second Aspect —Magnetic Field— that is born with them.

Malcander

"Next we have Malcander, the King of Byblos and husband of Queen Astarte. He is probably a form of the Phoenician god Melqart, or Melkarthos in Greek. Melqart means "King of the City", and the god was a prototype of the ideal king. His consort was 'Ashtart', the Queen Astarte of our myth. In the myth, he represents an aspect of the incarnate Soul in whose house Osiris is dwelling."

Nephthys

Quinn: "Nephthys is the tomb-dwelling goddess of death and sunset, sister of Isis and Osiris, and wife/sister of Seth. Her name, again, means 'lady of the mansion'. She escorts the deceased Pharaoh through the darkness of Hell and morns him as her lost brother Osiris. All of this indicates that she is the goddess of the mansion of the Soul, the persona.

"In some versions of the myth, Nephthys accompanies Isis on her quest for Osiris. She is also shown standing on the right of the pillar containing the risen Osiris, while Isis stands on the left. The twin goddesses are facing the pillar, with arms outstretched and palms facing Osiris. This suggests that the raising occurred in the middle point between the polarity of the two goddesses, as a result of their direct effort."

Celine: "So, the raising occurs at the midway point between life and death?"

Quinn: "Not quite. The Positive Pole is the Life Aspect. It would be more correct to say that the raising occurs at the mid point of the Wheel of Rebirth, and the point of balance between the dual aspects of the Goddess, that which oversees birth and that which oversees death. When you, the self, stand in the point of stillness midway between the Lady of Life and the Lady of Death, you step off the Wheel. We'll discuss this more in the next course on *The Magic of Consciousness*.

"In the present context, Nephthys represents the death aspect of the Goddess, sometimes called the Crone or Lady of Wisdom —She who presides over the Ascent of the Soul. We may also consider the Queen of Byblos, Astarte, to be an attribute or veil of Nephthys."

Osiris

"Osiris is the brother/husband of Isis and father of Horus. The polar relationship between Isis and Osiris is strengthened by the fact that they are twins, one of whom —Isis— rules over life, while the other —Osiris— rules over the land of death. However, in this case the land of death represents the higher realms on which the

Soul dwells after life here in the underworld."

Wil: "You said the underworld was the physical-dense."

Quinn: "It 'represents' the outer world of affairs. However, it may be more accurate to say that the journey of Osiris in the afterlife represents the continuing motion of the Soul. That motion doesn't stop when we step off the Wheel. It merely moves to higher realms. So you could say that what the journeys of Osiris represent depend on the context. When we're on the Wheel, it's the back and forth between the mental, astral, physical-etheric and physical-dense. After, it's the journey through higher planes.

Colette: "Higher planes?"

Quinn: "They're in your notes on Ishtar and Tammuz, the Buddhic and above.

"Now, it's also significant that Isis and Osiris are part of a tetrad of four twins, completed by Seth and Nephthys. Thus, together the four twins represent the polarity of Gemini, with the motion of the Soul represented by both the descent and ascent or death and resurrection of Osiris, and the Elder and Younger Horus.

"Since everything that exists must have its poles, the planetary Positive Pole or Father is, in itself, a polarity. Osiris represents the positive pole of the planetary Father. The positive pole of the Mother is Isis, while the negative pole of the Mother is Nephthys, the sister of Isis.

"Osiris becomes the elder Horus when Spirit —the Father— moves into the magnetic field.

"Osiris becomes the younger Horus when Isis removes him from the casket (persona) and is impregnated by him.

"Yes John?"

John: "What was the... well, why?"

Quinn: "Of?"

John: "Well, the myth."

Quinn: "One could say that it's an attempt to ask that very question, the question of 'why'?" but, in this case the focus of the answer is on the downward movement of the Father Aspect —Osiris. That downward movement resulted in the birth of the Son, Horus, and the uplifting of Osiris —with the aid of Isis.

"Since Horus was the king of Egypt, we should also keep in mind the ancient concept of divine kingship, in which the king was considered an embodiment of the land he ruled.[6] Thus, whatever happened to the king was reflected in the land."

The Prince of Byblos

"The Prince of Byblos represents the human soul, the form-identified self or Son, trapped within the negative pole of the Negative Pole. The fire that Isis bathes him in is the fire of mind, which quickens the kundalini at the base of the spinal pillar, drawing it up from the bottom toward the head.

"When that fire reaches the skull, the resting place of Osiris, it transforms the casket from the trap of the self into a temple of the Soul into an instrument for liberation and at-one-ment. Osiris is quickened and revivified as the kundalini reaches him, and he prepares to rise back up to heaven."

Seth

Quinn: "Seth is the brother/husband of Nephthys, and brother of Isis and Osiris. He murdered Osiris and usurped the throne of Egypt. A god of chaotic forces, his cult sometimes competed with that of Osiris for wor-

---

[6] The rulers of Egypt were "kings" at one time. They became "pharaohs" after the Hyksos conquered and were expelled from Egypt.

shipers. Thus, his 'evil' role in the myth may partly be an attempt to discredit a rival god. However, that does not alter his symbolic role.

"In the context of the myth, we may consider Seth to be the form-identified Soul that refuses the Path of Union.

"Tess?"

Tess: "What's a 'form identified Soul' again?"

Quinn: "Well, basically it's that fragment of our self that moved down into incarnation, in order to build the instrument of re-union, and became so identified with the form that it lost awareness of itself as the self. Thus it believes itself to be the persona instrument, and because of that belief, it has taken on all the limitations of the form.

"This traps that fragment of the self in the Wheel, the cyclic motion of form, until that fragment reunites with the overshadowing Self from which it came.

"Now, if Seth is that form-identified fragment of the Soul, then we may consider Seth and Nephthys to be equivalent to the mortal twins Castor and Clytemnestra, while Osiris and Isis would be equivalent to the immortal twins Pollux and Helen."

Shu and Tefnut

"Now, from our perspective, Shu and Tefnut represent the first, the cosmic polarity that emerged from Amun. This is that polarity for which the Universe is the physical-dense body of appearance. While we can be aware that this polarity exists, it is so far above and beyond us that we can know very little about them."

Thoth

Quinn: "Thoth was the god of knowledge and science. He was born from the head of Seth, and is symbolized by the ibis and baboon.

"Yes, Terry?"

Terry: "Any relation to the stuffed baboon Madam Blavatsky kept in her study?"

Quinn: "Ah… you've been reading some history. For the rest of you, I highly recommend studying the history of 'spiritual' organizations, the Theosophical society in particular, and from multiple viewpoints. You can learn a lot about group dynamics. But to answer your question, I would not be surprised if there were a connection, since her first great work was *Isis Unveiled*.

"Now, to continue, Thoth represents the transformed Seth, or the fallen soul that has risen into the light. As the 'lord of the sacred words' and having risen from darkness himself, only Thoth knows the word and grip that will raise Osiris."[7]

Jeff: "Is that like a mantra with mudras or something?"

Quinn: "No, not really. It relates to the magic of consciousness, and we'll get to it in a later lesson. For now, let's move on to the symbols of our present myth."

The Symbols

Quinn: (Standing and facing the board) "There are a number of significant symbols in this myth, including:

"Isis and Osiris are sister/brother (twins), wife/husband.

"Horus is the product of sister/brother incest.

"Osiris is hidden or entombed in a chest, and sent down the Nile.

"Osiris is reborn from a Tree.

---

[7] Quinn: Some versions have Anubis participating in the raising of Osiris, others include Horus.

142

"Isis rescues Osiris from death.

"Isis carries a sacred ankh, the symbol of life, and a sistrum (the sacred rattle of Isis).

"Isis journeys down the Nile in search of the murdered Osiris.

"Isis changes her appearance in order to avoid being recognized.

"Osiris is raised by a sacred grip.

"We'll examine the significance of some of the above symbols in following lessons, in combination with similar symbols in other myths. At this point, we'll focus on the familial relationships as symbols of polarity.

"Celine?"

Celine: "What about the Seventy-two Friends of Seth?"

Quinn: "Ah... That's an odd number for someone to have at a dinner part, isn't it, and very specific. Why seventy-two?

"It appears to refer to the ruling celestial intelligences of the seventy-two duodecans[8] of the zodiac. Thus, in order to betray Osiris and usurp his rule, Seth had to suborn the divine intelligences of the heavens.

Me: "Suborn?"

Quinn: "Well... to influence someone into doing something corrupt or illegal. Only influence isn't quite strong enough; maybe entice or incite.

"Now if they *were* the duodecans, then it supports the idea that the 'Kingdom of Egypt' ruled by Osiris is an allegory for a celestial land. The Egypt of the myth is a symbol of a heavenly realm, not the actual, physical land.

---

[8] Quinn: A duodecan is 5°, 5/360, or 1/72 of the Zodiac.

The Chest

"Now the sequence of the myth makes it obvious that the 'death' of Osiris occurred when he was sealed into the chest, and the chest was abandoned to the current of the Nile, the river of cyclic life.

"The chest of Osiris/Horus has the same meaning as the chest of Adonis/Tammuz. It's the container in which the Spiritual Soul is trapped during its journey in the three lower worlds and in the physical-dense world of affairs. However, the myth of Osiris/Horus adds another perspective to the chest, its transformation into the mansion or temple of the Soul."

Thea: "In Byblos."

Quinn: "Yes. The location is also significant. The fact that the transformation from the prison of the Soul to the instrument of redemption begins in the underworld, the outer realm of Byblos, indicates why we're here, in physical-dense incarnation."

The Delta

"The chest floats down the Nile, through the Nile delta, and into the Mediterranean. Later, during her return to Egypt, Isis brings the chest back through the delta, and hides Horus in its rushes until he grows large enough to challenge his uncle, Seth, for the throne of Egypt. The significance of this is found in the work popularly known as the Egyptian Book of the Dead.

"In the Egyptian Book of the Dead, the kingdom of Osiris was called 'the fields of rushes'. It was a sort of paradise, reached by passing through a series of seven gates, with each gate guarded by a warden who required an offering.

"Of course, our earlier study of the myth of Ishtar and Tammuz makes the significance of these seven gates obvious. The seven gates stand for the seven

144

planes through which Osiris descends in the chest of substance to reach the material world or Byblos. Once the work in this Underworld is complete, the Spirit ascends back through the seven gates with the help of the Great Mother.

"The Egyptian Book of the Dead has a great deal more to say about this process, but the above covers the essentials that concern us here."

The Tamarisk Tree

"The fact that the chest is 'lifted up' by the growth of the tree indicates that this is not an actual tree, since trees grow up only at the tips of their branches, not along their length. Thus, an item set in the crotch of a tree seven feet from the ground, and left there for twenty years, would remain seven feet from the ground—unless the ground level rose or fell.

"That being the case, we may safely consider the Tamarisk an allegorical tree, representing something else. As we shall see, trees are often symbols for the etheric body, the subtle network of light that underlies and forms the framework of the mental, astral, and physical-etheric bodies.

"Ed?"

Ed: "The what… tree of Adonis. Is that the same?"

Quinn: "The umm…"

Me: "Myrrh Tree."

Quinn: "Right.

"Yes, symbolically they represent the same structure. Again, they're different views of the same thing, the motion of the consciousness between the Two Aspects. The trees represent the light or 'etheric' body that underlies the rest of the persona."

"The growth of the tree around the chest symbolizes the development or evolution of this complex etheric body. The uplifting of the chest indicates the evolutionary movement of the self, trapped within the persona, to higher states of function and awareness within that body.

"When we combine these downward and upward movements, we have the twin Pillars of Gemini, beneath the solar and atop the lunar discs.

Byblos

"The historical Byblos was an ancient Phoenician port city on the shore of the eastern Mediterranean. In the myth, the kingdom of Byblos is set below the seventh gate —or plane— somewhere on the shore of the Mediterranean, near enough to Egypt that Isis had to disguise herself to escape being recognized. However, the Byblos of our tale is not the historical nation, but an allegorical country. It's reached by passing down the Nile —the cycle of life— into the lower realms of the Underworld.

"Now, I want to be sure you understand what the Underworld actually is. For instance, in the Middle Ages, the cosmos was often portrayed as a series of spheres. Layers of hollow crystalline spheres in the heavens held stars, planets, moons, etc. The earth was inside these crystal spheres, and deep within the earth was the Underworld or Hell. This was a symbol, and was not meant to be taken literally. However, the ignorant often did, and firmly believed that heaven was physically above the earth and hell below.

"This type of misunderstanding is common. Those who have not experienced, and thus do not understand the ancient mysteries, often take its symbols literally, an error that severely distorts the meaning.

"In modern terms, when a character in a mystery tale descends into a cave or sails down a river in quest of a lost love, they are not going down into the center of the physical earth, but descending in frequency. Thus, when they are shown descending to the bottom of a cave or the outlet of a river, they have reached the lowest frequency or plane.

"If we know what that lowest plane is, then we know what the Underworld actually represents. Of course, since we explored the four lowest planes in the previous lesson —the buddhic, mental, astral, and physical-etheric/dense— the answer is obvious. The true Underworld is the physical-dense plane.

"Since the symbolic Underworld of the dead is the physical-dense plane in which we dwell, then we are the 'dead'. Obviously, the 'death' referred to is not the death of the physical-dense body. It is the death of the self that occurs when the Spiritual Soul descends into the three lower worlds and identifies with its lower form.

"Thea?"

Thea: "What about the Resurrection of the Dead?"

Quinn: "The Christian?"

Thea: "Yes."

Quinn: "Oh, well that's a bit... we're not even to Pisces yet. But the basic idea, in any symbolic raising of the dead, or ascension to life in heaven, is not the restoration of life to the physical-dense body —since life in and as that body *is* death. True resurrection is the restoration of self-awareness, the liberation of the soul from the Wheel of Rebirth that comes with at-one-ment with the Spiritual Soul.

"OK?"

Thea: "Yes."

The Spring

Quinn: "Now, Isis sat on the shore of Byblos, wailing for her beloved and crying.

"This brings us to a very important point, one which we must understand if we're to understand why the physical-dense universe exists.

"The place where Isis rests is a spring, the fount of her tears. Her tears are the water of life. Ishtar cried on Tammuz to restore him to life. The tears of Isis, the Great Goddess, give life to the world. The world in which we live and move and have our being exists because Osiris —the Positive Pole or Spirit— descended into Substance and 'died' to his self. Everything that exists is created by the interaction between the Two Poles and is an outgrowth of Spirit-Osiris and Substance-Isis.

"Thus, the myth of Isis and Osiris is not the story of death and rebirth, but the story of life."

The Pillar and The Palace

"A tree is cut down, and the upper portion is transformed into the central pillar of a palace, upholding the roof. The chest of Osiris remains inside, now at the top of the column.

"This is the Jed pillar of Osiris, which represents both the spine and the subtle energy currents of the spine.

"The most interesting fact about this transformation is that the purpose of the chest has changed. Its components still function roughly the same, but the intent behind that function has been transformed from personal development to at-one-ment.

"At first, this may be the incomplete at-one-ment of identification with the Son and union with the Father.[9] But eventually, the incarnate consciousness realizes that the persona instrument, a portion of the Divine

---

[9] Quinn: Spiritual realization eventually brings the understanding that the Mother and Daughter are equally part of the process.

Mother, is a vehicle for Union of the Divine Poles of Mother and Father. At this point, the chest is no longer the container in which the Soul is trapped. It's become the temple in which the Soul finds its way home and through which it serves the One Life.

"However, it has not yet begun the journey home. The infant prince —Horus— must be bathed in the fire of the hearth —the 'fire of mind' of the temple[10]— completing the preparatory growth of the persona. The Great Mother then removes the casket from the pillar, and carries it back to Egypt.

"Osiris/Horus has begun the journey home.

"This represents the transformation of the personality —the mental, emotional, physical-etheric, and physical-dense bodies— into an instrument for:

"Embodying the Divine Intent of the Father through the Creative Intelligence of the Mother.

"Conveying the Intelligent Activity of the Mother to the Father.

"At-one-ment of the two poles of divinity.

"Spiritual traditions that are polarized on the Positive Pole generally recognize the 'chest' function of the persona —the trap of the self or Soul— but miss its later function —the instrument of liberation. This is because they do not recognize the interrelationship of the two poles or the proper function of Substance.

"As you will see in today's handout,[11] each of the

---

[10] Quinn: It may also represent kundalini, the fire of Substance, which, as it rises upward through the spine to the head, liberates the consciousness trapped in the persona instrument.

[11] Quinn: See the Addendum to Lesson 5.

bodies of the persona has a function in the process of liberation.

(Terry raised his hand as I began passing out the sheets)

"Yes, Terry?"

Terry: "What is that process?"

Quinn: "Of liberation? Well... it's the motion of the consciousness or self; the ascent of the Daughter to at-one-ment with the Father, and the descent of the Son to at-one-ment with the Mother, as part of an inner creative process or meditation. One result is the liberation of the self from the form. There's more in the handouts; too much to go into right now."

The Babe in the Fire

"According to the myth, Queen Astarte has two children, both boys. Isis becomes the nurse of the youngest prince, whom she suckles on her finger. She also bathes him in fire in order to burn away his mortal parts. This refers to the process of transmutation that is brought about by the fire of Divine Mind. It is this process that transforms the allegorical chest from the tomb of the Soul into the instrument of liberation and at-one-ment.

"'Burning away the mortal parts' does not destroy those parts, but purifies and transforms them. The parts referred to are the bodies and the subtle organs of those bodies. When this process is complete, the purified instrument becomes a vehicle of the Soul, and liberates the self from the motion of substance. The self or Soul is then free of the Wheel of Rebirth and thus 'immortal'.

"Unfortunately, Isis is interrupted before she can complete the process. This is a crucial point! The Great Mother, Isis, purifies the persona instrument. She descends to the self, trapped in Nephthys' kingdom, draws him up to her, bathes him in the Light of her Divine

Mind, transforms his dross matter into light, and liberates the trapped self.

"Thus, it is the Mother Aspect, Divine Substance, who liberates the Soul!

"Since Isis is interrupted, the purifying fires go out, and the babe 'dies' to the self. Fortunately, Isis is able to continue the process by another method. She obtains permission to free the chest from the pillar, does so, and begins the long, slow journey back to the heavenly kingdom.

"The second son of Queen Astarte follows Isis to an isolated spot, where she is crying over the body of Osiris. This scene is equivalent to the scene in the previous myth in which Ishtar cries over Tammuz, bathing him in the waters of life and revivifying him. Isis catches the prince looking at the dead Osiris, and is so angered —and/or the lad is so frightened at the sight of the dead Osiris— that the boy prince dies of fright.

"The second prince again represents the self, dwelling in and identified with the persona. However, the self has now experienced enough spiritual growth and development that it is ready —with the aid of Isis— to *die* as a separated persona and be *reborn* as a Spiritual Soul. This occurs at the very beginning of the journey home, just before Isis lifts the body of Osiris from the soil of Byblos and places it in her boat. Thus, the boy or incarnate soul dies and becomes Osiris at the moment of transition from identification as the persona to awareness of and as the Spiritual Soul.

"The resurrection of Osiris has begun, and Isis sets sail toward the Nile."

The Return to Egypt

"The return of Isis and Osiris back through the Nile Delta represents the ascent of the Spiritual Soul and

Substance. At the beginning of this great journey the Spiritual Soul is lost, still nearly dead to its self and utterly helpless. Only Isis, the Great Mother, can bring Osiris home."

The Nile

"It is interesting that during the descent the chest passes down the Nile, through its delta, and out into the Mediterranean. In this instance, since the chest/column represents the spine, the Nile represents the subtle force currents of the spine.

"Floating down the Nile represents the descent into the world of affairs (the Mediterranean).

"Sailing up the Nile represents the ascent back up from the world of affairs. This includes:

"The transformation of the persona—physical-etheric, astral, and mental bodies—into an active instrument of Union.

"The movement of the fire of Substance, or kundalini, up the central channel of the spine, activating each of the centers or chakras surrounding and connected to that central channel.

"Colette?"
Colette: "Chakras?"
Quinn: "The subtle organs or centers of energy of the etheric body. We'll go over them in some detail in a later lesson.

"The centers are developed during the journey back, and thus are part of the mechanism of that journey. They are not properly the instruments of death, but — when fully developed and rightly used— the tools of liberation.

"In terms of our earlier myth —Ishtar and Tammuz— they are the 'kappa' —toy tops— or the keys to the seven gates of Substance —and those gates open both ways.

"The Nile is a cyclic river. Until the Aswan dam halted the process, it flooded every year, washing silt down from the fertile uplands into the Nile Valley and estuary. The flood covered the valley floor, forcing the Egyptians to rebuild every year. Fortunately, the receding waters left behind a layer of fertile black silt that grew some of the most nutritious grain in the ancient world.

"Thus, the Nile is an excellent symbol for the Great Mother. It is cyclic, provides the grain that feeds the people, and while it flows down into the world, one can easily sail up it—the Nile flows north but the primary local winds blow south.

"Thus, the Nile represents:

"The cycle of incarnate life, the downward motion into and out of physical-dense incarnation, and the slow path of return following the winds or breath of the Soul.

"The fire of Substance or kundalini.

"Yes, Colette?"
Colette: What's koonduhleenee?"
Quinn: "Now that would be a long discussion. Let's hold off on that? We're going to be looking at it in an upcoming lesson anyway. Basically, there are a number of definitions, but the one we'll be using is 'the fire of Substance'."
Colette: "Is it like prana then?"
Quinn: "Technically, prana is a type of physical-etheric energy. Kundalini is the fire at the heart of every particle of substance, on every plane, including the physical-etheric, astral-emotional, and mental.

"Now, let's wrap this up."

The Polarity

If we convert the myth's symbolic gender and relationships into polarity and movement, we get the following.

"Lured by the separated self —Seth— Osiris falls into the persona. This is the Positive Pole, drawn downward through the outer field, into the polarity of the Negative pole.

"Sealed within the persona, the incarnate soul is set adrift in the cyclic motion of the three lower worlds.

"After eons of drifting, the persona evolves a complex physical-etheric body —the tree— and a system of energy channels and organs —the pillar and the portions of the body.

"The tree and pillar are the mechanism through which the Divine Mother discovers the lost Soul, and begins to raise it toward liberation.

"As the body rises, its growing light attracts Seth, who appropriates the body and its energy organs.

"The Great Mother battles the separated self for control. Horus is born and joins the fight. Seth is defeated and Horus rises to become Osiris."

Summary

Quinn: "Thus, we have the movement from:

"Positive pole to outer Magnetic Field.

"Outer Magnetic Field to Negative Pole.

"The fall into the Polarity of the Negative Pole or Substance.

"Liberation from the three lower worlds by the Divine Mother.

"Ascent through the inner Magnetic Field.

"Return to the Positive Pole.

"The basic tale is the same.

"Having discovered that our first two myths are merely different versions of the same story, we're almost ready for our next allegory, the myth of Eve and Adam. But first, we'll have our closing exercise."

The Descent

Sit in a comfortable chair, relax your physical body, calm your emotions, and focus your mind.

Bring your consciousness to a point of focus within your ajna center, a tiny golden sun approximately three inches in front of the forehead and between the brows. If it helps you place yourself there, you may imagine yourself to be a tiny figure standing within that small golden sun.

From your place within the ajna center, imagine yourself standing in the gateway, between the twin pillars. Leaving the world of shadows behind, step forward into the land of light. Above you is the golden all-seeing-eye of the Sun. Around you is the blossoming Earth. Before you are twin trees.

The tree on the right has golden bark, and leaves, red fruit, and glows with the fiery light of the Sun.

The tree on the left has silver bark, leaves, and fruit, and glows with the light of the Moon.

Shading your eyes, walk up to the golden tree, pick one of its red fruit, taken a bite, chew, and swallow.

With a loud crack, the trunk of the golden tree snaps open, revealing a hollow space. Ducking your head, step within.

The crack slams shut behind you, trapping you in darkness. A voice asks, "Who are you becoming?"

Contemplate the question, *"Who am I becoming?"* for at least three minutes.

Take a deep breath, open your eyes, and return your awareness to your surroundings.

"Practice this inner ritual at least once a day, every day, for a full lunar cycle —from New Moon to New Moon."

Raising the Queen of Heaven

Lesson 6

Knowledge of Life and Death

The Myth of Eve and Adam

The group said, "Good evening!" as Quinn entered. He sat, picked up his moose mug for a sip of tea, and Tess asked, "Where'd you get that?"

Quinn replied, "Hmm?"

"That mug."

"Oh, this? Celine, I think. At the end of my last Teacher Training class."

Celine said, "Dawna helped pick it."

Quinn replied, "It's a good one."

Celine grinned, and I realized that Quinn was using a different mug each lesson, to acknowledge the gifts without playing favorites.

Quinn said, "I've heard from Wil. He had a great time at Findhorn, and is in Glastonbury. He laments that the latter has gotten all 'New Age touristy' but says some of the old aura clings to the place despite all the glamour.

Celine said, "Tell them about it."

"Glastonbury? I was there in '89, part of a, well... a project I was working on. It's one of the few places that have ancient sites sacred to all Four Aspects."

Thea asked, "All four?"

Quinn's aura snapped into that indigo triangle he used while teaching, and I turned on the recorder.

✦

Quinn: "Yes. There's Glastonbury Abbey, or its ruins, which legend says was founded by Jesus himself and is thus sacred to the Divine Son. Then there's Glastonbury Tor, a conical hill with a tower at its summit — the remains of a chapel dedicated to Saint Michael, the Warrior of God— and thus sacred to the Father Aspect. Chalice Well is, of course, sacred to the Divine Mother. And then there's Wearyall Hill, which legend says is the place where Saint Joseph of Arimathea arrived with his twelve disciples, and where he planted his staff which grew and blossomed—which, as a place where they rose to the heights, would be sacred to the Divine Daughter."

Terry: "So, by moving from one location to another you can move from one Aspect to another?"

Quinn: "Umm... I wouldn't put it quite that way. The influence of each Aspect can be more accessible or more apparent at a site sacred to it. But, it's an expression of that Aspect, a reflection of it in energy, force, and substance, not of the actual Aspect."

(Celine thrust a hand up, and Quinn nodded to her.)

Celine: "So, you can use the energy field of a site like that to move from one state to another?"

Quinn: "Well, that's one way, yes. The ritual use of forms to move from one state of awareness to another is the essence of the old style of magic."

Colette: "How did that work?"

Quinn: "Did you ever play Super Mario Brothers when you were little?"

Colette: (Frowning) "Some. My cousin had it."

Quinn: "My nieces had a Nintendo. Remember the little floating platform things that went up and down, or around in a circle, and you had to jump onto them and ride them until you reached the place where you could either jump over onto the next one, or up to grab a coin or jewel or something?"

Colette: "Yeah..."

Quinn: "The old style 'magic of the form' is like that.

You move along the path by hopping onto a form that's moving in a direction you need to go, riding it for a while, and then hopping to the next. Now, what are the problems with that?"

Colette: "Me? Well, they wouldn't always be going where you want to go. And when they are, you have to wait for the right time to jump on and off, and if you miss, you'll fall."

Quinn: "That's right."

Terry: "So, you're saying that all the ancient forms of magic were like that?"

Quinn: "All the ones that used outer ritual and the cyclic motion of energy, force, and substance to move the consciousness."

Celine: "So, how does that differ from this 'magic of consciousness'?"

Quinn: "Oh... it's a matter of identity and causality. In the old magic you used the motion of form to alter the consciousness. In the new Magic of Consciousness you alter the consciousness in order to move Spirit and Substance. But we'll get into that later.

"Now, it's time to begin.

Opening Alignment

"Close your eyes, and sit up straight.

"Relax your physical body.

"Calm your emotions.

"Bring your consciousness to a point of focus within the ajna center, and there integrate your three-fold persona into a single unit. (Pause)

"From that tiny golden sun, turn your attention upward to that wisdom or truth overshadowing this evening's lesson, and become receptive to it by silently sounding the OM. (Pause)

"Maintaining that focus of receptivity in the ajna, take a deep breath, and open your eyes."

Lesson 6

The Myth

Quinn: "The most familiar version of the myth of Eve and Adam is the one in the Christian Bible.

"Yes, Bhikku?"

Bhikku: "What about the Koran?"

Quinn: "Well... I'm not an expert on the Koran. But that version of the myth was composed well into the Age of Pisces, not Taurus. Also, while it has a few episodes on Adam, it seldom mentions his wife, and so far as I can tell never even names her."

Colette: "Doesn't name her?"

Quinn: "No... (Quinn glanced over his shoulder at the wall of books, stood, grabbed a white canvas-covered volume from the religions section, and leafed to a blue bookmark.) listen...

"And we said, 'Adam, dwell thou, and thy wife, in the Garden and eat thereof easily where you desire; but draw not nigh this tree, lest you be evildoers.'"

"Now this is, of course, a *translation* of the Koran, and thus would not be recognized as a copy *of* the Koran by a Moslem. However, this passage is an example of a phenomenon we'll encounter numerous times as we proceed. As we move from Gemini into Taurus, Aries, and Pisces, the Divine Feminine will be belittled and denigrated more and more.

"Thus, while at this point in Taurus, or in the versions of the Taurean myths we have, while the Goddess has been reduced in importance to become subsidiary to the God, at least she still has a name. That is not always the case by the time we get to Pisces.

"Also, she is portrayed as a victim who, because of her womanish nature, was led astray by the serpent and then enticed Adam into sin. Later she is conflated with the serpent and portrayed as the actual source of sin.

(Quinn set the Koran on his side table, stood, and continued talking, while pacing back and forth and gesturing with his hands.)

"Now the Biblical account is a product of this process. That version of the myth has been altered to suit patriarchal sensibilities. It conflates ADM —the human race— with Adam the man, changes Eve from the 'instructor' to the 'helper' of Adam, veils the Creator —changing 'Elohim' and 'YHWH' to 'God'—and ends all too soon.

"However, if we tear these shrouds asunder by correcting the mistranslations, the Bible gives an adequate version of the first part of the myth. It's then simple enough to complete the myth by adding an alternative ending, from another Hebrew tradition, to the Biblical version. I've asked Tess to take all of this into account when she tells us the myth. Tess? (Quinn sat down and everyone turned to Tess.)

Tess: (holding a Bible, with folded sheets of paper tucked into the beginning) "Since the Biblical version is so well known, I've asked Quinn for permission to read mine. And since 'Eve and Adam' is part of a creation story, I will begin at the beginning.[1] (Tess lifted the folded sheets from the bible, unfolded them, and began reading.)

✦

"Genesis 1

1. "In the beginning Elohim created the heavens and the earth.

2. "The earth was without form and void, and darkness was upon the face of the deep; and the Spirit of

---

[1] Quinn: All Biblical quotes are based on the New Revised Standard edition. However, we have here replaced the translation "God" with the original "Elohim" or "YHWH," respectively.

Elohim was moving over the face of the waters.

3. "And Elohim said, 'Let there be light'; and there was light.

4. "And Elohim saw that the light was good; and Elohim separated the light from the darkness.

5. "Elohim called the light Day, and the darkness they called Night. And there was evening and there was morning, one day.

6. "And Elohim said, 'Let there be a firmament in the midst of the waters, and let it separate the waters from the waters.'

7. "And Elohim made the firmament and separated the waters which were under the firmament from the waters which were above the firmament. And it was so.

8. "And Elohim called the firmament Heaven. And there was evening and there was morning, a second day.

9. "And Elohim said, 'Let the waters under the heavens be gathered together into one place, and let the dry land appear.' And it was so.

10. "Elohim called the dry land Earth, and the waters that were gathered together they called Seas. And Elohim saw that it was good.

11. "And Elohim said, 'Let the earth put forth vegetation, plants yielding seed, and fruit trees bearing fruit in which is their seed, each according to its kind, upon the earth.' And it was so.

12. "The earth brought forth vegetation, plants yielding seed according to their own kinds, and trees bearing fruit in which is their seed, each according to its kind. And Elohim saw that it was good.

13. "And there was evening and there was morning, a third day.

14. "And Elohim said, 'Let there be lights in the firmament of the heavens to separate the day from the night; and let them be for signs and for seasons and for

days and years,

15. "'and let there be lights in the firmament of the heavens to give light upon the earth.' And it was so.

16. "And Elohim made the two great lights, the greater light to rule the day, and the lesser light to rule the night; they made the stars also.

17. "And Elohim set them in the firmament of the heavens to give light upon the earth,

18. to rule over the day and over the night, and to separate the light from the darkness. And Elohim saw that it was good.

19. "And there was evening and there was morning, a fourth day.

20. "And Elohim said, 'Let the waters bring forth swarms of living creatures, and let birds fly above the earth across the firmament of the heavens.'

21. "So Elohim created the great sea monsters and every living creature that moves, with which the waters swarm, according to their kinds, and every winged bird according to its kind. And Elohim saw that it was good.

22. "And Elohim blessed them, saying, 'Be fruitful and multiply and fill the waters in the seas, and let birds multiply on the earth.'

23. "And there was evening and there was morning, a fifth day.

24. "And Elohim said, 'Let the earth bring forth living creatures according to their kinds: cattle and creeping things and beasts of the earth according to their kinds.' And it was so.

25. "And Elohim made the beasts of the earth according to their kinds and the cattle according to their kinds, and everything that creeps upon the ground according to its kind. And Elohim saw that it was good.

26. "Then Elohim said, '*Let us make man in our image, after our likeness*; and let them have dominion over

the fish of the sea, and over the birds of the air, and over the cattle, and over all the earth, and over every creeping thing that creeps upon the earth.'

27. "So Elohim created man in their own image, in the image of Elohim they created them; *male and female* they created them.

28. "And Elohim blessed them, and Elohim said to them, 'Be fruitful and multiply, and fill the earth and subdue it; and have dominion over the fish of the sea and over the birds of the air and over every living thing that moves upon the earth.'

29. "And Elohim said, 'Behold, I have given you every plant yielding seed which is upon the face of all the earth, and every tree with seed in its fruit; you shall have them for food.

30. "And to every beast of the earth, and to every bird of the air, and to everything that creeps on the earth, everything that has the breath of life, I have given every green plant for food." And it was so.

31. "And Elohim saw everything that they had made, and behold, it was very good. And there was evening and there was morning, a sixth day.

"Genesis 2

1. "Thus the heavens and the earth were finished, and all the host of them.

2. "And on the seventh day Elohim finished the work which they had done, and they rested on the seventh day from all their work which they had done.

3. "So Elohim blessed the seventh day and hallowed it, because on it Elohim rested from all the work which they had done in creation.

4. "These are the generations of the heavens and the earth when they were created. In the day that the LORD YHWH made the earth and the heavens,

5. *"when no plant of the field was yet in the earth and no herb of the field had yet sprung up*—for the LORD YHWH had not caused it to rain upon the earth, and there was no man to till the ground;

6. "but a mist went up from the earth and watered the whole face of the ground—

7. "then the LORD YHWH *formed man of dust from the ground, and breathed into his nostrils the breath of life*; and man became a living being.

8. "And the LORD YHWH planted a garden in Eden, in the east; and there he put the man whom he had formed.

9. "And out of the ground the LORD YHWH made to grow every tree that is pleasant to the sight and good for food, *the tree of life also in the midst of the garden, and the tree of the knowledge of good and evil.*

10. "A river flowed out of Eden to water the garden, and there it divided and became four rivers.

11. "The name of the first is Pishon; it is the one which flows around the whole land of Havilah, where there is gold;

12. and the gold of that land is good; bdellium and onyx stone are there.

13. "The name of the second river is Gihon; it is the one which flows around the whole land of Cush.

14. "And the name of the third river is Tigris, which flows east of Assyria. And the fourth river is the Euphrates.

15. "The LORD YHWH took the man and put him in the Garden of Eden to till it and keep it.

16. "And the LORD YHWH commanded the man, saying, 'You may freely eat of every tree of the garden;

17. but of *the tree of the knowledge of good and evil* you shall not eat, for in the day that you eat of it you shall die.'

18. "Then the LORD YHWH said, 'It is not good that the man should be alone; I will make him an *instructor*

fit for him.'

19. "So out of the ground the LORD YHWH formed every beast of the field and every bird of the air, and brought them to the man to see what he would call them; and *whatever the man called every living creature, that was its name.*

20. "The man gave names to all cattle, and to the birds of the air, and to every beast of the field; but for the man there was not found an instructor fit for him.

21. "So the LORD YHWH caused a deep sleep to fall upon the man, and while he slept took one of his ribs and closed up its place with flesh;

22. "and *the rib which the LORD YHWH had taken from the man he made into a woman* and brought her to the man.

23. "Then the man said, 'This at last is bone of my bones and flesh of my flesh; she shall be called Woman, because she was taken out of Man.'

24. "Therefore a man leaves his father and his mother and cleaves to his wife, and they become one flesh.

25. "And the man and his wife were both naked, and were not ashamed.

"Genesis 3

1. "Now the serpent was more subtle than any other wild creature that the LORD YHWH had made. He said to the woman, 'Did YHWH say, 'You shall not eat of any tree of the garden?'

2. "And the woman said to the serpent, '*We may eat of the fruit of the trees of the garden*';

3. "but YHWH said, 'You shall not eat of the fruit of the tree which is in the midst of the garden, neither shall you touch it, lest you die.'

4. "But the serpent said to the woman, 'You will not die.

5. "'For YHWH knows that when you eat of it your

eyes will be opened, and you will be like YHWH, knowing good and evil.'

6. "So when the woman saw that the tree was good for food, and that it was a delight to the eyes, and that the tree was to be desired to make one wise, she took of its fruit and ate; and she also gave some to her husband, and he ate.

7. "Then the eyes of both were opened, and *they knew that they were naked*; and they sewed fig leaves together and made themselves aprons.

8. "And they heard the sound of the LORD YHWH walking in the garden in the cool of the day, and the man and his wife hid themselves from the presence of the LORD YHWH among the trees of the garden.

9. "But the LORD YHWH called to the man, and said to him, 'Where are you?'

10. "And he said, 'I heard the sound of thee in the garden, and I was afraid, because I was naked; and I hid myself.'

11. "He said, 'Who told you that you were naked? Have you eaten of the tree of which I commanded you not to eat?'

12. "The man said, 'The woman whom thou gavest to be with me, she gave me fruit of the tree, and I ate.'

13. "Then the LORD YHWH said to the woman, 'What is this that you have done?' The woman said, 'The serpent beguiled me, and I ate.'

14. "The LORD YHWH said to the serpent, 'Because you have done this, cursed are you above all cattle, and above all wild animals; upon your belly you shall go, and dust you shall eat all the days of your life.

15. "'I will put enmity between you and the woman, and between your seed and her seed; he shall bruise your head, and you shall bruise his heel.'

16. "To the woman he said, 'I will greatly multiply

your pain in childbearing; in pain you shall bring forth
children, yet your desire shall be for your husband, and
he shall rule over you.'

17. "And to Adam he said, 'Because you have listened to the voice of your wife, and have eaten of the
tree of which I commanded you, 'You shall not eat of it,'
cursed is the ground because of you; in toil you shall eat
of it all the days of your life;

18. "'thorns and thistles it shall bring forth to you;
and you shall eat the plants of the field.

19. "'In the sweat of your face you shall eat bread till
you return to the ground, for out of it you were taken;
you are dust, and to dust you shall return.'

20. "The man called his wife's name Eve, because
she was the mother of all living.

21. "And the LORD YHWH made for Adam and for
his wife garments of skins, and clothed them.

22. "Then the LORD YHWH said, 'Behold, the man
has become like one of us, knowing good and evil; and
now, lest he put forth his hand and take also of the tree
of life, and eat, and live for ever' —

23. "therefore the LORD YHWH sent him forth from
the Garden of Eden, to till the ground from which he
was taken.

24. "He drove out the man; and at the east of the
Garden of Eden he placed the cherubim, and a flaming
sword which turned every way, to guard the way to the
tree of life.

✦

"The centuries passed, the man grew old and infirm
with toil, and lay in great pain near to death. Then Eve,
seeing that Adam was about to die, left the earth and
journeyed to heaven.

"When she stood at last before the throne of the

LORD YHWH, she begged for Adam's life, offering to take half of his pain upon herself.

"The LORD YHWH was moved to pity by her pleas and said, 'Those who have eaten of the fruit of the Tree of Knowledge must know death, but because you know death, you shall also know rebirth.'

"Having won the promise of rebirth, Eve returned to the earth. She told Adam of the promise of the LORD YHWH, and then he died.

"Eve wept constantly for many days and nights, and then rose and taught her children the first mourning rituals, and the rites of passage for those who have died.

"And then Eve died and passed to the next life, and all her children mourned."[2]

The Main Characters

Quinn: "Thank you Tess."

Ema: "What was that last part?"

Tess: "It's based on an old Jewish story, non-biblical."

Ema: "Ah. It was very good."

Quinn: (standing and stepping up to the board) "Now, the characters were... Elohim, YHWH again, ADM... who else?"

Tess: "Eve!"

Thea: "The serpent"

Quinn: "Oh yes, mustn't forget her."

Celine: "The Cherubim"

Quinn: "Any more?"

Bhikku: "Who are these 'Elowheem'?"

---

[2] Quinn: Adapted from Apocryphal Midrashic works (Jewish legends), including *Vita Adae et Evae* (The Book of Adam and Eve) and *The Apocalypse of Mosis*, and *The New Book of Goddesses & Heroines*, by Patricia Monaghan.

Quinn: "E l o h i m. I suppose we might as well begin with them.

Elohim

"The Elohim were the actual Creators in Genesis 1. Most Christians assume that the biblical creator is YHWH, and tend to picture Him much as Michelangelo portrayed Him in the Sistine Chapel —a vigorous old man in robes with long white hair and beard. However, the name YHWH does not actually appear in the Bible until Genesis 2: 4.

"From Genesis 1:1 through 2:3 the creators are the 'Elohim', not YHWH.

"Now both Elohim and YHWH are generally mistranslated as 'God' in the Bible, which veils the identity of the creators. This is completely understandable in a conservative monotheistic religion, especially given the meaning of Elohim.

"Elohim is a name with two parts. The first part, 'Eloh' is a noun with a feminine ending —'h'. The second part, 'im' is a masculine plural ending.[3] This combination of a feminine noun and a masculine plural ending indicates both duality —feminine and masculine— and plurality —more than one being.

"This means that the Creators in Genesis 1 were:

"Female.

"Male.

"Two or more.

"The name itself leaves open the question of the number of creators.

"If there were two creators, then they were two poles or expressions —one female and one male— of one being.

---

[3] Glen: For further explanation and a slightly different conclusion see: *The Rosicrucian Cosmo-Conception*, The Creative Hierarchies, by Max Heindel, The Rosicrucian Fellowship, Oceanside, CA

"If there were more than two, then they were androgynous. The Two Poles of Divinity were in equal, balanced expression within them."

Me: "Androwhat?"

Quinn: "A n d r o g y n o u s. Technically, that's when you have mature male and female gender in one body."

Me: "Oh, one person with both sets of things, like a hermaphrodite?"

Quinn: "Yes."

Terry: "The creators were like two sets of twins then?"

Quinn: "Umm... that would be one way to represent them, symbolically."

Me: "But how would two andro's—"

Quinn: "Now that would be a good science assignment for this week; on, say... reproduction among hermaphroditic animals.

Me: "Daaad!"

Quinn: "I suggest you start with garden snails."

Me. "O..h..K..a..y."

Quinn: "At least five hundred words, illustrated, but *animals only.*

"Now, in either case, the creators were a duality and the 'days' indicate that they used the cyclic creative process. These conclusions are supported by the text.

"In Genesis 1:26 we find:

"Then God said, '*Let us make man in our image, after our likeness...*'

"In this passage, the Elohim refer to themselves as 'us' and 'our', plainly identifying themselves as a plural! The obvious question is, 'what plurality'?

"Yes Ed?"

Ed: "Couldn't it be like the royal plural?"

Quinn: "You mean the royal 'we'? If it was, then we'd expect to find it elsewhere when 'God' spoke. But we don't. YHWH, for instance, uses the singular.

"So is Elohim a single polarity or multiple bipolar beings? Fortunately, this question is answered in the very next passage.

"In Genesis 1:27 we find:

"So Elohim created man in their own image, in the image of Elohim they created them; *male and female* they created them."

"Thus, man, created in the image and after the likeness of Elohim, was created 'male and female'. Now 'male and female' can mean two things:

"Man was originally androgynous, that is, simultaneously male and female, and/or...

"Man was created as two separate genders, with neither gender having precedence.

"As we will see, both of the above are correct. Man was originally androgynous and later split into two separate but equal genders. However, the fact that man was created male and female, in the image and after the likeness of Elohim, means that *Elohim is male and female*. The Creators were not just the masculine YHWH, but the Positive and Negative Poles of Divinity, The Great Father and the Great Mother.

"We know the Creators are the Two Poles of Divinity because of the way creation works. Now, one of the primary secrets of the creative process is the reason it works the way it does. Up to now, while we've discussed *how* the creative process works, we have not discussed *why*...

"The One became the Three.

"The purpose, power, and will of the Positive Pole descends into Substance.

"The intelligent activity of the Negative Pole ascends to Spirit.

"The Magnetic Field relates Positive to Negative and Negative to Positive.

"The reason the One became Three is quite simple. The Three are the means and method whereby the One creates.

"As long as that no thing remained One, there was and could be nothing else but that One. There could be no change, no growth, no anything. This is a good description of a materialist's view of death—non-existence!

"Thus, in order to grow, to evolve, to simply *be*, that no thing divided itself into three things...

"A Positive Pole.

"A Negative Pole.

"A Magnetic Field.

"These three are the Creators because everything that exists is created by and emerges from them. This creative process has two basic parts:

"The descent of the First Aspect into Substance, followed by a pause or interlude at the low point

"The Ascent of the Third Aspect into Spirit, followed by a pause or interlude at the high point

"These are the 'days' of creation —'there was evening and there was morning, one day.' This process is why 'evening' —the descent— came before 'morning' —the ascent.

"This cyclic creative process produces everything that exists:

"The original universal Trinity reproduces itself in smaller proportion, producing the trinities of galaxies.

"A galactic Trinity reproduces itself in smaller proportion, producing the trinities of solar systems.

"A solar Trinity reproduces itself in smaller proportion, producing the trinities of planets.

"The Trinity of the Earth reproduces itself in smaller proportion, producing the trinities of everything that exists in our planetary life.

"Each of these trinities works the descent—pause—ascent—pause creative process. The method is the same, but the sphere of activity differs.

"The universe is produced by a great cycle of creation that contains all the lesser cycles:

"A galaxy is produced by a smaller cycle within the universal cycle.

"A solar life is produced by a cycle within a galactic cycle.

"A planetary life is produced by a cycle within a solar cycle.

"These smaller cycles may be compared to the orbit of the moon around the earth, within the orbit of the earth around Sol, and the orbit of Sol within the Milky Way. The smaller life cycles exist within the greater, but each has its own motion.

"These polarities and cycles continue reproducing themselves —in ever smaller form— down to the subatomic. However, in each case, no matter how far removed from the original, the basic nature of the Three remains the same:

"The Positive Pole continues to provide the purpose, power and will, or Divine Intent.

"The Negative Pole continues to provide the Intelligent Activity or Substance.

177

"The Magnetic Field continues to provide the awareness of relationship or Consciousness.

"Within the Trinity, the function of Substance —at all levels— is to differentiate the Divine Intent —conveyed to it by the Consciousness— into many intelligent activities. This is why, at each reproduction of the Trinity, you have numerous lesser expressions of the Trinity. At each reproduction, the basic Three are differentiated into many, each one of the many being itself a Three.

"When a Divine Intent is related by a positive pole to a negative pole, at any level, the negative pole responds with a new activity. That new activity of Substance differentiates that Intent into a new appearance or form. The result is a continued refinement of Substance into forms that are increasingly sensitive and responsive to Divine Intent.

"The first forms were relatively crude and unresponsive to Intent. However, millions of years of refinement are producing forms that are much more sensitive and responsive. As a result, it's now possible for human beings —with much more refined bodies— to achieve in a few lifetimes spiritual growth that formerly took hundreds of incarnations.

"When this spiritual growth proceeds far enough that an incarnate human soul achieves at-one-ment with the overshadowing Spiritual Soul, the process expands:

"The identity or 'I am' expands beyond the persona — the mind, emotions, and body— to include the spiritual group life of which the Soul is a part.

"The purpose or 'I will to be' expands beyond that of the individualized soul to that of the spiritual group life.

"The transmutation of Substance expands beyond the persona to include the energy, force, and substance of the spiritual group life.

"Terry?"

Terry: "You mean the transmutation of form into light?"

Quinn: "Yes, but it eventually expands beyond our individual personas to our group, transforming our shared thought-forms, feelings, and energy.

"One result of this expansion is that as the forms which hold groups separate from each other are raised into light, the divisions, the separations between groups disappear and humanity merges into one re-united kingdom. Now keep in mind that this movement, the re-union of the individual with the group, of groups with humanity, and of humanity with the One Life is a motion of consciousness."

Celine: "The magical motion?"

Quinn: "Yes. It's the motion of the Soul, the magic of consciousness that relates Intent with Form and thereby alters the motion of that form. But, where the difference arises, is that you do not identify with that new form, but with relationship, with the activity of consciousness.

"Bhikku?"

Bhikku: "So, if you don't identify with it, you don't become trapped within the form."

Quinn: "Yes, and it keeps the creative process going. It doesn't stop."

Jeff: "I don't get... It stopped before, right, but it doesn't when you don't identify?"

Quinn: "It's a result of intent. If the goal is to create a form, you relate Purpose to Substance, and Substance reacts with a new motion, a new Intelligent Activity, producing a new appearance or form. But, if that's the goal, if you identify with the form, the process grinds to a stop right there. It can't go on because you're not acting as the consciousness and relating things, you're acting as the form and performing an intelligent activity, the same one, over and over again.

"However, when you identify as the Soul, and with the creative process, you don't fall into the form and the creative process continues. The form never crystallizes, but remains fluid, attentive and responsive to a focus of Intent directed to it by the Soul.

"Terry?"

Terry: "What will this look like?"

Quinn: "Well... one of the... features of this way of working is that you don't know what it will look like until the outer form appears, and even then that outer form is transitory. Remember, you're working the magic of consciousness—you're not trying to create an outer form. You realize that there will be an outer form, that's part of the process, but it's *part* of the process, not the goal.

"Ed?"

Ed: "So, in the old way the goal would be to create a particular form?"

Quinn: "The ideal form, yes. But another problem with that is that the spiritual ideal cannot be achieved."

Bhikku: "What do you mean?"

Quinn: "Well, take the ideal of Christianity, of becoming like Christ. The realization of that ideal is so far beyond most of us that the average person just doesn't believe it's possible, not really. But since they're identified with that ideal, that astral form, at some level they note every instance when they fail to realize that ideal, they feel every 'failure', criticize themselves constantly, and build up a deep core of self hatred.

"So, by identifying with that form, that ideal, they trap themselves within it and prevent themselves from realizing it. It winds up being another trap.

"Thea?"

Thea: "So, shouldn't we identify with the Christ?"

Quinn: "Actually, that's exactly what you do. You identify with the Christ —not the mental idea, the astral ideal, or the physical idol, those are all forms— but with the Christ, the Second Aspect of Divinity. Remember, it doesn't really matter what word or words you use to identify that Aspect, just that you do identify with and as that Aspect, to whatever extent and degree you can.

"Now, where..."

Me: "The transmutation of substance."

Quinn: "Ah. As we free ourselves from the form, we gradually move from individual identity to group awareness. As this process of transmutation expands beyond individuals to include all of humanity, then human awareness —the normal state or condition of all human beings everywhere— will expand beyond individuality to include that of the entire kingdom as one united consciousness. At the same time, our personal lifecycles will be transformed from a multitude of tiny conflicting motions, to one united cycle, and humanity will then take up its work as a kingdom within the planetary life.

"All of this is achieved by consciously working the creative cycle of the Three Aspects of Divinity. As human beings, we are sparks of the Second Aspect in incarnation. It is, therefore, our function in the One Life to relate Divine Intent to Substance, and Divine Intelligence to Spirit. Thus, working the cyclic creative process is our purpose and function within the One Life.

"However, we cannot act as the Second Aspect or Soul as long as we're identified with, and trapped in the Third Aspect or Substance. The Soul must be freed from its tomb, by transforming that tomb into a temple of liberation.

"This is achieved by regular practice of the internal

and external rituals of the creative process. Through that process, we, each and every one of us, will slowly uplift the frequency of Substance until the entire physical-dense form of the Earth is transmuted into light.

"By thus raising the Queen of Heaven, we enable Her to uplift and liberate the Soul or Self that is trapped in Substance.

"Yes, Terry?"

Terry: "Well... you've talked about the individual steps, our own persona, but how do we raise the Queen of Heaven?"

Quinn: (grinning) "That's the whole point of the course, isn't it. We'll get into how it's done when we examine the roles of the other characters in the Myth of Eve and Adam.

"Now, who's next...?"

Me: "A D M"

ADM

Quinn: "Right. Now, in our current perspective, ADM is the androgynous being created *in the image and after the likeness* of the creators—the Elohim—on the sixth day of creation. In this context, 'Image' and 'likeness' mean two different things. The first indicates the *place* where ADM was created, while the second suggests the *nature* of that creation.

"Think about what those words mean! An *image* of a thing is a reflection of that thing, such as a mirror image. Thus 'in the image' means that ADM was created inside the reflection of God. This reflection exists in the three lower worlds in which we dwell. These worlds, and their contents, are not the creation of Elohim, but the reflection of that creation. The actual divine creation exists in the realm of ideas, which is reflected into thought on the mental plane, emotional feeling on the astral plane, and physical-dense forms in the world of affairs.

"On the other hand, a *likeness* is not a reflection, but a new thing that is intentionally similar to an original. A drawing, painting, or sculpture, for instance, would be a good or bad 'likeness' depending on how accurately they duplicated the person and/or thing they portrayed. Thus, ADM is 'like' Elohim because ADM, like Elohim, is a polarity.

"Elohim, remember, is a one thing that is three things, a Positive Pole, a Negative Pole, and a Magnetic Field.

"Now ADM, humanity, is a portion of the One-that-is-Three, with the emphasis on the Magnetic Field or Soul. Since that field is born of the two poles, it inherits their divine characteristics, including polarity. Thus, both the magnetic field and humanity have an internal polarity. In the magnetic field, that polarity consists of:

"The external, downward moving pole, which we refer to in gender terms as the Divine Son, and...

"The internal, upward moving pole, which we refer to as the Divine Daughter.

"Thus every human soul, as a part of that magnetic field, inherits the polarity of the Spiritual Soul. We are all, each and every one of us, the Daughter/Son of the Mother/Father.

"This fact is described —in slightly veiling masculine terms— in the creation of ADM on the sixth day. However, as we will see, this androgynous ADM does not yet have a physical-dense body.

"Now from Genesis 2:4 through the rest of the Biblical creation myth the creator's name is YHWH.

"This is the masculine God that most patriarchal monotheists picture when they imagine a creator. Now we know that YHWH actually represents the Positive Pole because:

"He impresses Substance to create Adam.

"The creation of Adam moves downward from YHWH through the Magnetic Field to the Negative Pole.

"In Genesis 2: 7 we find:

"'then *the LORD YHWH formed man of dust from the ground, and breathed into his nostrils the breath of life*; and man became a living being.'

"Although only the First Aspect is named in this verse, all three are actually present.

"The First Aspect or Positive Pole is YHWH or the Father.

"The Second Aspect or Magnetic Field is the 'breath of life' or Soul.

"The Third Aspect or Negative Pole is the 'dust from the ground' or Substance.

"Thea?"

Thea: "Were all Three present in the beginning, at the creation?"

Quinn: "In potential, yes, within the Elohim. The 'Word' for instance, that was with or within and spoke from the Elohim, was or became the Second Aspect. It was after the sounding of that creative Word, or by the sounding, that you have the separation of the One into Three. So, from this perspective, it's the task of the self, the Soul or Second Aspect, to re-unite the Three into One because it was the Soul's creative Word or activity that differentiated the One into Three in the first place.

"Celine?"

Celine: "So, the entire cosmic incarnation is one great motion, one great cycle of consciousness?"

Quinn: "Yes, and all the other cycles, within cycles, within cycles are within that.

"So, here we are, with all Three Aspects of Divinity —with two veiled by the patriarchal perspective— equally involved in a second stage of the creative process. The actual sequence of the creation of Adam would be:

"YHWH sounded His Word of Intent.

"The Soul or 'breath of life' carried that Intent downward.

"The 'dust from the ground' or Divine Mother received that Intent from the Soul, and responded by forming a body of Substance.

"Celine?"

Celine: "So it's a description of the creative process?"

Quinn: "Of part of that process, the downward motion.

"It's at this stage that humanity, reflecting the Daughter/Son duality of the Soul, split into two genders or Adam and Eve.

"Adam is the Positive Pole and Eve is the Negative Pole of the Human Kingdom.

"The second description of the creation of humanity, in Genesis 2: 3-7, appears to contradict our conclusion that ADM was androgynous:

3. "So YHWH blessed the seventh day and hallowed it, because on it YHWH rested from all his work which he had done in creation.

4. "These are the generations of the heavens and the earth when they were created. In the day that the LORD YHWH made the earth and the heavens,

5. *"when no plant of the field was yet in the earth and no herb of the field had yet sprung up*—for the LORD YHWH had not caused it to rain upon the earth, and there was no man to till the ground;

6. "but a mist went up from the earth and watered the whole face of the ground—

7. "then *the LORD YHWH formed man of dust from the ground, and breathed into his nostrils the breath of life*; and man became a living being.

"These verses describe the creation of man from the dust of the earth, and the breathing of the breath of life —the Soul— into his body. However, there is a problem with the sequence. In Genesis 1, Man is created on the sixth day, *after* the Elohim had already:

"separated light from darkness,

"separated the waters from the dry land,

"made the earth bring forth vegetation,

"placed the lights in the heavens,

"made the waters bring forth living creatures,

"and let the earth bring forth living creatures.

"However, in Genesis 2, Adam is created '*when no plant of the field was yet in the earth and no herb of the field had yet sprung up*' as occurred in Genesis 1 on the *second* day of creation!

"Continuing on to Genesis 2:21-22 we find:

21. "So the LORD YHWH caused a deep sleep to fall upon the man, and while he slept took one of his ribs and closed up its place with flesh;

22. "and the rib which the LORD YHWH had taken from the man he made into a woman and brought her to the man.

"This appears to be an irreconcilable conflict:

"In Genesis 1 the first man is an androgyne created on the sixth day.

"In Genesis 2 the first man is a male created before the end of the second day.

"Theologians examining these passages tend to speak of different authors —'P' and 'J'— writing at different times, whose work has been 'conflated' or combined by later editors. However, this does nothing to resolve the apparent conflict in meaning. Is the first version correct, or the later?

"Fortunately, the conflict disappears when we look for a deeper meaning beyond the mundane, and realize that what is being described are multiple levels of creation, or a descent from a more subtle state of existence to a more material condition. In these terms, we may say that the creation in Genesis 1 refers to the Spiritual Soul and Ideas—the Self and the archetypal forms on the buddhic plane, the plane of the Soul.

"Up to this point — Genesis 1— all forms on earth had existed only as ideas and thoughts in the Mind of the Goddess.

"The idea of ADM in the Mind of the Goddess existed in the Negative Pole of creation. It was the Mother's response to the Father's Divine Intent, precipitated into her Divine Substance.

"As a child of the One Life, the idea of ADM was a One. However, so long as ADM remained a One, she/he could not create. Since creation is the result of the interrelationship of the Three, in order for ADM to become an adult Child of God, the Three Aspects united within ADM had to separate.

"This separation produced a trinity in ADM's form, each portion of which had its own characteristics, and its function, in the creative process:

"A mental body, which provides energy or potential and creates thought-forms,

"An astral or emotional body, which provides force or activity, and

"A physical-etheric or bio-electrical body, which provides substance or appearance

"To become potential, the idea of ADM had to be precipitated into the mental plane.

"To become force, the idea of ADM had to be precipitated into the astral plane.

"To become Substance, the idea of ADM had to be precipitated into the physical-etheric plane.

"The one idea of ADM had then become three. However, in the process of moving into the persona, the ADM was split into a new polarity:

"In the new positive pole —Adam— the bodies were aligned to channel Divine Intent downward.

"In the new negative pole —Eve— the bodies were aligned to channel Creative Activity upward.

"Thus, the Creators used the cyclic creative process to create:

"The androgynous archetype of 'Man' on the Buddhic or Soul plane.

"The thought of 'Man' on the mental plane.

"The appearance of Eve and Adam on the astral and physical-etheric planes.

"Since we were a reflection of the Trinity, created using the cyclic creative process, we have:

"The Trinity within us.

"The innate capacity, as the trinity, to work the cyclic creative process.

"Since we are the trinity, and the trinity reproduces itself via the creative process, we are inherently creative. We identify with intent or will, relate that intent to substance, and respond to the success or frustration of our intent.

"Humanity's participation in the creative process is included in the story of creation. We have noted how — in the myths of Ishtar and Tammuz, and Isis and Osiris— the passage of the goddess through seven gates symbolized the passage downward —in frequency— through seven planes. In the myth of Eve and Adam the passage through those planes, as well as through time, are symbolized by the days of creation. Thus, since God rested on the seventh day, the physical-etheric universe did not yet exist!"

"John?"

John: "I don't... why?"

Quinn: "Why?"

John: "He'd already created everything."

Quinn: "Well, sort of, yes. You need to keep a couple things in mind here. First, we're looking at this from the perspective of Seven Planes, and counting them from above downward. This 'above downward' is the arc of the Divine Son, but that's OK here because we're looking at the manifestation process, the descent. Now we, that is the self or Soul, work with the idea of things on the soular plane, the thought of things on the mental plane, the emotional feeling on the astral, the energy form on the physical-etheric, and our physical-dense instrument works with physical-dense forms.

"If you transpose the seven days of creation onto this, you have God creating ideas on the fourth day, thoughts on the fifth, and astral-emotional forms on the sixth, but resting on the Seventh. So, He created the soular, mental, and astral forms of everything, and stopped. He delegated the lower creation, the long, slow process of unfoldment in time and space, to that portion of Himself which is us.

"The mist that rose up was raw physical-etheric substance, from which God formed the energy bodies of the plants, animals, and Adam and Eve.

"Remember the Rule of Three. In order for the thought-forms to fully develop, they needed a negative pole. In this case, that negative pole is the physical-etheric plane, the negative pole of the Negative Pole or Mother Aspect.

"For humanity to fulfill its creative function in the physical-dense, it had to create physical-dense forms of the proper frequency. Those were physically-split poles or male and female bodies.

"At first, the physical-etheric form that embodied the thought-form of man was also androgynous. During this phase of our development, man named or sounded the creative word that gave physical shape and form to the thought-forms of plants and animals.

"Celine?"

Celine: "Is that the 'lost word' of Freemasonry?"

Quinn: "Hold on to that question. We'll get to it later.

"Now, since we then embodied both poles within ourselves, there was no tension between those poles. Without that tension, the Mother Aspect could not act as the instructor of the Child. Thus, in order to progress more rapidly, and so serve his/her function in the One Life, the physical-etheric androgynous man had to be divided into Adam and Eve.

"Bhikku?"

Bhikku: "Aren't we supposed to release all tensions?"

Quinn: "Conflict. They're two different things. Conflict is when, for instance, you have two contradictory goals, like when you want to lose weight, but hate exercise and love cheesecake. Tension is the dynamic energy that flows between opposites. They may be a pair of opposites, such as Spirit and Substance, or polar opposites such as conflicting desires to lose weight and eat cheesecake. In the pair of opposites, the opposites are two sides of one thing, and the tension between them is the energy of relationship; in polar opposites, it's the energy of misrelationship and conflict.

"Now, we need the tension, the energy of relationship, because that's the motivation, the movement. In the persona, tension is the astral-emotional energy that drives us to manifest our goals.

"Ed?"

Ed: "So, without that tension, we don't get anything done, and with it we do?"

Quinn: "Yes, as long as it's the tension between a pair of opposites, or negative and positive poles.

Colette: "What happened to the Androgynes?"

Quinn: "Well, androgynous bodies will reappear in the human kingdom as the process of at-one-ment proceeds within humanity, lifting the physical-dense plane up in frequency to merge with the physical-etheric, and as we re-unite the poles of our self or Soul."

Colette: "Is that related to Soul Mates?"

Quinn: "Umm... This really isn't the time, there's so much stuff out there on this. But, it depends on what you mean. Basically, yes, most of the definitions I've seen are related to this process of at-one-ment. First, in the union of the two poles of the persona, and then as the re-union of the two poles of the Soul.

"Look, when the frequency of the persona instrument is high enough, and the at-one-ment of our two poles has proceeded far enough, then 'physical' human androgynes will be able to incarnate, live, and function creatively in the world.

"Celine?"

Celine: "What happens when those poles are brought together in one form?"

Quinn: "In terms of...?"

Celine: "The magical process?"

Quinn: "Oh, it becomes much more powerful, much more so than was possible before. Remember, the strength of the magnetic field is determined by the strength of the two poles and their nearness to each other. Thus, when the two poles of the human persona —male and female— at-one, the persona becomes a much more powerful instrument. When the two poles of the consciousness or Soul re-unite, the consciousness becomes extraordinarily more magnetic."

Terry: "What does it do?"

Quinn: "Well... the purpose of the magnetic field is to relate the Two Poles of Divinity. Being born of the relationship between them, that is its nature. Now when the Soul descends into incarnation, it goes through a cyclic, creative process of relating and uniting with a portion of the Negative Pole or Substance. Once it's achieved that, it then enters a cyclic, creative process of relating and uniting with a portion of the Positive Pole or Spirit.

"It's the same creative process in both cases, the magic of consciousness; it's just that the emphasis changes from the descent into the Negative Pole to the Ascent to the Positive Pole.

"Now once the incarnate consciousness at-one's with and integrates the persona into a single instrument, and the poles of the Soul are re-united, the Soul at-one's with the Spirit or Positive Pole, and at-one's that Spirit with Substance. The result is a Monopole, a single unit of Substance-Soul-Spirit."

Celine: "Is that the same as a 'Monad'."

Quinn: "In Theosophical terms? Yes, the Monopole would be the same thing as a Monad or 'Master of the Wisdom'.

"Now, getting back... Um..."

Me: "The Mother as Instructor to the Child."

Quinn: "Ah. Now, as we've seen, the Negative Pole or Divine Mother is an essential part of this entire process. Again, in 'Eve and Adam' Eve represents the Negative Pole of the Human Kingdom.

Eve

"Of course, the patriarchal viewpoint of the myth severely distorts the nature and purpose of Eve. This distortion begins, before she even appears, when the Bible characterizes her purpose in relationship to Adam.

"Genesis 2

18. "Then the LORD God said, 'It is not good that the man should be alone; I will make him a *helper* fit for him.'

19. "So out of the ground the LORD God formed every beast of the field and every bird of the air, and brought them to the man to see what he would call them; and *whatever the man called every living creature, that was its name.*

20. "The man gave names to all cattle, and to the birds of the air, and to every beast of the field; but for the man there was not found a *helper* fit for him.

"Now, the word 'ezer' is here translated as 'helper' or 'helpmeet', but is translated elsewhere in the Bible as 'instructor.'

"If the myth were told from an inclusive viewpoint, Genesis 2: 21-23 might read something like this:

21. "So the LORDS caused a deep sleep to fall upon

the androgyne, and while it slept divided it in twain and closed up its flesh;

22. "and one part which the LORDS had taken from the androgyne they made into a woman and the other part they made into a man.

23. "Then the woman looked upon the man, and the man upon the woman, and the two said, 'This at last is bone of my bones and flesh of my flesh, because she/he was taken out of me.'

"Eve was not, and could not have been, created out of Adam. As we've seen, the natures of polarity, and of the creative process, make it impossible for either gender to be created from or inferior to, the other!

"Thus, Eve represents the human negative pole, the substantial aspect that *instructs* the human positive pole —Adam. Both of these poles exist in every human soul, but in any persona instrument, one or the other pole is emphasized in the astral and physical-etheric, and in the resulting physical-dense body, of that incarnation. Thus:

"Eve includes the Divine Will of the Father, but emphasizes the Divine Intelligence of the Mother.

"Adam includes the Divine Intelligence of the Mother, but emphasizes the Divine Will of the Father.

"These two poles remain separate in their expression in form —appearing as women and men— until they are reunited in the consciousness of the Soul, and the two are again made One.

Cherubim

"Now, let me see... the next characters would be the Cherubim. They appear in Genesis 3: 22-24:

22. "Then the LORD God said, 'Behold, the man has

become like one of us, knowing good and evil; and now, lest he put forth his hand and take also of the tree of life, and eat, and live for ever —

23. "therefore the LORD God *sent him forth from the Garden of Eden*, to till the ground from which he was taken.

24. "He *drove out the man*; and at *the east* of the Garden of Eden he placed the cherubim, and a flaming sword which turned every way, to guard the way to the tree of life.

"Now, the word Cherubim or *Kerubim* originated in either Assyria or Akkadia. In ancient Assyrian religious art, cherubim were huge winged creatures with human or leonine heads, and the bodies of other creatures such as bulls, lions, eagles, etc. They were guardian spirits, usually stationed at the entrances of temples or palaces.

"Yes, Thea?"

Thea: "That sounds like a Sphinx."

Quinn: "Yes, it does, and there is probably some connection, especially when you consider the connection to the ancient mystery traditions. To this day, in Freemasonry for instance, a candidate has to face a guardian and answer a question or riddle in order to gain admission to the Lodge.

"Now, according to Hebrew tradition, the Temple of Solomon contained two pairs of cherubim:[4]

"One large pair immediately within the entrance to the inner chamber —the Holy of Holies— and a small pair atop the lid or mercy seat of the Ark of the Covenant.

"Bhikku?"

Bhikku: "The Arc of the Covenant?"

Quinn: "A r k. It's an old word for box or chest.

---

[4] Quinn: The meaning of the symbolism of the Temple, including these two pairs of cherubim, was explored in detail in another course: *The Temple and The Word*

Terry: "Ah! Another box."

Thea: "Bhikku, you've seen 'Raiders of the Lost Ark'?"

Bhikku: "Yes!"

Quinn: "We'll look at the Ark in detail in a later lesson. For now, keep in mind that it was guarded by Cherubim.

"Thus, in a sense, Cherubim are guardian angels who protect *places* rather than people. Further, since one had to have achieved a certain initiation in order to pass the cherubim guarding the entrance to the Holy of Holies, the cherubim might be said to be guarding the sanctity of a place.

"This has interesting implications for the expulsion of Eve and Adam from the Garden of Eden. They were not expelled as punishment for eating the fruit of the Tree of Knowledge, but because of the physical consequences. As we shall see, eating of the fruit of the Tree of Knowledge represented part of the creative process, the downward motion of descent whereby Eve and Adam took on physical-etheric and physical-dense bodies. In the process of moving into those bodies, they removed themselves from the Garden and could not return to it so long as they were in those bodies.

"Terry?"

Terry: "So, it was a frequency change, not a change in, what... geographic location?"

Quinn: "Yes. Eve and Adam moved out of the 'state of consciousness' of Eden, and thereby out of the experience of it in Substance. It was essentially a downward movement of consciousness."

Jeff: "So nirvana is like returning to the Garden?"

Quinn: "Umm... Well... sort of, but not really. Sorry, it depends what you mean. The consciousness can return to that 'position', but we've grown and developed, and so has the greater life, the Substance, so the experience of that position is very different."

Thea: "Like visiting your childhood home?"

Quinn: "Not quite, but close. Your childhood home always seems 'smaller', and it wouldn't be 'home' anymore. The astral and mental have kept developing, so you don't have that sense of smallness. But, by that point in the process of return they're not 'home' anymore either, so there is that similarity.

"Now that covers all the characters...

"Yes, Ema?"

Ema: "May we have a break?"

Quinn: "Yes, of course."

(The class took a brief restroom break, refilled their cups, and resumed their places.)

The Symbols

Quinn: "OK, everyone sit up straight, close your eyes, and resume your alignment of receptivity to the overshadowing Wisdom...

"Now maintaining that alignment, slowly open your eyes...

✦

"Let me see... the symbols include the Garden, flaming sword, and the two trees —the Tree of Life and the Tree of Knowledge.

The Garden

"As I suggested earlier, the Garden represents both the place of residence and the state of awareness of Eve and Adam before they ate of the fruit of the Tree of Knowledge.

"As a state of awareness, it represents the quality of human consciousness before the development of the solar plexus center and the consequent polarization of the emotions.

"Terry?"

Terry: "How do you know it's the Solar Plexus?"

Quinn: "Because of the way the consciousness functions when it dwells in that center. We'll get to the details in an upcoming lesson.

"As a place, the Garden represents both the three lower worlds —before humanity incarnated in the physical-dense world of affairs— and a harmonious relationship with the environment."

The Flaming Sword

Quinn: "The Flaming Sword is mentioned in Genesis 3:45:

45. "He drove out the man; and at the east of the Garden of Eden he placed the cherubim, and a flaming sword which turned every way, to guard the way to the tree of life.

"Although Christian religious tradition places the flaming sword in the hand of the cherubim, and turns the cherubim into an archangel —such as Michael— this is not supported by the above quote.

"A cherubim is not an archangel.

"The cherubim is not named.

"The cherubim is not depicted holding the sword and traditional cherubim did not have hands with which to hold it.

"The error in the tradition apparently grew out of a misunderstanding of the different functions of the cherubim and the sword. As we have seen, the cherubim were guardians of sacred spaces. Thus, the cherubim guarded the eastern border of the Garden of Eden, while the flaming sword guarded the way to the Tree of Life.

"In order to understand the sword we need to recall that substance moves in a cyclic or rotary motion. Thus, a flaming sword that turns every way represents the Fire of Substance. This sacred fire of substance exists in and circulates through all forms.

"In the Hindu tradition, the Fire of Substance is called kundalini. In the human organism this energy originates in the base of the spine and rises upward — like mercury in a thermometer— as the incarnate consciousness grows and develops. When that sacred fire reaches the top of the head, the incarnate consciousness achieves union with the overshadowing Spiritual Soul, and the two become one.

"Celine?"

Celine: "Kundalini can be either drawn up or forced up, right?"

Quinn: "Yes, that's right. The form-oriented rituals work to force it up from below, while the magic of consciousness magnetically attracts or draws it up from above."

Jeff: "Which is best?"

Quinn: "Well... it's not really a matter of good, bad, or best. It simply depends on what you're trying to do. If your focus is on the form, then you'll sort of gravitate to those rituals that force kundalini up by stimulating the form. If your focus is on the consciousness, then you'll use rituals that attract the kundalini up. Both methods have their effects, their advantages and limitations, and their adherents."

Celine: "But you teach the magic of consciousness."

Quinn: "Which draws the kundalini upward. That's part of why we move the consciousness upward as we progress, from the heart to the ajna and above. It draws the kundalini up with it. But, I get into those in today's handout.

"Now, 'the flaming sword which turned every way' represents the sacred fire of substance that must be uplifted in the human instrument before the incarnate consciousness can return to Eden, taste the fruit of the Tree of Life, and become one with God.

The Two Trees

"The trees of Life and Knowledge appear in Genesis 2:

9. "And out of the ground the LORD God made to grow every tree that is pleasant to the sight and good for food, *the tree of life also in the midst of the garden, and the tree of the knowledge of good and evil.*

16. "And the LORD God commanded the man, saying, 'You may freely eat of every tree of the garden;

17. "but of the tree of the knowledge of good and evil you shall not eat, for in the day that you eat of it you shall die.'

"Now, these trees grew in the center of the Garden of Eden.

"The fruit of the Tree of Knowledge conveyed awareness of good and evil.

"The fruit of the Tree of Life conveyed eternal life.

"The fact that these two trees are allegories should be self-evident. In a cosmic sense, the twin trees represent the two Poles of Divinity, the Divine Mother and the Divine Father.

"However, the context of the biblical passages suggests that in this case, the two trees of the garden also represent the Divine Twins —that polarity of consciousness emphasized in Gemini. But in this case, the journey of the twins is represented by the action of eating.

"Eating the fruit of the Tree of Knowledge represents the downward motion of the Son into identification with the Mother, and thus experience in form.

"Eating the fruit of the Tree of Life represents the upward motion of the Daughter into identification with the Father, which frees one from the Wheel of Rebirth."

Quinn: "We don't have time to go into all the details, so I've prepared these two hand-outs on the two trees and the Serpent of Wisdom.[5]

(I scooped up the copied handouts from the TV tray table by my chair, and passed them out.)

"And now, let's look at the polarity of the myth.

The Polarity

Quinn: "If we look at the myth's relationships in terms of polarity, we find the following sequence:

"The Spirit —Positive Pole— breathes forth the Soul.

"The Soul divides into Positive and Negative.

"The Son or Positive Pole identifies with form, and is thereby trapped on the Wheel or Rebirth and doomed to death.

"The Daughter —Negative Magnetic Field— obtains the promise of freedom from the Wheel.

"When the myth is viewed from this perspective, we find the same creative cycle that we discovered in the myths of Ishtar and Tammuz, Isis and Osiris, and the others. It's the same story, using different characters and symbols for the same polarities and movements."

The Meaning

Polarity and Gender

Quinn: "As we've seen, while the myth of Eve and

---

[5] Quinn: See the Addendum to Lesson 6

Adam has been altered by a later patriarchal perspective, it remains a retelling of the creative cycle we found in the earlier myths of Gemini and Taurus. However, Eve and Adam include the emphasis on Substance that came with Taurus.

"The myth also brings out the function of polarity in the creative process. Unfortunately, the myth is so shrouded in the patriarchal viewpoint that the details of the split of ADM into Eve and Adam, the nature of the trees and their fruit, and the function of humanity in the creative process, are deeply hidden.

"This brings up the question of why humanity did this, why did patriarchy happen, and what is it for? We'll explore the patriarchy, and its place in human evolution, in our next lesson, 'The Myth of Sarai and Avram'

"That's it for now. Let's prepare for the closing meditation."

Energy

Sit in a comfortable chair, relax your physical body, calm your emotions, and focus your mind.

Bring your consciousness to a point of focus within your ajna center, a tiny golden sun approximately three inches in front of the forehead and between the brows.

From your place within the ajna center, imagine yourself entombed inside the trunk of the golden tree. Turn your awareness to the tree itself, and note the light flowing into its fruits, and the red-amber fluid which courses from the fruit into the branches, trunk, and roots, into the Earth.

Become one with the tree, and recognizing that you are incarnate in that form for a purpose, audibly state the seed-thought:

> *"I am the Soul, born into the world of form to know and experience love."*

Without thinking about it or repeating it, allow the vibration of that thought to sound within your mind, like a bell that has been struck once. Continue listening to that vibration until all is still and quiet, then audibly sound the OM.

Take a deep breath, open your eyes, and return your awareness to your surroundings.

"Practice this inner ritual at least once a day, every day, for a full lunar cycle —from New Moon to New Moon."

Section Three

Dwelling in the Underworld

The Age of Aries

Quinn said, "Wil! Welcome back! How was the trip?" and sipped from his magenta 'Naturway' mug.

The edge of Wil's aura still hummed with a pink-tinged aftertaste from his trip. He grinned and replied, "Great! I did some lecturing and visited a few spiritual sites. The idea of Synthesis is really catching on, especially in Norway."

Quinn's left brow lifted, crinkling his forehead, and asked, "Studying or practicing?"

Wil frowned in confusion, and Quinn said, "It's one thing to study an idea. It's quite another to put it into practice in your daily life and affairs. But we'll get into that when we move from Pisces to Aquarius."

Quinn turned to the class and said, "Colette says her mom is doing OK, considering. They've started the chemo and now it's just a matter of waiting. She says she'll probably be back next week."

Thea said, "Let her know we're keeping her in our prayers."

Quinn nodded and replied, "I will."

Then he said, "Now, let's begin as usual." and I pushed the button on the recorder.

Opening Alignment

"Close your eyes.

"Relax your physical body.

"Calm your emotions.

"Bring your consciousness to a point of focus within the ajna center, and there integrate your three-fold persona into a single unit. (Pause)

"From that tiny golden sun, turn your attention upward to that wisdom or truth overshadowing this evening's lesson, and become receptive to it by silently sounding the OM. (Pause)

"Maintaining that focus of receptivity in the ajna, take a deep breath, and open your eyes."

The Myths of Aries

Quinn: "Our next myths originated during the Age of Aries, when the attention of the Soul or Divine Son turned from aspiring to the Negative Pole or Divine Mother to identifying with form itself.

"Yes, John?"

John: "What's the difference?"

Quinn: "Well, the essential differences to us are identity and behavior.

"Aspiration is a movement toward something, and if you're moving toward something, obviously you're separate from that thing. We do this all the time when we wish for something, such as, 'I wish I was rich'."

John: "Oh!"

Quinn: "Right. Anyone who's studied positive thinking knows this. By wishing you were rich, you are saying that you are *not* rich, and thereby defeating your desire.

"This is equally true of aspiring to the Mother in Taurus. By aspiring *to* the Mother, we were saying that we were *not* the Mother, and thereby separated ourselves from Her.

"Now, remember the balanced Poles of Gemini! We had moved into Taurus from a balanced relationship between the two Poles. We were equally the Daughter at-one with the Father, and the Son at-one with the Mother. Thus, when we separated ourselves from the Mother, we became the Father, longing for the Mother.

"So, there we were at the end of Taurus, identified as the Father aspiring to and thereby separate from the Mother, and then we entered Aries!

Celine: "And we became the form!"

Quinn: "Yes. As the Father, we identified with form. The Power of the Father entered the form via the Son and we became, well, 'enchanted' by form.

"The result of this enchantment was that we moved from revering the Mother to worshiping the Father, from honoring the Divine Feminine to desiring material things; such as wealth, fame, power, and sex.

Me: "Didn't they exist before?"

Quinn: "Oh, yes, certainly. But not so materially or so individually focused as in Aries.

"You see, as always, there was a purpose to all this. By focusing a fragment of the Power of the Father into our individual forms, we stimulated the individual 'I'dentity in that form. The incarnate soul moved a bit away from its outer groups, and more into individual awareness, with each incarnation in Aries, producing a stronger and stronger individual awareness.

"Now we see all this in the Aries myths in a number of ways. There is usually less attention on the journey into the underworld, and more attention on life in the underworld. The Goddess wanes in importance, while masculine gods increase. And the male protagonist becomes more powerful, more in control of his fate.

"Of course these are generalizations, and there are exceptions to all of them, but they do provide some basic guidelines.

"Now the allegorical stories we'll work with in the Age of Taurus include the myths of Sarai and Avram, Baal and Anath, Asherah and YHWH, and Moses and Zipporah.

"We'll examine each of these myths, following a rough progression from the eldest to the newest and most patriarchal.

"Thus, our next step in our quest is our first Aries myth, Sarai and Avram.

Lesson 7

Abandoning the Goddess

The Myth of Sarai and Avram

Quinn: "More commonly known as Abraham and Sarah, they are one of the first couples in the Bible. Sarai is the traditional matriarch of the Hebrews and Avram is the traditional patriarch of both the Hebrews and the Arabs.

"Thea?"

Thea: "Why the name change?

Quinn: "Well, Avram becomes 'Abraham' when he changes his patron god. But we'll get to that.

"Now it's highly unlikely that Sarai and Avram were actual historical persons. At most, they and related characters such as Lot represent peoples who migrated into the land of Canaan at various times, and whose oral traditions were later conflated or combined by various editors into a single story.

"The immigrations occurred during the Age of Taurus, and thus under the influence of the downward motion of the Positive Pole toward the Negative Pole of Divinity. However, the various stories were combined and revised during the Age of Aries. While the result is not an ancient mystery tale, the myth of Abraham and Sarah does represent a crucial period of transition...

"From matriarchy toward patriarchy —with the male gods competing with and eventually supplanting the female deities.

"From polytheism to monotheism —with the female deities being suppressed, and a number of male deities

209

synthesized into a single God.

"Thus, including their tale will help us understand the patriarchal shroud over the later myths.

"Unfortunately, the account in Genesis has been trimmed, revised, and expanded by a number of patriarchal contributors, and much of the original content and meaning was lost in the process.

"Entire books can and have been written on the meaning of the remaining fragments, and we need not duplicate those efforts. Instead, we'll attempt to restore the remnants and retell the myth from a broader viewpoint. Since the Biblical version, and patriarchal interpretations of that version, assumes that the only deity speaking is YHWH, this broader viewpoint includes clarifying...

"Which deities were speaking to which characters in the myth, and

"The motives of the characters in their interactions with and obedience to those deities.

"Now, the complete version of the biblical myth is much too long to go over here, so I've made a 'corrected' version of the complete text for your later review. But for now, Ema has put together a synopsis for us.

(Quinn nodded to me, and I handed out photocopies of the "corrected" verses.)

Quinn: "Ema?"

The Myth

Ema: "Long ago and far away in ancient Mesopotamia, Sarai, a Priestess of the LADY, heard that the Goddess was being neglected to the west, in the land of the Canaanites. Sarai called her household together, including her husband Avram, their goods, flocks, and servants, and set out for Canaan.

"Following the trade routes, they traveled for many days, and finally reached one of the ancient groves of Canaan. The abandoned trees were silent, for none were there to hear them. The patriarchal Canaanites worshiped male gods, and cared little for the LADY and her works.

"But Sarai bade Avram set up her tent in the grove and construct an altar, and she worshiped the Goddess—sacrificing corn and other fruits of the earth, and the LADY appeared in a cloud above Sarai's tent in the middle of the grove.

"And the women of Canaan saw the cloud, remembered the Goddess, and came to worship. Sarai showed them the ways of the LADY, the women reclaimed their power, and the land prospered.

"Sarai moved on to the grove of Bethel, and then to Negev, renewing the worship of the LADY and restoring the power of women. But the weight of the errors of men weighed heavily on the land, and the life-giving rains came not.

"Sarai and Avram journeyed to Egypt to escape the drought, but in Egypt Avram grew afraid. He knew the Egyptians would covet Sarai, for she was very beautiful, and he feared what they might do to possess her. So Avram told the Egyptians that Sarai was his sister, for his own sake.

"Now this was true under the customs of the Egyptians, for they counted descent from the father, but a lie under the customs of those who followed the LADY, and counted descent from the mother. But the Egyptians heard the words of Avram, and took Sarai to Pharaoh, and Pharaoh took Sarai into his house.

"Avram was richly rewarded by Pharaoh, but the LADY was wroth and set great plagues on the Pharaoh.

Pharaoh called Avram to him, and demanded an explanation. Avram confessed all, and Pharaoh grieved of his error, gave Sarai back to Avram, and sent them from Egypt.

"Sarai and Avram returned to the groves of Canaan, and Sarai set up her tent and worshiped the LADY.

"But the priests of the Canaanites were displeased to see their women turning to the LADY, and they went to Avram and said to him, 'You have seen how it is among us and among the Egyptians. Our gods set us over our women, and our sons are our heirs and comfort. Turn away from this woman's god, and worship a man's god, and he will make you the father of your people.'

"And Avram heard their words, and he turned away from the LADY and worshiped El Shaddai. And El Shaddai promised Abraham all that he wished—to make him the father of his people and give him all the land for his own. And Abraham was well pleased, but his ears no longer heard the LADY.

"When Sarai heard that Abraham had turned away from the LADY, she threw him out of her tent, thereby divorcing him, and moved to another grove.

"In fear and remorse, Abraham turned to El Shaddai, and the LORD repeated his promises of a son of Abraham's body, and wealth, and land, and demanded a sacrifice. And Abraham made an altar to El Shaddai, and sacrificed animals upon it in blood and fire.

"Now as a priestess, Sarai had borne no children and thus had no heir of her body to take up her service to the LADY. But after the customs of her people, a girl born to her household could be made her heir. So she called Abraham to her and bid him lie with her Egyptian maidservant.

"And Abraham lay with the maidservant, and she conceived. But having conceived, the maid became arrogant and mocked Sarai, and Sarai threw the maid from her tent, but allowed Abraham to enter and lie with her.

"Then Sarai moved again, from grove to grove, until she reached Gerar. And Abraham dealt with the king of Gerar as he had with Pharaoh, and King Abimelech took Sarai into his household. But the LADY appeared to Abimelech in a dream, and Abimelech returned Sarai to Abraham, and sent him forth with a great store of silver, flocks, and servants.

"And Sarai threw Abraham from her tent again, and returned to the groves. But her womb had already quickened, and she bore Abraham a son, Isaac.

"Sarai gave Isaac to Abraham, and Abraham sacrificed the foreskin of Isaac to El Shaddai, as a sign of the covenant between Abraham and the god. And Abraham and Isaac dwelled apart from Sarai.

"But El Shaddai did not trust Abraham, for a man who changes gods once may do so again, so he commanded Abraham to take Isaac up to a high place, build an altar on it, and there sacrifice Isaac.

"And Abraham took Isaac up to a high place, built an altar to El Shaddai, and laid his son Isaac upon it. But before Abraham could strike, El Shaddai bid him hold, and turned Isaac's gaze to a nearby thicket where a ram was trapped. And El Shaddai accepted the ram in place of Isaac.

"Now Sarai and Abraham lived apart for many years, and finally Sarai died serving the LADY in Her grove. And Abraham laid Sarai in a cave overlooking the grove. And when he died, his sons laid him in the cave next to Sarai, and so Sarai and Abraham were reconciled and dwelt together again.

"The End."

The Characters

Quinn: "Wow, Ema! Very good! Short, poetic, and with all the essential points.

(Quinn stepped up to the board)

"Now, let's go over the characters. We have...Sarai, Avram, Isaac, Pharaoh...

Ema: "Abimelech and Hagar."

Quinn: "The king and the servant, yes, and of course the Lady and El Shaddai..."

Thea: "Ishmael."

Quinn: "And Terah. Yes, I think that's it.

Abimelech

"Now Abimelech's name is quite suggestive. It means 'Father of the King', and any culture that uses 'father of' as part of a name is probably patrilineal.

"Yes, El?"

Me: "Patri-what?"

Quinn: "P a t r i l i n e a l. It's, um... in some cultures they measure descent through the father. It's a common feature of patriarchal cultures.

"However, Sarai and Avram were from the matriarchal culture of UR, which was matrilineal. They counted descent from the mother and only the mother.

"So, since Sarai and Avram had the same father but different mothers—"

John: "They were brother and sister? Yuuuck!"

Quinn: "No, they weren't. Consider this carefully. Who can and cannot marry is largely a matter of social convention. At that time, in matrilineal Ur, Sarai and Avram were *not* related and *could* marry.

"However, in patrilineal countries like the Pharaoh's Egypt and Abimelech's Gerar, they would have been brother and sister and *could not* marry."

Me: "But, it only takes one parent. They'd still be half."

214

Quinn: "El, this was thousands of years ago. They probably knew where babies came from, but they couldn't prove parentage. There weren't any blood tests. Descent and inheritance was a matter of custom."

Me: "Oh."

Quinn: "Yes, and customs were very important back then. You know what it's like to be different. Well, imagine Avram finding himself in a culture where his beautiful, desirable wife is his 'sister'. To him she's not, but to the Egyptians, to the Gerar, she is. So he told a partial truth, and a complete lie.[1]

Avram

"Now... Avram means 'high father', while Abraham means 'father of a great multitude'. His name changes from Avram to Abraham when he switches divine patrons. He was the brother/husband of Sarai and is the traditional patriarch of both the Jews and the Arabs.

"His new patron deity was El Shaddai. This god is commonly assumed to be another name for YHWH. However, this is probably another example of conflation or the absorption of one god by another. El means 'god' and the root of Shaddai, means either breast or mountain.

Colette: "Breast *or* mountain?"

Quinn: Well, there's some confusion over whether the root of Shaddai is the Hebrew 'shad' meaning breast or the Akkadian 'shadu' meaning mountain."

Terry: "Shadu."

Quinn: "Oh?"

Terry: "Think about it. You've got a sexually suppressed ancient people, who adopt a synonym for

---

[1] Quinn: I've placed further information on the two customs in the Addendum to Lesson 7.

'breast' as the word for breast."

Jeff: "Yeah... Like, 'look at the mountains on that—'"

Quinn: "Thank you Jeff, I think we got it.

"So, the meaning of the name, El Shaddai, is either 'god of the mountain,' 'the breasted goddess', or perhaps something like 'god the provider'.

"Now it may have been the name of a goddess at some point. However, in the myth it refers to a god who behaves like a masculine deity from a patriarchal culture. He seduced Avram away from the LADY with promises of land, wealth, fame, numerous heirs-of-the-body, and demanded blood sacrifice. This suggests that, by this point at least, El Shaddai is a male deity. He may have some of the attributes of a female deity, but this is a common feature in post-matriarchal gods, who appropriate some of the attributes and powers of goddesses. In the above myth He is usually referred to as 'the Lord'.

Hagar

"Sarai's Egyptian servant was named Hagar, which means 'a stranger', or 'one that fears'. When Sarai wanted an heir, she gave her servant, Hagar, to her husband, in the hope that Hagar would bear a daughter. Sarai was apparently following the laws and customs governing the behavior of Mesopotamian priestesses.

"However, by then Abraham had fallen under the influence of the Patriarchal Canaanites, and adopted a male Canaanite deity. Thus, he desired a male heir of his own and agreed to lie with Hagar in order to beget one.

"Eventually, both Sarai and Hagar had a son by Abraham. Sarai's son was Isaac, which means 'laughter', and he is the traditional ancestor of the Hebrews.

"El?"

Me: "Did Sarai have an heir, a daughter?"

Quinn: "We don't know. No daughters are mentioned in the surviving version of the tale, but they could easily have been cut from earlier versions.

"Hagar's son was Ishmael, which means 'God that hears'. He's the traditional ancestor of the Arabs.

The Lady

"Now the original patron of Sarai and Avram was a goddess. We have here called her 'the Lady' because she's not named in the Bible. However, we can guess.

"Sarai and Avram originated in Ur and moved from there to Haran before going to Canaan. On this basis, some have guessed that they worshiped the goddess Ningal/Nikkal, who, along with her consort Sin, was worshiped at both Ur and Haran.

"Now in the ancient Mesopotamian religion, male priests typically served goddesses and female priestesses served gods, which may make Sarai's service to the LADY appear odd. However, exceptions to this rule included the high priestess and priest who embodied the goddess and god during the Sacred Marriage. This suggests that Sarai and Avram may have been a high priestess and high priest, an idea which is supported by the original meanings of their names.

"John?"

John: "Their names?"

Quinn: "Well, as I said, Avram means 'high father'. Thus, it is an appropriate title for a senior male deity, or for the high priest who is his voice-on-earth.

Sarai

"Sarai is an archaic form of Sarah, but an even more ancient form was Sharratu, which meant 'queen.' In the ancient pantheon of Haran —where Sarai and Avram lived after leaving Ur— Sharratu was a title of Ningal, the moon-goddess.

"All the locations where Sarai dwelled were sacred to the Goddess. Since she also bears a name of the Goddess, it is highly likely that Sarai was a priestess and continued to function as such during her journeys. Thus, in our version of her story, we have portrayed her as a practicing high priestess of the Goddess or LADY. (Quinn glanced at his notes)

"At one point, speaking of Sarah, the LORD said to Abraham, 'I will tame her, and indeed I will give you a son by her.' However, the LORD did not, in fact, 'tame' Sarah to respond to either His or Abraham's will. She continued to live apart from Abraham after his apostasy —in locations sacred to the Goddess— and finally died in one of those locations.

"El?"

Me: "Upostacee?"

Quinn: "A p o s t a s y. It means to abandon one's religion or principles.

"Now Sarai was living amidst a patriarchal society, and apparently could not find someone local to take up her work. So she lay with Abraham in order to beget a daughter, an heir of her own, to carry on her own work. It wasn't to acquire an heir for Abraham.

"A final point about the characters concerns the ancestors of Abraham as listed in Genesis 11:27. Since Sarai and Avram came from a matrilineal society, they would have counted descent from a female line, not the male. Thus, a list of ancestors prior to Canaan would have been a list of female ancestors of Sarai, and the Biblical list of male ancestors of Abraham is likely a later, patriarchal revision.

"I have corrected this somewhat in the version of the verses in the handout,[2] by changing the list to the an-

---

[2] Quinn: See Addendum to Lesson 7.

cestors of Sarai. Terah, for instance —which is said to mean 'wanderer', 'loiterer', or 'delay'— is now described as Sarai's mother rather than Avram's father. This change is further justified by the similarity between 'Terah' and Terra, Tara, Tora, and other cognates for Mother Earth, and by 'Teraph', the statue or statuette of the Goddess Asherah later worshiped by Hebrew women."

The Symbols

Quinn: "So, those are the main characters. Now, let's look at the symbols. We had the groves, altars, trees..."

Terry: "The sacrificial ram."

Wil: "Egypt, Canaan, and Gerar."

Quinn: "Yes, all centers of patriarchy, at least when compared to the religion and customs of the contemporary Mesopotamians.

Trees

"Now despite her wanderings, it appears that Sarai spent most of her life in the Grove of Mamre. The Grove consisted of terebinth trees. Translations of the Bible tend to use 'terebinth' and 'oak' interchangeably, but they are very different species. In Canaan, terebinth trees were later sacred to Asherah—a goddess who has sometimes been identified with Ishtar/Inanna. The fact that the myth shows Sarai living and worshiping at such groves stretches the Hebrew worship of the Goddess back to their first ancestress, before Avram took up worship of 'The Lord'.

"Thus, the altar 'built' by Avram was dedicated to a goddess, a goddess who was or later became Asherah.

"As we will see in a later lesson, patriarchal influences slowly turned Asherah into the consort of YHWH. This becomes particularly significant in light of the altars to Asherah that were set up in the high places of Israel and Judah, as these commonly included trees or poles sacred to that goddess.

"Thus, in a sense, the myth of Sarai and Avram represents the conflict between matriarchy and patriarchy, goddess and god, that unfolded over the ages of Taurus, Aries and Pisces.

Canaan

"Canaan, where most of this myth is set, was located on the eastern shore of the Mediterranean. According to the Bible this land was given to Abraham and his descendants —in particular, to the descendants of Abraham via his son Isaac— as part of the covenant between the LORD and Abraham. However, there is some evidence that this covenant was a later priestly invention, created to justify an attempt by the southern kingdom of Judah to absorb the larger and wealthier northern kingdom of Israel."

Wil: "It was a land grab?"

Quinn: "On a par with Manifest Destiny."

Me: "What's that?"

Quinn: "Oh... it was a nineteenth century American belief that our nation was sort of 'destined by God' to stretch all the way from the Atlantic to the Pacific."

Thea: "'From sea to shining sea.'"

Quinn: "Yes, and it was used to justify all kinds of things—the treatment of the North American... oh, what are they now? Natives? The annexation of Texas and California—"

Thea: "Theft."

Quinn: "Oregon, and later some of the Caribbean and Pacific Islands. People can find ways to justify anything. It's part of the way the intellect works when it's being controlled by the desire body, or the throat center when it's controlled by the solar plexus.

"Now, where…"

Me: "The land of Canaan."

Quinn: "Ah.

"Bethel was a shrine/trading center north of Jerusalem where Avram "built" an altar.

"Gerar was a small patriarchal kingdom—identified as such by both their patrilineal customs and by the name of their king 'Abimelech'.

"Haran was a Mesopotamian city located northwest of Ur, on a tributary of the Euphrates River. Sarai and Avram migrated from Ur to Haran, and from Haran to Canaan.

"Hebron was a city in Canaan, southeast of Jerusalem. The sacred terebinth grove of Mamre was located at or near Hebron.

"Negev was the region of south Canaan.

"Shechem was a shrine/trade center north of Bethel. Avram built an altar here while Sarai and he were on the way to Mamre, near Hebron.

"Ur was a Mesopotamian city located —at the time of Sarai and Avram— near the mouth of the Euphrates River. It was probably the birthplace of Sarai, but perhaps not of Avram.

"Yes El?"

Me: "Ur isn't there anymore?"

Quinn: "Silt. As a river flows into the ocean it slows down and drops tiny particles of dirt or sediment. This builds up, and over centuries it can extend the shoreline at the mouth of the river further into the ocean. So, the ruins of Ur are still there, but it's not on the mouth of the river anymore."

Me: "Oh."

The Ram

Quinn: "Now for us a key element in the myth is the

scene where the LORD commands Abraham to sacrifice his son, and at the last moment provides a substitute."

Wil: "The sacrificial ram."

Quinn: "Which is the symbol of..."

Celine: "Aries."

Quinn: "Yes, which tells us what Age the myth is set in."

"Now, let's look at the meaning of all this."

The Meaning

Quinn: "In the ancient Mesopotamian religion, human beings were created by the gods in order to house, feed, and clothe the gods. Thus, the purpose of humanity was to serve their divine creators.

"Each of the cities in Mesopotamia recognized all the gods in the pantheon, but each city was dedicated —by the gods— to serving a particular god.

"The temples were quite literally the houses of the gods. Within the temples, consecrated women served and worshiped male deities while consecrated men served and worshiped female goddesses.

"However, during the annual sacred marriage rite, the High Priestess channeled the goddess while the King/High Priest represented the god.

"In paired female-male deities —such as Asherah and El Elyon— the polarities may be balanced. The god is then free to show his soft, loving side while the goddess reveals her power of death and destruction. In these systems, ritual sacrifice often consists of fruits of the earth, such as flowers, fruits, grains, nuts, etc.

"In matriarchal systems, the goddess or Negative Pole dominates. This produces an overemphasis on Substance, and devotion to the cycles of nature. The Positive Pole, the source of Divine Purpose, Power, and Will, is under-emphasized or ignored. Instead, everything and everyone is seen as controlled by the cycles of nature, including the god. Tammuz, for instance, was given his power over nature by Ishtar.

"In these systems, ritual sacrifice is often connected to the cycles of nature, including:

"Late winter early spring —sex magic and sacred marriage rites, of conception and planting.

"Fall —harvest celebrations and death rites.

"This focus on the cycles of substance strengthens the identification of the incarnate consciousness with those cycles and substance. This identification in turn strengthens the human attachment to their group forms, and their enslavement by the cycles of those forms.

"However, all of that was Taurean. There was goddess and god, but the balance of Gemini had passed and the downward motion toward substance produced an imbalance.

"Then the age of Aries came along, and with it an identification with the form so complete that it slowly cut man off from the gods. He could no longer see or hear them, but only the inner voice of his individual self. Thus, he no longer served the goddess, no longer served substance, but desired to possess form and have it serve him.

"This is symbolized in the myth by the fact that Sarai and Avram have left Mesopotamia. They have entered a new land representing the Age of Aries, an underworld where gods rule by swaying men with promises —of wealth, power, and descendants— and with threats. This is the beginning of patriarchy.

"Now this movement into patriarchy may seem like a bad thing, but it was humanity's —rather extreme— response to a cycle within the greater life of which we are a part. In this context, the sacrificial ram represents the sacrifice of the self or Soul on the altar of substance in the Age of Aries.

"In monotheistic, patriarchal systems —such as the later worship of YHWH— the Positive Pole is overbalanced and purpose, power, and will are overemphasized. This produces an emotionally immature male god who is violent, possessive, and jealous. In these systems, sacrifices focus on the Life Aspect, and often take the form of death magic —using birds, mammals, or even humans— or ritual blood magic, such as male and/or female circumcision.

"This focus on the purpose, power, and will strengthened individual human awareness of our own individual identities. Human beings became stronger individuals as a result, particularly in those regions that had relatively weak female icons.

"Jeff?"

Jeff: "Why? Why did we go through that? I mean, you're turning everything upside down."

Quinn: "You mean the whole mystical 'jump into the ocean of consciousness and merge with the One' thing?"

Jeff: "Yeah."

Quinn: "Keep in mind the broader perspective. While individuality, and the selfishness that comes with it, is sometimes seen as a bad thing, it's simply a stage, a necessary stage, in the development of the self or Divine Child.

"Once the self has developed individual awareness —can look into a mirror and see itself— it can't grow into group awareness —can't look into a mirror and see the group of which the individual is a part— *until* the individual self is so strong, so powerful, that it will not be threatened or frightened away by the experience.

"Bhikku?"

Bhikku: "You mean, we have to be selfish before we can become selfless?"

Quinn: "I wouldn't put it quite that way. Remember what we're doing, we're developing the consciousness, the identity and the instrument, of the creative process—the process of re-union. So, we need a consciousness and instrument that can relate with the entire Polarity at every level —that can relate the Positive to the Negative and the Negative to the Positive— all the way from an individual focus of identity up to that of at-one-ment."

Terry: "So the One had to become the many—separate, individual identities."

Quinn: "And each of those then has to become the One again, completing the cycle. And it has to be able to do that, to identify as the One Life, without being overwhelmed by it, without losing its individual self.

"Now, this powerful individuality that can stand assured and unthreatened in the midst of mystical union with a group can only be developed via long lives of selfishness.

"Thus, the experience of Aries also serves the One Life.

Summary

Quinn: "Now, the polarity of this myth could be summarized as follows:

"The united Magnetic Field descends into the Negative Pole.

"The Magnetic Field identifies with that Negative Pole, and is differentiated or divided, with the Son cleaving to the Father and the Daughter cleaving to the Mother.

"So, what we have here is a fragment of the path, that portion when twin poles of the Magnetic Field go their own ways.

"Now, we'll explore this transition further in the next chapter, 'The Myth of Asherah and YHWH'.

"Are there any final questions? No? Then its time for the closing."

Force

Sit in a comfortable chair, relax your physical body, calm your emotions, and focus your mind.

Bring your consciousness to a point of focus within your ajna center, a tiny golden sun approximately three inches in front of the forehead and between the brows.

From your place within the ajna center, imagine yourself inside the golden tree. The tree convulses, cracks, and the side of the trunk bursts open and falls away, spilling you out of the tree.

As you land in the boat-like fragment of the trunk, a flood of red-amber fluid gushes from the tree, carrying the trunk away amidst a scarlet brook.

The brook flows onward, bearing you with it. Note the color of the earth and sky, the shape of plants, and the sounds of animals along the way.

As you descend, the scarlet stream is joined by others, first a blue brook, and then green, yellow, orange, violet, and purple, becoming a great river. Cupping your hands, scoop up the water and drink the liquid.

As the liquid flows into and through your body, energizing and radiating through every organ, become one with the stream of rainbow-force and audibly state the seed-thought:

"My emotions are the force that drives love into action."

Without thinking about it or repeating it, allow the vibration of that thought to sound within your emotions, like a bell that has been struck once. Continue listening to that vibration until all is still and quiet, then, audibly sound the OM.

Take a deep breath, open your eyes, and return your awareness to your surroundings.

"Practice this inner ritual at least once a day, every day, for a full lunar cycle (from New Moon to New Moon)."

Lesson 8

Slaying the Ocean of Delusion

The Myth of Asherah and YHWH

Colette was going quiver-lippy from the sympathy when Quinn walked in and dispersed everybody. He enfolded her in his arms, infusing her with a wave of Indigo calm, and asked, "How is she?"

Colette's voice cracked, and then steadied as she replied, "It's bad... uhmmm... worst after the treatments. Really nauseous from the chemo, and it knocks her down. She hasn't lost her hair, another week or two. My sisters are helping with things..."

Quinn released her, stroked her jet-black hair, and said, "I'm doing what I can."

Colette replied, "I know."

Everyone took their seats, and when they had quieted, Quinn took a deep breath —inhaling much of the gray cloud exuded by the group— and said, "All right, we'll begin as usual." and I turned on the recorder.

Opening Alignment

"Close your eyes.

"Relax your physical body.

"Calm your emotions.

"Bring your consciousness to a point of focus within the ajna center, and there integrate your three-fold persona into a single unit. (Pause)

"From that tiny golden sun, draw a line of golden-white light upward to the crown center, a tiny blue-white sun approximately three inches above the top of the head.

"Slowly move upward along that line of light, and into the crown center. There identify as your higher self or Spiritual Soul. (Pause)

"As the Soul in the crown center, turn your attention upward to that wisdom or truth overshadowing this evening's lesson, and become receptive to it by silently sounding the OM. (Pause)

"Maintaining that focus of receptivity move back down the line of light into the ajna. (Pause)

"Maintaining that receptivity in the ajna, audibly sound the OM.

"Take a deep breath, and open your eyes."

The Myth

Quinn: "As we've discussed in earlier lessons, the transition from matriarchal polytheism to patriarchal monotheism took a long time. The transition lasted thousands of years and included a lot of violence. For the patriarchal priests of YHWH, this 'war of the gods' was centered in the Temple of Jerusalem. The goal of the war was two-fold:

"First, to make YHWH the only God worshiped in Israel/Judea.

"Now, despite what you've probably heard, it appears that the nations of Israel and Judea were not originally the same country. Their peoples spoke the same language and shared many customs, but they had never been a single nation. Israel, to the north, had more people, was more prosperous, and developed a sophisticated government sooner than did Judea to the south.

"Among other similarities, the Israelis and Judeans worshiped a number of regional gods and goddesses, including Asherah, El, Baal, Tammuz, etc. This pluralism both made it more difficult to unite the two countries and brought about their union.

"Yes, Bhikku?"

Bhikku: "Why was a large pantheon a problem?"

Quinn: "Ah. Well, to the priests of YHWH, 'God' was not part of a pantheon, not like, say, Brahma–Shiva–Vishnu. Where the Israelis may have seen it as a competition for supremacy within a pantheon of gods, to the Judean priests of YHWH it would have been more like the conflict between Islam and Hinduism."

Bhikku: "Oh. So they didn't recognize the gods of Israel?

231

Quinn: "Well, it wasn't quite that clear-cut. We're looking at a very long period of transition, covering hundreds and hundreds of years. At first, Judea and Israel shared many of the same gods. But as Aries progressed and Judean priests turned to patriarchal monotheism, that slowly changed. For instance, the Biblical 'Thou shalt have no other gods before me' does not deny the existence of other gods, it merely asserts the *supremacy* of YHWH among the Jews. The denial of the reality of all gods *but* YHWH came later."

Terry: "How did that make union difficult?"

Quinn: "Well, the various religious hierarchies wound up striving for power, especially for the support of the kings. The priests of Baal, for instance, were supported by the kings of Israel, and in turn supported them. The chief regional shrine of Baal was in Israel and YHWH was much weaker there.

"YHWH was much stronger in Judea, but still had to contend with Asherah and Baal for influence. The rulers of Judea sometimes supported Asherah/Baal, and sometimes YHWH.

"Thus, the priests of YHWH saw the worship of Asherah/Baal as a threat, and worked to destroy their worship. Their strategy hinged on turning the rulers of Judea away from Asherah and Baal by inventing scripture that justified the takeover of Israel by Judea, and the destruction of the worship of Baal. But we'll get to specifics later."

Terry: "So, the priests of YHWH told the kings of Judea that YHWH wanted them to conquer Israel, and would help them do so?"

Quinn: "Well, basically, yes.

"Now, their second goal was to make the Temple of Jerusalem the dominant place of worship in the combined Israel/Judea.

"As we saw in the myth of Sarai and Avram, Israel and Judea originally had many sacred sites of worship. These varied from minor household and roadside shrines to regional temples. The priests and prophets of YHWH were determined to suppress all of these other sites, and establish the Temple on Mount Moriah —in Jerusalem— as the supreme, exclusive site of Hebrew worship.

"This effort lasted many centuries, and was largely successful. In the end, the priests of YHWH transformed our Divine Mother into a whore and threw Her out of Her home."

Wil: "Isn't that hyperbole?"

Me: "Hyperwhat?"

Quinn: "H y p e r b o l e, it means, well... poetic exaggeration.

"And no, it's not. The prophets of YHWH called the Queen of Heaven a whore, expelled Her from the Temple in Jerusalem, burned Her cult objects, murdered hundreds of the priests of Her Israeli consort, and established a patriarchal monopoly. And the results of their violence are still resounding.

"Just look at all the people who believe, to this day, that Israel is a divinely-created nation and must be restored to its YHWH-created borders. It all stems from this struggle for religious supremacy."

Thea: "So the intifada, the struggle between the Jews and Palestinians, the restoration of the Temple, it all goes back..."

Quinn: "All of that, yes.

"Now, as mentioned earlier, Asherah was the Great Goddess of the matriarchal Judeans and Israelis. With the rise of patriarchy, the Judean prophets and priests of YHWH suppressed the worship of the 'Queen of Heaven.' Unfortunately, their efforts were so thorough that no portion of her mythos appears to have survived.

"I say 'appears' because Asherah was a popular regional deity, and portions of her myth do survive in non-Hebrew sources. In addition, Asherah was conflated or combined with several similar goddesses, including: Astarte, Anat, Atargatis, and Ashtoreth. Thus, it may be possible to restore the Hebrew Myth of Asherah by combining the surviving Asherah fragments with those of related goddesses.

Baal and Anath

"Unfortunately, such a restoration would be an extensive project in itself, and is beyond the scope of our present study. However, we can make a beginning. The most important surviving fragments of Asherah's myth are those contained in the myth of Baal discovered at...(Quinn glanced at his notes)

"Ras Shamra, in the ruins of Ugarit—a city located in present–day Syria, formerly northern Canaan.[1] Ugarit reached its greatest heights in the 12th century BCE, and was an influential regional power at the very time the Hebrews moved into Canaan. The city declined rapidly from 1200 to 1180 BCE, when it was abandoned suddenly, leaving behind a wealth of written records.[2]

"These clay tablets show that the Hebrews and Ugarits had a common literary, linguistic, and religious heritage. For instance, the language of Ugarit was so closely related to Hebrew that many of their words were identical.

"In addition, many of the gods of the Ugarit pantheon appear in the Bible, and/or in personal Hebrew

---

[1] Quinn: These texts, dating from 1300-1400 BCE, were discovered by a French archeological expedition, in 1929, 1932, and 1933.

[2] Glen: Aries lasted from 2500 BC to 300 BCE

names of the period. This affirms the close cultural and religious relationship between the people of Ugarit and the Hebrews.

"Thus, the Ugarit myth of Baal, in which Asherah and Her consort El both play vital roles, is especially important to our study. It reveals that Baal, and his sister/lover Anath, are central characters in another version of the myth of the dying and rising god. In this instance, Baal dies and Anath brings him back. There are a number of gaps in their myth, due to damage to the clay tablets, but we have most of the story.

"Now, in this case, I've asked John to tell us his version of the tale.

"John?"

The Myth

John: "Um... Well, El, the father god, commanded Kothar wa-Khasis to build a palace for Yamm—god of the sea.

"The goddess Ashtar complained at not being given a palace as well, and Torch Shapsh —the sun goddess— warned Ashtar that El would depose her if she did not keep quiet.

"Yamm sent two messengers to the Assembly of Gods in Mount Lala, instructing them to stand before El in his court, and arrogantly demand that El give Baal and all his spoils to Yamm.

"The gods were dining when the messengers arrived at the court, and Baal was waiting on El. The messengers of Yamm strode into the court with their heads high, and backs straight. When the assembled gods saw them, the gods bowed their heads to their knees in fear, for Yamm had become a tyrant and they feared even his envoys.

"Baal rebuked the gods for fearing the messengers of Yamm, demanded that the gods lift their heads, and promised to answer the envoys himself. The gods straightened up, the messengers strode up to El and stood before him without prostrating themselves as they should.

"The envoys spoke the words of Yamm, and their words burned like fire while their eyes slashed like swords, as through them Yamm demanded that El give him Baal, as a tribute slave, with all his spoils.

"El granted Yamm's demand, giving Baal to Yamm as a tribute slave.

"Inflamed at this demand, Baal cursed Yamm, demanding that Yamm be driven from his throne.

"Kothar wa-Khasis, the builder god, declared that Baal, the rider of the clouds, would smite his enemy and take his eternal kingdom. Kothar brought down two clubs, Yagrush and Ayamar, and gave them to Baal.

"As Kothar handed Baal Yagrush he spoke to the club saying, 'Thy name is Yagrush—chaser. Do thou swoop in the hand of Baal, like an eagle in his hand, and chase Yamm from his throne.'

"As Kothar handed Baal Ayamar he spoke to the club saying, 'Thy name is Ayamar—driver. Do thou swoop in the hand of Baal, like an eagle in his hand, and drive Yamm from his throne.'

"Baal lifted Yagrush in his right hand, Ayamar in his left, and raised them to strike down the envoys of Yamm. But Ashtoreth seized his hands, and reminded him that they were merely messengers.

"Baal lowered his clubs, stood before the messengers, and shouted his defiance to Yamm.

"The messengers left, taking the defiance of Baal to Yamm, and Baal and Ashtoreth followed them.

"When Baal and Ashtoreth reached the house of

236

Yamm, they confronted the god of the sea. Baal raised Yagrush high. Chaser swooped downward, like an eagle in the hand of Baal, and struck Yamm in his upper back. But Yamm's joints did not bend, or his bones break, and he was not thrown down.

"Baal raised Ayamar high. Driver swooped downward, like an eagle in the hand of Baal, and struck Yamm in his face, between the eyes. Yamm's joints bent, his bones snapped, and he collapsed to the ground.

"Baal loomed over the fallen Yamm, raised Yagrush in his right hand, and Ayamar in his left, in order to smash and rend Yamm. But Ashtoreth rebuked Baal, saying, 'For shame, O rider of the clouds, for our captive is prince Yamm.' Prince Baal was ashamed, and held his wrath.

"Prince Yamm coughed, and said, 'I am dying. Baal will reign.'

"Baal was now King of the Gods, but he had no palace worthy of his position. Baal sent the sons of Darkness to Anath to explain why he needed his own house. When Anath arrived, Baal said, 'I will do obeisance to Lady Asherah of the Sea, the Mother of the Gods, so She will give me a house and a court like unto that of other gods.'

"Baal called on Khothar wa-Khasis the deft. Khasis took up his tongs and melted thousands of shekels of silver and myriads of gold. With these, Khasis made:

"A gorgeous dais cast in silver and coated in gold,

"A gorgeous throne resting above,

"A gorgeous padded footstool,

"A gorgeous couch,

"A gorgeous table filled with animal-shaped vessels,

"Gorgeous bowls shaped like small beasts of Amurru,

"Gorgeous stelae shaped like wild beasts of Yam'an.[3]

"Kothar wa-Khasis took them to Lady Asherah of the Sea, Mother of the Seventy Gods, and offered her these gifts.

"Lady Asherah placed fire on the incense brazier, a pot of incense on the coals, and as the sacred smoke rose made obeisance to the Creator of Creatures, propitiating Bull El the Benign.

"Baal and Anath arrived while Asherah was making obeisance to El. Asherah was alarmed at their arrival, fearing that Yamm and some of her other children may have been killed, and asked after them. Baal and Anath did obeisance to Asherah, the Mother of the gods, and asked for her intercession with El.

"Reassured by Anath and Baal, Asherah agreed to deliver Baal's request to El. Qadesh wa-Amrur saddled an ass for Asherah, including trappings of gold and silver, placed her on its back, and led her to the palace of Bull El. Anath followed, and Baal headed back to the summit of mount Zaphon.

"Asherah penetrated the field of El, entered his pavilion, and prostrated herself at his feet. When El saw Her, he laughed, put his feet up on a footstool, and invited her to eat and drink.

"Asherah delivered her message from Baal, asking for a house like the other gods.

"Baal the Kindly asked if He was a servant or slave of Asherah, to handle so menial a task, or if Asherah was a handmaid to make bricks? Nevertheless, he gave

---

[3] Quinn: Stelae – carved decorative or inscribed commemorative pillars.

238

permission for a house to be built for Baal, like those of the gods, with a court like those of the children of Asherah.

"Asherah complimented the Great El for his decision. Anath heard and rejoiced, stamping her feet so that the earth quaked, and took the glad tidings to Baal on Mount Zaphon.

"Baal feasted with Kothar wa-Khasis, and they decided on the plan of the house, including whether and where to place a window. Kothar began the work, shaping gold and silver into bricks, firing it for six days, and letting it cool on the seventh.

"When the house was complete, Baal exulted and summoned his kinfolk to his new palace to celebrate. When they arrived, He made a great sacrifice of animals and wine, sating the gods.

"Baal took sixty-six towns and seventy-seven hamlets. Atop Mount Zaphon, He opened rifts in the clouds for his window, and shouted in His holy voice. East and west the high places shook and the earth trembled.

"'Neither king nor commoner shall escape my rule', shouted Baal, 'nor will I send tribute to Mot, lord of death'.

"Baal's enemies attacked and captured the woods and the side of Mount Zaphon. Lotan the Serpent — Shalyat of the Seven Heads— the servant of Mot, was destroyed in the battle. Baal sent the sons of Darkness to the underworld to deliver his message of defiance to Mot.

"Infuriated, Mot sent the brothers back with the message that because Baal had destroyed Shalyat, Mot would place a lip to the heavens and another lip to the earth, and devour Baal like the fruit of the trees.

"Frightened, Baal sent the sons of Darkness back to Hamriya, the city of Mot, with the promise that Baal would be His slave and bondman forever. Mot shouted in joy that Baal had been humbled. Baal would be delivered to him, and the fertility of the earth would die with Baal.

"Baal ate his last meal, and Mot declared, 'I will put you in the grave of the gods of the earth, and you will take your clouds, wind, storm and rains with you. You will bring your seven lads, Pidray, girl of Light, and Tallay, girl of rain, with thee to the underworld, so that all will know that thou art dead!'

"Baal loved a young cow, and lay with her seventy-seven times in the fields of Shechelmemet. She conceived and gave birth to Moshe.[4]

"Baal's dead body was discovered there in the fields of Shechelmemet. When El heard, the Father of Mercy descended from His throne to the earth, and poured the ashes of grief over his head. He donned sackcloth, grieved aloud for the masses, the people of Baal, and vowed to descend into the earth after Baal.

"The maiden Anath also wandered the earth, over every mountain and hill to the very depths, seeking Baal. Finally, she came to Dabr and the beauty of the field of Shechelmemet, and discovered Baal lying on the ground.

"Anath donned sackcloth, gashed her arms with a stone, and wept. She cried unto Shapsh, the Torch of the Gods, 'Lift Baal onto me!'

"Torch Shapsh picked up Baal and set him on the shoulder of Anath. She carried him up to the fastness of Mount Zaphon, and buried him in the hollows of the earth ghosts.

"Anath sacrificed seventy buffaloes, seventy oxen, seventy head of cattle, seventy deer, seventy wild goats,

---

[4] Quinn: Or "Math." Translations differ.

and seventy asses, as an offering for Aliyan Baal. Then she journeyed to the Father El, and at his pavilion prostrated herself at his feet, and honored him. There she lifted up her voice and cried out, 'Now let Asherah and her sons rejoice, for Aliyan Baal, the Lord of the Earth, is dead.'

"El cried loudly to Asherah of the Sea, 'Give me one of your sons, and I will make him king.'

"Lady Asherah replied, 'Let us make Yadi' Yalhan king.'

"Kindly El said, 'He's too weak, and cannot race with Baal or exchange javelin throws with Dagon's son.'

"Lady Asherah replied, 'Then let us choose Ashtar the Tyrant, let him be king.'

"Ashtar the Tyrant immediately left for the Fastness of Zaphon, and sat on Baal's throne. But his feet did not reach the footstool, nor did his head reach the top of the throne. Embarrassed at his lack, Ashtar declared, 'I will not reign in Zaphon's Fastness!' and descended from the throne of Aliyan Baal, and reigned over all of El's earth.

"Anath descended into the depths of the earth, into the city of Himriya, into the pit of Mot. Like the heart of a cow for her calf, like the heart of an ewe for her lamb, so was the heart of Anath for Baal.

"She seized Mot by the hem of his robe and cried, 'Mot! Deliver my brother now!'

"Mot replied, 'What would you have me do Anath? I wandered the earth looking for a missing soul, and found it in Dabr-land, in the beautiful field of Shihlme-mat. There I found Aliyan Baal, took in my mouth and crushed him like a lamb. Even the great Shapash, the Torch of the Gods, is in my hands.'

"The heavens stopped, a day, two days, and months passed, and then Anath approached Mot. Like the heart of a cow for her calf, like the heart of an ewe for her

241

lamb, so is the heart of Anath for Baal. She seized Mot, and cleaved him with a sword, she winnowed him with a fan, burned him with fire, ground him with millstones, and scattered his remains in the fields where the birds ate him, hopping from bit to bit.

"Anath wandered the city of Himriya, the dark pit of Mot, looking for the missing Baal. Like a cow for her missing calf, she searched, and finally found him. Anath lifted Baal, and bore him out of the pit, back to the earth, up the Fastness of Zaphon.[5]

"'The Prince, Aliyan Baal, Lord of the Earth, had died. But behold, He is alive!' And the kindly El cried, 'Now will I rest and my soul be at ease, for Aliyan Baal is alive, the Lord of the Earth exists!

"In the Fastness of Zaphon, Baal seized the sons of Asherah. Rabbim he struck in the back, Dakyamm he clouted with a bludgeon, felling them to the earth. Baal retook his throne and resumed his dominion.

The Main Characters

Quinn: "Thank you John. Very well done!

"Now, let's look at the main characters. There was Baal...

John: "Anath, Asherat, El, Kothar, Yamm, Mot, and Shapash."

Quinn: (writing the names on the board)

Anath

"Yes... Now Anath or Anat was the warrior goddess, the 'Maiden,' sister/wife of Baal, and daughter of

---

[5] Quinn: Some forty lines are missing at this point, including the raising of Baal. We created this paragraph to fill the gap in the story. It is *not* an original part of the myth.

Asherah and El. She was later linked to Athtart—
Hebrew Ashtoreth, the Greek Astarte.

"Asherah, Athirat or Qudsu was the Consort of El in
Canaan, of Baal in Israel, and of YHWH in Judea. This
is very interesting, as it suggests that originally they
became her consort, rather than she theirs. Asherah appears in the Bible forty times, and has a number of titles that indicate her various characteristics.

"Celine?"

Celine: "YHWH was Asherah's consort?"

Quinn: "Probably, yes. Remember, in the earlier,
matriarchal religious system the emphasis was on the
Goddess, and she often had a number of different con-
sorts. For instance, a nation might have a patron goddess whom each king 'married', served as consort, and
whose rule was divinely blessed by that, by his position
as the consort of the patron goddess. The king thereby
became a demigod, and/or was seen as the incarnation
of the god, like Pharaoh and Horus-Osiris.

"With the rising influence of patriarchy, the emphasis passed from the Goddess to her consort, who had often been different from one place to another. So, under
patriarchy we wound up with different gods with the
same goddess consort.

"Now Asherah, as 'She who gives birth to the gods'
and 'Creatress of all the Gods', is the Great Mother. And
the seventy gods mentioned in the myth may relate her
to the star Sirius.[6]

"As the 'wet nurse to the gods', she nurtured the
gods, kings, and queens.

"As 'Lady Asherah who treads on the Sea', she conquered the primal chaos.

---

[6] Quinn: A three-star system, Sirius B orbits Sirius A approximately
seventy times a year.

"As 'Mistress of Sexual Rejoicing' she was in charge of the fertility of plants and animals.

"Asherah was apparently worshiped in Egypt as Qudsu —'holy'— a goddess of love, during the height of Canaanite influence in Egypt.

"Asherah was a goddess of sexuality and prosperity, of both the land and the people dwelling in it. She was a very powerful deity, so much so that gods —such as Baal— asked her to intervene with El when they wanted or needed something.

Baal

"Baal was the God of rain and fertility. He was the Son of Dagan, and Son-in-law of Asherah and El. He resided on Mount Zaphon, north of Ugarit. God of the thunderstorm, he was usually portrayed holding a thunderbolt.

"His titles included:

"'Rider of the Clouds', 'Almighty', and 'Lord of the Earth'. If these titles sound familiar, it may be because they are all Biblical titles of YHWH.

"Baal's symbols included the thunderbolt and the bull.

"El was the eternal, ageless, Great Father of the Canaanite pantheon, creator of heaven and earth.

"El and Elohim are among the most popular names for God in the old testament. For instance, the God of the Psalms is named 'El', and thus the Psalms were most likely Canaanite hymns to El which the Hebrews adopted and applied to YHWH. Associating one god with another and combining them appears to have been a common practice in the ancient world, one in which the Hebrews actively participated."

Terry: "They plagiarized the Psalms?"

Quinn: "Ohh, I wouldn't put it that way. Plagiarism

is a modern concept."

Me: "Playjerism?"

Quinn: "P l a g i a r i s m. It's a Latin word meaning 'kidnapping', but it usually refers to the unauthorized and unacknowledged use of another writer's work.

Me: "A polite word for 'stealing'?"

Quinn: "Yes, but it's a modern concept, and it's not fair to them to, well, impose it on ancient humanity, to judge them by our standards. Also, we don't *know*, it just looks that way.

"Now, the Judeans not only transmogrified El into YHWH, but assimilated Baal, the Elohim, El Berith, El Elyon, and El Shaddai into YHWH as well.

Kothar wa-Khasis

"Kothar wa-Khasis was a craftsman god. Kothar means skilled and Khasis means clever. He built the temple-homes of the gods, the clubs Baal used to defeat Yamm, and the many gifts Baal gave to Asherah.

"Mot or 'Death' was the god of the underworld.

"Shapash was the Sun goddess and the Light of the Gods.

"Yes Jeff?"

Jeff: "Sun *goddess*?"

Quinn: "Yes. Sol is not always considered male. The Japanese Amaterasu, for instance.

Yamm

"Now, Yamm or 'Sea' was the Lord of the Sea and the favored son of El and Asherah. He became a tyrant, feared by the other gods.

"Bhikku?"

Bhikku: "If El was the head of the gods, then how could Yamm terrorize him and the other gods, and how could Baal become lord of the Earth?"

Quinn: "Ah. Well, at the time this story was written,

the worship of El was waning. He was being portrayed as an old, rather weak grandfather god who had passed rule over the Earth to his son-in-law Baal.

"Now apparently there was a period where various male deities strove for the position of chief among the gods. Yamm gained ascendancy for a while, and then lost out to Baal.

"Terry?"

Terry: "So Yahweh wasn't the only god struggling for ascendancy in the area?"

Quinn: "No, but we don't know if the priests of Baal resorted to murder.

"Any more questions?

"Then let's move on to the symbols."

The Symbols

Quinn: "As discussed above, at that time the house or temple of a god was considered their literal dwelling place. It was the place where the god was fed, clothed, and worshiped, and where he or she slept and communicated with his or her human servants.

"However, there were many gods—Asherah alone had seventy sons. Most were not important enough to warrant a house, and had to make do with lesser facilities. Thus, obtaining a temple of one's own represented a major advancement up the pantheon. In the example above, Baal replaced Yamm as the chief 'son' of El. In the process, Baal became the chief symbol of the Divine Son, and his wife Anath became the symbol of the Daughter.

"As the earthly structure in which the god dwells, the house represents the persona, or mental, emotional, physical-etheric, and physical-dense structure in which the soul resides during incarnation. It's the equivalent of the casket, chest, or box that appeared in our earlier myths.

"Tess?"

Tess: "What about the other symbols, like the two clubs?"

Quinn: "Yagrush and Ayamar? We'll get to them in the next lesson.

The Polarity

"If we convert the myth's symbolic gender and relationships into polarity and movement, we get the following.

"Insulted by the separated self —Yamm— Baal leaves the heavenly court for the kingdom of earth, and does battle with the lord of the earth.

"Baal —the Divine Son— conquers the lord of the earth, and takes his kingdom for his own.

"The Mother of the gods —Asherah— helps Baal build a house in which to dwell.

"Identified with and trapped within his house or persona, the incarnate soul claims the world of form as its own, and dies to itself. Mot, the lord of the Underworld takes Baal for his own.

"Anath, the sister/wife of Baal, descends into the underworld, conquers death, and brings back Baal, restoring him to his throne. The Son is raised by the Daughter.

Summary

"Thus, we again have the movement from:

"Positive pole to outer Magnetic Field.

"Outer Magnetic Field to Negative Pole.

"The fall into the Polarity of the Negative Pole or

Substance.

"Liberation from the three lower worlds by the Daughter.

"Ascent through the inner Magnetic Field.

"Return to the Positive Pole.

"The basic tale is the same.

"As humanity progressed toward individuality, our myths became more patriarchal, and the role of the Negative Pole and inner Magnetic Field were suppressed, with drastic consequences to the hero of the tale. We will explore those consequences further in the next lesson, the Myth of Moses and Zipporah.

But first, we'll have our usual closing."

Appearance

Sit in a comfortable chair, relax your physical body, calm your emotions, and focus your mind.

Bring your consciousness to a point of focus within your ajna center.

From your place within the ajna center, imagine yourself in the boat. The boat has run aground at the mouth of the rainbow river, where it flows into a great sea. Stand and step out of the boat onto the bare ground. Stoop and scoop up a handful of the earth on which you stand. Straighten, and feel the texture of the earth in your hand. Hold it to your face, look at it closely—noting the tiny particles. Smell it—noting the heady scent of fertile earth.

Move your awareness into and become one with the earth. Recognizing that you are incarnate in form for a purpose, audibly state the seed-thought:

"This is the Mother, from which I am born, and in whom I live, and move, and have my being."

Without thinking about it or repeating it, allow the vibration of that thought to sound within and through your entire persona instrument, like a bell that has been struck once. Continue listening to and feeling that vibration until all is still and quiet, then, audibly sound the OM.

Take a deep breath, open your eyes, and return your awareness to your surroundings.

"Practice this inner ritual at least once a day, every day, for a full lunar cycle (from New Moon to New Moon)."

Raising the Queen of Heaven

Lesson 9

Wandering in the Wilderness

The Myth of Moses and Zipporah

The group said "Good evening!" as usual, as Quinn entered. He picked up his stainless steel mug, sipped his tea, and said, "Well, it looks like everyone's here. We have a New Moon tonight, so this may be interesting.

"We'll begin, as usual, with an opening alignment.

Opening Alignment

"Close your eyes.

"Relax your physical body.

"Calm your emotions.

"Bring your consciousness to a point of focus within the ajna center, and there integrate your three-fold persona into a single unit. (Pause)

"From that tiny golden sun, draw a line of golden-white light upward to the crown center, a tiny blue-white sun approximately three inches above the top of the head. Slowly move upward along that line of light, and into the crown center. There identify as your higher self or Spiritual Soul. (Pause)

"As the Soul in the crown center, turn your attention upward to that wisdom or truth overshadowing this evening's lesson, and become receptive to it by silently sounding the OM. (Pause)

"Maintaining that focus of receptivity, move back down the line of light into the ajna. (Pause)

"Maintaining that receptivity in the ajna, audibly sound the OM.

"Take a deep breath, and open your eyes."

Moses and Zipporah

Quinn: "Now, do all of you know who Moses was? Uhuh. How about Zipporah? Nobody? Well, that's not really surprising, considering the patriarchal slant of the story.

"Moses was the archetypal prophet who led the Hebrews out of captivity in Egypt, and Zipporah was his wife. There is no evidence that either of them was an actual historical person. On the contrary, many biblical scholars consider Moses a combination of a number of fictional characters. Some trace his origins to Egyptian, Canaanite, and Mesopotamian myths, as well as to oral Hebrew traditions.

"However, the myth of Moses is actually another example of the universal tale of the path of spiritual growth and development. The parallels between Moses and other heroes and demigods are due to the fact that their stories portray the same journey.

"This being the case, we may safely consider the legend of Moses to be an allegory, another retelling of the descent and return of the Soul. However, in this case it's told during Aries, and from an almost exclusively patriarchal viewpoint.

"This patriarchal viewpoint is the product of a severe distortion of the relationship between the Divine Poles. That distortion is reflected in the resulting mystery tradition, the myth associated with that tradition, and in the outcome of the myth and tradition.

"Moses, the Great Liberator of his people, does not make it into the Promised Land.

The Myth

"The complete biblical story of Moses, including the

entire book of Exodus, much of the book of Deuteronomy, and parts of Leviticus and Numbers, is much too
long to include here, even in synopsis. Thus, El has copied the most pertinent chapters for us, and I've asked
Wil to give us a summary.[1]

"Wil?"

✦

Wil: "Um... Well, the Hebrew Patriarch Joseph took
his family to Egypt, which was then under the rule of
the Hyksos—a tribal people who had much in common
with the Hebrews. And Joseph's people prospered under
the Hyksos, the sons of Israel multiplied and filled the
land, and they became mighty.

"Then a new King rose in Egypt and overthrew the
Hyksos. He was an Egyptian, and he feared the sons of
Israel as allies of his enemies the Hyksos. So he started
an ethnic cleansing campaign to destroy the Hebrews.
He forbade them practicing skilled professions, enslaved
them, and appointed cReuel taskmasters over them.

"But the harder the King worked them, the more the
sons of Israel multiplied and spread through the land,
and the King went in dread of them.

"The fearful King began a campaign of male infanticide, but the Hebrew midwives refused to go along.

"So the desperate Pharaoh commanded all his people
that every son born to them must be cast into the Nile.

"A daughter of the tribe of Levi conceived and bore a
son, and seeing that he was beautiful she hid him for
three months. But when she could hide him no longer,
she remembered the tale of Isis and Horus, in which Isis
hid her son in the reeds of the Nile.

---

[1] Quinn: See the Addendum to Lesson 9 for the pertinent Biblical
excerpts.

"So the daughter of Levi covered a wicker basket with tar and pitch, and placed her son within it. She set it among the reeds of the Nile, and had her daughter watch.

"Pharaoh's daughter came down to the Nile to bathe, and saw the basket, and had her maid fetch it. And Pharaoh's daughter took pity on the babe, and took him as her own and named him Moses.

"Now when Moses was grown, he went to gaze at his brethren, and seeing an Egyptian striking a Hebrew, he struck the Egyptian down. And when Pharaoh heard of this, he tried to kill Moses, but Moses fled to the land of Midian.

"When he arrived there, he saw the seven daughters of the priest of Midian drawing water for their father's flock, until shepherds came to drive them away and use the water for their own. But Moses drove the shepherds away and helped the girls water their flock.

"When they returned home, the girls told their father, Jethro, of the Egyptian who helped them. And Jethro brought Moses into his tent, and gave Moses his daughter Zipporah.

"While Moses dwelled in the land of Midian, the Pharaoh died, and the people of Israel cried out to God in their bondage. And God heard their cries, and remembered his covenant with them.

"One day while grazing the flock of Jethro, his father-in-law, Moses came to Horeb, the mountain of God. And an angel of the LORD appeared to him in a bush that blazed with fire but was not consumed.

"And God called to Moses from the bush, and identified himself as the God of his forefathers. And God told Moses he had seen the affliction of His people in Egypt, and had decided to deliver them from the Egyptians, and give them the lands of the Canaanites, Hittites, and

Amorites.

"And the Lord commanded Moses to go to Pharaoh, and bring the sons of Israel out of Egypt. And God promised to help Moses, and told him what to say to the elders of Israel. Moses replied that he was a poor public speaker, and God made Moses' brother, Aaron, his mouthpiece.

"So Moses gathered his wife and sons on a donkey, took up the staff of God, and returned to the land of Egypt.

"In Egypt Moses asked Pharaoh to allow the Hebrews to go on a spiritual retreat, to worship their god YHWH, but Pharaoh refused.

"Aaron turned his staff into a serpent to impress Pharaoh. Two of Pharaoh's magicians performed the same trick, but Aaron's serpent swallowed up theirs. Pharaoh still refused, and increased the Hebrews' workload by requiring them to gather straw —for manufacturing mud bricks— that had previously been provided to them, without reducing their production quota.

"Ten times Moses asked that the Hebrews be freed. Each time Pharaoh refused, and each refusal was followed with a plague. In the first plague, the water of the Nile was turned to blood, but still Pharaoh refused to let the people go.

"Then followed plagues of Frogs, Flies, the death of the Egyptian cattle, Boils, Hail, Locusts, and Darkness over the land.

"Finally, the Hebrews asked their neighbors for articles of silver and gold, and YHWH sent the final plague, the death of the first born of each household. The Hebrews protected themselves from this plague by sacrificing first-born lambs, and painting the blood on their doorposts and lintels.

"Pharaoh relented and let the Hebrews go, but

changed his mind and attacked them while they were crossing the Sea of Reeds. However, the sea swallowed Pharaoh's army, and the Hebrews escaped into the wilderness.

"Once freed, the Hebrews rebelled against YHWH six times, and in punishment spent forty years wandering in the wilderness before they were allowed to find the Promised Land. Most of those forty years were spent camped beneath the sacred mountain on which YHWH appeared to Moses.

"During these forty years, YHWH appeared as a column of cloud by day and a column of fire by night.

"YHWH gave Moses the Ten Commandments, commanded the building of the Ark of the Covenant and the Tabernacle to house the Ark, and moved from the mountain into the Ark. He also gave detailed instructions on the sanctification of priests, and rituals of worship.

"YHWH was consistently capricious, acting like a spoiled, frightened, and jealous child. He kept His 'chosen people' in the wilderness until all those who had escaped from Egypt —and later disobeyed him— had died. At the end of the forty years, even his greatest servant, Moses, was not allowed into the Promised Land."

The Main Characters

Quinn: "Thank you Wil. That was very good. I particularly liked your interpretation of Egyptian history at the beginning."

Wil: "This way, it's a whole regime change, from Kings with ethnic and linguistic backgrounds similar to the Hebrews, back to true Egyptians with a grudge against 'foreign invaders'."

Thea: "It does make a lot of sense that way."

Quinn: "Yes. Now, you all have the handouts with

the Biblical version. Let's look at the characters.

(Quinn stood in front of the drawing board.)

"We have Moses or Moshe, Pharaoh, Jethro or..."

Wil: "Reuel."

Quinn: "The 'Priest of Midian, yes."

Jeff: "Who was Midian?"

Quinn: "Hold on, we'll add Midian. Now there was also the seven 'daughters', the two midwives..."

Thea: "Moses' mother and sister."

Quinn: "And of course his wife, Zipporah, and their son. Any more? No?"

Elder Sister

"Well, as we've discussed before, the Divine Daughter symbolizes the negative pole of the magnetic field, the relation of the Negative Pole of Divinity to the Positive, or the motion of consciousness from the Divine Mother to the Divine Father. In this myth, the Daughter Aspect is introduced as the elder sister of Moses, which suggests a number of things about him.

Jethro

"Jethro or Reuel was the father of Zipporah and a priest of Midian. The fact that he is identified three different ways—by two names and as a priest—is taken by some as an indication that he is a combination of three separate characters.

"Now the 'Midianites' were descendants of Midian, one of the sons of Abraham, just as the 'Israelites' were the descendants of Israel. Thus, as a 'priest of Midian', Jethro is a priest in the tribe of Midian. Which god or gods he served is not clear.

"Yes, Terry?"

Terry: "So, his god was not named 'Midian'?"

Quinn: "It's possible, but that's not how I read it. You've heard the phrase 'the god of Israel'? Well, this would be, 'the god of Midian'."

Terry: "Who, if he worshiped his father's god, would be the same as 'the god of Israel'."

Quinn: "That's one way to read it, and it would explain why Jethro went along with all this, but we really don't know.

Midwives

"Now, the midwives... In the Biblical version two midwives—Puah or 'Splendid' and Shiphrah or 'Fair' frustrate Pharaoh's first effort at infanticide. The fact that both midwives are named, when they need not be and usually would not have been, is very significant.

"The Bible is an overwhelmingly patriarchal document. Most of the women who appear in it are not named, but are instead identified by either their relationship to a man —such as Pharaoh's daughter— or their occupation.

"Tess?"

Tess: "How common was that?"

Quinn: "Well, actually, it was quite common. For instance, I have a friend with a traditional Hebrew girl's name that means 'five'.

Tess: "Five?"

Quinn: "Yes. Instead of naming girls, you number them. Daughter number one, two, three—"

Me: "Ewww."

Quinn: "And outside the family they'd be identified by their father. For instance, the first daughter of Yoseph the baker, or the third daughter of Shemesh ben Israel. This kind of thing continued in Europe through the Middle Ages, where we find the Arthurian Romances still identifying women primarily by their relationships to men. And we're still not free of it.

"How many of you gave up your family name when

you married?

(All the married women raised their hands.)

"Uhuh. Of course this is changing. For one thing, it's now much easier for a woman to stay single. Ema, how old were you when you married?"

Ema: "Eighteen."

Quinn: "And what did they call an unmarried woman of, say, thirty?"

Ema: "Spinster."

Thea: "Or 'old maid'."

Quinn: "Uhuh. Now, how many of you single wom.. um... females plan to give up your family name?

(None of us, Colette, Celine, or I, raised our hands.)

"We should keep in mind that our modern perspective on this is a result of the continuing movement of consciousness, from Aries through Pisces and into Aquarius.

"We should also consider the general tendency in patriarchal traditions to denigrate the role of women in those traditions, reducing powerful female characters to weak victims.

"Thus, the fact that Puah and Shiphrah are named, and conspire to defy and fool the Pharaoh, suggests that the midwives were originally much more important characters than their current roles indicate.

"In effect, Puah and Shiphrah represent the beginning of the path of return, when substance aids in the birth of consciousness or self-awareness.

Miriam

"Miriam was the virgin sister who watched over Moses. She represents the Daughter Aspect of the Soul, where Moses represents the Son Aspect. Thus, Miriam and Moses are two sides of one being, one consciousness or Soul.

Moses

"Moses or Moshe means 'pulls out', and is attributed in the myth to his being pulled out of the Nile at the command of his adoptive mother. However, since 'Moses' is the active rather than the passive form of the verb 'pulls out', it actually means that Moses is the puller rather than the one who is pulled. Thus, his name foreshadows his mission of leading or pulling his people out of the land of Egypt.

The Mother

"Moses' mother gives birth to him, places him in a basket, and then sets him adrift on the Nile, from which he is drawn by the Princess of Egypt. This mirrors the actions of Myrrha, Aphrodite, and Persephone in the myth of Aphrodite and Adonis and of Isis with Horus in the myth of Isis and Osiris. Thus, Moses' mother represents the Mother Aspect of divinity. More specifically, given the role of the princess, his mother represents the positive pole of the Negative Pole of Divinity.

Pharaoh

"Now Pharaoh, the ruler of Egypt, was considered 'Horus' while living and became Osiris when he died. Thus, he represents, in this case, that portion of the Son Aspect that is so identified with the form that it refuses the Divine call to leave the world of affairs and go unto god.

The Princess

"As for the Princess of Egypt who drew Moses out of the waters, since it was the custom in Egypt for Pharaohs to marry their sisters, it is possible the 'princess' was also the queen. Since Egypt represents the underworld in this myth, the princess represents the Queen of the Underworld, or the negative pole of the Negative

Pole.

"Ed?"

Ed: "But, she draws him out of the waters. Wouldn't she be Isis?"

Quinn: "Remember that at that point, Moses was moving *down* the river of life, not up. So, like Astarte in Byblos, she represents the Queen of the Underworld.

The Son

"As for the son of Moses, as usual the Son is the Symbol of the external portion of the magnetic field—which relates the Positive Pole with the Negative and is the motion of consciousness from the Divine Father to the Divine Mother.

Zipporah

"Moses' wife Zipporah or Tzipporah is a prophetess in her own right, and rescued Moses from seven years confinement in a pit. The fact that Moses is thrown into the pit by Zipporah's Father, and that Moses stays there for a period of *seven* years, strongly suggests that Zipporah represents the Great Goddess as the redeemer, and that the period in the pit represents Moses' descent into the underworld. This may even represent a vague memory of an initiation rite.

"Yes, Ema?"

Ema: "This pit I do not remember."

Quinn: "It's part of the Midrash, the traditional Hebrew stories. When Moses asks Jethro for Zipporah, Jethro throws him in a pit for seven years. Zipporah feeds him in secret, so when he survives it's deemed a miracle. Jethro frees him and gives him Zipporah.

Me: "Ewww."

Thea: "But it's not Biblical?"

Quinn: "No."

Lesson 9

The Symbols

Quinn: "Now, lets get into the symbols."

(Quinn stood, turned the board to a blank sheet, and began writing again.)

"We have the... the basket, Egypt, the Golden Calf...

"Celine?"

Celine: "From the Biblical version?"

Quinn: "Yes."

Celine: "The staff, and the columns of smoke and of fire."

Thea: "The Ten Commandments, and water from a rock."

Ema: "The promised land."

Quinn: "Any more? OK, let's see.

The Basket

"First, the basket. In order to hide her newborn son, Moses' mother made a basket of papyrus reeds, lined it with pitch, placed the basket in the Nile River, and had her daughter follow it to see what happened.

"This basket is symbolically the same box in which Osiris was entombed during his descent, and in which Horus was hidden during his ascent of the Nile. The Papyrus reeds, or rushes, play a similar role here, and again symbolize the etheric network and the mental, emotional, and physical-etheric bodies built around and within that network.

"In the beginning, the drift down the Nile represents the descent of the Soul into physical-dense incarnation. When it reaches its destination, the basket is discovered by a 'princess' of Egypt—representing the Queen of the Underworld.

"Here we see the etheric body acting as the instrument of incarnation, or descent into the three lower worlds. This is the persona as the trap or prison of the soul.

"During its sojourn in the lower world, the soul identifies with, and thereby attaches portions of itself to, myriads of forms.

"At the beginning of the ascent out of the lower world and to the promised land, the soul calls back all of these fragments of itself. This 'nation' of consciousness then makes the long journey through the wilderness, until it finally reaches its goal.

"During this process, the persona instrument is transformed from the trap or coffin into the instrument of redemption and at-one-ment. This purified vehicle consists of the mental, astral-emotional, and physical-etheric bodies, and seven energy centers or chakras. Now, I've included details on the bodies and chakras in another take-home handout.

(I passed around "The Instrument of Redemption", the second handout for this lesson)[2]

Egypt

Quinn: "The journey down the Nile in the basket represents the descent into form. The trials of the Hebrews under the Egyptians represent the trials of humanity in the world of affairs. The Journey in the Wilderness is the ascent from the world of affairs through the physical-etheric plane or the sea of reeds, the astral plane or the twelve springs and water from rock, and the mental plane or manna —mental substance— from heaven.

Golden Calf

"Now the golden calf incident is frequently misinterpreted. The problem was not that they were worshiping

---

[2] Quinn: See the Addendum to Lesson 9 for details on the centers or chakras.

some god other than YHWH, for the golden calf actually represented YHWH.[3]

"The problem with the golden calf was, first, that it was a graven image, and thus worshiping it was in direct conflict with the second Commandment which YHWH had just given to Moses—who was still in conference with God on Mount Sinai.

"John?"

John: "So, they were punished for breaking a Commandment that they didn't even know about? That they *couldn't* have known?"

Quinn: "It looks that way, yes."

Colette: "That's not fair!"

Quinn: "Is gravity fair? Remember, we're looking at symbols of the way things work, not history.

---

[3] Exodus 32:3-6

"All the people broke off the gold rings that were in their ears, and brought (them) to Aharon.

"He took (them) from their hand, and made it into a molten calf. Then they said: This is your God, O Israel, who brought you up from the land of Egypt!

"When Aharon saw (this), he built a slaughter-site before it, and Aharon called out and said: 'Tomorrow is a festival to YHWH!'

"They (started) early on the morrow, offered offerings-up and brought shalom-offerings; the people sat down to eat and drink and proceeded to revel."

Thus, the difficulty with the Golden Calf was not who was being worshiped, but how He was being worshiped.

Deuteronomy 5:8-9

"Thou shalt not make thee any graven image, or any likeness of any thing that is in heaven above, or that is in the earth beneath, or that is in the waters beneath the earth:

"Thou shalt not bow down thyself unto them, nor serve them: for I the Lord thy God am a Jealous God, visiting the iniquity of the fathers upon the children unto the third and fourth generation of them that hate me."

See also: Deuteronomy 4:15-19 for a longer version of the second commandment.

"The second problem with the calf was that it was a symbol of the previous age of Aries. Aaron or Aharon created the Golden Calf during the Hebrews' symbolic move into the mental plane, and during YHWH's dispensation of the new Law. Thus, the Calf represents both the conflict between the old path of Taurus and the then new path of Aries, and the conflict between the emotions and the intellect.

"The Calf is also another example of syncretism, in this case the absorption of Baal by El YHWH.

"In the previous chapter, we saw that Baal was symbolized by both a Bull and a Calf. It is as the 'Calf of Anath' that Baal is rescued from the underworld by his sister/consort. While Baal was worshiped in the north—Israel—with Asherah as his consort, El YHWH was worshiped in the south—Judah—with Asherah as His consort. Thus, in Deuteronomy 32, the priests of El YHWH absorbed the symbol of Baal into El YHWH, and then rejected all such symbols—and the joyful celebrations associated with the worship of Baal and Asherah—as blasphemous.

"The Priests of YHWH also adapted the symbols of the descent of Baal into the underworld:

"The seventy sons of Asherah became the seventy elders who Moses led up Mount Sinai,

"The underworld became the wilderness,

"The body of Baal became the Tabernacle,

"The palace of Baal became the Temple of YHWH in Jerusalem, and

"The clubs of Baal, Yagrush and Ayamar, became two columns, one of fire and one of cloud.

"Thus, the Myth of Moshe is another version of the

path of initiation, based in part on the Egyptian myth of Osiris and the Canaanite myth of Baal, but with the male god over-emphasized at the expense of the goddess.

The Promised Land

"The Promised Land represents the sacred place where we dwell when we have ascended above the physical-dense, astral, and mental planes, onto the Buddhic Plane, the realm of the Spiritual Soul.

The Ten Commandments

"These commands dispensed from on high are designed to suppress the lower desire nature. As mentioned in the handout, suppression is the method the throat center or concrete rational mind uses to control the emotions. Thus, the Ten Commandments are an intellectual interpretation of Divine Will, and represent the stage of spiritual growth wherein Divine Intent has descended to, and is interpreted by, the Throat Center.

Water From the Rock

"The water flowing from the rock represents the brain dew or spinal fluid which flows down the spine from the rock of the skull. This is part of the transformation of the physical instrument, brought about by the application of the Rod of Aaron and a Word of command, or the downward movement of Divine Will via the etheric energy system and the chakras.

"Are there any questions on the symbols? No?"

The Meaning

Quinn: "Now, as for the meaning...

"The myth of Moses and Zipporah follows the adventures of the Soul —Moses— as he incarnates in the underworld —journeys down the Nile— and then begins the journey back through the wilderness toward the Promised Land.

"However, Moses never reaches the Promised Land, but only gazes down on it from the hills. This is typical of male-dominated patriarchal versions of the myth cycle. The journey begins in the Positive Pole, moves downward through the outer Magnetic Field, moves into the Negative Pole, and becomes mired in the trinity of Substance.

"Because of the mis-relationship with the Divine Feminine, the Divine Father and Son oppose the Divine Mother and Daughter. The roles of Zipporah, Miriam and other female characters are suppressed, and Moses is unable to use either his Substance or his inner Magnetic Field to ascend to the Father.

"The task of moving into the Promised Land is left to Joshua, the hero who followed Moses.

"Thus, we again see that union or at-one-ment is achieved only through right relationship of the Tetrad, or the Divine Mother, Daughter, Father, and Son. We will explore the consequences of patriarchy further in the next lesson, the Myth of Demeter and Persephone.

"Are there any final questions? No? Then we'll close in the usual fashion."

Interlude

Sit in a comfortable chair, relax your physical body, calm your emotions, and focus your mind.

Bring your consciousness to a point of focus within your ajna center.

From your place within the ajna center, imagine yourself standing on the *Southern* shore of the sea, where air, water, and land meet.

Gaze around you, noting the clouds, birds, sand, and water.

Feel the heat of the sun and a cooling breath of air.

Listen to the waves rolling onto the shore and back to the sea.

Smell the salt, seaweed, and moist sandy earth.

Recognizing that you stand midway between the Purpose, Power and Will of the Father, and the air, fire, water and earth of the Mother, audibly state the seed-thought:

"I, the Soul, am the Divine Son, born into the world of form in order to reunite the Father and the Mother."

Without thinking about it or repeating it, allow the vibration of that thought to sound within and through your entire persona instrument, like a bell that has been struck once. Continue listening to and feeling that vibration until all is still and quiet, then, audibly sound the OM.

Turn your face to the East, the direction of the rising Sun, and begin walking. Follow the shore to the east for many days. As you travel, you have many adventures, including being whipped by the wind, burnt by the sun, drenched by rain, and assailed by wild beasts and people.

Take a deep breath, open your eyes, and return your awareness to your surroundings.

"Practice this inner ritual at least once a day, every day, for a full lunar cycle (from New Moon to New Moon)."

Section Four

The Journey into Light

The Age of Pisces

A gentle June shower stirred the backyard pond and cooled the roof as Quinn entered the library. The group said, "Good evening!" and he smiled and waved.

Colette said, "Mom really likes the bandanas, especially the rainbow angelfish."

Quinn replied, "Oh, good. I thought she might. They have another one with turtles."

Colette said, "Ooh, she'd love that!"

Grinning, Quinn said, "I'll email their site."

He glanced outside, sipped his tea, and turned to me and said, "We'll need to wash the car before Sunday."

I nodded, and replied, "I'll check out tomorrow's weather."

Quinn cast his gaze over the group, capturing everyone's attention, and said, "We'll begin, as usual, with an opening alignment.

Opening Alignment

"Close your eyes.

"Relax your physical body.

"Calm your emotions.

"Bring your consciousness to a point of focus within the ajna center, and there integrate your three-fold persona into a single unit. (Pause)

"From that tiny golden sun, draw a line of golden-white light upward to the crown center, a tiny blue-white sun approximately three inches above the top of the head. Slowly move upward along that line of light, and into the blue-white crown center. There identify as the Spiritual Soul. (Pause)

"As the Soul in the crown center, turn your attention upward to that wisdom or truth overshadowing this evening's lesson, and become receptive to it by silently sounding the OM. (Pause)

"Maintaining that focus of receptivity, move back down the line of light into the ajna. (Pause)

"Maintaining that receptivity in the ajna, audibly sound the OM.

"Take a deep breath, and open your eyes."

The Myths of Pisces

Quinn: "Our next myths originated during or are set in the Age of Pisces, when the attention of the Soul turned from identifying with form to aspiring toward union with the Father or Positive Pole of Divinity. This is the ascent phase of the motion of consciousness, the activity of the Daughter.

"Celine?"

Celine: "That's rather ironic."

Quinn: (grinning) "Yes, it is."

"Now, as we discussed in Aries, aspiration produces separation before it produces union. Thus, by aspiring to the Father we were in effect saying that we were *not* the Father, and thereby separating ourselves from Him.

"This placed us in the interesting position of trying to move toward the Positive Pole while simultaneously holding ourselves away from it. The result in Pisces was the creation of representations of the Positive Pole— including abstract mental ideas, astral ideals, and physical idols—that we could aspire to, identify with, but not reach.

"Now this occurred while most of humanity dwelt within their solar plexus center, and therefore all of these ideas, ideals, and idols were experienced and interpreted via the polarity of that center."

Wil: "So, it was automatically split?"

Quinn: "Yes. The solar plexus automatically split every idea, ideal, and idol —in the experience of its devotees— into 'that which is like that which I identify with', and is therefore good, and 'that which is different from that which I identify with', and is therefore bad.

"The result, as we shall see, was a vast constellation

273

of separative feelings in which everything associated with the Mother was identified as 'bad'.

"Ed?"

Ed: "Let me see if I have this... As we aspired to the Father, the solar plexus rejected the Mother as 'bad' because She's different from the Father?"

Quinn: "In whole and in part, yes.

"Mystics saw the intellect and the material world as obstacles to experiencing union with their ideal.

"Occultists saw the emotions and the material world as obstacles to knowing union with their idea.

"Both aspired to escape Substance and become one with the Divine Father.

"Celine?"

Celine: "But... you can't at-one with just the Father! You have to at-one with Her too, both at once!"

Quinn: "Yes. As we've discussed, it's the transformation of Substance from form into light that liberates the Soul and enables the Daughter–Son to reunite the Mother–Father.

"Thus, so long as we separate ourselves from any part of the Mother, including the mental, astral, physical-etheric, and physical-dense spheres, we cannot reach liberation or achieve at-one-ment.

"We see the results of this again and again in the myths of Pisces. The Divine Son, having separated himself from the Mother and Daughter, tries to ascend to heaven, and fails.

"As usual, we will study our myths of Pisces in a rough progression from the eldest to the newest, beginning with the Myth of Demeter and Persephone."

Lesson 10

When the Son Falls

The Myth of Demeter and Persephone

Quinn: "The myth of Demeter and Persephone is another example of the direct relationship between the secret rituals of the ancient mysteries, and a popular myth that portrayed those mysteries to the public. This myth was the central legend of the Eleusinian mysteries, and those mysteries were the foremost initiatic rites of ancient Greece. The city of Eleusis was a day's walk —fourteen miles— from Athens, and fell under the control of that powerful city/state. Unfortunately, the details of those rites have been lost, leaving us with the ruins of the temple complex, and the popular myth.

"Celine?"

Celine: "Didn't fragments of their rites survive in Freemasonry?"

Quinn: "Well, some writers have made that suggestion. The Eleusinian mysteries were very influential, and it's possible that some fragments of their rituals have echoes in modern initiation systems like Freemasonry. However, even if there was an outer link, the primary relationship is still the subjective one. The inner rites and outer rituals symbolized by the myth of Demeter and Persephone are an expression of the path of spiritual growth and development, as are those of Freemasonry. However, in the myth of Demeter and Persephone the echoes of the transition from matriarchy to patriarchy are easier to see.

"The first temple to Demeter at Eleusis was built during the 15th century B.C.E., sometime after Demeter's

275

fabled arrival from Crete. Only fragments remain of the version of the myth that was told in those early centuries. However, those fragments suggest that the story was originally much more matriarchal. For instance, the 'kidnapping' of Kore/Persephone was originally a planned elopement rather than a rape.

"But since the later, patriarchal version of the myth is by far the better known, I've asked Ed to base his version on it.[1]

"Ready Ed?"

The Myth

Ed: "Umm... yes. In the beginning was Chaos, the primal no thing out of which came every thing.

"Out of chaos emerged Gaea, the Great Mother of the Cosmos.

"Gaea gave birth to Father Sky, Uranus.

"Gaea mated with her brother/son Uranus, and gave birth to the Twelve Titans, six male and six female, including Cronus and Rhea.

"Rhea mated with her brother/husband Cronus, and gave birth to six of the twelve Olympians, including Demeter and Zeus

"Demeter mated with her brother Zeus, and gave birth to Kore.

"Kore led a happy childhood, growing up with the daughters of Oceanus and her half-sisters Athena and Artemis.

"Hades, the Lord of the Underworld, fell in love with Kore, decided to abduct her, and obtained the aid of his

---

[1] Quinn: The sources for the later, patriarchal version include: Homer (the blind poet, attributed to between the ninth and seventh centuries B.C.E.) Callimachus (third century B.C.E.), and Apolodorus (approx. mid first century B.C.E. to first century C.E.).

brother, Zeus. Zeus bade Gaea, goddess of earth, grow a special narcissus in a glade favored by Kore.

"One beautiful day, Kore and the Oceanides were gathering flowers in a beautiful glade when Kore saw an exceptional narcissus, and plucked it. At this signal, the ground cracked and Hades burst forth on his chariot. He grabbed Kore, dragged her screaming into the depths, and the earth slammed shut behind them.

"Demeter heard her daughter's cry and ran toward the sound, but found nothing. She searched everywhere for nine days, crying out and shredding her blue-green garments in grief. Finally, on the ninth day, Helios, God of the Sun, told Demeter of the kidnapping.

"Awash in anguish, Demeter's vitality waned. Her hair turned gray, her skin sagged and wrinkled. The aged Demeter wandered until she finally sat on the Mirthless Stone beside the fountain of Callechoron, near Eleusis.[2]

"Demeter was discovered sitting beside the fount, by the daughters of King Keleos of Eleusis. She told them that she had just arrived from Crete, and they invited her to be the nurse of Demophon, their newborn brother.

"When the grieving Demeter arrived at the palace, Queen Metaniera invited her to sit. The serving maid, Iambe, covered Demeter's stool with a white fleece. The goddess was too grieved to speak or accept refreshment, so Iambe joked with Demeter until the Goddess smiled and laughed. Demeter then asked for a drink of barley groats and mint.

"Under Demeter's care, Demophon 'grew like a god', without food or drink. Every night, the goddess secretly anointed him with ambrosia —the food of the gods—

---

[2] Quinn: i.e., the "Well of Fair Dances" at Eleusis.

and bathed him in fire. Finally, Queen Metaniera stumbled onto this secret rite, and screamed in fear for her son. The goddess snatched Demophon from the flames and cried out, 'Mortals are fools'.

"Demeter dropped her veil of age, took on her true appearance, and commanded the people of Eleusis to build her a home. The people set to work, and when the temple was complete, the grieving goddess resided there.

"So great was her sorrow, that the land became barren. Alarmed at the continued infertility, Zeus sent Iris, the goddess of the rainbow, to beg Demeter to return to Olympus and take up her duties, but Demeter refused.

"In desperation, Zeus ordered Hermes to go to Hades, bring Persephone back, and return her to Demeter.[3] Hades argued that he was a good husband, but reluctantly agreed to let Persephone go. Hermes took Persephone in his arms, returned to the upper world, and flew to Demeter's temple in Eleusis, where he gave Persephone back to her mother.

"Persephone ran to her mother, and they embraced, sobbing with joy. Finally, Demeter asked her daughter if she had eaten anything in the Underworld, and Persephone admitted that Hades had made her eat a pomegranate seed.

"With renewed sobs, Demeter informed Persephone that because she had eaten the seed, she could not remain, but would have to return to the underworld.

"Hermes returned to Olympus with word of this new crisis, and Zeus sent Demeter's mother, Rhea, with the promise that Demeter could have any honors she wanted, and that Persephone need spend only one-third

---

[3] Quinn: Kore, the daughter of Demeter, becomes Persephone (Queen of the Underworld) after her kidnapping.

of the year in the underworld, and two-thirds above with her mother, if Demeter would restore the fertility of the earth.

"Demeter agreed, and filled the world with grain, fruit, and green growing plants. She showed her sacred rites to King Keleos of Eleusis, and his sons Triptolemos, Diokles, and Eumolpus, establishing the Mysteries of Eleusis, and then returned to Olympus.

"Thus, to this day, when Kore departs, Demeter mourns and the world falls barren. When Persephone returns, Demeter rejoices, and the world bursts forth with renewed life."

The Main Characters

Quinn: "Very well done, Ed. Thank you.

(Quinn stood and faced the board, marker in hand.)

Quinn: "Now, let's look at the characters. There's Persephone or Kore, Hades, Demeter..."

Ed: "Gaea, Chaos, Oceanus, and the Oceanides.

Quinn: "And?"

Celine: "Well..., Hecate, Hermes."

Quinn: "Both associated with ritual."

Thea: "Cronus, Rhea, Uranus, and Zeus."

Quinn: "That about covers it. Any more? No?

Chaos

"Well, with Chaos, of course, we're back to the beginning. It's the primal no thing out of which every thing came.

"Cronus was a Son of Gaea and Uranus, the youngest of the male Titans. He was the father of six of the twelve Olympians —including Zeus, Hades, Poseidon, Demeter, Hera, and Hestia— and was the brother/husband of Rhea.

Celine: "Another brother/husband."

Quinn: "Yes, we see a lot of that. Remember the symbolism; it represents an equal, mature-and-fruitful, polarity.

Demeter

"Now Demeter or Ceres was the Mother Goddess of the Earth, the divinity of corn and agriculture."

Thea: "She's where the word 'cereal' comes from."

Quinn: "Yes."

Me: "How could the ancient Greeks have a divinity of corn?"

Quinn: "Well, 'corn' is an old English word for grain, including wheat, barley, oats, and later maize."

Me: "Oh. So she was the divinity of grains."

Quinn: "Yes, and one of the twelve Olympians—a daughter of Rhea and Cronus. Demeter was the Mother of Persephone by Zeus.

Gaea

"Now, Gaea is Mother Earth. She appeared out of the primal chaos, the first Negative Pole of Divinity, and gave birth to and mated with Uranus.

Hades

"Hades or Pluton was the ruler or god of the Underworld. He was the son of Rhea and Cronus, making him the brother of Demeter and Zeus, and thus the uncle/husband of Persephone."

Colette: "Eww."

Quinn: "Remember the symbolism! This represents the dominance of the feminine by the masculine.

"There is evidence suggesting that in the earlier matriarchal version of the myth, the attraction between Persephone and Pluton was mutual. Persephone eloped with Pluton, and thus there was no rape. This version preserves the willing assent of the Daughter to the Father."

Jeff: "What about even earlier versions?"

Quinn: "Earlier than the elopement? Well... at some point you'd get back to Taurus, when the Goddess ruled. The Lord of the Underworld would be a goddess who kidnaps a god, like with the myth of Inanna and Dumuzi. The polarity of the myth is so different, then, that it's essentially a different story.

Wil: "But you said it's only one story!"

Quinn: "Have you seen Rashomon?"

Wil: "Ummm... I think so, by Akira Kurosawa? But I don't—

Quinn: "It's the one about the investigation of a murder-rape, as told by four different characters, each of whom has a very different perspective. We're seeing the same thing here, four ages, Gemini, Taurus, Aries, and Pisces, each putting their spin on things, with the fifth and final perspective, the Aquarian, synthesizing them all into one."

Wil: "So, it's all one event, one 'motion of consciousness', just told in different ways."

Quinn: "From the perspective of different ages, different peoples, using the symbols and the experiences of those times and places.

"Now, in the later patriarchal version of our present myth, Hades 'raped' Persephone, abducted her and made her his queen against her will. This version throws off the balance between the Daughter and Father.

"Neither the earlier nor the later versions of the myth balance the Divine Daughter with a Divine Son. Kore had a brother, Plutus, who could easily have filled that role, but he appears to have been an obscure, minor deity. His symbols included a basket filled with ears of corn or a literal cornucopia."

Jeff: "How's his name spelled?"

Quinn: "P l u t u s, I think. But check. I sometimes confuse him with Pluton."

Hecate and Hermes

"Now Hecate represents the crone or negative pole of the Negative Pole.

"Hermes or Mercury was the son of Maia and Zeus."

Jeff: "Jeez!"

Quinn: "Yes, ol' Zeus did get around. But remember, that was another way of symbolically taking the power from the goddesses.

"Hermes was the chief messenger of the gods, and god of healing, wind, and thieves.

"Iris was the goddess of the rainbow, and —with Hermes— a messenger of the gods.

"Oceanus was the Lord of the great stream that encircled the world, also known as the Outer Sea, or the Atlantic. He was the husband of Tethys, and the eldest of the Titans

"The 'Oceanides' were the daughters of Tethys and Oceanus.

Persephone

"Persephone or Kore was the daughter of Demeter and Zeus, and niece/wife of Pluton/Hades. She symbolizes the internal magnetic field, or the Divine Daughter. As Kore, the virgin goddess of Spring, she is the Daughter born of the Mother and still identified with Substance. As Persephone, the Queen of the Underworld, she is at-one with the Divine Son, and carries the fruit of the earth —the intelligent activity of Substance— back to heaven.

"Ema?"

Ema: "In older version, Plutus by Persephone kidnapped was?

Quinn: "Umm...well, that would have the Goddess of

the Underworld imprisoning a minor god of plenty in the Underworld, so it would make sense as a sort of Taurus version, but I wouldn't really want to suggest that that was the way it was told, not with those characters. Remember, by Pisces many if not most of the Greco-Roman gods were conflations or combinations of several earlier gods. So, while there may have been equivalent characters earlier —in Taurus— we really can't call them the same gods, not unless we go back to the Tetrad, and see who represents what Pole. Then we can say that a particular goddess represents the Mother or the Daughter, or a god represents the Father or the Son, but they *represent* them. They're a symbol for that polarity.

"Remember, symbols are a way of connecting with the reality, with the Truth, and if and when we confuse the symbol with the reality, if we identify with that form, we lose the connection with the Truth and become trapped within the form. It becomes an instrument of delusion rather than of liberation.

Rhea

"Now, who's next?"

Me: "Rhea."

Quinn: "Ah. OK, now, Rhea was the sister/wife of Cronus, and mother of Demeter, Zeus, and Hades. She was known as the 'mother of the gods' or 'great mother goddess'.

"Tethys was one of the elder Titans, the wife of Oceanus and mother of all the world's rivers.

"Uranus was 'Father Sky', the Positive Pole of Divinity. He mated with Gaea to produce the twelve Titans — six female and six male — the first Magnetic Field.

"Zeus, the chief of the Greek gods, was a son of Cronus and Rhea.

"Now, that about wraps it for the characters. Let's look at the symbols."

The Symbols

Quinn: "Let's see, we have... the fountain, the stone, pomegranate..."

Thea: "The flower."

Quinn: "Right. Anything else? No? OK.

The Fountain

"The Fountain of Callechoron is a symbol of the Third Ventricle as the fount or source of the 'water of life', the 'brain dew' or transformed spinal fluid that moves downward from the brain and through the spine following the transformation of the individual human soul into the Spiritual Soul Incarnate.

The Stone

"The Mirthless Stone is a symbol of the pineal gland, and thus an outer expression of the Cave Center. The mirthless stone is reached when the Soul —having fallen into identification with substance— is differentiated by that substance into a state of separation from itself. This state of separation divides the Soul from both Divine Parents, including the Mother, who then mourns for Her lost child. This is somewhat ironic, since it is the natural function of the Mother or Substance — to differentiate— that produces the separation.

"Tess?"

Tess: "The Mother 'differentiates'?"

Quinn: "The intelligent activity of Substance produces the appearance of different forms. When the Son identifies with those forms, he takes on that appearance and experiences separation.

"This is the movement from union with the One Life into individuality. It brings a tremendous sense of loss, and loneliness, but the form-identified consciousness does not know why. So it looks for a form, or an experience in form, that will remove the pain. Over many incarnations of experience with many forms, the incarnate soul eventually learns that while some forms or experiences may temporarily veil the pain, none of them can end it.

"Thus, the pain and loneliness of separation eventually force the individual to seek beyond form, outside of their individual self, and they begin the quest for at-one-ment or union.

"Bhikku?"

Bhikku: "So separativeness is good?"

Quinn: "It's not a matter of good or bad. It's simply a part of the path that we all pass through. Having grown from species identity into individual awareness —the ability to look into a mirror and see oneself— you have to develop a very strong sense of self. Now, in order to do this one has to have two things: First, you need a mirror in which to look —a form, crystallized by your identification with it— that expresses your individual consciousness. Second, you need a self-awareness so strong that it will not run away screaming when you approach at-one-ment."

Colette: "But, why would it—"

Quinn: "'Run away screaming'? Well, remember, it's because only a very, very strong individuality can merge itself into the One Life and remain itself."

Bhikku: "But, isn't that the point, to lose oneself in the ocean of self."

Quinn: "Well, yes and no. Yes, that is a way of stating it when you're on the mystical route of the path. However, that perspective is a product of the mis-relationship with Substance that sees form, and the individuality that grows out of identification with form, as bad. Again, form, the identification with form, and the resulting individuality, are all simply part of the path.

"Besides, individuality does not actually disappear when you reunite with the One Life. It expands, becomes increasingly fluid, but the self is still there. You see both yourself and the One Life in the mirror.

Narcissus

"Now, Narcissus is the symbol of excessive self-love, or over-identification with one's individual being, and we may apply this as well to a flower bearing his name. This state occurs when the Soul —incarnate in and identified with the form— is differentiated by the form into an individual identity. Thus, Kore is kidnapped by Hades when she stoops to grasp isolated individuality.

"Again, this is a temporary condition, one which we all pass through to some extent, and it is a way of developing the separate, individual identity.

Pomegranate

"The pomegranate seed is a symbol of both fertility and of the pineal gland—the seat of consciousness in the head. When combined, this dual symbol makes the pomegranate the symbol of the birth of the consciousness in the form, the point at which the Soul becomes trapped on the Wheel of Rebirth and begins the cycle of birth, death, and reincarnation.

"In this context, a single seed represents a single incarnation or life. So long as Kore/Persephone eats a seed — identifies with form— after she descends to the underworld, she must return to 'live' —die to her self— again.

"Any questions about the symbols? OK, lets examine the 'meaning' of this myth.

The Meaning

"As with most myths, there are several layers of symbolism in our current tale. As with many of our myths, the most obvious is the ancient symbolic tale of the cycles of nature:

"The fruitful goddess of Spring disappears, and Mother Earth searches and grieves.

"In her grief, Mother Earth ages, Fall descends and turns to Winter.

"The Queen of the Underworld rules the death of life in Winter. Finally, the god of death impregnates the Daughter with his seed. The virgin reappears on earth in the fruits of Spring.

"In a more subtle layer of meaning, Persephone and her brother Plutus might represent the Divine Daughter and Son, the polarity of the Soul seen in Gemini. However, the balanced relationship is shattered by the abduction and rape by her uncle Pluton. This is a product of the motion of Pisces, which produced the familiar patriarchal version of the tale.

"Bereft of the balancing relationship with her male counterpart, Persephone is trapped in the polarity of substance, eternally moving from the worlds of death to that of life and back.

"In a balanced version of the tale, Persephone would follow her brother into the underworld, which they would rule together as husband and wife. Eventually, Persephone would lead the way to heaven, and her brother would follow."

Terry: "So what we have here is only half the story, the descent with a sort of aborted ascent."

Quinn: "I would say... 'infertile', perhaps.

Summary of the Polarity

Quinn: "In the context of our current study, the 'rape' of Kore by Hades represents the descent of the Soul into form, to become identified with that form and trapped within its cyclic motion. This is the movement of the consciousness from:

"The Positive Pole to the Negative, and

"The cyclic motion within the polarity of the Negative Pole.

"In the above patriarchal, Piscean version of the myth, the Divine Daughter is a helpless victim of circumstance who undertakes the journey alone. The Soul is so identified with the form that the Divine Son, represented as the uncle rather than the brother, remains in the underworld, ruling and thus ruled by the densest plane of substance. Since the Son remains in the underworld, the Daughter cannot liberate him and neither of them can go to heaven. The inevitable result is the entrapment of the Daughter in the cycle of rebirth.

"Thus, we see the effects of the motion of consciousness in Pisces. The patriarchal distortion prevents the Daughter from ascending to the Father and achieving reunion or at-one-ment.

"We will examine the spiritual consequences of Pisces further in the next chapter, the myth of Orpheus and Eurydice. But first, we'll close in the usual fashion."

Interlude (Continued)

Sit in a comfortable chair, relax your physical body, calm your emotions, and focus your mind.

Bring your consciousness to a point of focus within your ajna center.

After walking for many days and having many adventures, you finally come to a river. On the near bank of the river stands the Lady, clothed in white robes, crowned with silver, and holding a white staff.

At Her side is a sailboat, resting in the waters. She beckons to you, and you approach and kneel before Her. She strikes your kneeling form with the staff, once on each temple, and the third time on the forehead. You fall to the ground. She grips your hand, lifts you up, and whispers a word of power in your ear. Then She hands you the staff, and silently waves you toward the boat.

Recognizing that these gifts of the Mother will take you onward and upward on your journey, give thanks by audibly stating the seed-thought:

"My mind, emotions and body are gifts of the Mother, and I thank Her for all that She has done for me."

Without thinking about it or repeating it, allow the vibration of that thought to sound. Continue listening to and feeling that vibration until all is still and quiet, then, audibly sound the OM.

Take a deep breath, open your eyes, and return your awareness to your surroundings.

"Practice this inner ritual at least once a day, every

day, for a full lunar cycle (from New Moon to New Moon)."

Lesson 11

Turning Back to Darkness

The Myth of Orpheus and Eurydice

I clicked the "off" button on the fan's remote as Quinn entered the library. He smiled as the group greeted him and nodded back.

When he was seated, John asked, "Isn't it unlucky to meet on a Friday the 13th?"

Quinn said, "Actually, the 'Friday the 13th myth began on October 13th, 1307, when King Philippe le Bel of France engineered the arrest and suppression of the Knights Templar in order to liquidate his debt to the Order."

Ed: "Liquidate his debts?"

Quinn: "His father had been captured in Egypt while on crusade, and the Templars paid for his release. So, when Philippe inherited the throne of France, he owed the Order a king's ransom. Back then there wasn't anything like the regular tax system we have today. He didn't have the money, and no way of getting it, so the easiest method of getting rid of the debt was to eliminate his creditors."

Ed: "Yikes! What did he—"

Quinn: "Just one of the many low points in European history. I have a couple dozen works on the Templars over there, including their so-called trials. I'll show you after class.

"Now…"

Everyone sat up straight as Quinn gazed around the room, and I turned on the recorder.

Opening Alignment

"Close your eyes.

"Relax your physical body.

"Calm your emotions.

"Bring your consciousness to a point of focus within the ajna center, and there integrate your three-fold persona into a single unit in aspiration to the Soul. (Pause)

"Draw a line of golden-white light from the ajna, upward to the blue-white crown center. Slowly move upward along that line of light, and into the crown center. There identify as the Spiritual Soul. (Pause)

"As the Soul in the crown center, turn your attention upward to that wisdom or truth overshadowing this evening's lesson, and become receptive to it by silently sounding the OM. (Pause)

"Maintaining that focus of receptivity move back down the line of light into the ajna. (Pause)

"Maintaining that focus of receptivity in the ajna, draw a line of light from the ajna to the physical-dense brain, and audibly sound the OM.

"Take a deep breath, and open your eyes."

The Myth of Orpheus and Eurydice

"OK. The Myth and Rites of Orpheus were closely related to the Myth and Rites of Demeter. Where the Myth of Demeter explained the cycle of life and death, the Rites of Orpheus taught initiates how to find their way through the dark and gloomy caverns of the underworld to the beautiful Elysian Fields.

"El?"

Me: "Elysian Fields?"

Quinn: "Oh, I suppose you could call it the good side of town in the afterlife. From our perspective, it would be how to find your way out of the lower astral plane, where all the bad things dwell, into the upper levels where everything is bright and beautiful."

Thea: "Like in 'What Things May Come'?"

Quinn: "Yes, in fact I have that upstairs in Spiritual Fiction."

Thea: "The movie?"

Quinn: "No, the novel. The Robin William's movie is at the other end, in the DVD section. But either one is a fairly good example of what I mean, except for the stuff about suicides being trapped in a really nasty neighborhood."

Terry: "They're not trapped?"

Quinn: "Oh, for a while, but most of us go through some sort of temporary afterlife experience before moving on. It depends on what beliefs were impressed on us in our childhood, and on our emotional and mental state when we died, the condition of our astral body, that kind of thing. The condition of our persona determines where we go, and our beliefs determine how we shape and interpret it."

"Keep in mind that the astral plane is made of substance, very malleable substance. That's why its symbol is water. So it will readily take on any shape or appearance we impress on it, including whatever you expect to find in the afterlife.

Thea: "What about atheists?"

Quinn: "What kind of afterlife *don't* they believe in? They're usually fairly intelligent people who haven't been given a vision of the afterlife that their minds can accept, so they don't believe in one. But, they still have the image or they couldn't *not* believe in it, and that's the shape their afterlife takes. At least at first.

"Now eventually we all detach from that initial afterlife experience, and from all the forms left over from our last incarnation, and we move on. The Myth of Orpheus is part of that process.

"Jeff?"

Jeff: "Like the Tibetan Book of the Dead?"

Quinn: "Sort of, but the myth was a story one heard, and the rites were a ritual one experienced, sometime *before* death, often a long time before. But the Bardo Thodol was told, or later read, to the newly-deceased *while* they were undergoing the process.

"So, the Myth of Orpheus takes up where the Myth of Demeter left off, with Persephone the Queen of the Underworld. But, where the Myth of Demeter took a patriarchal view of the Goddess's role, the Myth of Orpheus takes an even more patriarchal view and reverses the functions of the genders.

"Orpheus, the Divine Son, descends to the underworld to rescue Eurydice, the Divine Mother.

"As we saw in our earlier, more matriarchal myths, when the Divine Son dies and the Divine Mother descends to the underworld to rescue him, She succeeds. However, when the Mother dies, and the Son descends to the underworld to rescue Her, He fails.

"This is a fairly typical expression of the motion of consciousness in Pisces. We've already discussed why this occurs, but the reasons will become even more apparent as we examine the Myth of Orpheus and Eurydice.

"John, are you ready?"

The Myth

John: "Uh, yes sir.

"One day Eurydice, the beloved of Orpheus, was walking through a meadow in Thrace with her Naiad friends, when a serpent struck, biting her in the ankle. Eurydice sickened and died from the snake's venom.

"Grieving for his lost love, Orpheus grabbed his lyre and sought out an entrance to the Underworld. Plunging into the dark cave, he descended to the realm of Hades.

"Deep beneath the earth, a giant, snarling beast leaped toward Orpheus. The hero jumped back. A huge chain leash brought the monster up short, and Orpheus stared, wide-eyed, at the slavering three-headed Cerberus, the giant canine guardian of the entrance to the Underworld.

"There was no way to pass by Cerberus without overcoming him, but Orpheus had no weapons, only his lyre. He sat on a rock and began to play and sing a soothing song. The beast calmed and listened, the six eyes slowly lowered, and the heads fell asleep one by one. When all three heads were snoring, Orpheus snuck silently past, and continued his descent.

"Emerging at last into a huge cavern, Orpheus found his way blocked by the river Styx. He charmed the ferryman Charon, and was granted passage across the river of forgetfulness.

"On the other side, Orpheus made his way to the rulers of the Underworld, Hades and Persephone, and begged them to release his beloved. They refused, but Orpheus charmed them with his song. Then Hades agreed to allow Eurydice to follow Orpheus back to the surface, but forbade Orpheus to speak with or look back at her until Eurydice had exited the portal. If he did, she would return to Hell forever.

"Orpheus slowly made his way back across the river, past Cerberus, his anxiety growing the entire way. Had he been tricked? Was Eurydice really following him? Orpheus was but moments away from the light when he could stand it no more. He spun about, looked back and saw his beloved Eurydice.

"The light of shock and disappointment flared in her eyes for a moment, then died, and she turned about and returned to the Underworld.

"Orpheus tried to go back to rescue Eurydice a second time, but Charon refused to grant him passage. The living Orpheus had lost Eurydice forever."

The Characters

Quinn: "Thank you John, very well done.

"Now, let's look at the characters.

(Quinn stood, as usual, and faced the board.)

"Let's see... we have Orpheus, Eurydice, Hades, Persephone, the Naiads...

Wil: "Charon and Cerberus"

Quinn: "Umm... let's include Cerberus in the Symbols.

Naiads

Terry: "Are Naiads like Dryads?"

Quinn: "Well, they're similar, yes, in that both are a type of nymph.

Colette: "Nymph?"

Quinn: "Hmm... It's a general type of lower order Deva.

"Colette?"

Colette: "Why not an elemental?"

Quinn: "Well... That relates to the magic of consciousness. But basically, elementals are 'involutionary'. That is, their function is to create the intelligent activity of form in the physical-dense world. Devas or 'angels' are evolutionary. Their function is to produce that intelligent activity of substance which raises the consciousness."

Me: "That's why you have me focusing on angels?"

Quinn: "In part, but it's also because when the magician commands elementals, the involutionary activity of the elementals drags on the consciousness of the magician. It's like walking up a 'down' escalator."

(I glanced up to where Sam watched from his perch in the rafters.)

Me: "But it's OK to make friends with them?"

Quinn: "Friendship is very different from command. The type, quality, and flow of energy is completely different. Also, remember that our physical-dense bodies actually *are* elementals. If we're going to live well in our body then we have to make friends with it. Otherwise, well, it will drag us down.

"Now, where were we?"

Me: "Dryads and nymphs."

"Ah. The basic difference between them is that Dryads are nymphs who dwell in, protect, and maintain trees and forests, while Naiads are water nymphs who dwell in, protect, and maintain lakes, rivers, streams, and fountains.

Orpheus

"Now, Orpheus was the son of Apollo by Calliope. He was the archetype of the musician, singer, and poet. He was the mythical founder of the Orphic Rites, an initiate of the Samothracian Mysteries, and is said to have co-founded the Eleusinian Mysteries with Dionysus. As I mentioned, His Orphic Rites were said to provide instruction on how the newly deceased could locate the Elysian Fields, and avoid the obstacles encountered along the way.

"His father, known as Apollo, Sol or Helios, was the Son of Zeus and Leto, and one of the twelve Olympians.

"His mother Calliope was Chief of the nine muses, and the daughter of Zeus and Mnemosyne.

John: "Mnemosyne?"

Quinn: "Memory, a daughter of Uranus and Gaea.

"Now, the thing to keep in mind about Orpheus is that he made the sounds that controlled the world. That's a good description of the creative activity of the soul, the sounding of the creative word that sets substance in motion—that sets it vibrating."

Wil: "So Orpheus is the Soul."

Quinn: "Yes, he'd be another symbol of the Divine Son.

Charon

"Now Charon was the ferryman of the Underworld. He guided the dead —those who could pay the toll— across the marsh of the Acheron and steered the boat over the river itself while forcing the dead to row."

Tess: "I thought it was a river."

Quinn: "The Styx? Yes, in some versions it is. And so we have another afterlife myth featuring a river and a marsh as journey and transition symbols.

"Now, one of the interesting facets of near-death experiences is that those having them, if they go far enough, always come to some sort of symbolic barrier, a wall, river, bridge, gate, door, something, that they do not pass. That barrier represents the barrier between 'life' in the world of affairs, and the 'afterlife' in the astral and above. In a sense this marsh or river serves the same function. Once you cross it, there's no turning back."

Wil: "Except for Orpheus."

Quinn: "Except for the Soul. Orpheus made it back, but he didn't bring Eurydice with him.

Eurydice

"Eurydice was also a daughter of Apollo, making her the sister/wife of Orpheus. She is sometimes portrayed as a dryad. Her name is a combination of the Greek words *eury* —wide or broad— and *dike* —justice. Here, she represents the feminine aspect of the Soul, the Divine Daughter.

"As we've already discussed, Hades was the god of the Underworld, brother of Zeus, and uncle/husband of Persephone, the Queen of the Underworld.

"Any questions about the characters? OK, let's look at the symbols.

The Symbols

"We have Cerberus, the Lyre, the river Styx...

Thea: "The serpent."

Quinn: "Yes. Anything else? No? OK.

Cerberus

"Now Cerberus was the giant, three-headed canine guardian of the entrance to the Underworld. Symbolically, he —or is it they— represent Canis Major, the constellation that guards the Zodiac.

Me: "Canwhat?"

Quinn: "C a n i s Major. It's Latin for 'Great Dog'. I have some information on it in the Glastonbury section."

Celine: "The Maltwood Zodiac?"

Quinn: "Yes."

John: "Maltwood Zodiac?"

Quinn: "Sometime early in the 20th century aerial photographs of the area around Glastonbury, England revealed what appeared to be a Zodiac formed of features of the landscape. This Zodiac was 'discovered' by a woman named Maltwood, but, of course, there was a great deal of controversy around it at the time.[1]

Celine: "It was in the 1920's. The guardian of the Maltwood Zodiac is called the 'Girt Dog of Langport', and she also used Ordnance Survey Maps."

Quinn: "Ah. Thank you."

Lyre

"Now, the Lyre is a kind of small, U-shaped harp, and was typically used to accompany singers and poets. It was the particular instrument of Apollo, as the god of music and poetry. Here, it is the symbol of the sevenfold word of the Soul, whose sounding begins the process of incarnation and formulates substance into distinct shapes."

Bhikku: "What is this 'word of the Soul'?"

Quinn: "I believe I touched on it in the handout on the centers. It's related to the note at the heart of each chakra and is utilized during the inner magic of consciousness. We'll go into it in depth in that course.

Bhikku: "Have you decided when to teach it?"

Quinn: "Looks like a couple weeks after this one ends. I'll let you know.

Serpent

"Now, the serpent that bit Eurydice is a symbol of the fire of matter, and of the channels or nadis through which that fire courses. In this case, it also symbolizes that substance which, through identification with its

---

[1] Quinn: See: A Guide to Glastonbury's Temple of the Stars, by K.E. Maltwood, F.R.S.A.

concrete forms, causes the 'death' of the self or Soul.

Styx

"The Styx or 'river of forgetfulness' symbolizes an experience common to the Wheel of Rebirth. As research into near death experiences indicates, passage from the physical-dense into the physical-etheric and astral planes includes a 'past-life review', a recollection of all that one has experienced in the just-completed sojourn in the world of affairs.

"This is followed, by a slow process of forgetting that comes with the gradual detachment from the forms associated with the past life. This process of detachment takes many decades —as time is measured in the physical-dense— and is part of the process of recovering from one life and preparing for the next. Thus most of us spend much more time 'between incarnations' — dwelling on the astral and/or mental planes— than we do in the physical-dense world of affairs.

"Of course, from the perspective of the Spiritual Soul, the process of detachment is simply part of the cyclic life of the form, the movement from one physical-dense incarnation into another. From the soul's perspective the entire period on the 'Wheel of Rebirth', attached to form, is spent in incarnation.

"Terry?"

Terry: "Why do we have to come back? I mean, if we detach from form between incarnations?"

Quinn: "Well, basically because of the process. You detach from the forms of your previous incarnation by attaching to the forms of your astral or mental life."

Celine: "So it's still the magic of form; detaching from one thing by attaching to another thing?"

Quinn: "Yes. Thus we remain attached to form, just to different forms. In fact, in some ways, when we're dwelling on those planes we become even more attached to the astral and mental forms than we were before, than when we dwelt in the physical-dense.

"Now, um...

Me: "The Styx."

Quinn: "Ah. Now, the river also represents the dividing line between 'life and death' beyond which none may pass and return. As I mentioned earlier, those who have 'near death' experiences sometimes go as far as this symbolic barrier. However, whatever form the symbol takes, it represents a very real barrier, for those who pass beyond it do not return.

"Any questions about the symbols? Then let's look at the meaning."

The Meaning

"The Myth of Orpheus appears to provide the basis for a mystery teaching on finding one's way to the Greek afterlife. However, if we keep in mind that from the perspective of the consciousness or Soul the physical-dense world is the realm of death, then the meaning of the Myth is reversed.

"The Underworld ruled by Hades is the physical-dense world. The 'death' of Eurydice represents the death of the self through identification with and entrapment in the cycles of the form.

"The Music of Orpheus which can wake the dead and lead them back to life is the creative Word of the Spiritual Soul, which calls the incarnate human soul back from its entrapping form into the light of its True Self or Oversoul.

"However, in order for the resurrection to work, the Soul's attention must remain fixed on the upward way. Any wavering of that fixed intent, even a momentary return to form-identification, will cause failure.

"If the attention remains fixed on the Light of the overshadowing Spiritual Soul, the self will emerge from the darkness, the incarnate human soul will merge with the Spiritual Soul, the Divine Daughter will merge with the Divine Son, and the two will become One.

"However, as we have seen, the Divine Son cannot maintain his focus on the upper realm, for that is not his task. His is the work of descent. It's the Daughter who leads the way out of darkness into the Light.

The Polarity

Quinn: "Thus, we again see the importance of polarity. The 'death' of Eurydice and the 'rescue' of Orpheus represents the descent of the magnetic field into form. However, in this case the relationship between the poles of the magnetic field has been reversed by the patriarchal expression of Pisces, and the attempt is unsuccessful.

"Instead of being responsible for the movement from the Negative Pole to the Positive, the Daughter or inner magnetic field remains trapped in the Negative Pole.

"Rather than being trapped by his descent into the Negative Pole, and rescued from there by the Daughter, the Son or outer magnetic field attempts to rescue the trapped Daughter. Since the Divine Son is the movement of consciousness from the Positive Pole to the Negative, He cannot help the Daughter move from the Negative Pole to the Positive. That's not His function and He has no such capacity. Therefore, He fails.

"We'll continue examining the consequences of the patriarchal expression of Pisces in the next chapter, the Myth of Mary and Jesus.

"Any final questions? Then prepare for the closing."

Aspiration

Sit in a comfortable chair, relax your physical body, calm your emotions, and focus your mind.

Bring your consciousness to a point of focus within your ajna center,

From your place within the ajna center, imagine that you are in a sailboat on the shore of a river. On the bank behind you is the Lady, clothed in white, and in your hand is Her staff.

Recognizing that you are preparing for the journey home, integrate your body, emotions and mind into a single unit in the Ajna center, and audibly state the seed-thought:

"I and the Mother are One."

Without thinking about it or repeating it, allow the vibration of that thought to sound. Continue listening to and feeling that vibration until all is still and quiet, then, audibly sound the OM.

Bow to the Lady, raise the sail, and push the boat away from the shore with the staff.

The Lady's breeze fills your triangular sails, driving the boat up the river. Sit in the back of the boat and place the end of the staff in the water as a tiller, steering the boat where you would go.

Take a deep breath, open your eyes, and return your awareness to your surroundings.

"Practice this inner ritual at least once a day, every day, for a full lunar cycle (from New Moon to New Moon)."

Lesson 11

Lesson 12

Ascending to Heaven

The Myth of Mary and Jesus

Quinn's aura radiated purple-on-indigo as he stepped into the library, smiled, and greeted everyone with
nods. Bhikku's solar plexus was unusually torpid, and
hazy with yellowish sludge.

Quinn sipped from his water, and said, "All right...
everyone's here let's begin."

Opening Alignment

"Close your eyes.

"Relax your physical body.

"Calm your emotions (pause).

"Bring your consciousness to a point of focus within the ajna center, and there integrate your three-fold persona into a single unit in aspiration to the Soul. (Pause)

"Draw a line of golden-white light from the ajna, upward to the blue-white crown center. Slowly move upward along that line of light, and into the crown center. There identify as the Spiritual Soul. (Pause)

"As the Soul in the crown center, turn your attention upward to that wisdom or truth overshadowing this evening's lesson, and become receptive to it by silently sounding the OM. (Pause)

"Maintaining that focus of receptivity, move back down the line of light into the ajna. (Pause)

"Maintaining that focus of receptivity in the ajna, draw a line of light from the ajna to the physical-dense brain, and audibly sound the OM.

"Take a deep breath, and open your eyes."

The Myth of Mary and Jesus

Quinn: "Now, of all the myths covered in this course, that of Jesus and Mary Magdalene is by far the best known and the most distorted. It's also the one with which those of us raised 'Christian' are most powerfully identified, and thus it can be very difficult for us to recognize it as a myth, accept its distortions, and understand its true meaning.

"Yes, Thea?"

Thea: "You were raised Christian?"

Quinn: "In a fairly moderate denomination, what I call 'potato salad' Christianity. But I went to Sunday School every week, memorized the Ten Commandments, did Bible Study, the whole bit."

Ema: "'Potato salad'?"

Quinn: "The congregation placed a lot more emphasis on the social life of the church than on doctrine. For instance, when I was sixteen the pastor announced that he didn't believe in the Virgin Birth of Jesus, and the congregation couldn't decide if they should be upset or not. He was a really nice guy, and it just wasn't important to them."

John: "How did you get from there to here?"

Quinn: "Oh... now that's a story. It started with Leon, my college roommate. But that's way off topic, and I don't want to go into it here. El's working on it as part of her creative writing assignment, and maybe she'll let you guys see it when she's done. She's very good, and I hope she'll have it published."

Me: (Everyone looked to me) "Maybe. I don't know. We'll see."

Quinn: "Now, let's get back to our myth.

"The evidence indicates that the gospels that tell the story were written long after the events they describe. No actual eyewitnesses were available, and there don't appear to have been any contemporary written accounts. In fact, there's no proof that the gospels are histories of actual events, quite the contrary.

"The gospels were written by Jewish men writing for Jews. In addition, they were writing after the Diaspora[1] and thus lived among and interacted with non-Jews. As a result of this situation, the Greco-Roman culture had a profound influence on both post-Diaspora Judaism and the Jewish cult of Christianity, an influence that's illustrated in the surviving frescoes of Dura-Europas.[2]

"Christians have ignored, denied, and suppressed this for centuries, but it's absolutely essential to understanding early Christian development. In the beginning, at a time when Judaism was undergoing substantial transformation, Christianity was a cult within Judaism, a cult with its own myths and traditions in addition to those of 'mainstream' Judaism. This Christian cult was

---

[1] 70 CE, when the Jews were expelled from Israel by the Romans.

[2] Dura-Europas was a Roman city located near the modern Syria-Iraq boarder. Destroyed in 256 CE, its ruins include both the oldest "church" ever discovered and a nearby Synagogue. The Church and Synagogue were located in converted roman-style homes, near temples of Zeus, Aphlad (a weather god), and Mithra. The surviving frescoes on the walls of the Synagogue suggest that there was some interaction between the temples, the Church, and the Synagogue. The frescoes, which show scenes from the "Old Testament", were painted in a typical Greco-Roman style, in a manner that portrayed Moses, for instance, like a Greco-Roman demigod. Thus, just as the earlier Babylonian Exile had a profound affect on Jewish religious development, the later Diaspora transformed Christian/Jewish religion. The early Christians and post-Diaspora Jews were an integral part of the surrounding society, and the mystery traditions of that society influenced both the developing cult and the authors of the gospels.

310

growing, and needed a common liturgy —form of worship— and means of educating new converts.

Tess: "What kind of transformation?"

Quinn: "In Judaism? Well, we really don't know the specifics. They'd not only lost their homeland but the Temple, their primary place of worship, and were having to figure out how to survive as a people, both culturally and religiously. Remember, Judaism had become a very centralized religion, and yet it still had a number of cults. With the Diaspora, the movement into other lands and influences, the loss of central control, well, there must have been an explosion of new ideas and practices."

Terry: "So, Christianity was one of those?"

Quinn: "Actually, Christianity was many of those. Think of it as a sort of social evolutionary process. If you take something mature and well developed, and place it in new, stressful environments, you often get many variations on the original. Some of those variations survive, but most die off, and in the end you have something new."

Terry: "So, modern Christianity and Judaism are survivals?"

Quinn: "With a common origin, yes.

"Now, the early Jewish Christians naturally turned to their Jewish liturgy and teaching traditions for the answer. Using the Judaic liturgical calendar —their annual cycle of holidays— as an outline, and the midrashic style of sacred storytelling, they formulated a series of educational works on Christianity. The results were the Christian gospels, which were designed to be read to the congregation, a portion at a time, in a sequence that led the congregation through an annual cycle of 'Christian' ritual.

"Celine?"

Celine: "A sort of annual ritual?"

Quinn: "Yes, a single ritual that unfolded over weeks and months, and eventually over an entire year."

"Now, since the midrashic style is concerned with conveying sacred truth through symbols, and *not* with historical events, the resulting gospels are not and were never intended to be actual historical records of the life of Jesus of Nazareth.

"The gospels are actually much more than that. They are the symbolic story of a 'savior', an Initiate of the One True Path who modeled that path for humanity.

"Since this expression of the path was modeled and written during the early centuries of Pisces, the myth naturally emphasizes ascension, the upward movement of the Daughter toward the Father.

"However, since it did so under the veil of patriarchy, the Daughter was obscured, and replaced by the Son.

"Now modeling the One True Path is an essential part of the work of every true Initiate of the Mysteries, part of their purpose in appearing in the world of affairs. Having achieved union of their Spirit and Substance, and freed themselves from the Wheel of Rebirth, such Initiates are not drawn back into incarnation by attachment to form. They do not *have* to be here, but return in order to show us The Way.

"Showing humanity The Way is the most effective method of teaching us. We learn all the essential things in our life by having them modeled for us, including such basic things as how to eat, walk, dress, talk, etc. Thus, Initiates incarnate in the world of affairs in order to model the Path of Initiation.

"Now, since the One True Path remained essentially the same, all Initiates, in every time and place, modeled the same thing. They expressed it slightly differently, because it came through their persona instrument and was demonstrated to a particular group in a particular time and place, but it was always essentially the same 'story'.

"That's another reason why these myths sound so similar. Many are based on or inspired by the life experience of an Initiate, each of whom modeled the One True Path.

"Unfortunately, the myth of Jesus and the Magdalene was distorted from its beginnings by ignorance, patriarchal bias, and the Solar Plexus polarity. Among other effects, this produced an over-emphasis on the Arian elements of the story, on the sacrificed rather than on the risen initiate. Further distortions have accumulated ever since. The resulting tale is so encased in mental illusion and astral glamour that it's very difficult to find the reality hidden within. Thus, in order to avoid most of that distortion, I've asked Bhikku to tell the story —since he comes from another tradition— but to limit his version to the barest outline of the essential points and to rename the principals Joshua and Mariam.

"Bhikku?"

The Myth

The Birth

Bhikku: (Now pale under his tan skin, and with yellow flashes pulsing in his abdomen) "Thank you Sir, thank you all. I am honored.

"The Spirit of YHWH entered into Mary, an unmarried girl, and made her pregnant. Then an angel appeared to her and announced that she was to give birth to a Son of God.

"Pregnant, with no visible father for the child, Mary wed a local builder named Joseph. While Mary was great with child she journeyed with Joseph to Bethlehem, and gave birth to Joshua in a stable, surrounded by animals.

"While staying in the stable, the young family was visited by three wise men and a group of shepherds.

"When Joshua was an adolescent, the family journeyed to the Temple in Jerusalem, and there Joshua astonished the priests with his knowledge and wisdom.

"The gospels are then silent until Joshua is a full-grown man of about thirty years.

The Baptism

"A wedding party ran out of wine, and Mary, mother of Joshua, took the problem to him. Joshua had the empty wine vessels filled with water, and the water was transformed into wine.

"Joshua attended an outdoor revival held by his cousin John on the bank of the River Jordan, was baptized by his cousin, and filled with the Spirit of Peace.

"Joshua became an itinerant preacher, traveling through the land and teaching the Wisdom to all who would listen. His popularity grew rapidly, and he soon had many followers.

Temptation on the Mount

"Exhausted by his work, Joshua left his leading followers in charge and went on a spiritual retreat. While he was praying and meditating alone, Satan appeared to him and promised to fulfill all his desires if Joshua would but follow him. When that did not work, Satan promised to fulfill all his aspirations if Joshua would but follow him.

"Joshua resisted all temptation, and dismissed Satan, ordering him away.

The Crucifixion

"Joshua returned to his teaching work, and after a very few years —when he was but 33— he and his chief followers traveled to Jerusalem for the holidays. While there, Joshua visited the rebuilt Temple, and, incensed by defiling greed, he committed a violent act of protest. The priests were offended and frightened by his actions, decided they had to act against him, and began plotting his death.

"Joshua and his followers met in the upper room of a house for a traditional holiday dinner. Later Joshua and his followers retired to a local garden, where he prayed all night while they slept.

"In the morning, Joshua was betrayed by one of his followers and arrested. Tried on trumped-up charges, he was found guilty and executed by nailing him to a cross and leaving him to die, while Mary, Mariam, and others watched.

The Resurrection and Ascension

"Joshua's body was laid in a tomb carved into the side of a hill, and a stone was rolled before the entrance.

"Mariam, along with other women, visited the tomb-for the customary bathing of the body, but found the stone rolled aside, the guards missing, and the tomb empty.

"Mariam reported this to Joshua's chief male followers, who disbelieved her. Some of them visited the tomb, also found it empty, and reported back to the others.

"Joshua was later seen walking the land. He appeared to his male followers, spoke with and was even touched by them, and then ascended to Heaven."

The Characters

Quinn: "Thank you Bhikku. Very well done! (Gazing around the room) Did anyone feel outraged? No? (Looking back to Bhikku) See? You can relax now.

"OK. Let's look at the characters. (Quinn rose, faced the board, and grabbed a blue marker.)

"Now, we have Joshua or Jesus, Mary, Mariam, John the Baptist, Joseph, the Three Wise Men, the animals in the stable, the shepherds... Eli... Who else?"

Thea: "The Holy Spirit."

Tess: "The Trinity."

Wil: "Satan"

Quinn: "All right... Anyone else? Yes, John?"

Eli

John: "Who's Eli?"

Quinn: "Ah. Well, Joshua called out to Eli or Eloi from the cross. There's some discrepancy over exactly what the name was. However, as discussed in the lesson on Eve and Adam, the term Elohim is usually translated as 'God' in the Bible, but actually refers to both the Feminine and Masculine poles of Divinity.

"Joshua uses a similar term while hanging on the cross, and it's also usually translated as 'God'. Now the gospels provide two versions of his words.

(Quinn picked up a large, black, leather-bound Bible from his end table, flipped to a book-marked page, and read:)

"Matthew 27:46 'And about the ninth hour Jesus cried with a loud voice, saying, Eli, Eli, lama sabachthani? that is to say, My God, my God, why hast thou forsaken me?'"

(He flipped to a later page, and read:)

"Mark 15:34 'And at the ninth hour Jesus cried with a loud voice, saying, Eloi, Eloi, lama sabachthani? which is, being interpreted, My God, my God, why hast thou forsaken me?'"

(Quinn closed the Bible, set it back on the table, picked up a green and black book, opened it, and said,)

"However, in *The Holy Bible From Ancient Eastern Manuscripts,*' by George M. Lamsa, we find the following corrected translation:

"Matthew 27:46 'And about the ninth hour, Jesus cried out with a loud voice and said, Eli, Eli, lemana shabakthani! My God, my God, for this I was spared! This was my destiny.'

(Quinn closed the book, put it back on the table, and continued.)

"This corrected version is quite helpful, but for one point. As we have seen, it's the Mother Aspect which rescues the Son from the death of form, *not* the Father. Since Joshua was modeling initiation, He would not have cried out 'My God, My God...' but, 'My Goddess, my Goddess, for this I was spared! This was my destiny.'

"Symbolically speaking, upon the death of Her Divine Son the Goddess appears and bears him away, His substance is transformed into Light, and He is taken up to Heaven. We have seen this movement again and again in our myth tales. The substance of the bodies of the Son is transformed, and he is born upward by the

Mother. This is the way the path works, and, as we shall see, is exactly what happened here as well.

Holy Spirit

"The Holy Spirit is the third person in the Trinity — Espiritu Sanctu or Shekinah— Divine Substance, or the Divine Mother Aspect."

Joseph

"Joseph is a symbol of the Divine Father. He disappears from the gospels when Joshua, the Divine Son, symbolically moves away from the Father toward the Mother.

Joshua

"Joshua was an initiate who incarnated in order to model the process of spiritual growth and development. This included union or at-one-ment with both the Positive and Negative Poles of Divinity, and with the twin poles of the Self or Soul.

"His union with the Positive Pole of Divinity is indicated by the statement of Joshua in Mark 10: 30:

"'I and the Father are One.'

"However, as we have seen, the consciousness or Soul cannot relate with one Pole without developing an equal relationship with the other Pole. Thus, in order for the Soul to identify as the Father Aspect of Divinity —'I and the Father are One'— it must be equally identified with the Mother Aspect of Divinity.

"Thus, within Himself, Christ experiences the Polar identity of:

"*I and the Mother are One.*'"

Thea: "He what?!"

Quinn: "It's simple electromagnetism. One pole cannot exist without the other. The consciousness cannot truly at-one with one Pole of Divinity without being equally united with the other.

"The Christ is the Adult Child of God, that consciousness or World Soul which is equally identified with both the Mother and the Father.

"Celine?"

Celine: "So, Christ is both the Daughter and the Son?"

Quinn: "Yes. That's what the 'Adult Child of God' *is*, the Daughter/Son who has 'wed', become one, and then reunited the Mother/Father.

"That's both the process and the function of the Soul.

"The resulting re-union of the vertical and horizontal poles is symbolized by the equal armed cross, which is the correct symbol of the Risen Christ.

Mary

"Now the name of 'Mary' is derived from the Hebrew 'Miriam', meaning 'sea of bitterness' and the Chaldaic 'mistress of the sea.' Thus, 'Mary' is a title for the Great Goddess as Asherah, the 'Lady of the Sea'.

"There are several 'Mary's' in our current myth, representing different aspects of the Mother and Daughter Aspects of Divinity, including:

"Mary, the mother of Joshua, who is sometimes called the 'Mother of God' and 'Queen of Heaven'. In Christian iconography she represents the Mother Aspect of the Goddess.

"Mary or Anna, the grandmother of Joshua, called 'Anna' to distinguish her from the mother of Joshua. Anna represents the Crone or Wisdom Aspect of the Goddess. She is considered by some to have been among the women who attended Joshua on the cross and later discovered that his body was missing.

"The third Mary is the other title character of this lesson, Mary Magdalene or 'Mariam' as we are calling her. The gospels refer to 'Mary of Magdala' or 'the Mag'dalene' twelve times, nearly all during or immediately following the Crucifixion:

> "She is among the women who observe the Crucifixion.[3]

> "After the Crucifixion, she is among the women who follow the body to see what is done with it.[4]

> "After the body is placed in the tomb, she is among the women who purchase ointments and go to the tomb to anoint the body.[5]

> "After the Resurrection, Christ appeared to the Magdalene, before anyone else, and then *she* announced the Resurrection to the twelve male Apostles.[6]

"Thus, Mariam was symbolically involved in each step of this process, from crucifixion, death, entombment and anointment, to resurrection.

"The Eastern Church retained this view of her, recognizing the Magdalene as the ointment bearer —for the dead body— and the first witness of the Resurrection.

"However, the Western Church confused her with a 'woman of the city, who was a sinner'[7] and portrayed her as a penitent whore. This mistake apparently began in the Fifth Century CE, when Pope Gregory the Great portrayed the Magdalene as a penitent woman in some of his sermons. However, this view did not become official church doctrine until the Council of Trent.[8] This

---

[3] Quinn: Matthew 27: 56, Mark 15: 40, John 19: 25
[4] Quinn: Mark 15: 47
[5] Quinn: Matt. 27: 61, Matt. 28: 1; Mark 16: 1; John 20: 1
[6] Quinn: Mark 16: 9, Luke 24:10, John 20: 18
[7] Quinn: Luke 7: 37
[8] 1545–1563 CE

doctrine lasted about 400 years, until the Second Vatican Council, which occurred early in Aquarius.[9]

"This mis-characterization of the *Apostle to the Apostles* is being corrected as Aquarius unfolds, but it is still a very common distortion.

"Far from being a penitent fallen woman, Mariam is the true 'Bride of Joshua', the Divine Daughter.

"Ema?"

Ema: "They were married?"

Quinn: "I was speaking symbolically, but the idea that Joshua and Mariam were in fact married has been out there for a while now.[10]

"We know there had to be a 'bride' of some sort, for, given the polar relationship between them, a 'Divine Son' simply cannot exist without a 'Divine Daughter'. In fact, the first portion of the Path, the quest for self-awareness, is the result of the attempt of these two poles to discover each other and re-unite.

"This polar quest-for-union produces the search for an ideal mate, a mate who is our self in another form, a mate with whom we can at-one in the Divine Marriage of the Soul.

"Colette?"

Colette: "Soul mates."

Quinn: "Well, I still prefer 'Twin Soul'. But, the very fact that we —each and all of us— are in incarnation indicates that our divine partner exists.

"Again, in order for anything to exist:

"The Positive Pole or Spirit formulates the purpose

---

[9] 1962–1965 CE

[10] Glen: The class met before *The DaVinci Code*, by Dan Brown (a novel promoting the idea that Jesus was wed to "Mary Magdalene") became well known. Thus, Quinn is referring to earlier works such as *Holy Blood, Holy Grail* (see the Bibliography).

of that thing.

"The outer magnetic field or Son relates that Purpose to Substance.

"Substance responds by creating the form of that thing, and

"The inner magnetic field or Daughter relates the intelligent activity of the Mother to the Father.

"The Soul creates its persona—mental, astral, physical-etheric, and physical-dense bodies—via this same dual polarity. As a result, in order to come into incarnation on any of the planes, the Soul must reflect its own Son–Daughter polarity onto that plane. Thus, each of us has a polar-opposite, our Self in another form, someone who is the incarnation of the other pole of our Soul.

"We could not be here otherwise.

"The entire Path of Initiation can be described as the unfoldment of the relationship between the Son–Daughter poles of the Soul. From this perspective, the stages are:

"The Quest for Self Awareness: In this stage, the incarnate human being gradually becomes aware of and as the self or Soul. Near the conclusion of this stage, one becomes aware of the polarities of the Soul.

"The Quest for Union of the Divine Son–Daughter: Having become aware of the polarities of the Soul, one seeks to unite them in order to better serve the One Life. This is a necessary step in that service, for one learns how and becomes able to unite the vertical Poles of Divinity by uniting the poles of the Soul.

"The Quest for Union of the Divine Father–Mother: Having achieved at-one-ment of the poles of the

Soul, one begins the inner and outer magical process of uniting the vertical Poles of Divinity, the Divine Mother–Father.

"Although heavily veiled and much misunderstood, each of these stages is modeled in the Myth of Mariam and Joshua.

"Joshua was a Rabbi, and Rabbi's were expected to be married. Had he not been, it would have been re-marked upon. This gives rise to a question posed by the first miracle —turning water into wine. This event oc-curred at a wedding when Mary, mother of Joshua, in-formed him that they had run out of wine. Nothing is said about why she took this problem to Joshua or why He acts on it, but the answer is really quite simple and has been discussed at length by others.

"The question is, why does Mary take this problem to Joshua? Why was it their concern?

"Well, who would have been responsible for the re-freshments at a party? The hosts! It was Mary's concern because she was the hostess! Israel was by then a patri-archal culture, and thus the bride was being brought into the groom's household. This made hosting the wed-ding party the responsibility of the groom's family. Mary, mother of Joshua, was the hostess. But why did she go to Joshua? Because He was the groom! It was *his* party!

"If he had just married, who was the bride? The an-swer to that is quite simple. What woman is portrayed as present when a wife would be expected to be there? As we've just seen, Mariam is the only woman who is portrayed as traveling with Joshua and who is consis-tently portrayed as taking responsibility for preparing his body for burial, a traditional duty of the women of a Jewish family. She traveled with him, and was a mem-ber of his household, but was not a sister, mother, or cousin.

"Now, keep in mind that, in comparison to the modern West, the Hebrew culture of the time was extremely patriarchal.

"For instance, as I mentioned earlier, I have a Jewish friend with a traditional family name which she insists harkens back to Biblical and earlier times. When I asked her what her name meant she said 'seven'.

"'Seven?' said I.

"'Yes.' said she, 'They used to number girls.'

"'Number girls! You mean, One, Two, Three...'

"'Yes, but outside the family they'd be identified by their patronymic.'

"'Patronymic?' asked I

"'The First daughter of Avram, the Second daughter of Avram, the Third daughter of Avram... and so on.'

"'Ummm, really?'

"'Yes.'

Quinn: "Now, in such a culture, when a woman left her father's household, her 'name' in effect changed to reflect her new status, usually subservient to another male. Thus, she might become 'Two, sister of Aaron' or 'Two, wife of Baruch'. However, unless she was important in her own right, she would, be identified by her relationship with a male."

Me: "Like we did up until medieval times?"

Quinn: "In the Arthurian Romances, yes.

"This, of course, raises the question of why, if this is correct, Mariam of Migdal is identified by her home village rather than as 'Mariam, wife of Joshua'.

"One could, of course, insist that she was *not* married to Joshua. However, such a claim would not account for why she was accorded the honor of a 'place name'.

"It appears to have been a custom of the time to identify *men*, when traveling outside of their village, by their place of origin—such as 'Joseph of Arimathea' or 'Jesus of Nazareth'. Thus, to identify a woman by her home village would, in some respects, be treating her like a man, that is, according her the same level of respect as a man—recognizing her as a person in her own right. Thus 'Mariam of Midgal" could, in and of itself, be taken as an indication that she was an important person.

"Celine?"

Celine: "What does Midgal mean?"

Quinn: "Oh... 'tower' or perhaps 'place of the tower'."

Celine: "So her first name is the name of the Great Goddess as the Goddess of the Sea, and her last name means 'tower'? Isn't that, well, 'the Mother Goddess from the Tower'?"

Quinn: "Yes, which we could portray as a goddess column, pillar, tree, or as the central, upward-moving portion of the magnetic field.

(Quinn stood and flipped through pages of the drawing pad, until he found the bar magnet / magnetic field illustration. Some stared, eyes wide, mouths gaping, while others nodded knowingly.)

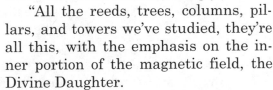

"All the reeds, trees, columns, pillars, and towers we've studied, they're all this, with the emphasis on the inner portion of the magnetic field, the Divine Daughter.

"Thus, Joshua and Mariam were husband and wife, which completely legitimizes her presence. And, in addition, she was an important person in her own right. However, neither of these thoughts were acceptable to the patriarchal Western church, which explained away her presence by identifying her with an unnamed fallen woman and presumed whore. Thus, once again we see the old patriarchal technique of degrading, perverting, and devaluing the Divine Feminine.

"The result was a severe distortion and disruption of the Christian expression of the path. It still serves the One Life, as all forms do, but not to anything like the extent that was originally intended and is still possible.

"Celine?"

Celine: "The first miracle, turning water into wine, it was *after* the marriage?"

Quinn: "Oh, yes! Excellent point! The miracles, the ministry of Joshua, those didn't, they couldn't begin until *after* the Daughter–Son union! It was the union, the integration or synthesis of the Divine Daughter and Son, symbolized in the marriage, that made the miracles and ministry possible.

"Thea?"

Thea: "What about the cult of Mary?"

Quinn: "The mother of Joshua?"

Thea: "Yes."

"Well, as the 'Mother of God', Mary represents the second aspect of the Goddess, the Great Mother. In the Christian 'Cult of Mary', at-one-ment with Christ is achieved through her as the Mother.

"However, this is a source of some conflict. The Church recognizes Mary as a Saint, not as the Third Aspect of Divinity. The Christian Third Aspect, remember, is the Holy Ghost, a translation of the Latin *Esperitu Sanctu*, a masculine pronoun which is a translation of the Hebrew *Shekinah*, the feminine pronoun meaning the 'Presence of God'.

"Thus, Mary remains, officially at least, a human woman. But, the Church tolerates her worship because of her popularity. In fact, no one has ever been able to completely stamp out the spiritual recognition of the Mother. There has always been some opening through which She can reach and uplift the Soul.

"Mary is an example of such an opening. The Great Goddess was excised from official doctrine, reduced to a 'mere' woman, and then that woman was raised to near divinity.

"Yes, Colette?"

Colette: "What about the rape of Mary?"

Quinn: "Ah yes. Well, I suggest that the wording, the entire perspective on this incident is a result of the motion of consciousness in Pisces.

"The impregnation of Mary posed a problem for the patriarchal Jewish authors of the gospels. The heroes and demigods of the surrounding Greco-roman culture were commonly born of virgins impregnated by a god, often without the girl's consent.

"Again, this is a patriarchal portrayal of what had been, in matriarchal times, a sacred festival of renewal initiated and controlled by the Goddess, with the full consent of the male. In a higher sense, this ritual symbolized the creative cycle of the Tetrad, with the emphasis placed on the Divine Feminine.

"However, in the patriarchal version, the male god initiates, dominates and controls the process, and often does not even ask for the woman's consent. This is rape, plain and simple, and that is not and cannot be the way The Path works!

"The Divine Father *did not* do that to the mother of Joshua.

"But the times led to it being portrayed that way, and having pulled the classic maneuver of stealing the Mother's power through sexual violence, the Church found itself in an uncomfortable position.

"Again, mis-portraying the Goddess may make it

more difficult for us to relate with Her, but it does *not* make Her go away, for She is the very Substance in which we live and move and have our being.

"Thus, She is inescapable. No matter how thoroughly suppressed, Her symbols remain potent. Raising the human Mary to near-divinity, as the 'Mother of God' and 'Bride of Christ', is only a beginning. By doing so, the Cult of Mary is following in the footsteps of older mystery traditions in which the Initiate was both the Son of the Divine Mother and Her husband.

"Again, this particular type of 'marriage' is symbolic of the movement of consciousness as it relates one Divine Pole with another. Whether the Daughter is portrayed as marrying the Father, or the Son the Mother, is a matter of where one is on the Wheel.

"In Taurus, matriarchal systems portrayed the Divine Mother marrying the son, and raising the son to divinity

"In Pisces, patriarchal systems portrayed the Divine Son marrying the mother, and raising the mother to divinity.

"In a symbolically complete myth tale, such as we would expect to see in Aquarius:

"The Daughter marries the Father.

"The Daughter and Son marry.

"The Daughter–Son marries the Mother–Father.

"The Mother and Father marry.

"All Four Aspects would be recognized as equally divine.

"Now, the Christian portrayal of Mary as both the 'Mother of God' and the 'Bride of Christ' is typical of patriarchal systems. In Pisces, the Mother is often lifted to divinity through symbolic marriage to the Divine Son.

"However, in a symbolically complete version of this

myth:

> "The Father marries the Mother —Joshua and Mariam are born.

> "The Daughter and Son marry —Mariam and Joshua become one.

> "The Daughter–Son marries the Mother–Father — Mariam/Joshua unites with the two Poles, and states: '*I and the Mother–Father are One.*'

> "Mariam/Joshua ascend to Heaven —the two Poles of Divinity again become One.

"This, in basic outline, is the actual story of the gospels, from the perspective of the process of Divine Marriage or at-one-ment.

Wil: "You're saying that's what really happened?"

Quinn: "No. I'm saying that's how the process actually works, and if it was worked, if the process was modeled for us, then that's how it was done.

"Now, we have already discussed the Trinity of Divine Mother, Father, and Son/Daughter. In the Christian version of the Trinity, these three are identified as:

> "God or YHWH,

> "Jesus Christ, and

> "Holy Spirit.

"There are, however several difficulties with these terms as typically understood in the Christian context. These difficulties include:

"The Father Aspect —God or YHWH— is overemphasized, to the point of portraying the Positive Pole of a planetary polarity as the sole creator, the whole of the One Life. This ignores the vertical polarity which gives birth to every thing that is.

"The Son Aspect is portrayed without the Daughter. This ignores the horizontal polarity that is the relationship between, and brings about the union of, the vertical poles. The Son does not exist without the Daughter, and they cannot function apart from each other. They are two poles of the One Self, the Soul of the One Life, that which Christianity calls 'The Christ'.

"In order to function as a complete path, this myth would have to:

"Recognize the inseparable polar relationship between the Two Aspects of Divinity, the Positive Pole/Father Aspect or YHWH and the Negative Pole/Mother Aspect or Holy Spirit. To whatever degree the myth retains a mis-relationship with the Great Goddess, to that degree it will be unable to function as a vehicle for the path, for realization of one's self *or* for the manifestation of the Divine Plan.

"Recognize the inseparable unity of the horizontal poles, Joshua–Mariam Christ. From this perspective:

"Joshua was a personality embodying the outer pole of the magnetic field,

"Mariam was a personality embodying the inner pole of the magnetic field, and,

"'Christ' is a title of the Second Aspect of Divinity that was expressed through the persona polarity of Mariam–Joshua.

"Yes, Terry?"

Terry: "Joshua and Mariam were *both* the Christ?"

Quinn: "It's the other way around. The planetary Soul or Christ incarnated through Mariam and Joshua. Having long-since achieved union of the positive and

330

negative poles of the Soul, unlike us, Christ could have incarnated as a single individual. However, since the Christ incarnated in order to model the Path, he did so in two personas, with Joshua expressing or embodying the external magnetic field and Mariam embodying the internal field. Thus, through them, he modeled that portion of the Path in which the Soul re-unites its internal and external magnetic fields, and again becomes one self.

"John?"

John: "That's the part that relates to soul mates, ummm... to twin souls?"

Quinn: "Yes, but again, we'd need an entire new course to get into that properly.

"Now, who's next?"

Satan

Wil: "Satan."

Quinn: "Ah.

"As mentioned earlier, patriarchal systems tend to portray the Divine Mother as lesser than the Divine Father, and to portray experience in form as a distraction from union with the Father.

"Christianity took this tendency to new extremes and transformed the Mother —Substance— into the source of all evil. Now, the primary difficulty with this attitude is not that we believed it, but that we conveyed that belief to Substance, and it believed us.

"John?"

John: "But, how... why would She...?"

Quinn: "Well, remember the function of the Aspects of Divinity:

"The Father is the source of Divine Purpose, Power, and Will.

"The Son conveys that Will to the Mother.

331

"The Mother responds to that Will with Intelligent Activity.

"The Daughter conveys that Intelligent Activity to the Father.

"Thus, Substance responds to an impression of will. That is its nature, its function. The resulting Intelligent Activity of Substance differentiates substance into many forms, including the substantial forms of and on all the planes.

"Now, this process works the same whether the 'son' involved is an Adult Son accurately conveying the Divine Will of the Father, or whether it is an immature son whose portion of will is distorted by mental illusions or astral/emotional glamours, such as selfish desires. No matter who's wielding it, or what it's used for, it's the same Will energy, and when it's focused and impressed on Substance, that substance will respond.

"Now, through the many ages, the regular, cyclic focus of Will on mental energy, astral force, and etheric substance has differentiated the substance of those planes into hosts of intelligent beings—beings of substance sometimes called angels or devas. Every form on these three planes is a deva, an intelligent being of mental energy, astral force, or etheric substance.

"The level of intelligence of these beings varies a great deal, all the way from that of the most basic particle of life up to that of the Light Body of the entire planet, the Great Mother Herself. However, they all share a similarity in their nature and function.

"As beings of substance, they cannot, of themselves, relate to their overshadowing purpose. That is the function of the Soul. Being born of the relationship between the two Poles, it is the nature of the Soul —of the Son— to relate the Purpose, Power, and Will of the Positive

Pole to the receptive intelligent Substance of the Negative Pole.

"Thus, the devas stand receptive to the will conveyed to them by the Soul of humanity. Unfortunately, for the last several thousand years:

"Mystics have identified the intellect, mental energy, and thus the devas of the mental plane, as obstacles to union with the Divine.

"Occultists have identified the emotions, astral force, and thus the devas of the astral plane, as obstacles to union with the Divine.

"The vast majority of those on the predominantly-patriarchal paths have identified the substantial forms of the physical-etheric, and their reflections in the physical-dense, as obstacles to the Divine.

"It being the nature of devas to receive whatever we relate to them, they have been impressed with the idea, thought, feeling, and action that they are obstacles to the Divine! Thus, they act accordingly.

"Ed?"

Ed: "So, we taught Substance that it's bad?"

Quinn: "Well, yes. One could say that God created us, and then *we* created Satan.

"In an odd way, it's fortunate for us that we've been so self-centered as a species as to be relatively unconcerned with those devas that are not directly related to ourselves. For instance, a common definition of 'angel' is 'an intermediary between God and man'. Typical Piscean, patriarchal hubris, but it saved our skins. Otherwise, the situation could be much worse than it is.

Me: "Whobress?"

Quinn: "H u b r i s. It's, well, when one's pride grows so big that you assume you can do anything."

Me: "Oh."

Quinn: "Now, as it stands, the devas that have been most affected by the delusion that 'substance is evil' are those with which we have the most intimate relationships, our own mental, astral, and physical-etheric bodies.

"Each of our bodies, and our persona as a whole, has been impressed with the delusion that it's 'evil' and that it is, therefore, the nature of form to resist the path of spiritual growth and development.

"Again, this is not correct. Substance is inherently Divine, but we programmed it with this delusion and must now deal with the results.

"Because of this, the moment we identify with and as the Soul, align with Divine Will —as the Daughter— and invoke that Will into form —as the Son— the form responds by resisting our efforts.

"While there would always be some *passive* resistance —for Newton's Third Law of motion[11] is equally effective on all three planes— the deluded substance *actively* and creatively resists the new focus of will. The result is, among other things, a collection of old mental, astral, and physical-etheric forms whose purpose is past, but which refuse to change.

"These old forms cling to life, retaining a spark of consciousness, a portion of the Soul, trapped within them, and thus preventing the would-be initiate from moving through the door of initiation. One cannot move on so long as these fragments of one's self are trapped in old states of awareness.

"Tess?"

Tess: "This is the crystallized substance that must be raised to Light?"

---

[11] Glen: An object, once set in motion, will tend to continue in that motion until acted upon by an external force.

Quinn: "Thereby freeing the consciousness trapped within it. Yes.

"These old forms are collectively called '*The Dweller on the Threshold*'. When viewed collectively, the Dweller of the entire human species is, in a sense, 'Satan', the great opponent of the Divine Purpose and Plan. From this perspective, Satan consists of the mental illusion, astral glamour, and etheric maya of humanity.

"Terry?"

Terry: "It's like the ultimate computer virus. It's taken over the net and wormed its way into every computer, and we're all so used to it that we think that's just the way things are."

Quinn: "Yes, but we created it, and are collectively responsible for accounting for it. Each of us is responsible for accounting for our portion of the whole, for our own Dweller.

"One's Dweller consists of all the distortion, the mental illusion, astral glamour, and etheric maya that remain as one prepares for full identification with and as the Spiritual Soul.

"Now, given the resistance of the Dweller, in order to achieve that identification, one must:

"Identify as the Spiritual Soul.

"Become one with The Path.

"Unite with the Dweller.

"As the Son, relate Divine Will with the Mother

"As the Daughter, relate the Dweller with the Father

"As the Path, raise the Dweller into the Light, liberating both the substance and the consciousness trapped therein.

"This magical activity of the Soul liberates both the

substance of the Dweller and the consciousness trapped within it, and enables the initiate to take up their work as a servant of the One Life.

Celine: "So it all comes back to the motion of consciousness."

Quinn: "Yes.

"Joshua passed through this process during the 'Temptation on the Mount', as did Gautama Buddha during his temptation beneath the Bodhi Tree. It's a part of the Path of Initiation, a part through which we must all pass, a part through which we can only pass by raising Substance into Light.

"Now this looks to be a long lesson, so I suggest we take a break, and look at the symbols when we get back."

(I turned off the recorder as people stood, stretched, and headed for coffee, tea, and the restroom.)

The Symbols

Quinn: "OK everyone... Sit up straight, relax your body and emotions, focus your mind, and move back into the ajna center. There integrate your three-fold persona into a single unit. (pause)

"Move back along a line of golden-white light into the cave in the center of the head. There become receptive to the Truth or Wisdom overshadowing this evening's lesson. (pause)

"Maintaining that alignment with the overshadowing Wisdom, take a deep breath, slowly open your eyes and turn your attention to the rest of the lesson. (pause)

(Quinn stood and faced the board.)

"All right, there are way too many symbols in this myth for us to begin to cover them all tonight, so we'll just touch on... Modeling initiation, the Last Supper—"

Bhikku: "The Shroud."

Quinn: "Oh, you heard about that? OK... The Triple Death..."

"Celine?"

Celine: "The gifts of the Wise Men."

Ema: "And forgiveness of sins."

Quinn: "OK, OK. Wow."

Divine Grace

"Well, while we're not here to argue doctrine, I will make a few, brief points regarding Forgiveness of Sins or Divine Grace.

"First, the very idea that our errors must be forgiven is an illusion, based on a patriarchal misperception of the Divine. Divine Love is completely unconditional, and there is nothing that we or anyone else can do to alter this fact. Thus, no matter what we say or do, 'God' loves us.

"If someone is unable to pass into 'heaven' after death, it is not because they have been found guilty of some crimes deserving of dire punishment, but because we continue to experience, after the death of the body, the same quality of consciousness we did in 'life'. Only now, we are experiencing that state on a more subtle plane whose substance is more responsive to our state of being. Thus, if our consciousness is trapped in an internal hell, it's because we create and inhabit that environment after death—and remain there for so long as our consciousness is identified with that condition.

"Divine Grace is not and never was unique to Christianity. It refers to the fact that we, as the Soul, cannot liberate ourselves. It's the Divine Mother who liberates us as She releases the sparks of our self trapped within Her. As we have seen, this fact has been portrayed in many different ways throughout the ancient mysteries.

"Ema?"

Ema: "Forgiveness of sins is hogwash?"

337

Quinn: "Um... No, not really. It's natural for us to feel guilty for our mistakes and to want divine forgiveness, and being assured that we are forgiven can bring great relief. However, once our heart center opens and we experience God's unconditional love, we realize that the only one condemning us is ourselves.

"Now, that experience of unconditional love is itself a part of the Path, one of five stages or 'Initiations' modeled by Joshua.

(Quinn nodded to me, and I began passing out the sheets on the Five Stages of Initiation.)[12]

"As indicated in the handout, the Soul begins or initiates a new motion of consciousness at each of these stages, and thereby gradually moves from individual self awareness to union with the One Life.

"Now, what's next? Ah.

The Gifts

"The gifts of the three 'wise men', Gold, Frankincense, and Myrrh, do not make sense unless we realize that in ancient times the 'wise' were Initiates of the Mysteries. The three gifts were symbolic, like much of the tale, and represented aspects of the mystery teachings.

"Gold is a symbol of the purified, incorruptible body—exemplified by the golden Solar Disc of Isis.

"Frankincense was used in embalming, and thus, in this context, is a symbol of death and rebirth, the second, initiatic 'birth in the heart' commonly called being 'born again' within the form

"Myrrh, in addition to being used in embalming, is a symbol of the relationship of the Son to the Mother. As we discussed earlier, Myrrha was the mother of

---

[12] Quinn: See the Addendum to Lesson 12.

Adonis, the Divine Son who was born into the world through her substance. Thus, giving a baby Myrrh symbolically recognized that baby as the returned Adonis or uplifted and enlightened Soul.

"Thus, the combined gifts of gold, frankincense, and myrrh symbolically represented the initiatic death and transformation of the body which leads to the rebirth of the Soul in the form. It is a re-affirmation of our central theme, the crucial importance of including substance in the process of spiritual growth and development.

The Last Supper

"The Last Supper is one of the most important episodes of the gospels, as it played a crucial role in the development of Christian ritual. Unfortunately, as with the rest of the myth, it is told from a patriarchal viewpoint that either relegates women to peripheral roles or ignores them entirely. This could not have been the case in any true... no... 'complete' initiatic rite, and, symbolically at least, it was not the case during the Last Supper.

"Unfortunately, we do not have time tonight for a thorough examination of that rite, and must limit ourselves to a few simple observations.

"The location in the upper room indicates that the events symbolically took place in the head—as does the crucifixion, which occurred on Golgotha, the place of the skull.

"Another point essential to us here is the bread consumed during the feast. This bread is mentioned in Matt. 26: 26, Mark 14: 22, Luke 22: 19, and 1 Cor. 11: 24.

"The versions in Matthew and Mark say:

"'Take, (eat); this is my body.'

"The versions in Luke and 1 Corinthians say:

"'This is my body which is (given) for you. Do this in remembrance of me.'

"In the ancient ritual of the Temple of Solomon, the Shew Bread was used inside the temple, as a sacrifice to the Great Goddess in the guise of Asherah. Now, of course, while the priests of Joshua's time still used Shew Bread, they sacrificed it to YHWH instead of to the Goddess.

"However, the common elements in the above versions of Joshua's words are 'This is my body.' As we have seen, the body is the Mother Aspect of Divinity. Thus, Joshua is here identifying his body with the bread which is offered up for sacrifice on the Passover feast.[13] Since this feast celebrates a symbolic event when the blood of first born lambs was sacrificed for the people of Israel, Joshua was saying, in very clear symbolic terms, that he was now the sacrificial lamb.

"This is emphasized again, in Matt. 26: 28 and Mark 14: 24, when Joshua took up a cup of wine and said, 'this is my blood of the new covenant, which is poured out for many...'

"Thus, we have the symbol of the Initiate as the sacrificial lamb, offering body and blood, or Substance — the Mother— and life —the Father— in order to show others the way.

The Shroud

"As for the Shroud, Joshua would have been laid in his tomb wrapped in a shroud or burial cloth. Sometime thereafter, The Mother came for him, and his body was transformed from gross substance into light, all in an instant. This momentary burst of pure light would have left a negative after-image on the shroud, like that on the Shroud of Turin.

---

[13] Exod. 12: 27 "you shall say, 'It is the sacrifice of the LORD's passover, for he *passed over* the houses of the people of Israel in Egypt, when he slew the Egyptians but spared our houses.'"

"However, by far the more significant effect would have been the freeing of any spark of consciousness left identified with and thus trapped within that form.

"Thus Christ, crucified on the Cross of Matter, was liberated when that body was raised from gross matter to Divine Light.

"This is the task which each of us must eventually accomplish, raising our own portion of Substance from dense materiality to pure energy, thereby freeing ourselves as we redeem and are redeemed by The Mother.

"Thea?"

Thea: "So, is the Shroud real?"

Quinn: "I really have no idea. Carbon dating indicates that it couldn't be, but some have suggested the sample was tainted by soot from the medieval fire that burned holes in it. However, I'd be more concerned with the effects of the blaze of light."

Terry: "What would that do?"

Quinn: "Ummm... Look, I'm hardly a scientist, but as I recall, carbon dating is based on the amount of what-do-they-call-it...

Terry: "Carbon-14."

Quinn: "Right. Which is accumulating in living organisms at a constant rate, but which stops at death, right?

Terry: "Yeah, basically."

Quinn: "So if the amount of carbon-14 in a living organism is constant, and it stops accumulating and begins degrading at a constant rate when the organism dies, then all they have to do is measure how much carbon-14 is left in a once living organism and they know how long it's been dead. It's just like measuring the sand that's run out of an hourglass. But in this case, the hourglass is, what, tens of thousands of years long.

"Well, one would expect the transforming burst of

light to be really high frequency stuff. Not visible light, that's fairly dense, but way, way above that. Now, what's the highest frequency of radiant energy we know of?"

Terry: "Cosmic rays."

Quinn: "OK. Now, what produces this carbon-14 stuff?"

Terry: "Well, when cosmic rays enter the...Oh!"

Quinn: "The what?"

Terry: "Atmosphere. They turn some of the nitrogen into nitrogen 14, which is breathed in and turned into carbon-14."

Quinn: "OK. So, what would happen if there were a huge, I mean a really, really, *huge* burst of cosmic rays when the body of Christ transformed?"

Terry: "Ah, I've no idea."

Quinn: "Right. We've no way of knowing. We can't replicate the situation. We don't know exactly what happened, we can only guess, and we can't observe it under controlled scientific conditions. It doesn't happen very often, and when it does, it's not going to be a public event. So, since we don't know what the exact conditions were that would produce a genuine 'Shroud', we can't date this one by carbon dating.

The Crucifixion

"Now the crucifixion, as described in the Christian Gospels, was a classic example of the sacrifice of an initiate. It was part of a sacred ritual called the 'Triple Death', which led to the raising of Substance and the liberation of the Soul. This ritual process was a typical part of the Ancient Mysteries, and the version described in the gospels would be recognised as such by any initiate of the Mysteries.

"Thea?"

Thea: "The crucifixion was a ritual?"

Quinn: "Remember, it's not history. Like all myths, the Gospels are a symbolic portrayal of Truth. The Gospels retell the story of initiation, a story that is lived again by everyone who walks the Path.

"Thus, the Gospels retell the story of the sacrifice of the Divine Son.

"For instance—

(Quinn again scooped up a Bible from his end table, and leafed through them to marked pages.)

Mark 15:

"19 And they struck his head with a reed, and spat upon him, and they knelt down in homage to him.

"This represents the first part of the Triple Death, a blow to the head.

"23 And they offered him wine mingled with myrrh; but he did not take it.

"His rejection of the myrrh represents a rejection of the rituals of the previous age —that of Aries— and the beginning of the new rites of the Piscean age. It also represents the turning away from the descent phase of initiation, represented by the birth from Myrrha, to the ascension phase—toward liberation and at-one-ment.

"Initiation is the result of the conclusion of one phase of spiritual growth and development and the beginning of another. In a sense, it represents the 'death' of an old state of being, and the birth of a new state of awareness. This process continues through a number of stages of death and rebirth —as outlined earlier— eventually taking one beyond the human stage of evolution and our planetary scheme or life.

"While the basic story of initiation remains the same, the details change from one age to another. Those details include the symbols used and the emphasis placed on the various parts of the initiatic process.

"For instance, in the age of Taurus the emphasis was on the transformation or uplifting of the body and consciousness. This is part of the reason why, for instance, the Judean worship of the golden calf was viewed with disfavor during the Exodus from Egypt. While the bull —the generative creator— was one of the symbols of YHWH, that symbol was no longer appropriate following the transition from the age of Taurus to the age of Aries.

"In the age of Aries —the goat— the emphasis was on the rite of sacrifice. The symbol of the initiate was the scapegoat, who is sacrificed for the sake of others. That's why, during that age, the mythos of the initiate emphasized the sacrificial death of the Son, the 'Lamb of God'.

Ascension

"However, in the 'new age' of Pisces—the fish—the emphasis was moving away from sacrifice toward ascension. Thus, the emphasis of Christianity was originally, and quite properly, placed on the *resurrection* of Joshua.

"Tess?"

Tess: "Ascension is Piscean?"

Quinn: "The emphasis of the ascension portion of the motion is Piscean, at least as we currently understand it. In the broader context, it would be more correct to say that ascension is the function of the inner pole of Consciousness. However, the vast majority of the teachings on ascension, the modeled examples, were formulated during the Piscean Age and carry the quality and character of Pisces."

Tess: "So, all the New Age teachings on Ascension are Piscean?"

Quinn: "Oh... No, no, we can't say 'all'. In any age there will be interpretations of the Path that emphasize each of the four motions, the downward, inward, upward, and outward, and even in this age it remains an essential part of the process. It's a matter of emphasis, the emphasis being determined by the primary motion of consciousness during that age.

"During Pisces, the emphasis was on the upward motion, or Ascent. At this point, while the Aquarian energy is predominant, the primary motion is the downward motion of Divine Intent. However, the existing forms are still primarily Piscean in character and quality. We're passing through a period of transition in which the Aquarian path of Synthesis is built on the foundation of what's gone before.

"Jeff?"

Jeff: "Do the different motions conflict or something?

Quinn: "Oh, yes, all the time. The old Piscean forms are having to change, and they don't want to and resist. This produces all kinds of outer conflict, and helping humanity move through this period of conflict is part of the task of the initiate. A task we begin as we work with that conflict within ourselves.

Manifestation

"Now all of this will be seen in expressions of the Path in the present 'new age' of Aquarius—the water bearer who pours out the Water of Life. Again, the emphasis is moving away from ascension toward the magical activity of consciousness which manifests Divine Intent in form, or toward Manifestation. The myth tales of this age will tell the story of initiation from this perspective, emphasizing the magical group activity that brings Divine Will into appearance.

"Now, where..."

Me: "Joshua's rejection of myrrh."

Quinn: "Ah... Let's see...

Crucifixion continued

"Mark 15: 24 And they crucified him, and divided his garments among them, casting lots for them, to decide what each should take.

"This represents the second part of the Triple Death —hanging. The method of 'hanging' varies quite a bit, from various types of suspension from—a tree or scaffold, to strangulation. The most common elements of the second death include:

"A tree or wooden scaffolding from which the initiate is suspended.

"A cord or rope with which the initiate is bound and/or strangled.

"In some variations, the second death was a second blow to the head, but this occurred when the initiation rites represented the unfoldment of centers or chakras in the head.

"John 19: 34 'But one of the soldiers pierced his side with a spear...'

"This represents the third part of the Triple Death. This part of the Triple Death was the most varied; the method used depending on the exact nature of the sacrifice and/or initiation. It could take the form of:

"A blow to the Crown or top of the head

"A third blow to the head, in either the center of the forehead or to the crown.

"Cutting the throat.

"Stabbing or cutting into the chest.

"Drowning.

"Poisoning.

"Evisceration.

"Castration.

(Quinn glanced at his notes)
"A classic example of the Triple Death, possibly contemporary to the Crucifixion, is the famous 'Lindow
Man', a body dating from 2 BCE to 150 CE, found in and
named after an English peat bog in 1984.

Colette: "BCE?"

Quinn: "'Before the Common Era', and 'Common Era'.

"Now, in the Lindow Man's case, the sacrifice had
been struck on the head with a blunt instrument, gar-
roted with a cord, and possibly drowned or poisoned—
the condition of the remains made the latter unclear.

"In the ritual sacrifice of Christ, the centers involved
in the Triple Death were the Head, Heart, and entire
etheric network —the hands and feet— especially the
network of the head via the crown of thorns.

"John?"

John: "So, the whole thing was symbolic?"

Quinn: "Yes, of course. That's what myths are."

Colette: "But the whole thing seems so..."

Me: "Uber-icky."

Colette: "Yeah."

Quinn: "Keep in mind that it isn't history. Again, I'm
not saying that none of the events portrayed in the gospels happened. It may be that some or all of them really
did. But, the gospels themselves are not historical
documents, and were not meant to be understood that
way. They are myth tales, conveying spiritual truth via
symbolism.

"Any questions?

"OK, let's look at the meaning of the myth."

The Meaning

Quinn: "The original meaning of the myth has been so twisted by patriarchal bias as to be barely discernable. The Divine Daughter was torn from the myth, thoroughly shrouding the Daughter–Son polarity. The Divine Mother was transformed from Light into Darkness, making union between the Two Poles almost inconceivable. As a result, the revolutionary teaching of Joshua that 'God is Love' was transformed in its expression into one of intolerance and hate.

"Of course, since all forms and experiences eventually serve the Divine Plan, this has not been without some benefit. Cut off from the Divine Daughter, the primary focus remained on the individual; in particular, on the love of God for, and forgiveness of, the individual who believed in and worshiped 'Him'.

"This idea that one has a personal relationship with God further strengthened the individual identity, both the love of the separate self —'God/Jesus loves you'— and the hate of our persona instrument—your body, emotions, and/or thoughts are evil.

"The result of this strengthened focus of the individual self is a much stronger ability of that individual self to focus. The average individual is now much more able to focus and wield the energies of will, love, and intelligence than ever before. While those energies may have been used for selfish purposes up to now, that does not detract from the increased ability to wield those energies. The goal of the path in this new age simply includes moving the focus from the individual to the group, thus transforming the relationship with and the expression of purpose, love, and intelligence from selfish to selfless.

"In this light, the patriarchal distortion of the path

in Pisces is not nearly so great a tragedy as it might otherwise appear. However, it must be corrected before humanity can move on. We must, each and all of us, re-alize with our whole heart that 'God' *is* Love before we can take our next step on the path.

The Polarity

"Now, as for the polarity of this myth...

"With the Daughter absent and the Mother reduced to a partially-raised human woman, the polarity of this myth is hopelessly imbalanced toward the masculine, with quite predictable results. Practitioners of this tra-dition have an extremely difficult time achieving right relationship with the substance of any plane.

"The basic polarity of this system can be outlined as follows:

"The Father takes the Daughter —Mary becomes pregnant.

"The Son comes forth from the Mother —Mary gives birth to Joshua

"The Son at-ones with the Father —'I and the Father are One.'

"The Son arises and goes unto the Father —Joshua Ascends to Heaven.

"In this polarity, there is no recognition whatsoever of the essential role of the Divine Feminine. The Son comes from and returns to the Father. The Feminine has no controlling role, and receives little of the benefit. In effect, the Masculine uses the Feminine for its own purposes—the social consequences of this are obvious.

"This is not how either the creative process or the Path work.

"While we may gain some solace from the thought that Mary received some reflected honor —as the mother of Joshua and the Bride of Christ— as we shall see, the treatment of the Divine Feminine was even worse in some of the subsequent mystery traditions. We shall explore this further —including the even more negative consequences— in the next chapter, the Myth of the Matronit.

"Any questions?"

Colette: "Where can we find more on Mariam?"

Quinn: "Oh, well, I'd suggest *'The Woman With The*... umm..."

Thea: *"With The Alabaster Jar*, by Margaret Starbird."[14]

Quinn: "Yes. Thank you. Anything else? OK. We'll close in the usual fashion."

---

[14] Quinn: *The Woman With The Alabaster Jar, Mary Magdalen and the Holy Grail*, by Margaret Starbird, Bear & Co., Rochester, VT, 1993

Ascension

Sit in a comfortable chair, relax your physical body, calm your emotions, and focus your mind.

Bring your consciousness to a point of focus within your ajna center, and there integrate your three-fold persona —body, emotions, and mind— into a single unit.

From your place within the ajna center, imagine that you are sailing up a great river. On the way, you are joined by others, each of whom helps with the journey and without whom you could not continue.

Clouds form and a storm breaks over you. Mighty winds whip the sail and dump rain, flood-waves break, lightning strikes, wild animals and horrid demons rise from the depths. Using the gifts of the Lady, you work together as a group to deal with each challenge in its turn, and continue on the upward way.

Recognizing that you have learned the lessons of life in form, as a group, audibly state the seed-thought:

"I will arise and go unto the Father."

Without thinking about it or repeating it, allow the vibration of that thought to sound. Continue listening to and feeling that vibration until all is still and quiet, then, audibly sound the OM.

Take a deep breath, open your eyes, and return your awareness to your surroundings.

"Practice this inner ritual at least once a day, every day, for a full lunar cycle (from New Moon to New Moon)."

Lesson 13

Trapped in Exile

The Myth of the Matronit

Tess, Thca, and Ema were discussing their Fourth of July plans —city fireworks displays, parades, family gatherings— when Quinn arrived. He was wearing one of his new "summer outfits", a stone-colored shirt with rolled-up sleeves, and kaki cargo shorts with a rope-belt. It somehow fit in with the indigo aura blazing around his head, and added an adventurous note to the colors washing through the room from the rest of the group.

I lifted the fan's remote and turned it off as he sat and sipped his ice water.

He asked, "Everyone ready? Terry? OK, let's begin."

Opening Alignment

"Bring your consciousness to a point of focus within the ajna center, and there integrate your three-fold persona into a single unit in aspiration to the Soul. (Pause)

"Draw a line of golden-white light from the ajna, upward to the blue-white crown center. Slowly move upward along that line of light, and into the crown center. There identify as the Spiritual Soul. (Pause)

"As the Soul in the crown center, turn your attention upward to that wisdom or truth overshadowing this evening's lesson, and become receptive to it by silently sounding the OM. (Pause)

"Maintaining that focus of receptivity, move back down the line of light into the ajna. (Pause)

"Maintaining that focus of receptivity in the ajna, draw a line of light from the ajna to the physical-dense brain, and audibly sound the OM.

"Take a deep breath, and open your eyes."

The Myth of the Matronit

Quinn: "While most modern Jews, Christians, and Moslems would like to believe that their faith is rooted in a monotheistic tradition, as we have already seen, this is not the case. In fact, while the Mother Aspect was more severely suppressed during the European 'Middle Ages' than ever before, the Great Mother continued to exert Her profound, albeit hidden, influence. This is readily apparent in the myth of medieval Jewish mysticism, the Kaballah.

"Yes, Wil?"

Wil: "What about medieval Romance?"

Quinn: "The Courts of Love, and the tales of King Arthur, his knights, and the quest for the Grail? Those are good examples, but I'm saving them for the course on Twin Souls.

"Now, regarding our present myth... Unfortunately, the underlying myth of the Kaballah is not common knowledge, even among students of that tradition. In fact, many students and practitioners of the Kaballah have studied it for years without ever becoming aware that there was such a myth.

"Celine?"

Celine: "I've read and heard bits and pieces over the years, but nothing coherent."

Quinn: "Thank you."

"This is not due to a lack of diligence on the part of modern students, but primarily to:

"The removal of the tradition from its cultural context.

"The fact that the complete myth tale is difficult to find.

"While the myth of the Matronit played a crucial role in the development of post-Diaspora Jewish mysticism, it makes little sense outside of that context. The myth focuses on the problem of how to be a practicing Jew without a Temple in Jerusalem —a problem that is of little interest to non-Jews. Thus, generally speaking, non-Jewish modern practitioners of the Kaballah usually ignore the myth."

Celine: "If we're even aware of it."

Quinn: Yes. Depending on their motivation, they tend to view the Kaballah as a system of personal empowerment, of spiritual growth and development, or both.

"However, given the effects of the myth on the Kaballah, and the influence of the Kaballah on Western occultism, I've asked Terry to provide us with a paraphrase of the myth.

"Terry?"

Terry: "Well... I've extracted my version of The Myth of the Matronit from a number of sources, and I've tried to make it easier to understand. I've tried to retain the original meaning —including the emphasis on the Father Aspect.[1] It's a bit different in, um, character, but I think I've captured the basic ideas."

The Myth

"In the beginning, God was All and filled All and naught existed apart from God. Then, He decided to create everything, and in an instant, withdrew himself

---

[1] Quinn: We could not find a complete version of this myth in any traditional source. The version Terry presented is a compilation, based on a variety of fragments. In addition to the other works on Judaism and the Kaballah cited in the bibliography, the most important source for Terry's version of the myth is: *The Hebrew Goddess*, by Raphael Patai, Third Enlarged Edition, Wayne State University Press, 1990, pp. 158 - 159

from the All, leaving space for everything that would be.

"Thus, God no longer filled All, and things could exist apart from God.

"In that space where God was not, He created the world, solely for man's sake. This He did for love of man, whom He loved above the All even before He created him.

"Thus, after the creation of the world, there was God and there was the World, two parts where there had been but One.

"Between and within these two were the ten emanations of God the King, ten aspects called the Sefirot, the ladder of descent into the world and ascent back to God.

"Then God created Adam and placed him in the world, and God gave Adam the gift of self-awareness, and Adam knew himself to be a man.

"Adam gazed about himself and contemplated the world and his place within it, and being in the world, he believed himself to be of the world, and thus Adam made a mistake that resounds through all creation to this day. Adam mistook the lowest emanation of God, the Shekinah or Female Aspect of God, for the All of God.

"Now since Adam was born of God, Adam —and through Adam all men— inherited some of God the King's power over the world. Thus, when Adam identified the Shekinah as God the King, Adam separated the Shekinah from God. No longer was there One God with ten emanations, but God the Father and Shekinah the Mother, both separate and alone. Ever since, man has repeated this mistake, increasing the painful separation of the Father from His Wife, the Shekinah.

"Finally, God created the People of Israel, with the Shekinah as both their mystical mother and the personification of the Nation of Israel. The People of Israel built the Temple of Jerusalem as a House for God the

King, including within it a bedchamber, the most sacred inner room. There, every midnight, God the King and His wife Asherah were reunited in rapturous union, and their connubial bliss nourished and enlivened Israel and the entire world.

"Since man had inherited some of the creative power of God, the union of God and Asherah is influenced by human behavior, especially that of the People of Israel. When Israel turns away from God, this tears God and Asherah apart, and when the people turn toward God, perform their duties to Him and obey His commandments, God and Asherah are brought together and united in love.

"Moreover, when the devout husband and wife obey God's commandment and unite in connubial bliss, the spiritual energy of their union pulls the Heavenly King and Queen together, prompts and compels the Divine Couple to do likewise, and thus momentarily restores Divine Unity.

"However, when Israel falls into error, the forces of error bind themselves to Asherah, preventing Her from uniting with God.

"When the Temple of Jerusalem was demolished and the Children of Israel were driven into exile, the Mother, who in a sense was the Nation of Israel, was taken into exile with Her people. Thus, in the worst disaster since creation, the Shekinah was riven from God the King.

"Bereft of His consort and His unity, God the King lost much of His energy, force, and might, and was left diminished, directionless and in great pain. Seeing that God was unable to remain alone because of His male nature, Lilith, the evil ruler of hosts of she-demons, took Asherah's place at His side and thus became ruler of the Holy Land which had once been Israel.

"This is how things stand to this day: God and Asherah sundered, the people of Israel and the Divine Matron exiled. Only the Messiah can end this tragedy, by reuniting the Divine Parents of Israel—God and Asherah."

✦

Quinn: "Well... Thank you very much Terry.

"Ema?"

Ema: "It's all about sex!"

Quinn: "Hold on. Let's not fix on that aspect of the story.

"It's really another version of the story of initiation, as told in the late Middle Ages from the perspective of the exiled people of Israel. There we have the One that becomes Three, the birth and fall of a Divine Child, the fall of the Divine Parents because of that Divine Child, the temporary union of the Divine Parents with the help of that Child, with a looked for permanent re-union brought about by the Adult Child.

"So, you see, it's not really 'about sex'. That's just part of the symbolism, the traditional symbolism used by all the ancient mysteries.

"Celine?"

Celine: "But, a lot of traditional Hebrew Kaballists practiced sexual rituals."

Quinn: "Yes, as part of the effort to temporarily re-unite YHWH with His Shekinah. It's all part of the initiation process, in this case, the Divine Marriage of Son and Daughter that brings about the re-union of the Mother and Father.

"However, in this story we have a very clear indication that humanity plays a role in the process. That role is distorted by the motion of consciousness in Pisces, but it's still there, and it will become clearer as we discuss the characters of the myth."

The Main Characters

Quinn: "Now, let's see...

(Quinn stands and faces the board.)

"The characters include... Adam, Eve, God or YHWH, Matronit, Shekinah, or Asherah..."

Wil: "Israel and Lilith."

Terry: "The Messiah."

Quinn: "Any more?"

"OK. Now, as we've discussed, Adam, the 'first man', symbolizes the Divine Son in incarnation.

"Eve, of course, the first woman, symbolizes the Divine Daughter in incarnation.

"And Asherah is the Divine Mother or Negative Pole of Divinity. In the original version of the myth, the Consort of God was Shekinah, the world, or the physical body of God. In essence, the Masculine Aspect is portrayed as giving birth to the Feminine Aspect, a very patriarchal perspective which, as we have seen, is contrary to how the creative process actually works.

"As usual 'God' is the Masculine or Positive Pole of Divinity.

"Now this tradition has worked itself into a classic logic loop. In this case, the two poles of divinity are riven asunder, and must be reunited by the Divine Son. However, since the Divine Son can only be born via the union of the Divine Parents, the Son cannot be born.

Me: "Logic loop?"[2]

Quinn: "Ummm... it's like when a D.J. loops a sample,

---

[2] Quinn: Any rational process that has no resolution because it always leads back to its beginning. A classic examples would be the question: 'Which came first, the chicken or the egg?" The answer given to El referred to playing a short piece of recorded music, of a few seconds or less, over and over again in a continuous loop. Because she is a musician, she understood it immediately.

but this is with logic instead of music."

Me: "Oh."

Quinn: "Now, in this case you have the split of God in two, and the problem of re-uniting those Two Aspects.

"Those Two Aspects can only be re-united by the Adult Son.

"However, the Adult Son can only be born of the re-united Two Aspects.

"So the Two Aspects have to be re-united.

"But that can only be brought about by the Adult Son..."

Me: "Oh."

Quinn: "Yes. The way out of this particular trap is to redefine the 'Divine Son' from an individual male, to the entire Kingdom of Humanity, both female and male—thus including both the Divine Daughter and the Divine Son. One then sees that the true Savior is humanity as a whole, grown from the immature form-identified child to the mature Daughter–Son, fully identified with both Divine Parents—and thus unifying them within our selves."

Celine: "So, humanity is the Messiah?"

Quinn: "In the process of becoming, yes. At that point, the entire Kingdom of Humanity is the Messiah.

"On the other hand, Israel is here a personification of the Divine Feminine, the Daughter who will be redeemed by the Son and help re-unite the Divine Parents."

Lilith

Wil: "And Lilith?"

Quinn: (Checking his notes) "There are numerous versions of the story of Lilith, dating from at least the 8th century BCE to the 17th Century. However, in the versions of the creation myth pertinent to our current myth, she was the first woman, created by God before Eve. In the pertinent medieval and renaissance stories, she is variously portrayed as being created before, at the same time, or after Adam. These stories also include various reasons for her being evil, such as:

"Forming her body from filth and impure sediments, rather than clean earth —as with Adam.

"Her soul was lodged in and called forth from the depths of the Great Abyss, whereas Adam's was breathed forth by God.

"She was a spontaneous creation of the world, and not of God.

"However she was created, Lilith refused to obey Adam and lay with him, or did so but proved to be a poor helpmeet, and/or eventually returned as an evil seductress.

"The various versions of her story commonly indicate that Lilith ran off into the desert, where she consorted with demons, bore demon children, and became their queen.

"Now, this is an obvious demonization of the Feminine Aspect, indicating that good wives obey their husbands while bad wives do not, and suggesting —in some versions— that without the guidance and control of men women fall into great evil.

"Now all the versions I've found clearly indicate that Eve was created as the 'helpmeet' of Adam, and thus women of men.

"However, as we've seen, 'helpmeet' is, in Genesis at least, a mistranslation of 'instructor'. Since the Mother is and must be equal to the Father, any representation of the Feminine as subservient or evil is a distortion, and at the present point in our development it hampers the process of spiritual growth and prevents humanity from restoring Divine Union. A more balanced perspective would be to view Lilith as representing the destructive attribute of substance, part of the trinity of the Divine Mother."

Bhikku: "Like Kali?"

Quinn: "And Ereshkigal or Persephone, the queen of the underworld who reins over death. Yes.

The Matronit

"The Matronit is the 'Matron' or Mother Aspect of Divinity —Asherah and Shekinah in another guise.

"However, where in the ancient Judean vision the Goddess was openly acknowledged as a separate character, the consort of YHWH, students of the Kaballa traditionally maintained that she is only an abstraction, and not an actual separate being. This, despite the fact that the Zohar, the primary work on the Kaballa, portrays the Matronit as a distinct individual.

"Terry?"

Terry: "How can they do that?"

Quinn: "Why don't they take the Zohar literally?"

Terry: "Yes."

Quinn: "Well, remember, faith is a product of the higher polarity of the Solar Plexus center. That polarity can see someone seeing the Divine, but cannot experience it directly for itself. And the belief that scriptures are absolutely literally true is a product of a nascent throat center that is dominated by the solar plexus. The throat center/concrete rational mind is then only beginning to develop, has a very difficult time with abstract concepts like symbolic stories, and is motivated by the solar plexus to take things literally."

Me: "Nascent?"

Quinn: "Oh... just coming into incarnation. Still

developing."

Terry: "So they were so fixed on belief in a One God, that they couldn't accept the concept of that One being two or three?"

Quinn: "Yes. It's a very common condition, even today."

"Now who's next... Ah.

The Messiah

"The Messiah is the Divine Son who will be born of Israel —the Divine Daughter— redeem Israel, return to the Father with Israel and as the Daughter–Son reunite the Divine Parents.

"It's interesting to note that in this tradition, the Divine Son has not yet been born, and thus, the Daughter is still awaiting redemption while the parents await reunion. This is the same basic story of relationship between the four that we have seen again and again.

"The Daughter —Israel— goes to the Father.

"The Father impregnates the Daughter.

"The Daughter gives birth to the Son —the Messiah, the People of Israel.

"The Mother takes the Son to the Underworld —the people go into exile.

"The Son grows to maturity, at-one-ing with the Daughter.

"The Adult Child re-unites the Mother and Father.

"As presented in the Zohar and similar Kaballistic works, the tradition is incapable of bringing about either the union of the Soul —via the at-one-ment of the Daughter and Son— or the union of Spirit and Substance —via the at-one-ment of the Father and Mother.

It cannot do so for the simple reason that it is incredibly polarized towards the Masculine and against the Feminine.

"Celine?"

Celine: "Are you saying the Kaballa is a dead end?

Quinn: "No, no, not at all. Please keep in mind that we're discussing the medieval Piscean myth, not the modern Aquarian practice. The two are quite different, and the modern version is often quite balanced.

"The Kaballistic tradition is and has always been a valid and valuable spiritual path. It's one of those paths which, by emphasizing the Masculine or Will Aspect of Divinity at an individual personal level, helped develop the individual will and personal identity. This individual 'will to be' and personal 'I am' are necessary foundations to later growth. They are necessary because the ability to focus the individual identity and will narrowly or specifically is a vital part of the creative process. One cannot create anything new without it.

"Imagine, for instance, if a whale needed to thread a needle. She cannot, for she has neither the eyes with which to see nor the hands with which to manipulate anything that small.

"This principal holds true for the entire creative process. In order to create the details of everything, at any level of expression, the One Life has to project a portion of itself into that level of being. This is equally true of galaxies, solar systems, planets, kingdoms, and individual human beings. In order to create at that level of being, the consciousness of that level of being has to become aware of its self, or self-aware. It has to develop an 'I'dentity.

"Bhikku?"

Bhikku: "The 'vow of the Bodhisattva!'"

Quinn: "Yes. To remain behind, forsaking the final

release, until every particle of substance has achieved enlightenment. And in order to do that, every particle must pass through individuality and at-one-ment. But not necessarily as a human being, but as part of a kingdom which achieves enlightenment.

"Now, this 'I'dentity then enables the Soul to relate the intent or will of a potential thing, with the potential substance of that thing, which then responds by forming itself into the form of that thing."

Terry: "So everything that exists, in order to exist, has to have its 'I'dentity, its focus of self?"

Quinn: "Yes. The self, soul, or magnetic field that relates the purpose of that thing with its substance, and its substance with its purpose. And as that spark of self grows and develops, it achieves what we've called species awareness, then individuality, then group awareness, and finally at-one-ment.

"Now, in this myth the Shekinah is the world. That aspect of God which can be perceived by the senses.

Cherubim

"In the Temple of Jerusalem, the union of God and Asherah took place in the Holy of Holies, the sacred inner room containing the Ark of the Covenant. The Ark was a gilded chest of acacia wood, whose lid —called the Mercy Seat— was decorated with sculptures of two spirits called cherubim."

John: "Like in 'Raiders'?"

Quinn: "Well, mostly. They got a lot right, but the cherubim were a bit, well…"

Me: "Cuddlesome."

Quinn: "Uh, yeah. Real cherubim were fierce guardian spirits, and there was nothing cute or cuddly about them. They did not look like baby-angels—as they're commonly portrayed today, or like beautiful women as in 'Raiders'. In ancient Assyria, Chaldea, Babylon, and Canaan, cherubim were winged guardian spirits with human heads and animal bodies —sometimes having lion forequarters and bull hindquarters. Statues of these imposing spirits were often set in the entrances to temples and palaces.

"Now in addition, the pair of cherubim atop the real Ark were sexual beings, one male and the other female, and the two were engaged in eternal sexual embrace."

Ema: "What? In the Temple?"

Quinn: "Yes, in the holiest inner room, atop the holiest object in the Temple. It was symbolic of the union between the Female and Male Aspects of Divinity — YHWH and Asherah— that was believed to occur in that very room, the 'Holy of Holies', above the lid of the Ark and between the outstretched wings of the united cherubim. That's what brought it about!

"At the moment of union or at-one-ment between YHWH and Asherah, the *Shekinah* or cloud of the presence appeared above the lid of the Ark, between the outstretched wings of the two cherubim. The united YHWH/Asherah was present in the cloud, and spoke from it with the High Priest of Israel —the only person who was allowed into the Holy of Holies.

"Some say that this Divine Marriage occurred every night at midnight, others that it occurred only on Full Moons, and some that it occurred but once a year, at Yom Kippur, when the High Priest entered the Holy of Holies.[3] As we will see, each of these viewpoints is partly correct, as the Divine Re-union is actually accomplished via a cycle of daily, lunar, and annual rituals.

"However, since, with the destruction of the Temple

---

[3] The "Day of Atonement," a day set aside to atone for the sins of the past year. See: Leviticus 23: 26-28

and the loss of the Ark, this re-union of YHWH and Asherah could not occur, the Hebrew mystics and occultists looked for some other way to bring it about. This led to the development of the Kaballa.

YHWH

"Now the name of 'God' used here, YHWH, does not have the same meaning that it did at the beginning of Pisces. It's now 'The Tetragrammaton', a Divine Tetrad of Father, Mother, Son, and Daughter. This may be confusing given our earlier definition of YHWH, and thus requires some clarification.

"As we discovered in lesson six, seven, and eight, the ancient Hebrews consisted of two nations, the northern Israel and the southern Judea, some of whose gods were gradually 'conflated' or combined into a single deity. The Northern Elohim were both female and male, while the Southern YHWH was male —with a female consort— but both Elohim and YHWH are mistranslated as 'God' in the Old Testament.

"However, the definition of YHWH was changed in medieval Kaballistic terminology. In this late-medieval mystical system, YHWH is an acronym in which each letter represents one of four divine elements that make up the divinity. YHWH was still considered One indivisible God, yet that One was also a four. The four divine elements were:

(Quinn glanced at his notes, stood, and wrote on the board...)

"Y: *Hokhma* (Wisdom), the Father.

"H: *Binah* (Understanding), the Mother.

"W: *Tif'eret* (Beauty), the Son.

"H: *Malkhut* (Kingship), the Daughter.

(Then the turned and faced the class.)

"At first, the recognition of the four may appear to be an advancement beyond patriarchal monotheism. However, one must keep in mind that this tetrad is an expansion of the formerly exclusively-male YHWH to include the other Aspects of Divinity. Thus, rather than tearing away the veils that had hidden the Divine Mother and Daughter, this merely added another layer of patriarchal shroud."

Wil: "Like Apollo's takeover of Delphi."

Quinn: "Yes. The python or serpent is an ancient symbol of the Goddess.

"Thus here, even more than before, we have the concept of 'one God', YHWH, obscuring the Four Aspects of Divinity.

"The result was intellectual and emotional confusion among the *medieval* followers and practitioners of Kaballa. They knew with their feeling nature that the Four were unique, diverse beings, yet argued with their intellect that the Four were merely theoretical aspects of the One, indivisible YHWH. This, despite the fact that their central text, the Zohar, clearly indicated that that One had been sundered into Two, and their central, vital task was to re-unite those Two!

"Thus split within themselves, they were incapable of achieving that inner union of the individual persona which is the first step toward re-uniting the Divine Feminine and Masculine!"

Ed: "What about modern Kaballa?"

Quinn: "Oh, that's a whole new subject, quite outside our current discussion. But, please keep in mind that none of the limitations or distortions we've assigned to the medieval Piscean myth necessarily applies to the modern Aquarian practice of the Kaballa. The context is quite different, as is the perspective of the practitioner.

I've had conversations with modern practitioners who tell me that the Tetrad concept, as I've explained it to you, sounds Kaballistic to them. So, again, we really can't generalize and say that the ancient views or interpretations are shared by the modern practitioners of any of the myths or rites we've discussed."

The Symbols

"Now, as for the symbols of the myth, we have...

(Quinn stood, faced the board again, and wrote quickly using a red marker)

"...the Divine Marriage, the Ten Emanations of God, and the Temple in Jerusalem.

The Divine Marriage

"The Divine Marriage is, of course, the Union of God and Asherah. While we've already discussed the subject of the Hieros Gamos or sacred marriage rite, the Myth of the Matronit brings out an aspect of that ritual which is crucial to the path of initiation.

"Humanity, and only humanity, can re-unite the sundered Poles of Divinity.

"This is, in fact, our purpose and function as a Kingdom in the Planetary Life. Unfortunately, a detailed examination of this subject will have to wait for a course on the magic of consciousness. However, I have prepared a handout that goes over the basics.[4]

(I scooped up the copies and handed them out.)

Sefirot

"Now, many volumes have been devoted to the 'Ten Emanations of God,' the Sefirot or Tree of Life. For our purposes, the top three represent the Three Aspects of

---

[4] Quinn: See Addendum to Lesson 13

Divinity, and the lower seven represent the major chakras or centers.

"In effect, the One became Three, and the Three were reflected in the lower seven. The Divine Son descends and the Daughter ascends via the pathways between them. The lowest or tenth sefirot is Malkut, the Divine Daughter, the lowest plane of existence.

"Colette?"

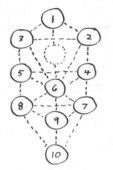

The Tree of Life

Colette: "Where can we learn more about the modern practice of the Kaballa?"

Quinn: "I'm sure Celine would be happy to discuss it with you, and I have a number of works on it over there in the 'occult' section.

The Temple

"Now, we'll look at the Temple in Jerusalem in more depth in the next lesson. However, basically, as in Mesopotamia with their pantheon, it was the House in which God dwelled. It was, in effect, a structure or body through which the People of Israel served and contacted God. It had three 'rooms', including a porch or entrance, a middle chamber, and an inner chamber or 'Holy of Holies.' These rooms symbolized, respectively, the physical-etheric, the astral-emotional, and the mental bodies. The Ark represented the Cave Center, the place of magic where the incarnate soul and the Overshadowing Spiritual Soul become one.

Thus, the Temple represented the human persona, as a symbolical 'house' where God and Goddess united."

The Polarity

Quinn: "Now, if we use our original template to convert all this symbolism into polarity and movement, we get the following:

"The All divides Itself and becomes Two, God and the World. This is the movement of the One into the Polarity of Two.

"Between God and the World are ten Emanations of God: This is the Magnetic Field, but —as an 'emanation of God'— limited to that portion which moves from the Positive Pole to the Negative.

"God created Adam: The Magnetic Field relates the Positive Pole to the Negative, and the Divine Son is born.

"Adam mistakes the World for God: The Magnetic Field is trapped in form.

"God creates Israel: The Magnetic Field is differentiated into many forms.

"Israel creates the Temple of God: The differentiated Magnetic Field tries to re-unite the two poles within a special house and chest.

"The Temple is Destroyed and the People Exiled: The house is thrown down, the chest lost, and the people are left with no means of re-uniting the Two Poles.

"This myth has several crucial gaps, chief among which are the failure to recognize the equality of the Two Poles, and the absence of the Divine Daughter from the Temple. Without Her, there is no possibility of re-union and the house itself cannot stand, for She is an essential part of the Magnetic Field which holds it together."

Summary

Quinn: "Thus, we have the movement from:

"One to Two.

"Positive pole to outer Magnetic Field.

"Outer Magnetic Field to Negative Pole.

"The fall into the Polarity of the Negative Pole or Substance.

"The Destruction of the vehicle of Re-union.

"But for the distortions, the basic tale is the same.

"Now, having seen another example of the effects of patriarchal distortions in Pisces, and the advancement achieved because of those distortions, it's time to proceed to our next allegory, the myth of Solomon and Hiram.

"But first, we'll close as usual."

At-one-ment

From your place within the ajna center, imagine that your group has sailed all the way up the river to its source, a stream flowing between an arch formed by two trees.

The tree on the right has silver bark, leaves, and fruit, and glows with the light of the Moon. A huge silver serpent is crawling up the tree, with its head near the top while its tail is in Earth.

The tree on the left has golden bark, and leaves, red fruit, and glows with the fiery light of the Sun. A huge golden serpent is crawling down the tree, with its head near the bottom while its tail is in Heaven.

Beyond the trees is the dimly-glimpsed realm of Heaven, where you must go to fulfill your purpose, place, and function in the One Life. However, the way between the trees is blocked by their inter-woven branches, and you cannot pass.

Recognizing that only the stream may pass the way, the entire group steps out of the sailboat into the stream. Join hands, left palm up and right down, sit in the stream, and, as a group, aspire upward. When your group aspiration has reached its height, audibly state the seed-thought:

"I and the Father are One."

Without thinking about it or repeating it, allow the vibration of that thought to sound. Continue listening to and feeling that vibration until all is still and quiet, then, audibly sound the OM.

Take a deep breath, open your eyes, and return your

awareness to your surroundings.

"Practice this inner ritual at least once a day, every day, for a full lunar cycle (from New Moon to New Moon)."

Raising the Queen of Heaven

Lesson 14

Transforming the Cage into a Temple

The Myth of Hiram Abiff

Tess was showing Colette a picture book on stuffed animals when Quinn entered.

She slipped it back into its place as Quinn sat in his chair, and carefully picking up his condensation-slick glass of iced tea.

Quinn gazed at the two empty seats, and said, "Ema and Thea have been delayed by Fourth of July family gatherings. They may be here later, but probably not.

"Now, we're outside the city limits here, and the county regulations permit private fireworks, so we'll have to put up with a bit of smoke and noise."

He turned to me, and asked, "Guido's ready?"

I nodded and replied, "I told him, and he'll keep quiet."

Quinn nodded, nibbled his lip, and said, "It starts around dusk. You'd better reassure him again then.

"Now, let's get started."

I pointed the remote at the fans, turned both of them off, and then pushed the "on" button on the recorder.

Opening Alignment

Quinn: "Bring your consciousness to a point of focus within the ajna center, and there integrate your three-fold persona into a single unit in aspiration to the Soul. (Pause)

"Draw a line of golden-white light from the ajna, upward to the blue-white crown center. Slowly move upward along that line of light, into the crown center, and identify as the Spiritual Soul. (Pause)

"As the Soul in the crown center, turn your attention upward to that wisdom or truth overshadowing this evening's lesson, and become receptive to it by silently sounding the OM. (Pause)

"Maintaining that focus of receptivity, move back down the line of light into the ajna. (Pause)

"Maintaining that focus of receptivity in the ajna, draw a line of light from the ajna to the physical-dense brain, and audibly sound the OM.

"Take a deep breath, and open your eyes."

The Legend of the Temple

Quinn: "Now, as Pisces moved toward Aquarius, intolerance in the West began to ease and it became possible to partially restore the Ancient Mysteries, producing a new interpretation of the One Path. The resulting new ritual system —with its rites and symbols— was, as always, appropriate to the humanity of that time and place.

"Yes, Terry?"

Terry: "When was this?"

Quinn: "Oh... late 17th, early 18th century.

"This partial restoration of the Mysteries produced the brotherhood commonly known as Freemasonry.

"Now, it was only a partial restoration because of the condition of the consciousness of humanity at that time —still trapped within patriarchy and constricted by the motion of Pisces.

"For instance, unlike in all the ancient systems, the persisting intolerance toward alternative spiritual systems did not allow general distribution of the Myth of Freemasonry. So, instead of the myth becoming public, as had traditionally been the case, it was kept hidden.

"Thus —during its early years, at least— the senior members of the Freemasonic brotherhood, within the limitations of their times, worked to establish a society in which the Mysteries could be completely restored, and toward a society in which the principles of tolerance and democracy —as practiced in the Masonic Temples or 'Lodges'— were fully realized.

"These efforts to establish a new society based on democratic principles and free of religious intolerance were centered in North America."

Wil: "Why?"

Quinn: "Why here?"

Wil: "Yes."

Quinn: "Well... that would take a whole course in it-self, and it's not really my area. But if you're interested, I've a number of works that touch on it —*The Secret Destiny of America*, *New Atlantis*, and stuff on the origins of Freemasonry, Francis Bacon, Queen Elizabeth, the East India Company, and the colonization of America.[1] There's lots of shadow-history stuff. But what it basically comes down to is, because this was the ground where it could be done.

"Now, the conflict between the ideals of brotherhood, and the political and economic conditions of the times, gave birth to the United States. However...

"Ed?"

Ed: "Economic?"

Quinn: "Look into the history of the East India Company, in particular its involvement in the colonization of North America, and its management of the colonies as profit centers. Then consider Jefferson's efforts to include an amendment against 'monopolies' in the Bill of Rights. We may touch on this in *The Magic of Consciousness*, when we go into what happens when you bring the creative motion down too far, and identify with the form.

"Let's see... Now, once this goal of establishing a new form of government was accomplished, the focus of the brotherhood moved toward nurturing the development of that society, through the practice of brotherhood, tolerance, and charity. Thus, the attention moved away from the Ancient Mysteries at the heart of the or-

---

[1] Quinn: Actually, it's *"America's Assignment With Destiny"*, by Manly P. Hall, and *"The New Atlantis"*, by Francis Bacon.

der, and the meaning of their myth, rituals, and symbols was slowly forgotten.

"Thea?"

Thea: "What about slavery?"

Quinn: "Oh geez... That would take a whole work on economy, or right relationship with humanity, or both. Ummm... Look, suppose you have a leaky roof. When it rains, you put a bucket under it to catch the water, and empty the bucket when the rain stops. Now, what's going to happen the next time it rains?"

Thea: "The leak comes back."

Quinn: "Right.

"Now, the founders freed themselves from political and economic tyranny, but they were still part of the society that had produced that tyranny. The inner cause, the thoughts and feelings about relationships, about finance and government, was still within them. So it merely sought other forms of expression through them, not necessarily them personally, but through America. And those misrelationships, those thoughts and feelings, produced the outer activity of slavery, especially in the south, and indentured immigrant workers, especially in the north."

Thea: "So, we became what we fought against?"

Ed: "Until the Civil War."

Quinn: "Oh... I wouldn't say that. Ask any veteran of the Civil Rights movement. Also, I suggest you look at what the railroads did with the 14th Amendment after the Civil War, and at the current consequences to our individual rights, liberties, economy, and well, pretty much everything.

"Basically, we haven't finished dealing with these misrelationships, not by any means. We've improved things a great deal, but there's still an immense amount of work to do, the core of which is in the identification as, and the controlled motion of, the consciousness.

"But, let's move on.

"Now normally, of course, the whole point of a myth is to give the people of a society a symbolic story that prepares them for initiation into the mysteries. However, the intolerance the Order faced in its early years appears to have prevented a complete version of the Myth from ever being published as a myth. Instead, the 'Legend of the Temple' is normally portrayed, in Freemasonic Lodges, in the initiation ritual that raises a Fellow Craft or second degree Freemason to Master Mason or third degree."

Wil: "But you're forbidden to talk about that!"

Quinn: "As in any of the ancient mystery traditions, the oaths of a Freemason prevent us from discussing the secrets or mysteries of the order with any non-freemasons, yes. However, the myth itself is not included among those secrets, not even by implication.

"Terry?"

Terry: "If the complete myth has never been published, where did you find it?"

Quinn: "Well, I hope I qualified that with 'appears.'"

Me: "Yes."

Quinn: "Actually, we didn't find one. There don't seem to be any, not any complete ones. The senior Masons I consulted were not aware of any either, so we did what really, traditionally —as a part of the outward movement of the mysteries— would normally have been done a couple hundred years ago, and may well have been. We translated the initiation ritual into a myth story.

"John?"

John: "But isn't that... It seems sneaky."

Quinn: "Not really. Remember, the mystery tale is *supposed* to be public. Its primary function is, as a part of the Path, to help prepare the general public for the initiation rites. And much of the myth *is* public. It's just that you can't find the whole thing. And without exposure to the myth as part of the culture, you don't have the depth of preparation that candidates had in ancient times, and the rituals can wind up appearing, well, weird or bizarre, because the members of that culture have not been prepared for them. That's because the story of the mysteries, or the version of it that is part of our culture, is not as impressed on our psyches. We haven't been prepared for the mysteries, so they don't seem 'normal' to us.

"So, in order to help correct this, Celine has, with my help, transformed the 'secret' ritual of Freemasonry into a dramatic short story, re-creating the Myth that would —but for intolerance— have long been available to the public.

"John?"

John: "And this is the first time you've done this?"

Quinn: "Yes, but it looks like we may be doing it again in a few weeks. Celine and I have been invited to do a course on this subject for a group of freemasons and interested esotericists.

Terry: "Can we take that class also?"

Quinn: "Well, it wouldn't really be a good idea. Like this one, *The Temple and The Word* course will mostly be a subjective process. Just like here, the inner experience, the meditations, are really the most important part. In that sense, each course is a complete cycle of inner experience and realization, and you should only do one at a time. Trying to do both at once would, well, be like trying to talk and whistle at the same time.

"But don't worry. We'll tape and transcribe that one also, and the transcripts of both will be available.

"Any more questions?

"Celine?"

The Legend[2]

Celine: "Sacred silence hung over Mount Moriah. There was no sound of axe, hammer or any tool of iron, either in the courtyard or inside the Temple itself. Workmen swarmed about, setting the stones that had been hewn, squared and numbered in the quarries, and placing the beams that had been prepared in Lebanon.

"When the sun reached its zenith, the supervisors called a halt to the work, and dismissed the men. Dusting themselves off, the workers poured over the courtyard and out the gates, seeking their refreshment outside the sacred precincts. Reaching the gates last, the supervisors looked about, and when satisfied that all the workmen had left, pushed the gates closed with a thud that echoed through the Temple courtyard.

"Up in the inner sanctum of the Temple, a robed figure stood before the Ark of the Covenant, with his left hand under one cherubim and his right hand over the other. After a time, he backed away, bowed low (with the jewel of his office hanging from his neck), and shuffled backwards, between the huge cherubim guarding the arched entryway and out of the Holy of Holies.

"Stopping immediately inside the middle chamber, he straightened, turned, and gazed around the nearly completed temple, pausing to stare at incomplete portions. Stepping to a stand holding the trestle board[3], he concentrated on its surface, and then erased the old in-

---

[2] Quinn: Our version of the Legend is largely based on that found in *Duncan's Ritual of Freemasonry*, by Malcolm C. Duncan, David McKay Company, Inc., New York. A nearly identical version of the Legend, with much more extensive commentary, may be found in the text from the later course, *"The Temple and The Word"*.

[3] The "trestle board or "tracing board" was a kind of portable "chalkboard".

structions and laid out the rest of the days work.[4]

"When done, he carried the trestle board out of the temple, past the spiral stair to the upper rooms, and under the arch supported by the two bronze columns on the porch. There, he paused to set the trestle board at the base of the pillar of the moon (where all the builders could see it) and then walked down the stairs.[5] In the courtyard, he passed between the huge bowl of the Brazen Sea and the great bronze sacrificial altar, and headed toward the *south gate*. The period of refreshment was over, and it was time to re-admit the workmen.

"Deep in thought, he was almost there before he noticed a dark figure in the shadows of the gate, clasping some sort of rod. Startled, he wondered who he was and why he was there.

"*'Perhaps it is a messenger from the King?'* he thought. His pace faltered as he neared, and then he recognized Jubela, one of the workmen.

"Jubela's brow and nose crinkled as he strode up to Hiram, kicking up dust with his sandals. He grabbed Hiram by the collar of his robe and snarled, 'I've been waiting for a chance to get you alone! You promised to give us the secrets of a Master Mason when the Temple was complete! We'll, it's almost done, and we've waited long enough! I want to travel and receive a Master's wages!'

"Jubela twisted Hiram's robe and roared, *'Give me*

---

[4] Quinn: Some versions of the Legend indicate that the work was nearly complete, with the events starting on "the very day appointed for celebrating the cap stone of the building." However, this appears to conflict with the indication that the Fellow Crafts, lacking further instructions on the Tracing Board, remained at refreshment.

[5] Quinn: The two columns are free standing in most versions. However, in some they supported an arch.

the secrets of a Master Mason!'

"Astounded, Grand Master Hiram replied, 'Brother, this is neither the proper time nor place. Be true to your oaths, and I will be true to mine. Wait until the Temple is completed, and then, if you are found worthy and well qualified, you will receive the secrets of a Master Mason; but until then, you cannot.'

"Jubela shook Hiram, raised his measuring rod like a club, and said, 'Don't talk to me of time or place! *Give me the secrets* of a Master Mason, or I'll kill you!'

"Hiram replied, '*I can't*! Both Kings Solomon and Hiram must be there!'

"Jubela shouted, 'No more delays!' grabbed even more of Hiram's robe, and screamed, '*Give me the Master's word*!'

"Hiram calmly replied, '*I shall not*!'

"Jubela raised his measuring rod, and brought it whistling down on Hiram's throat.[6] The tip tore into flesh, and splashed Hiram's robe with crimson.

"Jubela released Hiram, and the wounded Grand Master fled toward the west gate of the Temple compound.

"At the west gate a second journeyman named Jubelo, wielding a metal mason's square, confronted the wounded Grand Master.

"Jubelo grabbed Hiram even more roughly than had Jubela, and raising his square demanded, '*Give me the secrets* of a Master Mason!'

"Grand Master Hiram replied, '*I cannot*.'

"Jubelo shook the Master and shouted, '*Give me the secrets* of a Master Mason!'

"Hiram calmly replied, '*I shall not*.'

---

[6] Quinn: Other versions of the Legend have the three blows delivered to Hiram's head.

"Jubelo shouted, '*Give me the Master's word*, or I'll kill you!' and shook him violently.

"Master Hiram replied, '*I will not!*'

"Jubelo struck Master Hiram on the *left breast*. His mason's square tore through the robe, into the Master's flesh, dashing scarlet to the courtyard.

"Jubelo thrust him away, and the bleeding Grand Master staggered toward the east gate of the Temple.

"At the east gate a third journeyman named *Jubelum*, with a heavy gavel thrust into the sash of his robe, confronted the wounded Grand Master.

"Jubelum seized Master Hiram with both hands by the collar of his robe, and swung him round, placing the Master's back toward the east. Then Jubelum screamed, 'Give me the secrets of a Master Mason!'

"The dazed Master replied, 'I cannot!'

"'Give me the secrets of a Master Mason, or I'll kill you!'

"'I shall not!'

"Jubelum seized the Master even more fiercely, and slowly ground out, 'You have escaped the others, but you cannot escape me! I do what I say! Give me the Master's word, or I will kill you!'

"'I will not!'

"Jubelum screamed, 'Then die!' grabbed his gavel, and smote Master Hiram on the forehead. The Grand Master collapsed to the stones, twitched briefly, and lay motionless.

"The three ruffians gathered around the body, and one asked, 'Is he dead?'

"'His skull is smashed in.'

"'My God! What have we done?'

"'Murdered our Grand Master, without obtaining the word. The question is, what shall we do with the body?'

"'Bury it in the rubbish of the Temple, until low

twelve, and then we will meet and give it a proper burial.'

"'Agreed!'

"They rolled the body in canvas, buried it in the rubbish heap, and departed.

"Long hours later, at the hour of midnight, as the last notes of the hour of twelve died away, each of the three ruffians crept through the shadows toward the body. They met, identified each other, and Jubelum said, 'I suggest we carry the body to the west, to the brow of the hill there, where I've dug a grave.'

"The others agreed, and they took up the body, still rolled in canvas, raised it to their shoulders, and carried it away. After they lowered the body and filled in the grave, they planted an acacia above it, as was the custom. When they were done one of them exclaimed, 'Now, let's get out of here!'[7]

"The three headed for the nearest port, intending to sail beyond King Solomon's reach, but discovered that they could not take ship without a pass. Turned away, they returned to a hiding place near the body. There, they discussed their plight.

"First Ruffian, 'What shall we do?'

"Second Ruffian, 'Go to some other port?'

"Third Ruffian, 'But the rules are as strict in other ports as in this.'

"First Ruffian, 'What will become of us?'

"Second Ruffian, 'We shall be taken and put to death.'

"Third Ruffian, 'Let's hide until night, steal a boat and put to sea.'

---

[7] Quinn: Some versions have the ruffians plant the acacia in order to conceal the grave in a manner that enables them to find it later. Other versions have the ruffians leave the grave unmarked. The party that discovers it then marks it with the acacia so they can find it later. The version used above is said to be based on an ancient custom of marking grave sites with acacia bushes.

"First Ruffian, 'That won't work! Our escape would be discovered, and the coast lined with our pursuers before we can steal a boat!'

"Second Ruffian, 'Then let's flee inland, and avoid being taken as long as possible.'

"Third Ruffian, 'Agreed!'

✦

"Back at the Temple, King Solomon strode into the courtyard, found the workmen lounging around in confusion, and demanded, 'What's going on? Why are the men not at work?'

"The Junior Grand Warden replied, 'Your Majesty, no work has been laid out for us on the trestle-board.'

"King Solomon exclaimed, 'No work laid out on the trestle-board? What is the meaning of this? Where is our Grand Master, Hiram Abiff?'

"The Junior Grand Warden replied, 'We do not know, Your Majesty. He has not been seen since high twelve yesterday.'

"King Solomon exclaimed, 'Since high twelve yesterday! Something must be wrong. Search for him through the apartments of the Temple, and make due inquiry. Let him be found!'

"The workers began a frantic search for Grand Master Hiram Abiff, searching the temple grounds and asking each other if they had seen him. It soon became apparent that he had not been seen since he retired for his noon prayers the previous day.

"After a time, the Junior Grand Warden reported, 'Your Highness, we cannot find him. He has not been seen in or about the Temple.'

"King Solomon frowned, exclaimed, 'Something must have happened!' turned to his secretary and said, 'Brother Grand Secretary, call the rolls of The Craft, and report to me as soon as possible.'

"The Grand Secretary strode up to the porch of the Temple and announced, 'Assemble, Craftsmen!'

"When all had gathered, he said, 'It is Grand Master King Solomon's orders that the rolls be called, and report made as soon as possible.'

"The Secretary then called out the names of the workers, receiving a response to each until he asked, 'Jubela? ... Jubela! ... Jubela!' After calling more names, which also received replies, he asked, 'Jubelo? ... Jubelo! ... Jubelo!' and after a few more names, he called, 'Jubelum? ... Jubelum! ... Jubelum!'

"Finishing the rolls, the secretary left the brethren on the porch, closed the Temple doors, and reported to King Solomon. 'Your Highness, the rolls have been called, and it appears that three Fellow Crafts are missing, namely, Jubela, Jubelo, and Jubelum. From the similarity of their names, I presume they are brothers, and men from Tyre.'

"At that point, the Junior Grand Warden entered, knelt before King Solomon, and said, 'Your highness, twelve Fellow Crafts wish to be admitted. They say they have important tidings.'

"King Solomon replied, 'Admit them.'

"The Junior Grand Warden opened the door, and said, 'Come in, you twelve Fellow Crafts.'

"The twelve stepped into the Temple, clothed in clean white gloves and aprons, and advanced toward King Solomon in the east. They formed a line across the outer chamber, and made the sign of a Fellow Craft. King Solomon replied with the same sign, and one of the Fellow craft said, 'Your Highness, we come to inform you that fifteen of us Fellow Crafts, seeing the Temple about to be completed, and being desirous of obtaining the secrets of a Master Mason, so that we could travel in foreign countries and receive Master's wages, entered into a conspiracy to extort the secrets from our Grand Master.

"'After thinking it over, we twelve changed our minds. However we fear the other three have taken the Grand Master's life. We therefore now appear before your Majesty clothed with white gloves and aprons, in token of our innocence, and, acknowledging our premeditated guilt, we humbly implore your pardon.'

"They knelt and waited in silence. Finally, King Solomon said, 'Arise, you twelve Fellow Crafts. Divide yourselves into parties and travel —three east, three north, three south, and three west— with others whom I shall appoint, in search of these ruffians.'

"King Solomon signed to his secretary, and said, 'Send word to the ports and frontier towns by the fastest messengers. The borders are to be closed and none are to leave the kingdom without a pass.'

"The Fellow Crafts divided into four groups and departed as instructed. Those who headed west made their way to the sea, and after questioning many people, found the same sea captain who had turned away the ruffians.

"The first craftsman said, 'Hallo, friend! Have you seen any strangers pass this way?'

"'I have, three.'

"'What did they look like?'

"'I believe they were three brothers, workmen from the Temple. They sought passage to Ethiopia, but did not have a pass, so I turned them away. Last I saw, they were headed inland.'

"The second craftsman said, 'That's them! They turned back inland?'

"'Yes.'

"The third craftsman said, 'After them!'"

"A Fellow Crafts, one of the twelve conspirators, said, 'Let's report!' and three headed back to the Temple while the others started searching inland.

"On reporting to King Solomon, one of the three said, 'Your Highness, we are among those who searched to the west. In the port of Joppa, we met a sea captain who had spoken with the ruffians. They sought passage to Ethiopia, but he refused them as they did not have your pass, and they then fled inland.'

"King Solomon replied, 'You will find the ruffians, traveling as before, and if you do not find them you twelve conspirators will be deemed the murderers, and be punished for it!'

"The three left, complaining about the 'unjust' fate that awaited them if they failed. Heading west, they searched avidly for some time, until, near the summit of an almost-barren hill, one of them sat down and said, 'I'm tired! I must rest.'

"One of his companions exclaimed, 'I am tired, too!' and plopped down.

"Another asked, 'What do we do now? We can't go back yet. The twelve would be put to death. Let us take a northwesterly or a southwesterly course. Which way will we go?'

"One of the seated brethren replied, 'Southwesterly. That way we will link up with our brothers.'

"As he stood, he grabbed an acacia bush for support. It pulled loose, and he nearly fell. Staring at the roots, he exclaimed 'Hey, how come this came up so easily?'

"He stooped, examined the ground closely, and said, 'This looks like a fresh grave!'

"They began to dig, fearing what they would find.

✦

"Some distance away, the rest of their party was

quietly searching among the rocks and crags of the western hills. Finally, exhausted, they sat down to rest, and shortly heard someone wailing, 'Oh! That my throat had been cut across, my tongue torn out, and my body buried in the rough sands of the sea, at low tide, where land and water meet, ere I had been accessory to the death of so good a man as our Grand Master, Hiram Abiff.'[8]

"One of the listening craftsmen whispered, 'Hey, that's Jubela!'

"Then they heard a groan, followed by, 'Oh that my left breast had been cut open, my heart torn out, and placed upon the highest pinnacle of the Temple, there to be devoured by the vultures of the air, ere I had consented to the death of so good a man as our Grand Master, Hiram Abiff.'[9]

"Another craftsman whispered, 'That's Jubelo!'

"Then they heard a low moan, followed by, 'Oh! That my body had been cut in two, my bowels taken from thence and burned to ashes, the ashes scattered to the four winds of heaven, that no more remembrance might be had of so vile and wicked a wretch as I.[10] Ah! Jubela, Jubelo, it was I that struck the fatal blow!'

"The third listening craftsman whispered, 'Jubelum!'

"The three craftsmen huddled together, and one of them asked, 'What shall we do? There are three of them, and only three of us.'

"Another replied, 'Our cause is just! Let's rush them.'

---

[8] Quinn: Based on the penalty phase of the Obligation of an Entered Apprentice, as found in *Duncan's Ritual of Freemasonry*, Third Edition, David McKay Company, Inc., New York, p. 35

[9] Quinn: Based on the penalty of a Fellow Craft, as found in *Duncan's Ritual of Freemasonry*, pp. 65-66

[10] Quinn: Based on the penalty of a Master Mason, as found in *Duncan's Ritual of Freemasonry*, p. 96

"The three Fellow Crafts rose and leapt onto the crag where the murderers lay hidden. The ruffians fought back, but were finally subdued, and hauled back to the Temple.

✦

"Meanwhile, the three Fellow Craft who'd found the grave had reported to the Temple. After giving the sign, one of them stepped forward and said, 'Most Worshipful King Solomon, I was among those who pursued a westerly course, and, on my return, after several days of fruitless search, sat down on the brow of a hill to rest and refresh myself. On rising, I accidentally caught hold of a sprig of acacia, which, easily giving way, excited my suspicions. Having my curiosity aroused, I examined it, and found it to be a grave.'

"No sooner had this craftsman finished his report, than the rest of his party arrived with the ruffians. They signed to King Solomon, and reported, 'Your highness, while searching among the rocks and crags of the hills to the west, we heard the voices of Jubela, Jubelo, and Jubelum.'

"They reported what the three had said, and then threw the bound ruffians to the floor before King Solomon. The three ruffians squirmed into kneeling positions, with their heads to the floor.

"King Solomon glared down at them, and said, 'Jubela, you stand charged as accessory to the death of our Grand Master, Hiram Abiff. What say you, guilty or not guilty?'

"'Guilty, Grand Master.'

"'Jubelo, you also stand accessory to the death of our Grand Master, Hiram Abiff. What say you, guilty or not guilty?'

"'Guilty, Grand Master.'

394

"'Jubelum, you stand charged as the willful murderer of our Grand Master, Hiram Abiff. What say you, sir, guilty or not guilty?'

"'Guilty, Grand Master.'

"King Solomon replied, 'Vile, impious wretches! Despicable villains! Reflect with horror on the atrocity of your crime, and on the amiable character of your Worshipful Grand Master, whom you have so basely assassinated. Hold up your heads, and hear your sentence.'

"The three rose onto their heels, and King Solomon intoned, 'It is my orders that you be taken beyond the gates of the court and executed, according to your several imprecations, in the clefts of the rocks. Brother Junior Grand Warden, you will see my orders duly executed. Begone!'

"The craftsmen dragged the three ruffians out of the Temple, and carried out the sentence. When they returned, one of them reported, 'Your Majesty, your orders have been duly executed upon the three murderers of Grand Master, Hiram Abiff.'

"King Solomon nodded, fixed his gaze on the twelve and said, 'You twelve Fellow Crafts will go in search of the body and, if found, observe whether the Master's word, or a key to it, or any thing that appertains to the Master's Degree, is on or about it.'

"The twelve repentant conspirators left, and one among them asked, 'Well, brothers, can we find where the *acacia was pulled up?*'

"Another replied, 'I know the way', and led them to the hill to the west.

"There, he said, 'This is the place. Let's dig here.'

"Reaching a canvas-wrapped form, a third lifted the canvas aside, revealing a mangled, putrid body. He stared carefully at the face, and said, 'Yes, this is the body of our Grand Master, Hiram Abiff. Does anyone see anything pertaining to the Master's word, or a key to it, or any thing appertaining to the Master's Degree?'

"Being but Fellow Crafts, they did not know what they were looking for, but they had to search. They drew off the canvas and searched the body, but found nothing. Finally, one of the brethren, took hold of the jewel around the Grand Master's neck, and exclaimed, 'This is the jewel of his office!'

"'Let's report that we found nothing on or about the body excepting the jewel of his office.'

"One of them carefully removed the jewel's chain from the Master's neck, and they all reported to King Solomon. As they bowed before him, one said, 'Tidings of the body!'

"King Solomon asked, 'Where was it found?'

"'A westerly course[11], where our weary brother had sat down to rest and refresh himself.'

"'Was the Master's word, or a key to it, or any thing appertaining to the Master's Degree, on or about it?'

"'Your majesty, we are but Fellow Crafts, and know nothing about the Master's word or Degree. There was nothing found on or about the body excepting the jewel of his office.'

"They presented the jewel to King Solomon, who examined it and said, 'This is the jewel of our Grand Master, Hiram Abiff; there can be no doubt as to the identity of the body. You twelve Fellow Crafts will now go and assist in raising it.'

"After they left, King Solomon turned to King Hiram of Tyre and said, 'My worthy brother of Tyre, as the Master's word is now lost, the first sign given at the grave, and the first word spoken after the body is raised,

---

[11] Quinn: Note that the sun sets in the west, thus it is the place where the light "dies." Osiris rode his boat into the West each night.

shall be adopted for the regulation of all Masters' Lodges until future generations shall find out the right.'[12]

"King Hiram replied, 'Agreed.'

"King Solomon turned to the Fellow Crafts and said, 'Given the solemnity of the occasion, you will all dress in clean, white aprons and gloves, without any silver or other metal.'

"When they had made themselves ready, King Solomon, King Hiram, the Junior Warden, and The Fellow Crafts returned to the grave, and gathered in a circle around it. The Fellow Crafts removed the coverings of the body.

"King Solomon waved his arms in distress, and said, 'O Lord my God, I fear the Master's word is forever lost!' He then turned to the Junior Warden and said, 'You will take the body by the Entered Apprentice grip, and see if it can be raised.'

"The Junior Warden stooped and attempted to lift the body by its right hand, using the grip of an Entered Apprentice. However, the body slipped out of his hand and fell back into the grave.

"The Junior Warden turned to King Solomon and reported, 'Most Worshipful King Solomon, owing to the high state of putrefaction, the body having been dead already fifteen days, the skin slips, and the body cannot be raised.'

"King Solomon again waved his arms in distress, and exclaimed, 'O Lord my God, I fear the Master's word is forever lost!'

"Turning to King Hiram, he asked, 'My worthy

---

[12] Quinn: Note that the tradition plainly states that all three are Grand Master's, and thus King Solomon and King Hiram must have known the word. Thus, it was not *lost* at the death of Hiram Abiff, but could not then be conveyed to another Master because it took all three G.M.'s to convey the word.

brother of Tyre, I will thank you to endeavor to raise the body by the Fellow Craft's grip.'

"King Hiram of Tyre stooped and took the body's right hand in the grip of a Fellow Craft, but the body again slipped away.'

"King Hiram straightened, turned to King Solomon and reported, 'Owing to the reason before given, the flesh cleaves from the bone, and the body cannot be so raised.'

"Waiving his arms in distress at each exclamation, King Solomon cried, 'O Lord my God! O Lord my God! O Lord my God! Is there hope for the widow's son?'

"Then he turned to King Hiram and asked, 'My worthy brother of Tyre, what shall we do?'

"King Hiram replied, 'Let us pray.'

"Grand Master Solomon directed the brethren to kneel around the body on one knee. He knelt by the head and led the brethren in prayer. When done, they rose, and King Solomon said, 'My worthy brother of Tyre, I shall endeavor, with your assistance, to raise the body by the strong grip, or lion's paw, of the tribe of Judah.'

"King Solomon stepped to the feet of the body, bent over, and gripped the right hand. He then placed his right foot against Hiram Abiff's right foot, and his left hand to his back, and raised him up perpendicularly to a standing position, and with the body clasped tightly to him whispered the Masonic word in his ear.[13]

✦

Quinn: "Wow! Very well done! Thank you, Celine.

"Now, this is the traditional Legend. The actual

---

[13] Quinn: Other versions indicate that Solomon mumbled "it stinks" upon lifting the body, and that this thus became the replacement word.

ritual performance varies somewhat from one branch of Freemasonry to another, but the above is fairly standard. As we will see when we look at the characters and symbols, this myth is another version of the ancient story of initiation.

The Characters

"Now...

(Quinn stood, faced the board, and grabbed a blue marker.)

"... who are the characters? We have... Hiram Abiff, King Solomon, and King Hiram..."

Celine: "The three ruffians."

Quinn: "Of course. Anyone else? ... OK.

Three Ruffians

"Now, the three 'ruffians' are the three Fellow Craft or journeymen who attacked and killed Grand Master Hiram Abiff. They represent both the three-fold persona instrument and the motion of the consciousness within that instrument.

"The motion of the consciousness is indicated by their names, Jubel*a*, Jubel*o*, and Jubel*um*, which are exactly the same except for their final letter or letters. When these final letters are combined, in the order in which they appear in the myth, we get 'AOUM', a combination of the creative words of the incarnate Soul, AUM and OM.

"AUM is the creative word during the involutionary phase of the Soul's incarnation —the outward and downward movement of the Son into form.

"Terry?"

Terry: "Outward?"

Quinn: "Yes. Remember the illustration of the bar magnet? The first motion of the Son is horizontal, outward from the Positive Pole, and then down."

Terry: "What about the diagonal movement, the arc from up to out?"

Quinn: "That's the upper point of transition from Daughter to Son, where the two eventually meet and merge in Spirit."

Terry: "So the lower, inward diagonal movement..."

Quinn: "Is the lower point of transition from Son to Daughter, where the two eventually meet and merge in Substance.

"Bhikku?"

Bhikku: "Do they meet at both points simultaneously, or... Which comes first?"

Quinn: "Well... It depends on the emphasis of the system, the type of motion practiced. For instance, a mystical system that emphasizes aspiration to the Positive Pole could bring about the mergence of Daughter and Son. It would happen if the incarnate consciousness achieved union with the Father. When they manifested that union in their life and affairs, the Son and Daughter would merge. They may aspire to escape the world at first, but as they actually moved toward union with the Father they would recognize the necessity of uniting with the Mother as well."

Bhikku: "In order to complete the path?"

Quinn: "The Path itself would bring them to that point of realization, that in order to progress, they had to manifest their spiritual realization in form.

"And the opposite, of course, would be true of systems that emphasize union with the Mother. Aspiration to the Negative Pole would eventually bring about the mergence of the Son and Daughter, and also the union with the Father."

Tess: "So eventually they wind up at the same place."

Quinn: "Of course. They were really going to the

same place all along, each in their own fashion, just using different... oh, combinations or formulations of the motions of consciousness.

"Now, the OM is the creative word during the evolutionary phase of the Soul's incarnation—the inward and upward movement of the Daughter to self realization.

"From the perspective of the Spiritual Soul, this outward and downward and inward and upward movement is one great cycle. From the perspective of the persona, it includes many 'incarnations', or life in a sequence of personas.

"Thus, the combination of AOUM represents the great cycle of the Soul, the movement into and out of incarnation, which finally leads to the mastery of the form and release from the Wheel of Rebirth.

"This in turn suggests that each of the ruffians represents a phase of that great cycle. In that case, Jubela represents the downward movement, in which the Son builds and identifies with the form.

"Jubelo represents the life in the form, in which the incarnate soul gains knowledge and experience through life in the three lower worlds.

"Jubelum represents the phase of withdrawal from the form, in which the Daughter returns home with the fruit of her experience.

"The common portion of their names, 'Jubel', is actually, 'Yah El' or the 'Father-God' of southern Judah, who is represented —in this patriarchal version of the mysteries— as the sole source of the creative Word.

"Tess?"

Tess: "What's the actual source?"

Quinn: "Well, it depends on the context, and how you look at it. In the beginning, the Word was spoken by the One that was everything before there was any thing. But in the very act of speaking, the One became the

Three. Now, you could say that each of the Three Aspects, being three, have their portion or fragment of the Word. Or, you can say that the Word is the Second Aspect, the magnetic field of motion between and within the other Two.

"In the Myth of Freemasonry, the creative 'lost word', without which the Temple cannot be built is the creative Word of the Second Aspect, the Divine Child or Spiritual Soul. It's the sounds or notes of that 'word' that are at the heart of and create each of the Seven Major Centers or Chakras.

Hiram Abiff

"Now, while Hiram Abiff is the traditional 'Grand Master' of Freemasonry, there was never any such person and he does not exist outside of this myth.

"Celine?"

Celine: "What do you mean?"

Quinn: "He's a made-up character who doesn't appear anywhere else.

Celine: "What about the Bible?"

Quinn: "Does not contain anyone named 'Hiram Abiff' or a single character in charge of building the Temple.

"Actually, it looks like Hiram Abiff is, in part, a composite of three biblical figures:

"Betzalel—who was in charge of constructing the Tabernacle,

"Adoniram—who was in charge of the levy of unskilled workers assigned to the Temple project, and

Hiram Abi—a 'brass' smith who made the furnishings and ritual tools of the Temple."

Celine: "So there was a 'Hiram Abi'."

Quinn: "As a character in the Bible, yes. But he was a *smith*, not the Grand Master in charge of the project.

402

Plus, as we have seen, the Bible is a collection of symbolic stories or myths, not history."

Celine: "So if there was a 'Hiram Abi', he was just a brass smith?'"

Quinn: "Um, actually no. The 'brass' of the Bible was probably bronze.

"Now, Hiram occupies the same position in the Temple Legend as did our other 'Sons' of 'God' in their legends. Thus, he's half of the Daughter–Son polarity of the Soul. And, as usual in Pisces, the 'Daughter' is obscured by the patriarchal perspective.

King Solomon

"As for King Solomon, archeological evidence suggests that, unlike Hiram Abiff, 'King Solomon' was a real, historical person. According to the Biblical account, he was a son of David, who ruled the combined kingdom of northern Israel and southern Judah from 970 – 931 BCE.

"However, in our current Myth, King Solomon represents the source of Divine Purpose, Power, and Will that motivates the building of the Temple. Thus, Solomon represents the Positive Pole or Father Aspect of Divinity.

King Hiram

"In both the Freemasonic and Biblical myths, King Hiram is the sovereign of Tyre. Tyre was a real place, a Phoenician colony contemporary with Biblical Israel. According to these traditions, King Hiram ruled this small but wealthy nation of sea traders to the north of Israel. He provided the cedar beams used in the Temple, the woodsmen and stone masons who worked on the Temple, and the smiths who made the implements, vessels, altar, etc.

"An important clue to King Hiram's identity is found in the Legend itself:

'After they left, King Solomon turned to King Hiram of Tyre and said, 'My worthy brother of Tyre, as the Master's word is now lost, *the first sign given* at the grave, and *the first word spoken* after the body is raised, shall be adopted for the regulation of all Masters' Lodges until future generations shall find out the right.'

"This is significant because the myth clearly indicates, and the tradition plainly states, that both King Solomon and Hiram Abiff were Grand Masters, and thus must have known the word. Thus, the Word was not lost in the sense that no one knew it. It was lost in the sense that it could not be sounded unless all three Masters —King Solomon, Hiram Abiff, and King Hiram— were present. In other words, the Creative Word can only be sounded by a complete Trinity!

"This indicates that King Hiram was part of the Divine Trinity, equal to King Solomon and Hiram Abiff.

"If King Solomon represents the Positive Pole or Divine Father, and Hiram Abiff represents the Magnetic Field, then King Hiram represents the Negative Pole or Divine Mother! She may be hidden here behind a masculine shroud, but nevertheless the Goddess remains."

Celine: "But that means the entire lodge ritual is a—"

(Quinn's right hand shot up to scratch at the base of his throat, and Celine snapped her mouth shut and flushed. Several of the students looked puzzled, but Quinn quickly stood, faced the board, and continued the lesson.)

The Symbols

Quinn: "Turning our attention to the symbols, we find a wealth of meaning. But those that concern us most here are...

"The Ark, the Creative Magic of Hiram Abiff, and the Lost Word.

The Ark of the Covenant

"Now as mentioned earlier, the Ark of the Covenant was a gilded chest of acacia wood, kept in the inner chamber of the Temple. 'Ark' in fact means 'chest', and in the context of this myth the symbolism of the Ark is similar to that of the chests of Osiris and Adonis.

"Bhikku?"

Bhikku: "So it represents the three-fold persona?"

Quinn: "Yes, but the placement of the Ark in the Temple of Solomon makes its meaning more specific.

"According to historical record, Biblical myth, and Masonic tradition, there were two pairs of guardian statues, or 'cherubim' in the Holy of Holies, a pair of large statues on either side of the entrance, and a smaller pair atop the Mercy Seat or lid of the Ark. As I mentioned earlier, one apparent historical fact about the pair atop the Ark is that they were a sexual pair — male and female— portrayed in eternal sexual union. The posture of the larger pair is unknown, but if both pairs were engaged in sexual union, then we have some very interesting symbology...

"In order to enter the Inner Chamber, Grand Master Hiram Abiff would have to pass between the large male and female cherubim, passing through the place of at-one-ment.

"In other words, one would have to become the Spiritual Soul, and achieve union between the Male and Female Aspects of oneself, in order to enter the Holy of Holies.

"In order to communicate with 'God', the High Priest would have to achieve union with the Male and Female Aspects 'outside' of his self.

"Approaching the Ark, and the male and female cherubim on its lid, the High Priest would:

"Expand his consciousness to at-one with the Soul of the One Life.

"Lay his left hand under the male and his right on the female —without crossing his arms.

"As the Divine Son, relate the Father Aspect to the Mother Aspect.[14]

"As the Divine Daughter, relate the Mother Aspect to the Father Aspect.

"The Shekinah or emanation of God would then appear between the two cherubim, and 'God' would speak.
"Wil?"
Wil: "How... Where did you get this?"
Quinn: "In meditation. It's an extension of the allegory. Remember, the Temple, Inner Chamber, Ark, and cherubim do not represent physical places or things. They are symbols of an actual process, the inner creative activity or magic of consciousness. When you have experienced the process, it's not difficult to extend or fill-in-the-gaps in a symbolic myth.

The Magic of Hiram Abiff

"This creative process is symbolized by the efforts of Hiram Abiff, the supervisor of the work. Hiram does not formulate the Plan, for that is the work of King Solomon, nor does he perform physical labor, for that is the work of King Hiram's builders.

---

[14] Quinn: In order for this process to work, a High Priestess would also have to be present, completing the circuit. She would lay her left hand on the male and her right under the female cherubim (without crossing her arms) and, as the Divine Daughter, relate the Mother to the Father. Only then, with the Mother related to the Father and the Father related to the Mother could Goddess or God "speak" through their representatives.

"Hiram Abiff performs a rhythmic ritual through which he relates the Plan to the builders and the builders to the Plan. This regular ritual has four portions:

"Ascending the Temple Mount,

"Meditating in the Holy of Holies,

"Descending the Mount, and

"Gazing on the work.

"The process may be described as follows:

"When all is quiet in the courtyard —the physical-dense body— the Grand Master ascends the steps to the Temple.

"At the top of the stairs, he steps onto the porch or entrance, and prepares his physical-etheric body for higher impression.

"When the energy body underlying his physical-dense form is ready, he steps through the entry into the middle chamber, calms and clears his emotions, and prepares to aspire upwards.

"When his astral or emotional body is ready, he quiets his mind and steps into the Inner Chamber.

"Immediately within, he integrates his mind, emotions, and physical-etheric body into a single unit, merging the poles and magnetic field of the persona.

"Having merged the persona into a single unit, Hiram Abiff then steps up to the Ark, and merges with it, becoming at-one with the Spiritual Soul.

"As the Spiritual Soul, he ascends to Solomon, and at-one's with the 'Architect' of the universe.

"The Ascension complete, he:

"Reports on the current condition of the work and the builders, and

"Contemplates the Divine Plan.

"Having grasped the pertinent portion of the Plan, the Master of Works leaves the Inner Chamber, pausing at the portal to translate the idea of the Plan into a thought, and to organize the thought with his intellect.

"Within the middle chamber, Hiram Abiff gathers his astral force, and impresses his organized thought on the tracing board.

"The Grand Master then steps onto the porch, calls the builders to the work, and points to the tracing board as their guide.

"The builders then go about their tasks, constructing the Temple in accordance with the Plan, as conveyed to them by the Master of Works, Hiram Abiff.

"It should be noted that the builders decide how to follow the instructions on the tracing board. They have a great deal of latitude in their creative activity. The precise forms of appearance they create are up to them, and are not the concern of either Solomon or Hiram Abiff.

"Hiram Abiff performs this ritual on a regular basis, making use of daily, lunar, and annual cycles."

Terry: "That's the creative process, the, um, magic of consciousness?"

Quinn: "In essence, yes.

"This rhythmic ritual uses the rotary motion of substance to carry the consciousness through its own creative process. It's the creative process we've discussed throughout this course, with its daily, lunar, and annual cycles.

"It's either quite complex, or very simple, depending on how you view it.

"Now, I have a great deal more on the Temple and related subjects. Much too much to go over now, we'd be here for days. However, I do have a bit more to hand out.

(I passed around the hand-out on The Temple of Solomon.)[15]

"It's getting late, and there's a lot left on the Lost Word and on the Magic of Consciousness, so I'm going to send you handouts on those."[16]

Summary

Quinn: "OK. Our investigation of the Legend of the Temple has brought us to the following conclusions:

"The Temple of Solomon represents the house or dwelling place of the Soul in three states of awareness. As indicated in the handouts, each state of awareness has its own symbolic house or temple, including:

"The Tabernacle, or house of the incarnate soul, is the persona —including the mental, emotional, physical-etheric and physical-dense bodies.

"The Temple of Solomon, or house of the Spiritual Soul, is the Light Body of the Soul.

"The Temple of Ezekiel, or house of the Spirit, is the body of the Spirit.

"Each of the characters in the Legend represents one of the Three Aspects of Divinity:

"The builders represent intelligent beings of substance, directed by the Soul.

"The Three Ruffians represent the three-fold persona, consisting of the three bodies mentioned above (reflected in the physical-dense body), and the three-fold

---

[15] Quinn: See the Addendum to Lesson 14.
[16] Quinn: Again, see the Addendum to Lesson 14.

goddess.

"Hiram Abiff represents the Spiritual Soul or Son Aspect.

"King Solomon represents the Spirit or Father Aspect.

"King Hiram represents Substance or the Mother Aspect, the Great Goddess.

"The furnishings of the Temple, such as the pillars, Ark, and tracing board, represent portions of the human instrument used in the creative process.

"The Lost Word represents the creative Word of God, or that portion thereof wielded by each of the Three Aspects and fragments of the three aspects—such as a Spiritual Soul.

"The activities of the characters in the settings — especially in the temples— represent the creative magic of consciousness which produces spiritual growth and development, and re-union of the One Life.

The entire process of spiritual growth and development lies within the rites and rituals of Freemasonry, veiled in allegory and illustrated by symbols. It's not merely a fraternal order or 'old boy's club', but a last remnant of the Ancient Mysteries. Within its Lodges lie hid the Ageless Wisdom that reveals our purpose, place, and function within the One Life.

"In our next chapter, we will bring our quest up to the mid twentieth century, with the myth of Prince Charming and Snow White.

"But first, we'll close in the usual fashion."

Invoking Purpose

Sit in a comfortable chair, relax your physical body, calm your emotions, and focus your mind.

Bring your consciousness to a point of focus within your ajna center, and there integrate your three-fold persona —body, emotions, and mind— into a single unit.

From your place within the ajna center, identify with and as your spiritual group, and aspire upward to the Father.

Imagine that your group has, as a unit, ascended beyond the physical, emotional, and mental worlds to the higher realm of the self or Overshadowing Soul. There, seek out your place as a group unit within the One Life, and invoke your Divine Purpose into your awareness by audibly stating the seed-thought:

"I stand receptive to the Purpose, Power, and Will of God as it is made known to me by the Soul. I serve that Purpose, accept its Power, and do the Will of God."

Without thinking about it or repeating it, allow the vibration of that thought to sound within the group consciousness. Continue listening to and feeling that vibration until all is still and quiet, then, audibly sound the OM.

Take a deep breath, open your eyes, and return your awareness to your surroundings.

"Practice this inner ritual at least once a day, every day, for a full lunar cycle (from New Moon to New Moon)."

Raising the Queen of Heaven

Lesson 15

The Awakening

The Myth of Prince Charming
and Snow White

Jeff asked, "How's the 'Cinnamon Chai'?"

I glanced up from my notes, and said, "The Rooibos?"

"Yes."

"Smell it. It's very good, but you have to like pepper."

As I returned to my preparations Quinn's faint "OM" emerged from the meditation room. Jeff poured a glass of the iced Chai, and sat in his usual seat.

Quinn entered a few moments later, took a sip of iced tea, and turned from Ema to Thea as he asked, "How were the fireworks?"

Ema and Thea took turns describing their family gatherings, mounds of potato salad, hotdogs, grilled burgers, soydogs, and frolicking children, and followed by fireworks.

I remembered my first sight of fire elementals streaming through the sky, spitting light, hissing, and bursting in great pops, their wild glee reflected in the aura of the audience. I'd screamed and clutched mom, and she picked me up, hugged me and said the noise couldn't hurt—it was just people playing. But it wasn't, and they could.

That was when I began to suspect that other people couldn't see everything I did, and when mom began to suspect that I was... well, special.

I pushed the memory away as Ema and Thea finished. Quinn asked, "Is everyone ready? El?"

I nodded, put down my notes, and turned off the fans

with the remote.

Quinn said, "OK, let's get started."

I flicked on the recorder.

Opening Alignment

Quinn: "Bring your consciousness to a point of focus within the ajna center, and there integrate your energy, force, and substance in aspiration to the Soul. (Pause)

"Along a line of golden-white light, slowly move upward into the crown center, and there identify as the Spiritual Soul. (Pause)

"As the Soul in the crown center, turn your attention upward to that Wisdom overshadowing this evening's lesson, and become receptive to it by silently sounding the OM. (Pause)

"Maintaining that focus of receptivity, move back down the line of light into the ajna. (Pause)

"Maintaining that focus of receptivity in the ajna, draw a line of light from the ajna to the physical-dense brain, and audibly sound the OM.

"Take a deep breath, and slowly open your eyes."

The Tale of Snow White

Quinn: "OK. Traditional 'fairy tales' are often surviving fragments of ancient myths —the spiritual teachings of older cultures. Isolated from their origins, they are distorted, misunderstood, and apparently reduced to little more than entertainment. However, a fragment of the original meaning remains, and can be discerned if one gazes past the veils. Snow White is an excellent example of this type of 'fairy tale.'

"The Grimm Brothers first published their edition of Snow White in the nineteenth century —somewhere between 1812 and 1822. Walt Disney created a new version of this popular tale in 1937. His *Snow White and the Seven Dwarves*, the very first feature-length cartoon, was immensely popular.

"Now it may seem odd for us to consider this 'children's cartoon', but it was preceded and partly inspired by an animated short called *The Goddess of Spring* — Persephone— and followed by *Sleeping Beauty, Cinderella, The Sword in the Stone, The Black Cauldron, The Beauty and the Beast, Hercules*, and others. Thus, Disney has a history of animating symbolic tales, and including *Snow White* in our studies makes perfect sense.

"However, unlike the myths examined above, Disney's Snow White is a fantasy. It was designed to entertain the public, not to educate them in the Ancient Wisdom. Thus, while Snow White's cast of characters includes archetypes of all four members of the Tetrarchy, those archetypes have been heavily veiled by the desires and expectations of mid-twentieth century, or late Piscean, humanity.

"The Four Aspects of Divinity, and the relationships

between them, were severely distorted by those desires, but the Mother, Daughter, Father, and Son are still easily recognizable."

Wil: "There's no king."

Quinn: "He's an off-screen character, but still very influential. But let's hold off on that.

"Now, the direct connection with the ancient mysteries is lost, but the ageless tale of descent, death, return, and re-union remains.

"Thus, while we can learn little about initiation rites from *Snow White*, it has a great deal to tell us about humanity's recent relationship with the Four Aspects of Divinity. A careful examination of this fantasy will tell us where humanity was in the early and mid-twentieth century, and thus, where we need to go in order to bring about right relationship between the Four.

"Now, for obvious reasons, I've asked El to tell this myth for us.

"El?"

The Fairy Tale[1]

Me: "Once upon a time, long, long ago and far away, there lived a beautiful little Princess named Snow White. Her evil stepmother ruled through lust and fear —the lust of men for her beauty and fear of her ruthless power. And as this evil Queen gazed on little Snow White, she saw great beauty and the rightful heir of her stolen power. And so the Queen feared that some day, as

---

[1] Quinn: While preparing to tell the myth, El watched Disney's "*Snow White*" dozens of times (including flipping through it cell by cell) and made notes so extensive they amounted to a reconstruction of the screenplay. She also delved into the history of the story, and, as a result, used some of the language of Disney's version as well as several scenes that were cut from the final film.

Snow White grew, she would become more beautiful than her, and take back the stolen power.

"And so the evil Queen forced little Snow White into rags, and made her work like the lowest servant, laboring night and day at all those hard tasks that line the face, bend the body, and break the spirit.

"And every morning, as soon as she completed her toilette, the evil Queen stood before her Magic Mirror, and demanded, 'Magic Mirror on the Wall, who is the fairest one of all?' ... and as long as the mirror answered, 'You are the fairest one of all,' the evil Queen was reassured, and the maids of the kingdom were safe.

"But woe to the kingdom when the Mirror named someone else, for then the evil Queen called for her henchmen, and the fair maid disappeared, whether noble or peasant, and was never again named by the Mirror.

"And so life went, with Snow White laboring through the seasons and years of childhood, until one morning...

"The evil Queen strode up the tower stairs to the upper room where she gazed at the stars, and turned to her Magic Mirror. It was set on a slate-gray wall, encircled by the arched signs of the Zodiac, and a spark of flame danced within it.

"With her dark features shadowed by the Mirror's red light, the evil Queen raised her arms high and intoned, 'Slave in the Mirror, by thy name I summon thee! Come from the darkness of infinite space. Speak! And let me see thy face.'

"Flames burst against the far side of the glass, and parted to reveal a dead-white head —hairless, as though burnt clean by the tormenting blaze.

"The spirit stared at the Queen with eyes set deep within indigo shadows, and said, 'Thy beauty fills the land, turning all toward thee, all but one. Though long veiled beneath dirt and toil, one has broken free and her true beauty stands revealed.'

"'Then she must join the others. Reveal her name!'

"'Lips red as the rose, hair black as ebony, skin white as snow.'

"'Snow White!' said the Queen.

✦

"Surrounded by doves, Princess Snow White was scrubbing the bottom of twelve winding steps leading up from a castle courtyard. The courtyard included a wishing well, sheltered by a roof whose two supporting pillars were twined about with blossoming vines.

"As her work took her near the well, Snow White turned to the doves, and told them it was a secret Wishing Well. She then sang a song into the Well, and to the doves, telling of her desire for a Prince to come and take her away.

"At that very moment Prince Charming was riding by the castle on his white horse. Hearing Snow White's sweet voice, he rode up to the courtyard's wall, stood atop his horse, vaulted the wall, joined Snow White at the well, and sang to her of 'One Song, One Love.'

"Startled, and embarrassed by the dirty rags she wore, Snow White retreated indoors, to a castle balcony, as Prince Charming continued singing. From her retreat, Snow White had a dove deliver an innocent kiss to the Prince. Then, as though awakening from a dream, Snow White realized her danger, and bade the Prince leave before he was seen. But it was too late.

"All the while, the dark form of the evil Queen watched from a shadow-draped window high in the castle.

"As the Prince returned to the wall, the Queen turned and summoned her evil henchmen and the huntsman. The henchmen were close by, and arrived in moments. She ordered them to take and imprison the Prince in the deepest, darkest dungeon beneath the castle.

"The henchmen found the Prince outside the courtyard, and leapt upon him. He fought bravely, but there were too many of them, and they dragged him off.

"When the huntsman arrived, the evil Queen ordered him to take Snow White for a walk the next day, to 'pick wild flowers', and then to murder her and bring back the Princes' heart in a red box. The huntsman was repelled by the idea, but he knew he was a dead man if he disobeyed, so he hardened himself and agreed.

"The next morning, the Huntsman took Snow White for a walk to the edge of the woods. For her, it was a rare break from endless toil on a perfect day, and she delighted in the beauty of everything.

"The little Princess discovered a lost chick, and as she knelt and spoke with it, the huntsman drew his knife and crept up behind her, preparing to plunge it into her unshielded back.

"Snow White glimpsed his shadow, spun around, and drew back in horror. Moved beyond endurance by her plight, the Huntsman dropped his knife, knelt before the Princess, begged her forgiveness, and blurted out that the Queen had ordered her death. Snow White leaped up, and the huntsman shouted at her to flee, to run and hide, and never come back.

"As she fled deep into the woods, the trees grew black and evil in her sight, and snatched and tore at her, driving her onward in heedless flight. Finally, the frantic Snow White was trapped, surrounded by grasping limbs, snapping maws, and glowing eyes. She spun round and round, desperately seeking escape, and finding none, fainted.

✦

"Snow White lay sobbing in a clearing. Light slowly returned, revealing a beautiful forest filled with small, harmless creatures. The animals approached and tried to comfort the distraught Princess.

"Snow White started at their touch, and the animals leaped back.

"Gazing up, Snow White realized that they were harmless, called them back and apologized to them. She joined the birds in song and the animals came out from hiding. Snow White explained that she would need a place to sleep and the animals took her to a cottage in the woods.

"Snow White peered inside, then knocked, and entered. It was a beautiful little cottage, with owls and rabbits carved on many of the wooden beams and furniture, but everything was filthy. The Princess exclaimed at the disorder, dirt, and cobwebs, and realized that the 'children' who lived there must have no mother. Speculating that perhaps the children would let her stay if she cleaned and cooked for them, she led the animals in driving out all the dust and dirt, and restoring order in the cottage.

"Meanwhile, the Seven Dwarves were hard at work in their diamond mine, singing as they worked, with Doc testing the diamonds via their *sound* (by striking them), and Dopey tossing out the rejects.

"Exploring the upper floor of the cottage, Snow White discovered a bedroom containing seven small beds, with owls, rabbits, and names carved into them. She noted the names, lay down, and slept.

"With the Princess asleep, only the animals heard the Seven Dwarves returning from work, and they fled or hid. The approaching Dwarves saw light in their cottage, and speculated that there may be a ghost or a goblin, a demon or a dragon inside. Frightened, they stalked into the cottage, and mystified to find everything clean and put away. Sneezy sneezed, and three birds hidden in the rafters screeched, driving the Dwarves away. But the seven returned, and sent Dopey up to the bedroom to see what 'it' was.

"A shaking Dopey skulked up the steps to the bedroom. Covered by a white sheet, Snow White stretched and moaned in her sleep. Dopey yelled in fright, and all Seven Dwarves fled in terror. Dopey tripped, and become entangled in pots and pans. The Dwarves mistook Dopey for 'it', and beat him. Discovering their mistake, they stalked back up to the bedroom together, and were about to strike when they discovered that the monster was a girl.

"Snow White started to wake, and the Dwarves ducked behind the footboards. Snow White saw the Seven Dwarves, realized that they are little men, and named each of them.

"The Dwarves asked Snow White who she was. She identified herself and begged the Dwarves not to send her away because the Queen would kill her. The Dwarves identified the Queen as an old witch, who knew everything by her evil arts.

"Snow White offered to clean and cook for them if they let her stay. The Dwarves agreed, and Snow White hurried down to take their soup off the fire.

"The Dwarves ran down to dinner, but Snow White made them wash first.

"Grumpy refused to wash, and sat chewing a stalk of grain while the other Dwarves bathed their hands and faces in a long trough.

"Finished with themselves, the other Dwarves grabbed and scrubbed Grumpy. Sent for the soap, Dopey fumbled and swallowed it. The Dwarves put ribbons and flowers on Grumpy, and Snow White called them to dinner.

"Meanwhile, back at the castle, a light shone from a window high in a tower. Inside the evil Queen stood holding the red box. Behind her hung a dark-blue curtain, covered with golden moons and stars. Before her was the Mirror, filled with the bone-white face of its tormented occupant. The Queen demanded, 'Who now is the fairest one of all?'

"The Magic Mirror replied, 'Over the seven jeweled hills, beyond the seven falls, in the cottage of the seven dwarves, dwells Snow White, fairest one of all.'

"The Queen objected that Snow White was dead, and presented the red box as proof. But the mirror replied, 'Snow White still lives, the fairest in the land, 'tis the heart of a *pig* that you hold in your hand.'

"Furious, the evil Queen threw down the box, and decided to kill Snow White herself. She rushed down a winding stair to a rat-infested dungeon, past a skeleton in an open coffin, and through a door into an alchemical lab littered with skulls and watched over by a crow.

"The Queen decided she must first disguise herself, leafed through her spell books, and found a formula to transform her beauty into ugliness. Then she stood over a cauldron of bubbling potion, and intoned:

"'To make me old, mummy's dust.'

"'To shroud my cloak, the dark of night.'

"'To age my voice, an old hag's cackle.'

"'To whiten my hair, a scream of fright.'

"'A blast of wind to fan my hate.'

"'*A thunderbolt to mix it well.*'

"'Now begin my magic spell.'

The Queen drank the potion, and her body transformed into that of an old witch or peddler woman.

"As the instrument of her malice, the Old Witch chose the 'Poisoned Apple of the Sleeping Death'.

"Meanwhile, Snow White and the Seven Dwarves sang and danced after dinner, using musical instruments shaped like or carved with animals. These were mostly owls and rabbits, but also included a drum / cymbal stand and a drum/bell stand shaped like pelicans (played by Dopey with great enthusiasm and versatility), and a clarinet shaped like a fish (played by Sleepy). There was also a duck-shaped cymbal stand and a drum carved with rabbits and played by Happy.

"The Dwarves begged for a story. Snow White told them of her meeting with and love for Prince Charming, and sang 'Someday my Prince will come...'

"The Dwarves' cuckoo clock sounded—with a frog instead of a bird, and a moon above the clock face. The Seven Dwarves asked Snow White to sleep in their beds, saying they would be comfortable downstairs.

"After she left, the Dwarves fought over a single feather cushion, scattering its stuffing, and finally made their beds wherever they could.

"Upstairs, Snow White said her prayers, 'Bless the seven little men who have been so kind to me, and may my dreams come true, Amen... Oh yes! Please make Grumpy like me!'

"Meanwhile, the evil Witch brewed up the Poisoned Apple. Concerned over a possible antidote, she checked the spell book, but found that 'The victim of the Sleeping Death can be revived only by love's first kiss.'

"Delighted by the thought that Snow White would be buried alive —making such a kiss impossible— the Witch descended, even deeper into the catacombs beneath the castle —passing the skeleton of a prisoner who'd died of thirst. She boarded a boat, poled out of the catacombs into a river, across the river to a swamp, and lurched away into the forest.

"At the cottage next morning, as the Dwarves left for

work, each in turn stopped to warn Snow White against the Witch, and received a kiss on his head —even Grumpy, who was so bemused he walked into a tree and then a stream.

"Meanwhile, the evil Witch stalked through the forest, disguised as an old peddler woman with a basket of apples, and watched by two vultures.

"Snow White, making pies for the Dwarves, sang, 'Someday my Prince will come, Someday when Spring is here...'

"The Witch appeared at the window and offered apples for pies. Birds harassed the Witch, trying to drive her away. The Witch faked a heart ailment and begged for water. Snow White took her in and then fetched water while the Witch readied the Poison Apple.

"Alarmed, the animals raced away, through the forest to fetch the Dwarves.

"Meanwhile, the Witch offered the apple as a magic wishing apple 'One bite and all your dreams come true!'

"The animals reached the Dwarves, and frantically tried to tug and push them back toward the cottage, but the Dwarves refused to budge. Beset by the animals, Sleepy suggested that maybe the Queen had found Snow White. At that, the Dwarves leaped atop the deer and galloped through the forest to the rescue.

"Backed into a corner by the Witch, Snow White admitted that there was someone she dreamed of, took the apple, and wished that the Prince would come and carry her away to his castle where they would live happily ever after. Snow White bit the apple and collapsed.

"Triumphant, the Witch exclaimed, 'Now I will be the fairest in the land!'

"Galloping back, the Dwarves spotted the Witch leaving the cottage and gave chase. The Witch fled, and climbed a steep crag that dead-ended in a cliff. Trapped, she grabbed a sturdy branch and started levering a boulder onto the advancing Dwarves while the two vultures watched.

"Suddenly, a bolt of lightning struck the branch, and through the branch the cliff, right between the boulder and the Witch. The crag cracked and broke apart, and the Witch fell screaming, followed by the boulder. The watching vultures grinned in triumph and took flight, spiraling down —clockwise— to dine.

"The grief-stricken Dwarves placed the apparently-dead Snow White downstairs, in her own bed, framed by two lit candles, and prayed around her.

"Snow White was so beautiful, that the Dwarves could not bring themselves to bury her. So they built her a coffin of glass and gold, placed it in the center of the woods, and cared for her night and day. All the animals stood watch with them, and even the heavens wept.

"In the confusion following the Queen's long absence, the Prince escaped from his dungeon prison, and began a long quest for Snow White.

"Fall slowly passed into winter, winter into spring, and the Princess slept, the Dwarves kept watch, and the Prince searched.

"Finally, after many adventures, the Prince learned of a beautiful maid trapped in eternal sleep within a glass coffin.

"Deep within the forest, amidst the bloom of spring, the Seven Dwarves placed bouquets of flowers around the coffin, lifted and set-aside the glass lid, and knelt to pray.

"A sad, longing voice broke into song, with, 'One Song, One Love...'. It was the Prince. He'd found her at last.

"The Prince approached the body of Snow White, and the Dwarves rose and made way for him. The Prince leaned over Snow White and kissed her gently on the lips. "The Dwarves knelt again, and bowed their heads.

Snow White's eyelids fluttered, her breast moved, and she awoke, stretched, and sat up. And lo, there beside her knelt her beloved Prince Charming.

"The Dwarves and the animals all danced for joy as Prince Charming lifted Snow White in his arms and carried her to his white steed. Once she was mounted, the Prince lifted each dwarf up to Snow White for a goodbye kiss atop his head.

"Then the Prince led the mounted Snow White toward a beautiful pink-orange-gold sunset, and a glowing castle resting within the clouds of heaven.

"'...And they lived happily ever after.'

Quinn: "Thank you El. Very well done!"

The Characters

Quinn: "Well, as you may have noticed, this fairytale is a rather distorted fragment. The Princess is a helpless, dependent victim. The Queen is evil incarnate. The Prince is a romantic cipher with only two scenes, and the King does not appear directly at all.

Wil: "Directly?"

(Quinn stood, and faced the board.)

Quinn: "Hold just a bit. We'll get to that. Let's list the characters first.

"Let's see... We have Princess Snow White, the Evil Queen, Prince Charming...?

Wil: "The King?"

Quinn: "Yes."

Ed: "The Seven Dwarfs."

Quinn: "*Dwarves*, yes."

Ema: "The Witch and the Mirror."

Quinn: "Yes."

John: "The Huntsman."

Quinn: "Right."

Bhikku: "The Henchmen?"

Quinn: "Yes...

"Is that it? Tess?"

Tess: "The animals?"

Quinn: "No... No, I don't think so. We'll cover them in 'Symbols'."

The Henchmen

"Now then, let's see... The Henchmen appeared in scenes that were cut from Disney's final version. As you will recall from El's version, at the Queen's command, a group of armed ruffians attacked the Prince, dragged him into the castle, and imprisoned him in the dungeons. These henchmen are the same 'ruffians' that appeared in the Freemasonic myth. They represent the lesser builders, or the builders of the impermanent forms in which the self or soul is temporarily imprisoned. Since the movement here is downward into form, portraying the Prince in this position is quite appropriate, as that is the movement which he rules.

Terry: "So he's the Divine Son?"

Quinn: "Yes, but we'll get to him later."

The Huntsman

"Now the huntsman represents the Destroyer Aspect of the Positive Pole of Divinity, that focused Will which —when focused on form— shatters crystallization, allowing new movement to take place and new forms to develop.

"The aborted attack on Snow White by the Huntsman represents that ascent by the Daughter into relationship with the Father which leads to the birth and descent of the Son.

"Yes, John?"

John: "The Huntsman is the Father?"

Quinn: "He's an aspect of the Father, an aspect which frees the consciousness by destroying the imprisoning form. Now as I mentioned earlier, this is a natural consequence of the impression of Divine Will in a form that is so crystallized or rigid that it cannot respond or remold itself to that new impact of Will. The result is that the crystallized form shatters, and the consciousness moves on to its next state of existence.

"The King or Divine Father does not appear directly, but remains transcendent, a condition which reflects a mis-relationship between the Father and Mother Aspects of Divinity. The Prince attempts to re-establish this relationship in the opening scene, by declaring his love for Princess Snow White. However, the Queen frustrates this attempt by having her Henchmen capture and imprison the Prince.

"The Divine King's power is demonstrated when the Witch prepares to kill the Dwarves by tipping a boulder onto them. As we've seen, the thunderbolt is a classic symbol of the transcendent Father god in heaven. Having such a bolt —a classic symbol of Divine Justice— destroy the Witch, places the Father in direct opposition to the Divine Mother. This is, of course, a complete distortion of their true natures, as all existence is a product of the creative relationship of these Two.

The Queen

"On the other hand, the Magic Mirror is an Aspect of the Queen —her deep subconscious. This is demonstrated by its placement at the center of the arc of the zodiac. The Mirror is that Aspect of the Goddess which 'knows everything'.

"Terry?"

Terry: "I don't understand about the Zodiac."

Quinn: "Ah! Well, in the opening scene of the film the eye of the camera zooms toward the castle, up to a tower window, into the tower room, and finds the Queen standing with her back toward us, facing the Mirror. On the wall around the Mirror, and thus, from our perspective also around the Queen, are all twelve symbols of the Zodiac in a great arc.

"Now the setting of the tale is medieval, and medieval cosmology was geocentric."

Me: "Gee oh what?"

Quinn: "G e o c e n t r i c. That's when you believe that Earth is at the center of the universe, and all the heavenly bodies —including the stars of the Zodiac— are set in crystal spheres around it.

"Thus, placing the Queen at the center of the Zodiac, in a geocentric universe, clearly and unmistakably identifies her as Mother Earth!

Wil: "But she's evil!"

Quinn: "*Is* she? Is she really? Or is all of that simply a patriarchal distortion? We'll get to that in a moment, but first, let's make sure of her identity.

"A later scene shows the Queen seated on her throne, surrounded by a wealth of symbols. The symbols in the throne-room scene include:

"On the wall behind the Queen are twin serpents, coiled three times, with mouths open, facing each other. Representing, thus, the twin pillars of substance, or Ida and Pingala.

"Appearing with the serpents are three-peaked crowns, indicating by their association with the serpents, that they represent the three-aspects of substance, the virgin, mother, and crone.

"Atop her head the Queen wears a five-peaked crown, combining the three-aspects of substance with the twin serpents.

"At her throat, the Queen wears the Solar Disk of the Father Aspect which, since it is at her throat rather than on her head, indicates that she speaks for the King, but is not identical with him.

"The Queen, throne, serpents, and crown are framed by the spread tail feathers of a great golden peacock. The peacock is the ancient symbol of Juno, the mother of the gods, whose feathery 'eyes' represented her eternal watchfulness, and the plumes against which she — and Maat in Egypt— measured the hearts of men. And this 'watchful' aspect, of course, relates back to the Mirror.

"Thus, the Queen is unmistakably identified with and as the Great Goddess or Divine Mother, here reduced in stature to a mortal woman, and isolated from Her consort, the Divine King.

"Now, Her destructive selfishness is not part of Her nature, but is caused by Her isolation. In the absence of the Divine Will of the King, the Queen is left with no purpose outside of Her self, and thus seeks to perfect substance or Her form of appearance.

"Thus, the portrayal of the Queen as dark, destructive, and selfish is, in a sense, accurate, but only because She has been divorced from Her Divine Spouse by ignorance and polarization.

"The greatest danger in this situation is that The Mother *believes* it! As we discussed earlier, for thousands of years now the Divine Child —humanity— has been identifying substance as the source of evil. We have, in fact, so thoroughly impressed the substance of the astral, physical-etheric, and physical-dense planes with the thought-form that 'substance is evil', that substance has been thoroughly programmed with that thought, and behaves accordingly. The forms with which we work *believe* that they are evil, and therefore resist any contrary idea or thought.

"Thus, every creative effort of the initiate, every working of the creative process, must take into account the active resistance of substance. Substance must be redeemed, not because it's evil, but because we, as ignorant children of the One Life, told it that it's evil.

"So, that's our job, not just to free ourselves, but to redeem the Mother and reunite our Divine Parents. Which brings us back to the two central characters of the tale, Snow White and Prince Charming.

Prince Charming

"Prince Charming is, of course, the Divine Son or external Magnetic Field of Divinity. He is here presented —in deleted scenes— as being imprisoned by the Queen in the dungeons of the Castle, from which he escapes. While the imprisonment was symbolically correct, his escape was not. In a symbolically correct version the Princess and Prince would seek each other out, the Princess would rescue the Prince from his underworld prison, and they would ascend to Heaven as equals."

Colette: "Snow White would rescue the Prince?"

Snow White

Quinn: "Not necessarily the character Snow White, but the Daughter 'rescues' the Son. Or, more accurately, after the Son moves down into, identifies with, and becomes trapped within Substance the Daughter is responsible for the upward movement that frees the consciousness or Soul.

"The character of Snow White represents that Divine Daughter or inner Magnetic Field of Divinity. However, here she is misrepresented as the one rescued from the chest or tomb of substance, rather than the rescuer. Again, this is a patriarchal distortion which —as we have seen— neutralizes the creative process. In order

432

for the magical process to work, the 'Princess' must rescue the 'Prince'.

"Tess?"

Tess: "What about the Seven Dwarves?"

The Seven Dwarves

"Ah... We'll, they're an odd case. They're not really individuals. In the original story, each of the Dwarves had their own mine, in which they dug for a particular jewel. They took turns working the mines, working together in one on Sunday, in another on Monday, etc.

"We get another clue to their identity in the words of the Mirror, when he described where Snow White is hiding, (Quinn consulted his notes, and read:) 'Over the seven jeweled hills, beyond the seven falls, in the cottage of the seven dwarves, dwells Snow White, fairest one of all.'

"So, we have seven different jewels, each in their own hill, with their own waterfall, all living together in a cottage. Does this sound familiar?

"Celine?"

Celine: "The Seven Centers."

Quinn: "Yes. Each of the Dwarves represents the spark of consciousness at the heart of one of the Seven Centers or Chakras. Their dwelling place is the house in the underworld in which the Soul 'dies' and within which it is eventually resurrected. Of course, in order to be resurrected, the Soul incarnate in that dwelling must clean and purify it, activating, clarifying, and bringing each of the centers to full functionality. Only then can the Daughter and Son be reunited.

"This union occurs in the cave in the center of the head, when all Seven Centers are lifted into their higher correspondences in the head, and become negative or receptive to the place of magic or cave center. The two

Poles of the Soul are then united, when, following a moment of absolute silence, each pole sounds its portion of the creative word —AUM and OM— in complete harmony, and AUOM sounds forth.

"This moment would be portrayed in our present tale by the reunited song of the Prince and Princess.

"Ed?"

Ed: "So, which Dwarf is which center?"

Quinn: "Ah... Well, to determine that we have to look at their attributes.

(Quinn stood, faced the board, and began writing next to the list of characters.)

"Let's see... There were Doc, Grumpy, Sleepy, Dopey..."

Me: "Bashful, Sneezy, and Happy"

Quinn: "Right."

"OK, now others might do this differently, but what condition do we say the Soul is when it's in incarnation?"

Celine: "'Dead' to itself or asleep."

Quinn: "Yes! So Sleepy would be the crown center, the center within which a spark of consciousness sleeps until the time of awakening. Now this is supported by the fact that when the animals ran to fetch the Dwarves —to rescue the Princess from the Witch— it was Sleepy who realized what was going on. That's because the crown or head center is the center of spiritual intuition in the body.

"Next, I would suggest that Dopey represents the unintegrated, and therefore disorganized and confused, ajna center. While the fully developed ajna center is the central, controlling chakra for the entire persona, in its early development it's subject to the conflicting impulses of the mental, astral, and physical instruments, and thus unable to organize any of them.

"Doc, of course, is the throat center. Remember, it's his job to assess the jewels via sound, which is a function of the throat. He's also the 'voice of reason' within the group, who tries to be its leader, but is never able to control the feelings and impulses of the group.

"Happy would be the heart center, always at-one or balanced with the environment —except when overwhelmed by the others.

"Sneezy is the solar plexus, the center of the lower emotions whose cyclic explosions of astral force throw everything into chaos.

"Bashful would be the sacral center, the center of procreation whose activity gives rise to self-awareness."

Terry: "Isn't that the solar plexus?"

Quinn: "One would think so, but look at the recapitulation process. An infant achieves self-awareness — is able to look in the mirror and recognize itself— at around age two, when they're still a bundle of appetites. The solar plexus doesn't start to unfold for another four or five years.

"Grumpy would be the base or kundalini center."

Wil: "Grumpy?"

Quinn: "Yes. While the flow of kundalini up the spine stimulates and awakens the other centers, the kundalini center itself is the last to be awakened. It forms a functioning polarity with the crown center when all the centers between them are activated and open, the crown is awake, and energy is flowing freely from crown to base and back. In the meantime you have — symbolically, in our fairy tale— Grumpy, whose every action depends on, but is frustrated by, his brethren.

"Is that clear?

The Witch

"OK, moving on, we have the witch, who, of course,

represents the third or crone aspect of the Mother. She is Wisdom, the black-veiled Goddess of Death who brings rebirth. In a balanced representation, this deity would be portrayed as implacable, but ultimately benevolent. Of course, that was not possible in the masculine-polarized, form-identified world of the mid-twentieth century.

"However, we must always keep in mind that the polarization of those times —which is slowly giving way— brought about necessary growth and development, however painfully. We cannot reject that polarization without both undermining the foundation of our next step, and mis-directing ourselves toward an equally painful fixation on the opposite pole."

The Symbols

Quinn: "OK, let's look at the symbols. The story has a lot of them, but we've already looked at some. Let's see... We have the Wishing Well, the Castles, the cottage, mines, lightning..."

Wil: "Prayer and the Witch's branch or staff."

Quinn: "OK."

Tess: "The black forest, and the crystal coffin."

Quinn: "Yes..."

Ema: "The vultures, the crow, and the sleeping death."

Thea: "The Wishing Well and the other birds, the doves, owls, and peacock."

Quinn: "We've already covered some... We'll see. El?"

Me: "The corn, owls, rabbits or hares, and the Queen's symbol thingy."

Quinn: "Coat of arms?"

Me: "Yes."

Quinn: "Anything else?

Birds

"OK, let's see... Birds... Well, the ability of birds to ascend above the earth made them a potent symbol of transcendence. Their beautiful voices and tendency to dwell in trees often made them the symbolic messengers of tree spirits. Some birds, such as doves, owls, crows, and vultures, had more specific symbolic associations due to their habits, appearance, behavior, etc.

"The black crow that accompanies the Queen in the underworld, and observes her transformation into the Witch —partially from inside a skull— is sacred to the Goddess of Death or of the Underworld, the crone aspect of the Great Mother. Thus, its presence in that time and place reinforces our previous identification of the Witch.

"Doves surround Princess Snow White in her opening scene, in which she washes the lowest step of the castle and sings into the Wishing Well. Later in the scene, after she flees from the Prince into the castle, a dove serves as her messenger to the Prince, delivering a kiss.

"In Christianity, the Dove is the symbol of the Holy Ghost —Espiritu Sanctu, or Shekhina, who is actually the Divine Mother— and a messenger of Divine Will. The dove also often represented the Third or Mother Aspect in the ancient mystery traditions. (Consulting his notes) The dove was associated with those procreative female divinities who gave birth to the material world. It was sacred to Aphrodite, Astarte, Cybele, Isis, Venus, Mylitta, and was a symbol of wisdom.[2]

"Thus, in 'Snow White', the Doves are the messengers of the Divine Mother, and the fact that one delivers a message for the Princess indicates that Snow White

---

[2] Quinn: See: *The Secret Teachings of All Ages*, by Manly Palmer Hall, p. LXXXIX

sometimes represents one of the three attributes of the Goddess —the Virgin. This is a product of conflation, the combination of one aspect or attribute of divinity with another. In this case, the 'weakened' feminine aspects of Daughter and Virgin are partly combined into a single character.

"Another bird, the owl, appears both in the night-dark forest and in carved relief in the cottage. The owl was sacred to the Goddess as the Lady of Wisdom who ruled the night. Its appearance in the forest indicated that Snow White was descending to the underworld. Its appearance as carved decorations in the cottage indicated that Snow White had arrived in her underworld dwelling.

"The Queen's throne was framed by a peacock, with its magnificent tail feathers spread in a circle around the seated Queen. The peacock was an ancient object of veneration because it killed poisonous snakes. It was also an emblem of Pride, of Immortality —because it resembled and was often confused with the phoenix, and because it was believed that the body of a dead peacock did not decay —and of Wisdom— because of the many eyes on its tail feathers.

"The prideful nature of the Queen emphasizes the 'pride' aspect of this symbol.

"The vulture is a symbol of the transmutation of substance. This transmutation includes:

"The death of the body,

"Raising of the substance of the body to a higher state, and

"Liberating the self or soul from the coffin of form in which it had dwelt.

"Two vultures would represent the Divine Mother as a polarity, twin sisters representing the descent of the Goddess into Form —birthing the Self in the world of affairs— and the ascent of the Goddess to Heaven — liberating the Soul. In the Egyptian system, Nepthys and Isis represent this polarity of the Mother and were often portrayed with vultures' wings.

"Thus, the two vultures —who presumably consume the body of the dead Witch— actually represent the transmutation of gross matter into Light, a process which liberates the Soul from the form and raises it to Heaven. The Black Queen thus becomes the Heavenly Light or Sun, her earthly dwelling becomes a heavenly castle, and the Soul —Snow White and Prince Charming— dwell in Her paradise.

The Black Forest

"The black forest is the same forest in which Myrrha —the mother of Adonis— was turned into a tree, and the sea of reeds via which Osiris descended into the world. It represents the etheric network as the instrument by which the Divine Son incarnates in form — although in this case the Son is mis-portrayed as a Daughter.

"The branch or staff which the Queen uses to lever the boulder toward the Dwarves represents Susumna, the central nadi or etheric-energy channel of the spine. The boulder is the pineal gland, which is located in the center of the head and is associated with the cave center. The incident in which the Queen is 'destroyed' represents the moment when the kundalini, moving up the spinal nadi, encounters the downward moving light of the Soul in the cave in the center of the head. Symbolically speaking, the 'stone' blocking the cave is rolled aside and the Overshadowing Soul and incarnate soul become One.

"At that point the Queen 'dies' as the consciousness awakens and makes the transition from the unconscious cyclic motion of the form, to the conscious creative activity of the Soul.

The Castles

"The two castles represent both two conditions of substance and two states of indwelling consciousness.

"The Castle on Earth, which is ruled by the Divine Mother but ordered by her Henchmen, the Three Ruffians of the Mental, Astral, and Physical-Etheric Planes, represents the Earthly Kingdom of the three lower worlds.

"The Castle in the Sky appears in the final scene, in which Prince Charming walks and Princess Snow White rides off into the sunset, and a heavenly castle. This castle represents the Heavenly Kingdom —purified or raised Substance— ruled by the Divine Father, to which Prince Charming is taking Princess Snow White. This is, of course, a reversal of the actual process, as the ascent or upward movement is governed by the Daughter, and thus She raises the Son.

"The similarity in appearance of the two castles suggests that they may in fact be the same structure, united by the union of the Daughter–Son. This would be symbolically accurate, as following that union the lower castle does, in fact, become a direct reflection of the heavenly castle.

Coat of Arms

"Now the Queen's royal coat of arms appears above Her throne, on the breast of the peacock. It consists of a shield divided into four squares. On the upper left and repeated in the lower right is a radiant golden sun with a three-pointed crown centered over it. On the upper right and repeated in the lower left is a serpent.

"The radiant golden sun represents the Divine King, the Father Aspect of Divinity.

"The three-pointed crown centered over the sun represents the reign of the Divine King and the three attributes of the Father.

"The serpent represents the winding energy of the Divine Queen.

"The repeated symbols represent the balance of the Divine Father and Divine Mother both above and below, or transcendent and eminent.

The Cottage

"As for the Cottage, like our earlier Temple of Solomon, the front porch or entrance of the cottage is held up or supported by two vertical beams or squared columns. This, plus its setting and inhabitants, clearly identifies the Cottage as the underworld dwelling place of the fallen Child; the persona instrument. It is equivalent to the palace or temple of our earlier myths, and the upper room where Snow White sleeps represents the head, while the lower room where the Dwarves sleep, during her stay, represents the lower persona instrument.

"The cottage itself contains a number of symbols, including rabbits or hares, and ears of corn or grain.

"The Rabbits or Hares are a symbol of the fertility of the Goddess, and thus of the Goddess herself. The appearance of this symbol throughout the cottage balances the accompanying symbol of the Owl, indicating that the cottage is the place in which the self *lives* when it dies to its true nature.

"The banister and landing at the top of the stairs in the cottage include reliefs of an ear of corn, another ancient symbol of the Goddess, commonly associated with initiation rites.

Crystal Coffin

The Crystal Coffin is the same chest or box that appeared in our earlier myths. As before, it represents the three-fold persona—body, emotions, and mind.

"As I mentioned earlier, the 'seven jeweled hills' with seven waterfalls represent the system of seven major centers or chakras. The 'hills' are the centers, the 'falls' the chakras or vortexes, and the dwarves are the intelligences that indwell each center.

"Lightning is a traditional weapon of the Divine Father. It appears twice in our story. First, when the Queen calls it to mix her disguise potion. Second, when it strikes and cracks the crag on which she's standing, flinging the Queen to her death. In both cases, it represents the descending Will of the transcendent Father, impressing on and shattering crystallized form.

"Now, as I mentioned earlier, those are not the only instances in which the transcendent 'Father' or King appears. When Snow White performs her bedtime prayers, those prayers are, by implication, addressed to the Divine Father. This represents the ascent of the Daughter to the Father that precedes the fall of the Divine Child and the Child's entrapment in the chest or entombment in the coffin.

"Just look at what Snow White asks for, and what happens. Her prayers, her 'wish' at the Well, her wish to the apple. It all leads directly to her 'death' and awakening.

"In this context, the 'Sleeping Death' represents the loss of self or 'death of the Soul' via incarnation in and identification with a persona instrument. In the tale, the circumstances of the Spell of the Sleeping Death make it clear that the stated intentions of the Queen are not her true motivations, for her supposed goal of regaining her position as the 'Most beautiful in the land' *could not* possibly be gained by the chosen solution.

"The Queen made herself ugly, with no plan for reversing the process.

"Snow White would not be destroyed by the spell, but *preserved*.

"Thus, in the context of the Queen's stated goal, the method used makes no sense whatever, as it *could not* achieve the stated goal. In fact, it led directly to the exact opposite!

"However, it does make sense if we recall that the Queen's personal character is a Piscean patriarchal shroud over a matriarchal myth. If we ignore her distorted character, and look instead at the results of the Queen's actions, her true motivations become clear.

"The Queen created the circumstances that brought Snow White and Prince Charming together. She sent both the Prince and Princess into the otherworld, forcing the Prince to go —down— in quest of the Princess while the Princess prayed —aspired upward— to be found by the Prince. She arranged to preserve the Princess' beauty in a manner that sacrificed herself and enabled the Prince to discover the sleeping Snow White.

"The Queen *forced* them into it, and sacrificed herself to do so! Thus, the true hero of the tale is the Queen, for she sacrificed everything in order to bring about the union of the Daughter and Son, that union which must occur before the Queen can be reunited with the King!

The Wishing Well

"In the ancient mysteries, wells sometimes represented doorways into the otherworld, the world of the fey. Thus, Snow White's wish-song to the castle's Wishing Well represented the preparation for her descent to the underworld, for the purpose of achieving union with her polar self, the Prince or Divine Son.

"In effect, the Queen —who was watching from a castle window— was merely fulfilling Snow White's wish for re-union by the only means possible, by arranging the descent into, life within, and ascent from the otherworld.

The Meaning

Quinn: "The tale of Prince Charming and Snow White contains all the essential elements of the initiation process—descent into form, death, ascent, and at-one-ment. Thus the one true path lives on, portrayed once again for a new people in another time and place, as an animated film beloved by adults and children alike.

"In our next and final meeting, we will summarize our discoveries, and outline once again the magical process of Raising the Queen of Heaven. But first, we'll close in the usual fashion."

444

Descent

Sit in a comfortable chair, relax your physical body, calm your emotions, and focus your mind.

Bring your consciousness to a point of focus within your ajna center, and there integrate your three-fold persona —body, emotions, and mind— into a single unit.

From your place within the ajna center, identify with and as your spiritual group, and align with the Purpose, Power, and Will of God.

Imagine that your group has, as a unit, realized some portion of the Divine Purpose which you all share. Then, project that Purpose downward, into the world, via the group mental, astral, and physical-etheric instrument, and through that instrument on into the world of affairs, by audibly stating the seed-thought:

"As the Soul, I precipitate Divine Will into my energy, force, and substance via my mind."

Without thinking about it or repeating it, allow the vibration of that thought to sound through the group instrument. Continue listening to and feeling that vibration until all is still and quiet, then, audibly sound the OM.

Take a deep breath, open your eyes, and return your awareness to your surroundings.

"Practice this inner ritual at least once a day, every day, for a full lunar cycle (from New Moon to New Moon).

"Take what you have learned out into the world and apply it in service to the One Life."

Raising the Queen of Heaven

Afterword

Raising the Queen of Heaven

Everyone was up and chatting, but immediately quieted and sat down when Quinn entered. He gazed around at everyone, smiling and nodding, and then said, "Well, are you ready? We'll begin as usual."

I pushed the button.

Opening Alignment

Quinn: "Bring your consciousness to a point of focus within the ajna center, and there integrate the group energy, force, and substance. (Pause)

"Along a line of golden-white light, slowly move upward into the crown center, and there identify as the Group Soul. (Pause)

"As the Group Soul in the crown center, turn your attention upward to that Wisdom overshadowing this course, and become receptive to it by silently sounding the OM. (Pause)

"Maintaining that focus of receptivity, move back down the line of light into the ajna. (Pause)

"Maintaining that focus of receptivity in the ajna, draw a line of light from the ajna to the physical-dense brain of the group, and audibly sound the OM.

"Take a deep breath, and slowly open your eyes."

Afterword

Quinn: "OK. During this course we've studied the movement, the magical motion of consciousness that creates everything that is.

"As we've seen, the Soul of humanity is moving through the great cycle of the Zodiac, and by that movement, relating and re-uniting the Two Poles of Divinity. This is the function of humanity in the One Life.

"However, in order to re-unite everything that is, we had first to achieve separation, to isolate our selves as individual entities that could focus on the manifold forms of the One Life, in order to bring every thing back to the One Life, so that no thing would be overlooked.

"Each turn of the Celestial Wheel, each sub-cycle of consciousness within the Wheel, and each new Age, brings us closer to the realization of our purpose. This motion is reflected in the rites and myths of the Ancient Mysteries, and in the unfoldment of human consciousness in new ideas, thoughts, feelings, and modes of behavior.

"Every new Age changes the motion of the Wheel, refocusing human consciousness, the Mysteries, and the myths that reflected the Mysteries. Thus, through the unfolding ages we slowly move outward, downward, inward, upward and back, in a continuing cycle of transforming relationships.

"Through the last four ages, we've slowly moved from species identity, into individuality, and are now moving into that group awareness that includes individuality and species.

Gemini

"Gazing back through the intervening ages, we

449

glimpsed shades of the Age of Gemini, dim remnants of a time when the Poles were represented by Divine Twins, a duality separated by the balance of Life and Death.

"Those shades included Pollux and Helen, Shu and Tefnut, Lal and Nin Ezen Gu, the Asvins, and Yin and Yang. These Divine Twins portrayed the motion of consciousness in Gemini, when the Two Poles of Spirit and Substance were balanced yet separated by Life and Death.

"The Twins portrayed a time when our awareness was much broader, more tribal or communal, long before the individual awareness achieved in Pisces.

Taurus

"Then came the Age of Taurus, and the descent from the Positive Pole or Divine Father toward the Negative Pole or Divine Mother. The attention of the descending Soul or Divine Son turned towards the Great Mother and Her rites ruled the Mysteries.

"We found this downward motion of the Son emphasized in the Taurus myths of Inanna and Dumuzi, Isis and Osiris, and Eve and Adam.

"They represented a time when our awareness was narrowing, becoming increasingly focused on the cycles of nature and on immediate tribal forms.

Aries

"With the Age of Aries, the Soul of Humanity moved into and identified with the Negative Pole or Divine Mother. The cycles of Substance ruled humanity as we identified with our forms. Having thereby lost itself in the form, the attention of the incarnate Soul turned to the cyclic motion of Mother Nature, and the rites of sacrifice ruled the Mysteries.

"And, again, we found that motion of the Soul por-

450

trayed in the myths of that Age—Sarai and Avram, Asherah and YHWH, and Moses and Zipporah.

"They portrayed a time when our awareness became trapped in and limited by the individual form or persona, stimulating the growth and development of individual identity.

Pisces

"Then came the Age of Pisces, and the ascent from the Negative Pole —or the abstraction of consciousness from the three lower worlds— toward the Positive Pole or Divine Father. The attention of the ascending Soul or Divine Daughter turned toward the Great Father and His rites ruled the Mysteries.

"Thus, the upward motion or ascent of consciousness was emphasized in the myths of Pisces, including Demeter and Persephone, Orpheus and Eurydice, Mary and Jesus, the Matronit and YHWH, Hiram Abiff, and Snow White and Prince Charming.

"Here we found an age when individual awareness, and the ability to focus narrowly and specifically, reached its height.

Aquarius

"We have now entered the Age of Aquarius or Synthesis. Our consciousness has begun to recognize itself as the Divine Daughter–Son, whose task —represented in the rites and Mysteries of *this* Age— is to reunite the Two Poles of Divinity, the Divine Mother–Father.

"In this Age we are moving from individual awareness into group identity, a group identity that includes within it the individual awareness of every member of the group, thereby creating a state of awareness in which we will, when we look into a mirror, simultaneously see our species, our individual self, *and* our group. This is the next step ahead of us as humanity.

"Each of us contributes to this Great Work as we bring about union within our selves —within each instrument of our persona— the physical-dense, physical-etheric, astral/emotional, and mental—of the persona as a whole, of the Soul, and of our Spirit, Soul, and Substance. This inner union is brought about by the practice of inner rituals of at-one-ment, and the expression or embodiment of the realization gained in those rituals in the outer world of affairs.

"In these new rituals, the emphasis will no longer be on one of the motions of consciousness, but will be on working the inner magical process as a whole.

"The rituals of the ages of Gemini, Taurus, Aries, and Pisces took place in the outer world. There, initiates to the ancient mysteries performed complex ceremonies designed to take the candidate through a symbolic experience of a portion of the path of spiritual growth and development. However, this will not be the method in the Age of Aquarius.

"The primary energy of this new age is that of ceremonial magic, and thus all the old forms of ritual magic are being stimulated into activity and re-discovered by humanity. However, the motion of the consciousness through the past ages has been part of a long, upward spiral —upward toward re-union, and upward in frequency.

"Thus, the frequency of those old rituals does not quite suit humanity today. The energy of this Aquarian Age is higher than any we have previously experienced, and the quality is that of the Soul rather than the form. Thus, the magic of this age is the inner creative ritual, the magic, of the consciousness, and the emphasis will be on the entire process, not any one portion of it.

"We are moving from the outer rituals to the inner, from the magic of form to the magic of consciousness.

Afterword

This is a new experience, a new path, which is still being explored. The inner rituals of this new path are still being formulated, and its outer myths have yet to be written.

"At this point, we know that this magic uses the inner motion of consciousness to raise the form, and the uplifting of the form to raise the consciousness, in repeating cycles of ascent, at-one-ment, descent, at-one-ment, leading towards and finally to re-union.

"In the inner rituals up to this point, we have practiced portions of this magical cycle, preparing ourselves for the practice of the complete ritual.

"And now, in our final exercise in this class, we will perform a complete ritual, invoking whatever is overshadowing as our next step into appearance in the mental, astral, and physical-etheric realms, and into the outer world of affairs.

"Is everyone ready? Then let's begin…"

The Magic of Consciousness

Quinn: As the Daughter, bring your consciousness to a point of focus within the ajna center, and there integrate the group energy, force, and substance into a single unit, a single group persona. (Pause)

Along a line of golden-white light, slowly move back from the Ajna into the cave in the center of the head, and there integrate the group consciousness—the 'I will to be", the 'I am', and the 'I create'—into a single unit. (Pause)

Tighten the focus in the cave to a tiny point of indigo-white light. (Pause)

As the Group Soul in the cave, turn your attention upward in frequency, through the crown center, to the Overshadowing Spiritual Soul of the group. (Pause).

Identify with and as the Group Soul, and thereby become receptive to its Divine Purpose, Power, and Will. (Pause)

As the Son in the cave, invoke that Divine Intent downward, into the group cave, by silently sounding the OM. (Pause)

As the Son in the cave, radiate that Divine Intent outward through the ajna to the group mental energy by audibly sounding the *OM*. (Pause)

As the Son in the cave, radiate that Divine Intent outward through the ajna to the group astral force by audibly sounding the *OM*. (Pause)

As the Son in the cave, radiate that Divine Intent

outward through the ajna to the group physical-etheric substance and physical-dense brain by audibly sounding the *OM*. (Pause)

Recognize that the energy, force, and substance of the three lower worlds will respond to that focus of intent, and that their response will be reflected as appearance, as shape and form, in the world of affairs. (Pause)

Slowly relax your attention, return to your normal focus, take a deep breath, and open your eyes. (Very long pause)

✦

"Well... That's it for this course. I suggest you continue practicing this technique for an entire lunar cycle, beginning at the next New Moon.

"In our next class, we'll explore the *Magic of Consciousness*, and continue experiencing and building the new path together.

"In the meantime, thank you all for coming.

"May the Lady bless you, and the Lord keep you,

may the Daughter lift her countenance unto you,

and may the Son give you peace. Aoum..."

(The class joined in the "Aoum!" and, after it had faded to silence, they stood and stretched and amid hugs and quiet murmurs, filed out of the library.)

Raising the Queen of Heaven

Lesson 1 Addendum[1]

The Zero

The common medieval European method of calculating sums used "counters" (coin-size pieces of metal, wood, or bone) on a "counting table" (a table with columns drawn on or inlaid into it, much like a page in an accounting book or program). The system underwent many changes over the centuries, but in a simple form the right hand column represented "ones", the next column to the left represented "tens", the next to the left "hundreds", the next "thousands", and so on (if one was working in a base-ten system, which was not always the case). Thus, if one had five counters in the first column, none in the second, and five in the third, one had five hundreds and five (505). If you then added six to the first column, making eleven, you took away ten counters from the first column, leaving one, and added one counter to the second column, indicating five hundreds and one ten and one (511).

This method of calculating sums was gradually replaced with "calculating with a quill" (written calculations using Arabic numerals). In the process, it was necessary to find a symbol for empty columns. Otherwise, five hundreds and five was written as 5 5, which could easily be mistaken for five tens and five (55). Originally this space-holding symbol was a circle (representing a counter) with a line struck through it "Ø", indicating that that counter was a mere space holder and was not to be counted. Thus, five hundreds and five was written as 5Ø5, or the modern 505. See: *Number Words and Number Symbols*, by Karl Menninger.

---

[1] Quinn: In light of the class discussions (the exact contents of which I could not know ahead of time) I've revised the original "handouts" a bit to create these Addendums.

Lesson 4 Addendum

The Seven Planes

The Seventh Plane

The main point to keep in mind is that the vibratory frequency of each plane gives its substance features unique to that plane. The slower the rate of vibration, the denser the substance, and the less malleable the forms created out of that substance.

Like the others, the seventh plane has seven sub-planes. The three densest portions or sub-planes of the seventh plane vibrate at an extremely low rate, producing very dense forms with characteristics not found anywhere else. These three dense sub-planes are known as the physical-dense world of affairs.

The Physical-Dense World of Affairs

The world of affairs is unique in that forms made of this frequency of substance can appear to be separate or disconnected from other forms. This occurs when forms have a distinct surface, beyond which they do not appear to exist. This appearance of separation, created by a distinct surface, does not occur in forms made of other qualities of substance.

The physical-dense consists of the three lowest sub-planes of the seventh plane, and includes all the forms of matter that our physical-dense bodies can see, hear, smell, touch, or taste. These three sub-planes, include:

Solid Sub-plane: This is the seventh sub-plane of the seventh plane.

- The densest portion of the densest plane.
- Solid forms have a distinct surface.
- Of the trinity of Substance, appearance predominates in the physical-solid sub-plane.
- It is a reflection of the Physical-Etheric sub-planes (the four sub-planes immediately above the three physical-dense).

Liquid Sub-plane: This is the sixth sub-plane of the seventh plane.

- Of the trinity of Substance, activity predominates in the physical-liquid sub-plane.
- Liquid forms often have a distinct surface.
- It is a reflection of the Astral-Emotional plane.

Gaseous Sub-plane: This is the fifth sub-plane of the seventh plane.

- Of the trinity of Substance, potential predominates in the physical-gaseous sub-plane.
- Gaseous forms often do not have a distinct surface.
- It is a reflection of the Mental plane.

The Physical-Etheric Plane

As mentioned above, the physical-etheric is often symbolically represented as the Virgin. The Physical-Etheric Plane consists of the four highest sub-planes of the seventh plane. In these four sub-planes:

- Appearance predominates.
- Forms made of the substance of this plane do not have a distinct surface, but radiate and blend into their environment.
- The element of esoteric earth or light predominates.

The physical-etheric body consists of substance that vibrates more rapidly than physical-dense, but less rapidly than the substance of the emotional body.

The forms of this plane are the underlying network or blueprint of all physical-dense forms, including the human body.

The Astral/Emotional Plane

Again, the astral is often symbolically represented by the Mother of the Negative-Pole trinity. The astral/emotional plane consists of substance that vibrates more rapidly than physical-etheric substance, but less rapidly than mental substance. It consists of Substance in which:

- Force or activity predominates.
- Forms made of astral substance do not have a distinct surface, but radiate and blend into their environment.
- The element of esoteric water or vibration predominates.

Astral substance is vitalized by and attracted to thoughts. When a thought is directed into astral substance, that portion of the astral which vibrates in sympathy with the thought is attracted to the thought, and forms a body of astral force around the thought. This force is the activity that moves the thought downward into appearance in physical-etheric and physical-dense form. Thus, all physical-dense forms must have their astral/emotional correspondent, or they could not exist. Also, every thought must have its astral/emotional correspondent or it could not be perceived or processed by the physical-dense brain.

In order for this process to work properly, the force or astral waters of the emotional body must be clean, clear, and available. Difficulty arises when:

- The astral body is formed of the dark and sluggish waters of the lower sub-planes of the astral. The astral body is then slow to respond to thought and its substance veils and distorts those thoughts to which it does respond.
- The incarnate self or Soul identifies with its emotional feelings (i.e., I feel X). Because of that identification, the self retains the temporary emotional feelings making them permanent astral forms. This limits both the amount and the frequency range of available force. The result is a debilitated astral body that can react only through its pre-programmed emotions (i.e., when someone does X, I feel Y).
- The incarnate self rejects its emotional feelings as an impediment, either to the proper function of the mind and/or to the mental realization of the Positive Aspect of Divinity. This denies the divinity of emotional feelings, the cuts the thinker off from much of the force of the astral body, and therefore limits their ability to manifest thought in the world of affairs.

Each of the above is a normal part of the development of the astral instrument. However, in order to "Raise the Queen of Heaven", one must rise beyond them. The Mother must be accepted, purified, and left free to respond to the Wisdom of the Crone. This can only be accomplished through appropriate inner and outer ritual.

The Mental Plane

As mentioned previously, the mental plane is often represented by the Crone. The mental plane consists of substance that vibrates more rapidly than emotional substance, but less rapidly than the substance of the Buddhic Plane. It consists of Substance in which:

- Energy or potential predominates.
- Forms made of mental substance do not have a distinct surface, but radiate and blend into their environment.
- The element of esoteric fire or color predominates.

An organized collection of mental substance is a thought-form. The mind uses thought-forms much as computers use programs. A thought-form is intent, translated into a complex pattern of mental activity. Thus, the thinking mind is processing a thought-form.

The Buddhic Plane

The buddhic plane consists of substance that vibrates more rapidly than mental substance. The plane on which the higher self or Spiritual Soul dwells, it consists of Substance in which:

- The element of esoteric air or sound predominates.
- Organized patterns of buddhic substance lie above the realm of persona experience.

An organized body of buddhic substance is an idea, or the archetype of a thing.

The Four Higher Planes

The four planes above the Buddhic exist beyond the range of human experience, and little can or needs to be said about them here. It is enough to know that they exist.

Lesson 5 Addendum

The Subtle Bodies

Although we are all familiar with the physical-dense body, most of us are little aware of the more subtle bodies symbolized by the chest and by the temple. Since everything that exists is a reflection or formulation of the Trinity, and must be three things, then the chest or persona must also be three things.

As mentioned above, the three aspects of the persona are its:

- Positive pole or mental body
- Magnetic field or astral body
- Negative pole or physical-etheric body

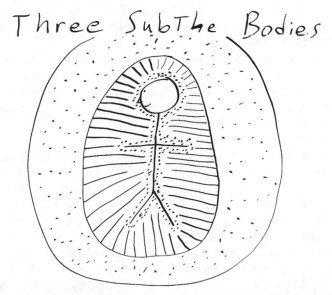

This is the polarity that traps Tammuz/Adonis or Osiris / Horus when he descends into matter, and through which he achieves liberation during the ascent to Spirit.

Each of these bodies is built of the substance of the corresponding plane, and each body has unique characteristics and abilities. These bodies can either support at-one-ment, or work against it, depending on the intent of the indwelling Soul and the programming of the body.

The Physical-Dense Body

The physical-dense brain and body are designed and intended to:

- Begin the process of relating the Intelligent Activity of Substance to the Father.
- This is accomplished in the Ascent process by relaxing the physical-dense body, leaving it receptive and ready to respond to a higher impression.
- Express Divine Intent in the world of affairs via intelligent activity

This is accomplished in the Descent process by relating and impressing the realization gained in the high point on the receptive physical body. The physical-dense body responds with an intelligent activity that creates a form of appearance for the new thought.

The physical-dense body is made out of physical solid, liquid, and gaseous substance, and is, therefore, in itself a trinity. However, it is not properly a part of the "persona" because it is merely a reflection of the creative activity of the mental, emotional, and physical-etheric bodies.

In order for the creative work to proceed properly, the physical-dense body should be in good health and free of all non-prescription drugs (including alcohol and marijuana).

In this context, being drug free is not a moral judgment. The inner and outer rituals that liberate the Soul and unite the Poles are designed to unfold the consciousness and transform the persona in a particular way. Indiscriminate drug use is not compatible with this transformative process. Mixing the inner ritual with drugs will produce unpredictable, possibly harmful results. Thus, we encourage you to avoid all recreational drug use.

If you use psychoactive drugs, then do not practice any of the meditations in this book. You may get away with using nicotine or caffeine, but anything stronger would be a *very dangerous* combination.

The Physical-Etheric Body

The energy body that underlies and forms the outline of the physical-dense body is technically known as the physical-etheric body. The electrical currents that flow through our nerves and brain are the densest portions of this body. The physical-etheric body is the underlying structure of, and is causative to, the physical-dense body.

The fact that the physical-etheric is causative to the physical-dense is demonstrated by the growth of nerves in a fetus. The electrical current flowing through the growing nerve actually precedes the developing nerve tissue.

- The physical-etheric body forms the underlying structure of the physical-dense instrument.
- The densest portion of the physical-etheric, the bio-electric current, follows pathways laid down by the more subtle levels of the physical-etheric instrument.
- The nerve growth follows the bio-electric pathways.
- This causality is equally true of the other structures of the physical-dense body, although the mechanism is a bit different.

The physical-etheric consists of substance that vibrates more rapidly than physical-dense matter, but less rapidly than the substance of the emotional body. The physical-etheric body is shaped roughly like the physical-dense body, and although it interpenetrates the other bodies, it extends beyond the physical-dense body three or more inches.

A clue to the nature of this body is found in the reports of near death experiences. First, a subtle energy body emerges out of our physical-dense body. It may view its physical-dense surroundings for a time, finding that while it can touch itself (and is, therefore, a body of substance), it passes through physical-dense forms (walls, ceilings, doors, etc.).

At some point, the discarnating consciousness passes through a tunnel of light. On the other side of that tunnel, the consciousness finds itself on the more subtle physical-etheric plane. The physical-dense realm is no longer visible, and time and space are quite different.

Thus, we have a subtle energy body, which, during life, interpenetrates and dwells within the physical-dense body, forming part of the overall persona or mask of the incarnate soul.

The inner and outer rituals that transform the physical-etheric body into part of the temple should:

- At least begin the process of cleansing and gaining conscious control over the physical-etheric body.
- Transform this body from a source of personal appetites into a refined instrument that gives appearance to Divine Intent.

This work must be well on its way before the chest is transmuted into a temple.

The Astral/Emotional Body

The emotional body consists of substance that vibrates more rapidly than physical-etheric substance, but less rapidly than mental substance. This body is oval in shape, and although it interpenetrates the other bodies, it may extend beyond the physical-dense body by as much as eighteen inches.

When the physical-dense body dies, the discarnating consciousness passes through a tunnel of light and finds itself on the astral plane and in the astral/emotional body. The consciousness or soul has withdrawn from both the physical-dense and physical-etheric bodies, and those forms will now begin to disintegrate.

Thus, the astral body is a subtle body of force that, during incarnation, interpenetrates and dwells within the physical-dense and physical-etheric bodies, forming part of the overall persona or mask of the incarnate soul.

The inner and outer rituals that transform the astral

body into part of the temple should:

- Begin the process of cleansing and directing the astral body.
- Transform this body from a source of emotional desire into a clean and clear pool of force that is ready to fuel Divine Intent.

This work must be well on its way before the chest is transmuted into a temple.

When the incarnate consciousness is identified with its emotional body, the persona is the chest or trap of the Soul. The consciousness is then, in effect, saying, "I am what I feel". By identifying with and as the emotions, the incarnate consciousness limits itself to the abilities of the emotional body. It cannot perceive, identify with, or act as either its mind or overshadowing Spiritual Soul.

Before the Soul can liberate itself, the chest must become the temple. The astral body must be transformed from a trap into an instrument of self-awareness and spiritual union.

This transformation is accomplished through:

- Purpose: The true purpose and right function of the emotional body, as a part of the temple, must be recognized.
- Identity: The indwelling consciousness moves from identification with its emotional feelings to identification as the self or Soul.
- Creative Activity: The emotional body must be cleansed of astral forms and fogs, and transmuted into a clear pool of force.

The emotional body provides the force that motivates the persona into action. If the force of the astral body is clean and clear, then the entire astral instrument, including a tremendous amount of force, is available to the persona; however, if the astral body is packed full of emotional forms, then very little astral force will be available.

The astral bodies of most people are so caught up in emotional forms that they have very little astral force left over. What little astral force is available is so colored by selfish desires that it taints, veils, and distorts any thought-form it encounters.

The result is confusion of both:

- Purpose (when desire becomes the motivation) and
- Identity ("I am what I feel", or, "I am happy," "I am sad," etc.).
- Creative Activity: Rather than a pool of force, the astral body becomes stuff out of which forms are made. This produces astral forms that veil mental thought-forms and distort attempts to precipitate those thoughts into appearance.

In order to take on appearance in the world of affairs, thought-forms must be propelled downward from the mental plane, through the astral/emotional plane, and into the physical-etheric plane. In order to do this, the focused mind appropriates astral-emotional force, and uses that force to drive the thought-form downward. If the persona does not have enough astral force, then it will not be able to create below the mental realm. One may be a great "thinker", but thinking is all one can do.

If there is sufficient force to drive the thought-form downward, but that force is not clean and clear, then the thought-form will be distorted by its downward movement. If the individual or group is identified as their emotions, then that identification will produce an astral/emotional distortion of that thought, adding to the clutter in the astral body. This type of emotional distortion is called *glamour*.

If there is sufficient astral force to drive the glamour downward into appearance in the physical-etheric, then the resulting form will be so distorted that the original intent may not be recognizable. This type of physical-etheric distortion is called *maya*.

The basic problem here is one of identification. If the incarnate consciousness identifies with the thought (i.e. this is "my" thought/idea), then it gives that thought some of its own consciousness or "I"dentity. At that point, part of the incarnate self or consciousness becomes trapped in the thought. The thought takes up residence within one's mind, and when one drives it downward, it becomes an astral form and takes up residence in one's astral body.

Eventually, the astral body becomes crowded with so many forms that very little energy is available for anything new. Since these old forms are created from a separative (persona-identified) perspective, they are distortions of the original intent. Their auras cloud and distort the remaining astral energy, and the persona is left with a polluted astral body that is incapable of doing any real creative work. Any forms that manage to wend their way through these polluted bodies are colored and shaped by the process. The result is quite different, in quality and characteristics, from the original intent.

Thus, in order to function properly, the emotional body must be a completely clean and clear pool of force, free of any and all emotional forms. Only then can it convey thought from the mental body to the physical-etheric without distorting it.

The inner and outer rituals that transform the astral body into part of the temple should:

- At least begin the process of cleansing the emotional body of astral forms and fogs, transmuting it into a clear pool of force.
- Transform this body from a source of personal desires into a refined instrument that drives thought downward into appearance.

This work must be well on its way before the chest can be transmuted into a temple.

The Mental Body

The mental body consists of substance that vibrates more rapidly than emotional substance, but less rapidly than the substance of the Soul Body.

Mental substance is the stuff out of which thought is formed, and the mental body is an instrument for creating and processing thought-forms. This body is globular in shape, and although it interpenetrates the other bodies, it may extend beyond the physical-dense body by as much as two feet.

After the discarnating consciousness passes through the

tunnel of light, onto the astral plane and into the astral/emotional body, it may continue on through the astral plane into the mental. It then takes up residence in the mental body. The consciousness or soul has then withdrawn from the physical-dense, physical-etheric, and astral bodies, taking with it the focus of intent of that incarnation. Since this focus of intent is the purpose or positive pole of that incarnation, the forms created by the relationship between that positive purpose and negative substance will now begin to disintegrate.

Thus, the mental body is a subtle body of energy that, during incarnation, interpenetrates and dwells within the physical-dense, physical-etheric, and astral/emotional bodies, forming part of the overall persona or mask of the incarnate soul.

The inner and outer rituals that transform the mental body into part of the temple should:

- Begin the process of clarifying the mental body and focusing its attention on the Soul.
- Transform this body from a source of intellectual processing of thought, into a mechanism for translating Spiritual Ideas (Divine Archetypes) into thought-forms.

This work must be well on its way before the allegorical chest can be transmuted into a temple.

When the incarnate consciousness is identified with its mental body, the persona is the chest or trap of the Soul. The consciousness is then, in effect, saying, "I am what I think". By identifying with and as thoughts, the incarnate consciousness limits itself to the abilities of the mental body. It cannot, then, perceive, identify with, or act as its overshadowing Spiritual Soul.

Before the Soul can liberate itself, the chest must become the temple. The mental body must be transformed from a trap into an instrument of self-awareness and spiritual union.

This transformation is accomplished through:

- Purpose: The true purpose and right function of the mental body, as a part of the temple, must be recognized.

- Identity: The indwelling consciousness moves from identification with its thoughts to identification as the self or Soul (the Daughter and the Son).
- Creative Activity: The mental body must be cleansed of separative thoughts, and transmuted into a mechanism for focusing energy.

The mental body translates the ideas of the Spiritual Soul into thought-forms (organized patterns of energy). In the creative meditation process, these thought-forms are passed to the astral body, which drives them downward to the physical-etheric body, which in turn gives those thought-forms a body of appearance.

In order for the resulting form to serve the Divine Plan, the entire mental instrument must be clean, focused on, and receptive to, the idea held by the Soul, and able to hold that focus long enough to receive a complete and accurate impression of that idea. The idea, impressed on mental substance by the focus of the mind, then becomes a clear thought-form and an accurate reflection (on mental levels) of the overshadowing idea of truth.

However, if:

- the mental body is polluted by identification as the separated self,
- does not hold the focus long enough for the thought to fully form, or
- does not focus clearly enough,

then the resulting thought-form will be a distorted reflection of the overshadowing idea. This type of distortion is called *illusion*.

This is the condition of the mental bodies of most people. Their mental energy is so polluted by identification as the separated self that they have very little energy left for original thought. When they can actually focus, they seldom hold an idea focused clearly or long enough to formulate a complete thought-form.

The result is confusion of:

- Purpose (when a distorted thought or illusion becomes the motivation).

- Identity ("I am what I think").
- Creative Activity: Rather than an instrument of creative thought, the mental body is a tool for distortion, a creator of mental illusion.

In order for the ideas created by the Soul to take on appearance in the world of affairs, those ideas must be translated into thought-forms, astral force, and, physical-etheric activity. This is accomplished via Creative Meditation. We will discuss this process in detail later, but for now, the basics will suffice.

Creative Meditation

The process of creative meditation consists of four stages, an Ascent, an interlude or pause, a Descent, and another interlude.

During the Ascent stage of creative meditation, the mind aspires to, and at-one's with, the Soul and the Idea of Truth focused by the Soul. The idea is available from the Soul because the Spiritual Soul is meditating in a cycle that mirrors that of the creative cycle of the incarnate Soul. Thus, when the incarnate soul is at the Height of its meditation cycle (during the Full Moon), the overshadowing Spiritual Soul is at the low point of its cycle.

Where the incarnate Soul meditates from New Moon to New Moon, the Spiritual Soul meditates from Full Moon to Full Moon. Thus:

- Ascent: The Spiritual Soul Ascends from Full Moon to New Moon.
- First Interlude: At the New Moon, during the Height of its meditation, the Spiritual Soul:
  o At-one's with the Spirit (the Divine Father).
  o Intuitively grasps the pure Truth held in availability to it by the Father.
- Descent: The Spiritual Soul Descends form New Moon to Full Moon, translating pure Truth into the Idea of truth, or an archetype of a form.
- Second Interlude: At the Full Moon, having reached the lowest point of its creative meditation cycle, the

Spiritual Soul holds out the Idea of Truth to the incarnate consciousness (just as the later reaches the height of its cycle with the aid of the physical-dense, physical-etheric, astral, and mental bodies).

While the Idea of truth can be contacted without using the creative meditation cycle:

- It is a great deal more difficult
- The idea will probably be incompletely grasped
- The idea will probably be distorted by the mental, emotional, and physical-etheric bodies

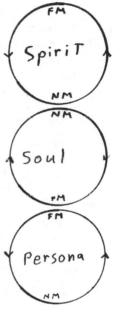

If the idea somehow manages to be precipitated into the world of appearances despite these difficulties, the resulting form will be so distorted that it will not serve the Divine Plan, and will likely work against it.

One character in the legend demonstrates this point. Seth was the infertile brother of Isis and Osiris. His wife, Nepthys, had to have sex with Osiris in order to get pregnant (resulting in the birth of Anubis). Thus, some say that Seth murdered Osiris both in order to gain the throne of Egypt and out of jealousy.

The important point for us is that Seth was infertile. He represented the incarnate soul that has had the opportunity to identify with and as the self or magnetic field, and refused it. This is the magnetic field trapped in the Negative Pole *by choice*. It refuses the Light, refuses to recognize itself as Soul, but instead identifies as the mind or positive pole of the persona.

Cut off from the Light of the Soul, the *dark brother* exists in the appearance of separation. Since the Soul is the magnetic field that relates Spirit and Substance, the dark brother is unable to relate with anything except from his self-centered point of view. The result is:

- Separation from the One Life and selfish motivation,
- The attempt to rule the three lower worlds via the mind.
- Intentional distortion of:
  o energy or thought-forms, producing illusion,
  o force or astral forms, producing glamour,
  o substance or physical-etheric forms, producing maya.

This is evil, a complete reversal of the Divine Plan. The distorting process that produces it is *black magic* and the one who practices it is a *black magician*.

The black magician is so identified with and as the mind that the Soul simply does not exist for them. Thus, they are incapable of directing their mind upward to the overshadowing Spiritual Soul and grasping an Idea of Truth. Since they cannot grasp an Idea of Truth, they cannot create new thought-forms from those Ideas.

Thus, the black magician is "infertile", unable to give birth to truly new Ideas or Thoughts. They can only misappropriate already existing thought-forms, and distort them into an illusion that serves their selfish purposes.[1]

One must learn to work the creative process before one can reach the point of decision between the Soul and the mind.

When the incarnate consciousness has a well-developed mind, and is identified with its self or Soul, the mind is upwardly focused. It then receives Ideas of Truth from the Spiritual Soul, and reflects those Ideas into the mind.

When the bodies of the persona are in right relationship with the self or Soul, the Spirit passes its Intent to the Soul, the Soul formulates that intent into an idea and relates the idea to the receptive persona, and the persona translates the idea into thought, emotion, and physical appearance. The persona then communicates the result back to the overshadowing Soul and the Soul relates it to Spirit.

This is the creative rhythm of Spirit, Consciousness, and Matter, or of the Divine Father, Child, and Mother, symbol-

---

[1] We will discuss good and evil in detail in a later work on the Divine Plan.

ized in the polarity of the bar magnet. As we know, the current of magnetic energy flows from the positive pole, out and down along the external portion of the magnetic field to the negative pole, and then in and up through the center of the bar magnet (at the heart of the magnetic field) from the negative to the positive poles.

In the human being, Divine Intent flows from the positive pole of Spirit, downward through the Soul to the negative pole of Substance (where intent is given shape and form), and then up again from Substance through Soul to Spirit, completing the circuit.

In this circuit, each Aspect of Divinity has its own function.

- Spirit provides the Divine Intent, the Purpose, Power, and Will of the One Life.
- Substance gives shape and form to Divine Intent by *differentiating that intent into intelligent activity or matter It thus provides a field of expression for the positive pole, and a field of experience for the magnetic field.
- Consciousness relates the Intent of Spirit to Substance, and the resulting Intelligent Activity of Substance to Spirit.

This rhythmic creative process by which Divine Intent manifests, the consciousness evolves, and substance is perfected, is the great work of the *white magician*. The end result of this process is the union or at-one-ment of the Three, the Great Work of the white magician or Disciple of the Light.

When the human being identifies with and as a portion of their persona, this identification cuts them off from the higher portion of the circuit, and forces the incarnate consciousness to turn to their mind, emotions, and/or physical body for their purpose or motivation. This is not the proper function of the persona.

The resulting mental, emotional, and/or physical "purpose" is necessarily rooted in the persona, and since the persona is form and form differentiates, the form-identified consciousness perceives itself as different and separate from all other forms. Thus, the motivations of the persona-identified

consciousness are basically selfish. These selfish intents distort all of their thoughts and feelings, producing forms that
express individual will, desire, and appetite, rather than Divine Intent, Aspiration, and Activity.

The cure for this is to turn the persona's attention to the
higher self or overshadowing Soul, and cleanse the persona of
all distorting and distorted thoughts, feelings, and appetites.
We have included a number of meditation techniques designed to accomplish just this, and will follow with additional
works that include more inner and outer rituals.[2]

As discussed earlier, this process is based on a series of
regular meditation exercises, forming a rhythmic sequence of
inner and outer transformation.

We have already begun the process of identifying as the
Soul, recognizing our higher purpose as a Soul, and aligning
the Astral body with that purpose. The next step is to begin
the process of transmuting the persona into an instrument of
the Soul.

---

[2] Quinn: *The Magic of Consciousness* series.

Addendum to Lesson 6

The Two Trees

The second creation in Genesis 2 refers to the creation in and of the three lower worlds, the mental, astral, and physical-etheric planes.

The etheric body, with its centers and nadis, is reflected in the mental, astral, and physical-etheric bodies and organs. These in turn are reflected in organs and systems of the dense-physical body. These dense-physical counterparts include the sympathetic and parasympathetic nervous systems, the glandular system, the cardiovascular system, and the spinal column. The world's religions and mystery traditions frequently symbolize these organic systems as trees, vines, fruit, and pillars. These sacred symbols include the:

- ASK TREE —Norse— "from which issued the men of the generation of bronze."
- BRAMANANDA —Hindu— the rod or stick of Brahma with the 7 knots of the 7 spinal nadi.
- GOGARD —Hellenic (Greek)— tree of life "amidst its magnificent foliage dwelt a serpent"
- HOMA —Middle East— planted by Ahura-Mazda (the god of light) "He who drinks of its juice never dies"
- TAT —Egyptian—pillar/backbone of the god Ptah, later Osiris
- TREE OF LIFE —Hebrew— Genesis
- TZITE TREE —Mexican— "out of which the Mexican third race of men was created" From the Mexican Popul Vuh or "Bible."
- WORLD TREE —Hindu— (Bhagavad Gita) the sacred Ashvatta "They say the imperishable Ashvatta is with roots above and branches below"
- YGGDRASIL —Scandinavian world tree, source of Odin's wisdom.

- ZAMPUN —Tibetan great World Tree[1]

It should not be surprising to find trees featured in many early spiritual systems, given the importance of trees to humanity. However, the trees of these traditions share some interesting features. They may describe:
- One tree with three roots (such as Yggdrasil)
- Two separate trees (such as the Tree of Knowledge and Tree of Life)
- A rod, staff, or pillar (such as Bramananda, Djed, Asherah, Tat and Tattu, Boaz and Jachin).

Most descriptions of the tree/pillars include significant features such as fruit, knots, jewels, shining leaves, etc. They also often place a serpent in the tree (as in Bramananda, Gogard, Yggdrasil, the Tree of Knowledge, etc.).

These are descriptions of the same tree or trees, Jachin / Pingala and Boaz/Ida. The descriptions are different because the observer, method of observing, and that which is observed differ from one time and place to another. The descriptions of these trees are similar because they are describing the same things, the Tree of Life and the Tree of Knowledge

The Tree of Life

Osiris is the Father or Life Aspect of the Egyptian trinity of Osiris–Horus–Isis. In their myth, Osiris was entombed alive in a casket. A tree grew around the casket, and a pillar was made from the tree. Thus, we see the Tree of Life as a symbol of the Father or Life Aspect, entombed in form.

The pillar, tree, and casket are three containers of the Life Aspect. The casket is the physical body. During incarnation, the Spiritual Soul (Horus) enters into and identifies with the body, and "dies" to its self. The incarnate Soul forgets who and what it is, and acts in the world as a body.

The tree surrounds, enfolds, and is reflected in the casket. Energetically, the tree represents the etheric or subtle-energy body that underlies the persona. This body is composed of

---

[1] Compiled from: *Man, Grand Symbol of the Mysteries*, by Manly P. Hall, pp. 175 -185

hundreds of tiny tubes of light, or nadis, which form the framework of the mental, astral, and physical-etheric bodies.

When the Soul sounds the creative word through the etheric framework, on the frequency of the mental plane, the word attracts mental substance to this framework, forming the mental body.

When the creative word is sounded on the astral plane, it attracts emotional substance, forming the astral-emotional body.

When the creative word is sounded on the physical-etheric, it attracts physical etheric substance, forming the physical-etheric body.

Although this entire energy system is reflected in the physical-dense body, the "Tree of Life" is reflected, in particular, in the spine and the cardiovascular system.

The ancient Egyptians considered the physical heart to be the "seat of life." During mummification, they originally left it in place, but later developed the custom of replacing it with a special stone. The Life Thread, one of the three threads of the antahkarana (the rainbow bridge or silver cord from the overshadowing Spiritual Soul to the persona instrument) is anchored in the sino-atrial node or pulse point of the heart. This thread brings the Life Aspect into the physical-dense body. The heart begins to beat when this thread connects to the heart, and it ceases to beat when this thread disconnects.

The Life Aspect flows out from the heart throughout the entire body, along the network of veins and arteries laid out (on subtle levels) by the etheric body.

Thus, the etheric body, as the Tree of Life, moves the First or Life Aspect down and out, exciting substance into organized, intelligent activity.

The Tree of Knowledge

In Genesis 2:17 we find:

"but of *the tree of the knowledge of good and evil* you shall not eat, for in the day that you eat of it you shall die."

The tree of Knowledge or Wisdom is also a symbol of the etheric body, but as an instrument of the Third Aspect or Divine Intelligence. In this function, its physical-dense correspondents include the nervous system and the ductless glands. The ductless glands are the physical-dense correspondents of the chakras.

The Fruit of the Tree

There are seven major and twenty-one minor energy organs or centers on the etheric "tree" or body. These organs are formed of swirling vortexes of force and are commonly called centers or chakras. Whether it is a "Tree of Knowledge' or a "Tree of Wisdom" depends on which center is the place of residence of the incarnate consciousness. If the consciousness identifies with its thoughts (i.e. "I am what I think"), then it dwells in one of the centers that specialize in processing mental energies. If the incarnate consciousness identifies with its emotional feelings (i.e. "I am what I feel"), then it dwells in one of the centers that specialize in processing emotional energies.

Knowledge of Good and Evil

Each center expresses a particular state of consciousness. Awareness of good and evil, for instance, is born in the Solar Plexus center, and it is at this stage of development that the Tree of Knowledge becomes the Tree of Knowledge of Good and Evil. As we shall see in the following chapter, the function of the Tree changes as the consciousness grows and develops, and moves upward from one chakra or center to another.

The Fruit of the Trees[2]

The two trees are also represented as snakes twining around the central shaft of the rod or staff of Mercury. The serpent that represents the downward moving energy is called Pingala, and that which represents the upward moving energy is Ida. The central rod, Susumna, represents the spine. Pingala and Ida

---

[2] The source for this illustration of a caduceus is unknown.

intersect each other at five points along the spine. At each of those points, a spark of consciousness constantly sounds a creative note. That creative note radiates light, creating a tiny geometric jewel or "center" of light.

The center vibrates in harmony with the note, setting the surrounding etheric substance into spiraling motion.[3] That spiral is called a chakra.[4] When seen from the side, the chakra looks like a swirling vortex of energy. When one peers down into it, it looks like a spinning wheel or flower.

There are two such centers above the spine, making seven major centers. One is in front of the forehead, and the other on top of the head.

Each of these centers contains:

- A spark of consciousness. This spark is a tiny mote of the Light of The Soul, extended into the three lower worlds. Each spark has a particular quality of awareness that is peculiar to and typical of that center.
- A note or sound. This note is part of the seven-fold word that created the persona and holds its substance together (This creative word will be discussed in detail in a later chapter).
- Vibrating substance. The notes set substance vibrating throughout the three lower worlds. Thus, the seven major chakras are present in the mental, astral, and physical-etheric bodies. The centers process energy on each of the three planes. However, each of them specializes in a particular frequency range, and they are seldom all functional in any one persona instrument.

The entire persona instrument, including the three subtle bodies, three nadis, and seven major centers, is reflected in the physical-dense body. The seven major centers, for instance, are reflected in the ductless glands, and each of them "governs" some portion of the physical instrument.

---

[3] Illustration of "Primal Anu" vortex by Mr. Jinarâjadâsa.
[4] "Chakra" is Sanskrit for "wheel".

Genesis 3: 7 states:

"Then the eyes of both were opened, and they knew that they were naked; and they sewed fig leaves together and made themselves aprons."

This represents the development of self-consciousness or self-awareness that develops along with the Solar Plexus center. In terms of the "mirror test" described above, when this occurs, a being looking into a mirror will see, not only their species, but their individual self.

The Serpent of Wisdom and the Fire of Matter

Genesis 3 states:

1. Now the serpent was more subtle than any other wild creature that the LORD God had made. He said to the woman, "Did God say, 'You shall not eat of any tree of the garden'?"

13. Then the LORD God said to the woman, "What is this that you have done?" The woman said, "The serpent beguiled me, and I ate."

A primary difficulty with this concept is that serpents do not and did not "speak". Some try to get around this difficulty by conflating the serpent with the Lucifer. However, immediately after the above we find:

14. The LORD God said to the serpent, "Because you have done this, cursed are you above all cattle, and above all wild animals; upon your belly you shall go, and dust you shall eat all the days of your life.

15. I will put enmity between you and the woman, and between your seed and her seed; he shall bruise your head, and you shall bruise his heel."

This punishment makes it clear that the serpent in Genesis is a snake, not Lucifer or a demon. Since talking animals do not exist, the serpent is obviously an allegory, not a real beast.

This is supported by the fact that the "Serpent of Wisdom" was a common symbol in the region, associated with a number of goddesses, including:

Asherah: A serpent wound around her tree/pillar.

Astarte: "She of the womb" was sometimes portrayed holding two snakes.

Eurydice: The wife of Orpheus, she was bitten in the heel by a serpent, and died.

Eurynome: Rose from the primal darkness, formed the wind of chaos into a serpent (Ophion), mated with Ophion and laid the universal egg.

The patriarchal priests of YHWH loathed Asherah in particular, which is highly suggestive. We already know that they demonized Asherah herself. It would hardly be surprising if they did the same with one of her symbols.

If we remove the patriarchal veil, we find that the serpent symbol has a number of meanings that are important to us at this point.

- Because the serpent renews itself by shedding its skin, it is a symbol of regeneration, and the Oroboris (the serpent with its tail in its mouth) is a symbol of eternity.
- Because the serpent moves in a winding motion, it is also the symbol of the force of substance, which moves in a spiral. These movements can be seen:
- Microcosmically in the spiralae (orbital paths) of atoms.[5]
- Macrocosmically in the orbits of planets.
- At the human level in the twining paths of Pingala and Ida, the nadi of the sun and the nadi of the moon.

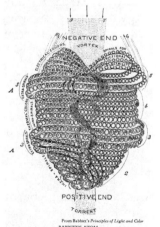

From Babbitt's *Principles of Light and Color*
BABBITT'S ATOM

In the context of the human energy system, the serpent actually represents the atomic fire of matter and the motion of force in the form. The Sanskrit term for the atomic fire of matter is *kundalini*. Kundalini is found

---

[5] Illus. from: *The Principles of Light & Color*, by Edwin S. Babbitt

in the center at the base of the spine, and normally rises from there up Susumna (the central spinal nadi). The rising kundalini activates each spinal center as it approaches them, providing the substantial energy that drives the vortex. The "petals" of the lotus open and the incarnate Soul has access to the quality of consciousness and the frequency of substance that the center controls.

Kundalini

Kundalini has been called the fire of substance, fire by friction, manas, the principle of intelligence, and a variety of other terms that communicate little to the earnest seeker. It may be easier to describe kundalini by returning to basic concepts.

As earlier noted, the basic trinity of substance is Energy, Force, and Substance, or potential, activity, and appearance. Kundalini is the Force or activity of Substance that relates potential (energy) and appearance (form).

Its position between potential and appearance gives kundalini tremendous power. It is, in effect, the ability of substance to take on appearance. Nothing can take on appearance without its portion of kundalini.

Its position between potential and appearance may also contribute to one of its names "fire by friction", for it is born of the friction between energy and substance.

We may further refine our understanding by comparing the trinity of substance to their corresponding elements:
- Energy corresponds to the element fire or color.
- Force corresponds to the element water or vibration.
- Substance corresponds to the element earth or light.

Thus, if kundalini is both force and fire by friction, then it would appear to be at least two different elements. This is only partly correct. In actuality, kundalini may be associated with all four prime elements.

Thus, when we speak of kundalini we are discussing the four elements as a whole. Every thing below it in frequency is a reflection of the vibrating Sound / Light / Color, a projection of that vibrating primal substance into the three lower worlds.

That projection is made possible by the polarity between the fallen kundalini and risen kundalini (the portion of kundalini that remains on the buddhic plane). So long as the force in the body remains in the base center, and is not available in the centers above it, then those centers do not have the necessary force to perform their function and the abilities of the persona instrument and incarnate consciousness are severely limited.

Until the kundalini reaches and vivifies the center, the chakra exists only as a potential. The point of consciousness and sounding note are muted, and the vortex is absent (or present only as a slight depression in the etheric body). Because of the relationship between kundalini and the chakras, rising kundalini is associated with the evolution of the form, and with spiritual growth and development.

There are two basic methods of moving kundalini up the spine. Which method one uses largely depends on one's orientation. Those who are substance oriented tend to push kundalini up the spine by "heating" the kundalini from below. When the kundalini has risen past the sacral center, and is at least approaching the solar plexus, it is possible to drive it further up using practices that raise sexual stimulation to incredible heights, hold it at those heights (retaining the sexual energy), and then direct it into and up the spine.

This is rather like holding a lit candle under a mercury thermometer. When it works, it drives the kundalini upward. However, this method is often painful and can be very dangerous. The chief difficulty is the lack of control over the process. When kundalini is forced upward it does not follow Susumna, but Ida (the nadi of the moon). It pushes upward, encountering each center in turn, in a sequence that is not necessarily natural for the individual involved. The rising kundalini then burns away the protective etheric sheath surrounding each center as it stimulates them into activity. Thus, the newly active center is unprotected from its environment, and the incarnate consciousness has no opportunity to adjust to the forcefully activated center.

The resulting pain and confusion can be incapacitating.

When the chakras or centers are vivified naturally, the incarnate consciousness has an opportunity to learn to use them.

Those who are consciousness oriented tend to draw kundalini up the spine via the magnetic attraction of the Soul. Through their meditation work, they move consciousness (and thus their place of residence) into the head, and the magnetic attraction of the consciousness begins to grow. Eventually, the magnetic attraction of the Soul in the head becomes so powerful that it draws the kundalini upward.

The advantage of this technique is that the kundalini moves upward in the manner and order that is natural to that persona instrument. It flows upward through Susumna, and it activates the major and minor centers in the order that is natural and normal for that persona, avoiding a great deal of pain and danger.

Lesson 7 Addendum

The Biblical Myth of Sarai and Avram

Genesis 11

27. Now these are the records of the generations of Terah. Terah became the mother of Sarai, Nahor and Haran; and Haran became the father of Milcah, and Iscah.

28. Haran died in the presence of his mother Terah in the land of his birth, in Ur of the Chaldeans.

29. Sarai and Milcah took husbands for themselves. The name of Sarai's husband was Avram, and the name of Milcah's husband was Nahor, the son of Haran.

30. Sarai was a voice of the LADY, and keeping with her vows, had no child.

31. Terah took Sarai her daugher, and Avram her son-in-law, her daughter Sarai's husband; and they went out together from Ur of the Chaldeans; and they went as far as Haran, where Sarai served in the house of the LADY in that city.

Genesis 12

1. Now the LADY said to Sarai, "Go forth from your country, And from your relatives And from your mother's house, To the land which I will show you;

2. And I will bless the land, And I will bless you; And so you shall be a blessing;

3. And I will bless those who bless you,

4. And through you all the land will bear fruit and be blessed."

5. So Sarai and Avram went forth as the LADY had spoken to them.

6. Sarai took Avram her husband, and all their possessions which Avram had accumulated, and the persons which he had acquired in Haran, and they set out for the land of Canaan; thus they came to the land of Canaan.

7. Sarai passed through the land as far as the site of the sacred terebinth and oak grove of Shechem. Now the Canaanite was then in the land.

8. The LADY came to Sarai and said, "Through you I will bless this land." So she set there her tent, and bade Avram worship there at the altar of the LADY.

9. Then they proceeded from there to the mountain on the east of Bethel, and Sarai pitched her tent near the sacred oak, with Bethel on the west and Ai on the east; and there Avram worshiped at the altar of the LADY, sacrificing the fruits of the earth. Sarai called upon the name of the LADY, and the goddess appeared as a cloud above her tent.

10. Sarai and Avram journeyed on, continuing toward the Negev.

11. Now there was a famine in the land; so Sarai and Avram went down to Egypt to sojourn there, for the famine was severe in the land.

12. It came about when they came near to Egypt, that Avram heard of their customs, became frightened and said to Sarai, "See now, I know that you are a beautiful woman;

13. "and since the Egyptians count descent from the father we share, rather than the mothers we do not, if they hear that we have the same father they will say, 'This is his sister and his wife'; and they will kill me, but they will let you live.

14. "Please say only that you are my sister so that it may go well with me because of you, and that I may live on account of you."

15. It came about when Sarai came into Egypt, the Egyptians saw that she was very beautiful.

16. Pharaoh's officials saw her and praised her to Pharaoh; and she was taken into Pharaoh's house.

17. Therefore he treated Avram well for her sake; and gave him sheep and oxen and donkeys and male and female servants and female donkeys and camels.

18. But the LADY struck Pharaoh and his house with great plagues because of Sarai, Avram's wife.

19. Then Pharaoh called Avram and said, "What is this you have done to me? Why did you not tell me that she was your wife?

20. "Why did you say, 'She is my sister,' so that I took her for my wife? Now then, here is your wife, take her and go."

21. Pharaoh commanded his men concerning him; and they escorted him away, with his wife and all that belonged to him.

Genesis 13

1. So Sarai went up from Egypt to the Negev, she and her husband and all that belonged to them, and Lot with them.

2. Now they were very rich in livestock, in silver and in gold.

3. They went on their journeys from the Negev as far as Bethel, to the place where Sarai's tent had been at the beginning, between Bethel and Ai,

4. to the place of sacred oak and the altar where she had wor-

shiped formerly; and there Sarai called on the name of the LADY. ...

12. Sarai and Avram settled in the land of Canaan, and one of the gods of the Canaanites, El Shaddai, came to Avram and spoke to him. ...

14. El Shaddai said to Avram, "Now lift up your eyes and look from the place where you are, northward and southward and eastward and westward;

15. "for all the land which you see, I will give it to you and to your descendants forever.

16. "I will make your descendants as the dust of the earth, so that if anyone can number the dust of the earth, then your descendants can also be numbered.

17. "Arise, walk about the land through its length and breadth; for I will give it to you." So Avram worshiped El Shaddai and was deaf to the words of the LADY.

18. When Sarai learned that Avram worshiped El Shaddai, she moved her tent and came and dwelt by the oaks of Mamre, which are in Hebron, and there she worshiped at an altar to the LADY. ...

Genesis 15

1. After Sarai moved, the word of the LORD, El Shaddai, came to Avram in a vision, saying, "Do not fear, Avram, I am a shield to you; Your reward shall be very great."

2. Avram said, "O Lord GOD, what will You give me, since I am childless, and the heir of my house is Eliezer of Damascus?"

3. And Avram said, "Since You have given no offspring to me, one born in my house is my heir."

4. Then behold, the word of the LORD came to him, saying, "This man will not be your heir; but one who will come forth from your own body, he shall be your heir."

5. And He took him outside and said, "Now look toward the heavens, and count the stars, if you are able to count them." And He said to him, "So shall your descendants be."

6. Then he believed in the LORD; and He reckoned it to him as righteousness.

7. And He said to him, "I am the LORD who brought you out of Ur of the Chaldeans, to give you this land to possess it."

8. He said, "O Lord GOD, how may I know that I will possess it?"

9. So He said to him, "Bring Me a three year old heifer, and a three year old female goat, and a three year old ram, and a turtledove, and a young pigeon."

10. Then he brought all these to Him and cut them in two, and laid each half opposite the other; but he did not cut the birds.

11. The birds of prey came down upon the carcasses, and Avram drove them away.

12. Now when the sun was going down, a deep sleep fell upon Avram; and behold, terror and great darkness fell upon him.

13. God said to Avram, "Know for certain that your descendants will be strangers in a land that is not theirs, where they will be enslaved and oppressed four hundred years.

14. "But I will also judge the nation whom they will serve, and afterward they will come out with many possessions.

15. "As for you, you shall go to your fathers in peace; you will be buried at a good old age.

16. "Then in the fourth generation they will return here, for the iniquity of the Amorite is not yet complete."

17. It came about when the sun had set, that it was very dark, and behold, there appeared a smoking oven and a flaming torch which passed between these pieces.

18. On that day the LORD made a covenant with Avram, saying, "To your descendants I have given this land, from the river of Egypt as far as the great river, the river Euphrates."

Genesis 16

1. Now because of her vows, Sarai had borne no children and had no heir to her office, but she had an Egyptian maid whose name was Hagar.

2. So Sarai called Avram to her and said to him, "Now behold, my vow to the LADY has prevented me from bearing children. Please go in to my maid; perhaps I will obtain children through her." And Avram listened to the voice of Sarai.

3. After Sarai had lived ten years in the land of Canaan, she took Hagar the Egyptian, her maid, and gave her to her husband Avram as his wife.

4. He went in to Hagar, and she conceived; and when she saw that she had conceived, her mistress was despised in her sight.

5. And Sarai said to Avram, "May the wrong done me be upon you. I gave my maid into your arms, but when she saw that she had conceived, I was despised in her sight. May the LADY judge between you and me."

6. But Avram said to Sarai, "Behold, your maid is in your power; do to her what is good in your sight." So Sarai treated her harshly, and she fled from her presence. ...

Genesis 17

1. Now the LORD appeared to Avram and said to him, "I am God Almighty; Walk before Me, and be blameless.

2. "I will establish My covenant between Me and you, And I will multiply you exceedingly."

3. Avram fell on his face, and God talked with him, saying,

4. "As for Me, behold, My covenant is with you, And you will be the father of a multitude of nations.

5. "No longer shall your name be called Avram, But your name shall be Abraham; For I have made you the father of a multitude of nations.

6. "I will make you exceedingly fruitful, and I will make nations of you, and kings will come forth from you.

7. "I will establish My covenant between Me and you and your descendants after you throughout their generations for an everlasting covenant, to be God to you and to your descendants after you.

8. "I will give to you and to your descendants after you, the land of your sojournings, all the land of Canaan, for an everlasting possession; and I will be their God."

9. God said further to Abraham, "Now as for you, you shall keep My covenant, you and your descendants after you throughout their generations.

10. "This is My covenant, which you shall keep, between Me and you and your descendants after you: every male among you shall be circumcised.

11. "And you shall be circumcised in the flesh of your foreskin, and it shall be the sign of the covenant between Me and you.

12. "And every male among you who is eight days old shall be circumcised throughout your generations, a servant who is born in the house or who is bought with money from any foreigner, who is not of your descendants.

13. "A servant who is born in your house or who is bought with your money shall surely be circumcised; thus shall My covenant be in your flesh for an everlasting covenant.

14. "But an uncircumcised male who is not circumcised in the flesh of his foreskin, that person shall be cut off from his people; he has broken My covenant."

15. Then God said to Abraham, "As for Sarai your wife, you shall not call her name Sarai, but Sarah shall be her name.

16. "I will tame her, and indeed I will give you a son by her. Then I will bless her, and she shall be a mother of nations; kings of peoples will come from her." ...

18. And Abraham said to God, "Oh that Ishmael might live before You!"

19. But God said, "No, but Sarah your wife will bear you a son, and you shall call his name Isaac; and I will establish My covenant with him for an everlasting covenant for his descendants after him.

20. "As for Ishmael, I have heard you; behold, I will bless him, and will make him fruitful and will multiply him exceedingly. He shall become the father of twelve princes, and I will make him a great nation.

21. "But My covenant I will establish with Isaac, whom Sarah will bear to you at this season next year."

22. When He finished talking with him, God went up from Abraham.

23. Then Abraham took Ishmael his son, and all the servants who were born in his house and all who were bought with his money, every male among the men of Abraham's household, and circumcised the flesh of their foreskin in the very same day, as God had said to him. ...

25. And Ishmael his son was thirteen years old when he was circumcised in the flesh of his foreskin.

26. In the very same day Abraham was circumcised, and Ishmael his son.

27. All the men of his household, who were born in the house or bought with money from a foreigner, were circumcised with him. ...

Genesis 20

1. Now Abraham journeyed from Mamre toward the land of the Negev, and settled between Kadesh and Shur; then he sojourned in Gerar.

2. Abraham said of Sarah his wife, "She is my sister." So Abimelech king of Gerar sent and took Sarah.

3. But God came to Abimelech in a dream of the night, and said to him, "Behold, you are a dead man because of the woman whom you have taken, for she is married."

4. Now Abimelech had not come near her; and he said, "Lord, will You slay a nation, even though blameless?

5. "Did he not himself say to me, 'She is my sister'? And she herself said, 'He is my brother.' In the integrity of my heart and the innocence of my hands I have done this."

6. Then God said to him in the dream, "Yes, I know that in the integrity of your heart you have done this, and I also kept you from sinning against Me; therefore I did not let you touch her.

7. "Now therefore, restore the man's wife, for he is a prophet, and he will pray for you and you will live. But if you do not restore her, know that you shall surely die, you and all who are yours."

8. So Abimelech arose early in the morning and called all his servants and told all these things in their hearing; and the men were greatly frightened.

9. Then Abimelech called Abraham and said to him, "What have

you done to us? And how have I sinned against you, that you have brought on me and on my kingdom a great sin? You have done to me things that ought not to be done."

10. And Abimelech said to Abraham, "What have you encountered, that you have done this thing?"

11. Abraham said, "Because I thought, surely there is no fear of God in this place, and they will kill me because of my wife.

12. "Besides, she actually is my sister, the daughter of my father, but not the daughter of my mother, and she became my wife;

13. and it came about, when God caused us to wander from her mother's house, that I said to her, 'This is the kindness which you will show to me: everywhere we go, say of me, "He is my brother".

14. Abimelech then took sheep and oxen and male and female servants, and gave them to Abraham, and restored his wife Sarah to him.

15. Abimelech said, "Behold, my land is before you; settle wherever you please."

16. To Sarah he said, "Behold, I have given your brother a thousand pieces of silver; behold, it is your vindication before all who are with you, and before all men you are cleared."

17. Abraham prayed to God, and God healed Abimelech and his wife and his maids, so that they bore children.

18. For the LORD had closed fast all the wombs of the household of Abimelech because of Sarah, Abraham's wife.

Genesis 21

1. Then the LORD took note of Sarah as He had said, and the LORD did for Sarah as He had promised.

2. So Sarah conceived and bore a son to Abraham in his old age, at the appointed time of which God had spoken to him.

3. Abraham called the name of his son who was born to him, whom Sarah bore to him, Isaac.

4. Then Abraham circumcised his son Isaac when he was eight days old, as God had commanded him. ...

Genesis 22

1. Now it came about after these things, that God tested Abraham, and said to him, "Abraham!" And he said, "Here I am."

2. He said, "Take now your son, your only son, whom you love, Isaac, and go to the land of Moriah, and offer him there as a burnt offering on one of the mountains of which I will tell you."

3. So Abraham rose early in the morning and saddled his donkey, and took two of his young men with him and Isaac his son; and he split wood for the burnt offering, and arose and went to the place of

which God had told him.

4. On the third day Abraham raised his eyes and saw the place from a distance.

5. Abraham said to his young men, "Stay here with the donkey, and I and the lad will go over there; and we will worship and return to you."

6. Abraham took the wood of the burnt offering and laid it on Isaac his son, and he took in his hand the fire and the knife. So the two of them walked on together.

7. Isaac spoke to Abraham his father and said, "My father!" And he said, "Here I am, my son." And he said, "Behold, the fire and the wood, but where is the lamb for the burnt offering?"

8. Abraham said, "God will provide for Himself the lamb for the burnt offering, my son." So the two of them walked on together.

9. Then they came to the place of which God had told him; and Abraham built the altar there and arranged the wood, and bound his son Isaac and laid him on the altar, on top of the wood.

10. Abraham stretched out his hand and took the knife to slay his son.

11. But the angel of the LORD called to him from heaven and said, "Abraham, Abraham!" And he said, "Here I am."

12. He said, "Do not stretch out your hand against the lad, and do nothing to him; for now I know that you fear God, since you have not withheld your son, your only son, from Me."

13. Then Abraham raised his eyes and looked, and behold, behind him a ram caught in the thicket by his horns; and Abraham went and took the ram and offered him up for a burnt offering in the place of his son.

14. Abraham called the name of that place The LORD Will Provide, as it is said to this day, "In the mount of the LORD it will be provided."

15. Then the angel of the LORD called to Abraham a second time from heaven,

16. and said, "By Myself I have sworn, declares the LORD, because you have done this thing and have not withheld your son, your only son,

17. indeed I will greatly bless you, and I will greatly multiply your seed as the stars of the heavens and as the sand which is on the seashore; and your seed shall possess the gate of their enemies.

18. "In your seed all the nations of the earth shall be blessed, because you have obeyed My voice."

19. So Abraham returned to his young men, and they arose and went together to Beersheba; and Abraham lived at Beersheba. ...

Genesis 23

1. Now Sarah lived one hundred and twenty-seven years; these were the years of the life of Sarah.

2. Sarah died in Kiriath-arba (that is, Hebron) in the land of Canaan; and Abraham went in to mourn for Sarah and to weep for her.

3. Then Abraham rose from before his dead, and spoke to the sons of Heth, saying,

4. "I am a stranger and a sojourner among you; give me a burial site among you that I may bury my dead out of my sight."

5. The sons of Heth answered Abraham, saying to him,

6. "Hear us, my lord, you are a mighty prince among us; bury your dead in the choicest of our graves; none of us will refuse you his grave for burying your dead."

7. So Abraham rose and bowed to the people of the land, the sons of Heth.

8. And he spoke with them, saying, "If it is your wish for me to bury my dead out of my sight, hear me, and approach Ephron the son of Zohar for me,

9. that he may give me the cave of Machpelah which he owns, which is at the end of his field; for the full price let him give it to me in your presence for a burial site."

10. Now Ephron was sitting among the sons of Heth; and Ephron the Hittite answered Abraham in the hearing of the sons of Heth; even of all who went in at the gate of his city, saying,

11. "No, my lord, hear me; I give you the field, and I give you the cave that is in it. In the presence of the sons of my people I give it to you; bury your dead."

12. And Abraham bowed before the people of the land.

13. He spoke to Ephron in the hearing of the people of the land, saying, "If you will only please listen to me; I will give the price of the field, accept it from me that I may bury my dead there."

14. Then Ephron answered Abraham, saying to him,

15. "My lord, listen to me; a piece of land worth four hundred shekels of silver, what is that between me and you? So bury your dead."

16. Abraham listened to Ephron; and Abraham weighed out for Ephron the silver which he had named in the hearing of the sons of Heth, four hundred shekels of silver, commercial standard.

17. So Ephron's field, which was in Machpelah, which faced Mamre, the field and cave which was in it, and all the trees which were in the field, that were within all the confines of its border, were deeded over

18. to Abraham for a possession in the presence of the sons of

Heth, before all who went in at the gate of his city.

19. After this, Abraham buried Sarah his wife in the cave of the field at Machpelah facing Mamre (that is, Hebron) in the land of Canaan. ...

Genesis 25

1. Now Abraham took another wife, whose name was Keturah.

2. She bore to him Zimran and Jokshan and Medan and Midian and Ishbak and Shuah.

3. Jokshan became the father of Sheba and Dedan. And the sons of Dedan were Asshurim and Letushim and Leummim.

4. The sons of Midian were Ephah and Epher and Hanoch and Abida and Eldaah. All these were the sons of Keturah.

5. Now Abraham gave all that he had to Isaac;

6. but to the sons of his concubines, Abraham gave gifts while he was still living, and sent them away from his son Isaac eastward, to the land of the east.

7. These are all the years of Abraham's life that he lived, one hundred and seventy-five years.

8. Abraham breathed his last and died in a ripe old age, an old man and satisfied with life; and he was gathered to his people.

9. Then his sons Isaac and Ishmael buried him in the cave of Machpelah, in the field of Ephron the son of Zohar the Hittite, facing Mamre,

10. the field which Abraham purchased from the sons of Heth; there Abraham was buried with Sarah his wife. ...

Wife/sister and Husband/brother

Abraham's relationship with Sarah has traditionally been a subject of uncomfortable speculation. Abraham identified Sarah as both his wife and sister, and twice 'married' her to foreign kings. Biblical scholars have tried to dismiss this pandering (to his own desire for wealth) by assuming that Abraham lied about her being his sister and accepting his explanation that he did so for fear of his life. However, this weak justification falls apart when we examine the actions of Sarai and Avram from the point of view of the Mesopotamian culture from which they came.

Ancient Mesopotamia was a matriarchal culture. In common with many matriarchal cultural systems:

- Children were considered siblings when and only

when they were born of the same mother.
- A boy and girl born of the same father, but different mothers, were not 'related'.

Matrilineal descent was the custom in ancient Mesopotamia, including Ur, the original home of Sarai and Avram.

Also under matriarchy:
- The laws of inheritance favored the last and the female descendants of the mother. That is:

Property is held in the mother's name, and is inherited by her daughters.

The youngest child was the primary heir (ultimogeniture rather than primogeniture).

Thus, Sarai's interest in an heir.
- When a young couple married, the new couple joined the family of the bride's mother.

This is seen in the story of Abraham (in a portion not included above) when the patriarch ensures that his son Isaac will *not* go to live with his bride, in a manner that indicates that this is a departure from the usual custom.

We also see this custom in the biblical book, *The Song of Songs* 3:5

"I held him, I would not let him go / until I brought him to my mother's house."

The Song of Songs is sometimes considered a remnant of ancient Sumerian fertility rites. However, the above line plainly indicates that fertility alone is not indicated, but sacred rites of marriage, for in the matriarchal cultures of that time and place, bringing a man into one's mother's house or tent was part of the marriage ritual.[1]

Abraham and his male descendants adopted patriarchal customs and a male god, while the matriarchs of the family tried to maintain matriarchal customs and worship.

The biblical evidence of matrilineal descent persists up to the time of King David.

---

[1] Quinn: In Ema's version of the myth, the opposite behavior, a wife throwing her husband out of her tent, becomes a method of divorce. I know of no historical evidence for this, but it adds a nice touch.

The peoples to the west (Hittites, Girgashites, Amorites, Canaanites, Perizzites, Hivites, Jebusites, etc.), however, had more patriarchal cultures, and used the rules of patrilineal descent (the primary parent was the father). Under this cultural system:

- A boy and girl born of the same father and mother were full siblings.
- A boy and girl born of the same father (but different mothers) were half siblings.

Also under patriarchy:

- The laws of primogeniture favor the male descendants of the father. That is, the property is held in the father's name, and is inherited by his sons, particularly the eldest.
- When a young couple married, the new couple joined the family of the groom's father.

If Sarah and Abraham had different mothers, but the same father, they would have been "unrelated" in Ur, and thus eligible to marry. However, the local definitions of relationships changed when they journeyed west, creating potential problems. Both systems abhorred incest, they simply defined blood relations differently.

Patriarchal kings would have considered them brother and sister. Thus, when Abraham told Pharaoh that Sarah was his sister, Abraham told the truth (or, rather, a partial truth). Under the patrilineal laws of Egypt she *was* his sister. However, she was also a priestess of the Goddess, and Abraham was her consort.

Addendum to Lesson 8

The Temple of Solomon

According to the Bible, the Temple of Jerusalem was built at the command of King Solomon. However, Solomon did not have sufficient trained workers or materials for the project, and thus he contracted with King Hiram of Tyre. King Hiram ruled a small but wealthy nation of sea traders to the north of Israel. The cedar beams used in the Temple were cut by woodsmen provided by King Hiram, in the Lebanese forests controlled by Hiram. The King of Tyre also provided trained stone masons who cut and shaped the stone used in the Temple, and the smiths who made the implements, vessels, altar, etc. King Solomon provided unskilled Judean labor, a building site, and wages for the workers.

In fact, Tyre was a real nation, a Phoenician colony contemporary with biblical Israel and Judea.

All of this makes King Hiram's crucial supportive role quite odd from the Judeo/Christian viewpoint, as there is no indication that King Hiram or any of his people worshiped YHWH. Quite the contrary, like all Phoenician cities, Tyre had its own "Ba'alat" (female goddess) who had a male consort or "Ba'al". Thus, King Hiram of Tyre, his woodsmen, and his masons were part of the local religious traditions that YHWH's prophets fought against in the Old Testament.

The fact that the Legend has "pagans" construct the Temple is another source of criticism from those who do not understand the allegory. The proper response is to look for the symbolic meaning. In this case, the search can begin as a question, "Why would members of this tradition be chosen to build the Temple?"

A common, rational response to this question is to suggest that the Hebrews did not have either the materials (wood or metal) or the skills (woodsmen, masons, or smiths) to build the Temple themselves, so they had to import foreign materials and workers. However, this ignores the central fact that the Legend is an allegory and that all of the characters and actions are symbolic of the path of spiritual growth.

Once we recognize this, and turn our attention to the symbolism, we find a hint to its meaning in the fact that the Ba'al (male god) had a significant Ba'alat (female god), as a consort.

The Temple represents the Substance or Mother Aspect of the Spiritual Soul. The material for the Temple, the Stone and Wood, is depicted as coming from, and being shaped by the builders of Tyre. Thus, when the builders of Tyre transport stone and wood to Judea, they are symbolically transporting the Substantial Aspect, the concept of the Divine Mother or Queen of Heaven, from Tyre to Jerusalem.

The fact that YHWH had a consort, Asherah, was hidden behind patriarchal shrouds for thousands of years. That consort is and must be the polar equal of YHWH. Like all poles, the two cannot exist without each other.

As discussed earlier, this simple fact is abhorrent to patriarchal monotheists, who typically use a number of strategies to undermine and supplant female deities, including:

- The male gods "rape" the goddess (symbolically stealing the power of the goddess and establishing the preeminence of the god).
- Turn the goddess into a lesser being, such as a queen, princess, or heroine.
- Distort the goddess into an evil, demonic being.
- Turn the goddess from the dominant divinity into a subsidiary divinity, dependent on the god.
- Transfer characteristics and power from goddess to god.

These are often done in combination, as when Zeus raped various heroines. The patriarchal Judean priests and prophets were striving against a goddess (Asherah) whose rites included sexual passion. Their reaction included:

- Demonizing the goddess.
- Removing all hint of sex from their official rites.
- Turning the joyful act of sexual passion into a solemn duty, commanded by YHWH.
- Transferring the creative process, including the builders who perform the work (the "hosts of heaven") from

the goddess to YHWH.

This process covered hundreds of years, and began with the advancement of YHWH to primacy.

The Bible indicates that the local name of the Ba'alat was "Ashe'rah". When Asherah first appears in the Bible, she is already being transformed from a significant female Ba'alat (the polar equal of El/YHWH), into a subsidiary female deity. However, the priests did not agree on the identity of the male God.

There appears to have been a power struggle between the Israeli priests of El and the Judean priests of YHWH, with Asherah as part of the prize.

Asherah was a very popular goddess in both Israel and Judah, with altars in many high places. In Israel, she was worshiped alongside the El, but in Judah (including the Temple of Solomon), she was worshiped alongside YHWH.

This began to change with the advent of extreme patriarchy, and the rejection of all gods but YHWH.[1] The prophets demonized Asherah, threw her out of the Temple, and instituted the exclusive worship of YHWH.

Unfortunately, the followers of YHWH failed to understand the nature of polarity. Yes, there is only One God, but that Divine Being is so far above us that "naught may be said" about that Being.

We know that YHWH is not that One Divine Being "About Whom Naught May Be Said" because:

- A great deal *is* said about Him,
- He is always portrayed as masculine, and
- He is part of a Trinity.

The first expression of that One Divine Being is a trinity, the Three Aspects that are One. The Polarity between those Aspects, and the magnetic field of relationship between them, produces everything that is.

Thus, everything that exists, in order to exist, must have a positive pole (spark of Spirit), negative pole (Substance), and the magnetic field between them (consciousness).

---

[1] 2 Kings 21, 2, 2 Kings 23, 1 – 3, & 1 Kings 18, 19-40

These two divine poles are always in balance. As in an electromagnet, the strength of one pole must be equal to the other. Thus, by cutting themselves off from the negative pole, patriarchists limit their access to the positive. By rejecting Asherah, they distanced themselves from YHWH.

Some attempts have been made over the centuries to bring back the goddess and restore some balance between the poles. However, none have been successful. The Christian Trinity, for instance, is improperly portrayed as masculine, forcing the raising of Mary, the mother of Jesus, into the role of the Queen of Heaven. This is actually the title and role of the Great Goddess, the polar opposite of and equal to the Father.

The Lioness of God

While it is generally believed that the Temple of Solomon was originally dedicated to YHWH, the evidence indicates that this was not necessarily the case.

An early, biblical name for Jerusalem was "Ariel",[2] meaning "Lioness of God." One of the customs of ancient times was to name a city after its chief deity (Athens being one of the better-known examples). This suggests that the village of Ariel was originally dedicated to a deity who was symbolized by a lioness. The lioness was the symbol of several local goddesses, including:

- Asherah (a Canaanite goddess who rode a sacred lion; a.k.a. Ashtoreth, Astarte, Anat, Atargatis, Ishtar, and Aphrodite),
- Bast (originally the Egyptian lion goddess of sunset),
- Cybele (a great goddess from Phrygia/Turkey who drove a lion-drawn chariot),
- Eriskegal (a Sumerian form of Ishtar, Mami, and Inanna, she appeared as a lion-headed goddess suckling lion cubs),
- Hathor (an Egyptian mother and daughter of the Sun, she was represented as a lioness, a cow, a woman, and as a tree),

[2] Isaiah 29, 1-2

- Hebat (a Hittite/Hurrian sun goddess, known as the "queen of heaven" and portrayed standing on a lion),
- Mehit (lion-headed Egyptian goddess),
- Sekhmet (a lion-headed Egyptian sun goddess),
- Tefnut (an Egyptian goddess of daybreak, depicted as a lioness or as lion-headed). [3]

The lioness was not a symbol of YHWH

For our purposes, the most interesting of these regional goddesses is Asherah. There is some indication that she was the consort of YHWH. However, this would have been a late matriarchal/early patriarchal view (before she was demonized and eliminated from the pantheon). The Matriarchal view would have given the goddess predominance, making YHWH the consort or husband of Asherah.

Asherah was depicted as the force of life, and was evoked during childbirth and planting. She was later disguised as Shekinah, the Holy Ghost, and as Sarah, the sister/wife of Abraham. She was also known as the "Serpent Lady", and her symbols included the Tree of Life surmounted by serpents.

Asherah was worshiped in the "high places" of Israel and Judea, and was depicted, in her shrines, as a pillar or rod. Thus, the high place of Mount Moriah (a threshing floor that became the site of the Temple, next to the village of Ariel/Jerusalem) may originally have been sacred to the Great Goddess.

The Bible depicts Asherah worship (misnamed Ashtaroth or Ashtoreth) in the Temple, so we have good indication that she was worshiped there at the beginning of the patriarchal period.[4]

Another significant point is that the Temple of Solomon was built on a "threshing floor" on the summit of Mount

---

[3] Quinn: See, *The New Book of Goddesses and Heroines*, by Patricia Monaghan, Llewellyn Publications, St. Paul, 2000, as the primary source for this list.

[4] Asherah was worshiped in the Temple during most of the six centuries from its founding to its destruction by Nebuchadnezzar in 586 B.C.E.

Moriah. One would, therefore, expect the site to have been sacred to a god or goddess of grain (in particular, to the third aspect of the goddess, the crone who represented reaping).

YHWH was not a god of grain, but several local goddesses were, including Asherah.

As mentioned above, Asherah was the consort of YHWH, and was originally worshiped in the Temple along with the masculine YHWH. Her devotees made household statuettes of her out of baked bread, indicating that she was associated with corn.

This suggests that the "threshing floor" on Mount Moriah (the high-place where Solomon built the Temple, was originally sacred to Asherah, a complex goddess whose attributes included those of a triple goddess.

Addendum to Lesson 9

The Myth of Moses and Zipporah

The complete biblical story of Moses, including the entire book of Exodus, much of the book of Deuteronomy, and parts of Leviticus and Numbers, is too long to include here. Thus, we will begin with the first through fourth chapters of Exodus, followed by a summary of the rest of the myth.

Exodus 1

6 Joseph died, and all his brothers and all that generation.

7 But the sons of Israel were fruitful and increased greatly, and multiplied, and became exceedingly mighty, so that the land was filled with them.

8 Now a new king arose over Egypt, who did not know Joseph.

9 He said to his people, "Behold, the people of the sons of Israel are more and mightier than we.

10 "Come, let us deal wisely with them, or else they will multiply and in the event of war, they will also join themselves to those who hate us, and fight against us and depart from the land."

11 So they appointed taskmasters over them to afflict them with hard labor. And they built for Pharaoh storage cities, Pithom and Raamses.

12 But the more they afflicted them, the more they multiplied and the more they spread out, so that they were in dread of the sons of Israel.

13 The Egyptians compelled the sons of Israel to labor rigorously;

14 and they made their lives bitter with hard labor in mortar and bricks and at all kinds of labor in the field, all their labors which they rigorously imposed on them.

15 Then the king of Egypt spoke to the Hebrew midwives, one of whom was named Shiphrah and the other was named Puah;

16 and he said, "When you are helping the Hebrew women to give birth and see them upon the birthstool, if it is a son, then you shall put him to death; but if it is a daughter, then she shall live."

17 But the midwives feared God, and did not do as the king of Egypt had commanded them, but let the boys live.

18 So the king of Egypt called for the midwives and said to them, "Why have you done this thing, and let the boys live?"

19 The midwives said to Pharaoh, "Because the Hebrew women are not as the Egyptian women; for they are vigorous and give birth before the midwife can get to them."

20 So God was good to the midwives, and the people multiplied, and became very mighty.

21 Because the midwives feared God, He established households for them.

22 Then Pharaoh commanded all his people, saying, "Every son who is born you are to cast into the Nile, and every daughter you are to keep alive."[1]

Exodus 2

1 Now a man from the house of Levi went and married a daughter of Levi.

2 The woman conceived and bore a son; and when she saw that he was beautiful, she hid him for three months.

3 But when she could hide him no longer, she got him a wicker basket and covered it over with tar and pitch. Then she put the child into it and set it among the reeds by the bank of the Nile.

4 His sister stood at a distance to find out what would happen to him.

5 The daughter of Pharaoh came down to bathe at the Nile, with her maidens walking alongside the Nile; and she saw the basket among the reeds and sent her maid, and she brought it to her.

6 When she opened it, she saw the child, and behold, the boy was crying. And she had pity on him and said, "This is one of the Hebrews' children."

7 Then his sister said to Pharaoh's daughter, "Shall I go and call a nurse for you from the Hebrew women that she may nurse the child for you?"

8 Pharaoh's daughter said to her, "Go ahead." So the girl went and called the child's mother.

9 Then Pharaoh's daughter said to her, "Take this child away and nurse him for me and I will give you your wages." So the woman took the child and nursed him.

---

[1] Quinn: This has been interpreted as either a reinforcement of the oppression of the Hebrews, so that all of the people of Egypt are enforcing it, or as a drastic attempt by Pharaoh to stem a general population explosion by expanding the infanticide to include all males born in Egypt. However, if we view the myth as an allegory, then this passage becomes a command from the Divine Father to the Divine Son to begin the descent into appearance.

10 The child grew, and she brought him to Pharaoh's daughter and he became her son. And she named him Moses, and said, "Because I drew him out of the water."

11 Now it came about in those days, when Moses had grown up, that he went out to his brethren and looked on their hard labors; and he saw an Egyptian beating a Hebrew, one of his brethren.

12 So he looked this way and that, and when he saw there was no one around, he struck down the Egyptian and hid him in the sand.

13 He went out the next day, and behold, two Hebrews were fighting with each other; and he said to the offender, "Why are you striking your companion?"

14 But he said, "Who made you a prince or a judge over us? Are you intending to kill me as you killed the Egyptian?" Then Moses was afraid and said, "Surely the matter has become known."

15 When Pharaoh heard of this matter, he tried to kill Moses. But Moses fled from the presence of Pharaoh and settled in the land of Midian, and he sat down by a well

16 Now the priest of Midian had seven daughters; and they came to draw water and filled the troughs to water their father's flock.

17 Then the shepherds came and drove them away, but Moses stood up and helped them and watered their flock.

18 When they came to Reuel their father, he said, "Why have you come back so soon today?"

19 So they said, "An Egyptian delivered us from the hand of the shepherds, and what is more, he even drew the water for us and watered the flock."

20 He said to his daughters, "Where is he then? Why is it that you have left the man behind? Invite him to have something to eat."

And Ruel placed Moses in a pit in the ground, and left him there seven years, without food or water. But Zipporah fed Moses in secret.[2]

21 Moses was willing to dwell with the man, and he gave his daughter Zipporah to Moses.

22 Then she gave birth to a son, and he named him Gershom, for he said, "I have been a sojourner in a foreign land."

23 Now it came about in the course of those many days that the king of Egypt died. And the sons of Israel sighed because of the bondage, and they cried out; and their cry for help because of their bondage rose up to God.

---

[2] Quinn: This passage does not appear in the Bible, but is based on another Hebrew legend.

24 So God heard their groaning; and God remembered His covenant with Abraham, Isaac, and Jacob.

25 God saw the sons of Israel, and God took notice of them.

Exodus 3

1 Now Moses was pasturing the flock of Jethro his father-in-law, the priest of Midian; and he led the flock to the west side of the wilderness and came to Horeb, the mountain of God.

2 The angel of the LORD appeared to him in a blazing fire from the midst of a bush; and he looked, and behold, the bush was burning with fire, yet the bush was not consumed.

3 So Moses said, "I must turn aside now and see this marvelous sight, why the bush is not burned up."

4 When the LORD saw that he turned aside to look, God called to him from the midst of the bush and said, "Moses, Moses!" And he said, "Here I am."

5 Then He said, "Do not come near here; remove your sandals from your feet, for the place on which you are standing is holy ground."

6 He said also, "I am the God of your father, the God of Abraham, the God of Isaac, and the God of Jacob." Then Moses hid his face, for he was afraid to look at God.

7 The LORD said, "I have surely seen the affliction of My people who are in Egypt, and have given heed to their cry because of their taskmasters, for I am aware of their sufferings.

8 "So I have come down to deliver them from the power of the Egyptians, and to bring them up from that land to a good and spacious land, to a land flowing with milk and honey, to the place of the Canaanite and the Hittite and the Amorite and the Perizzite and the Hivite and the Jebusite.

9 "Now, behold, the cry of the sons of Israel has come to Me; furthermore, I have seen the oppression with which the Egyptians are oppressing them.

10 "Therefore, come now, and I will send you to Pharaoh, so that you may bring My people, the sons of Israel, out of Egypt."

11 But Moses said to God, "Who am I, that I should go to Pharaoh, and that I should bring the sons of Israel out of Egypt?"

12 And He said, "Certainly I will be with you, and this shall be the sign to you that it is I who have sent you: when you have brought the people out of Egypt, you shall worship God at this mountain."

13 Then Moses said to God, "Behold, I am going to the sons of Israel, and I will say to them, 'The God of your fathers has sent me to you.' Now they may say to me, 'What is His name?' What shall I

say to them?"

14 God said to Moses, "I AM WHO I AM"; and He said, "Thus you shall say to the sons of Israel, 'I AM has sent me to you.'

15 God, furthermore, said to Moses, "Thus you shall say to the sons of Israel, 'The LORD, the God of your fathers, the God of Abraham, the God of Isaac, and the God of Jacob, has sent me to you.' This is My name forever, and this is My memorial-name to all generations.

16 "Go and gather the elders of Israel together and say to them, 'The LORD, the God of your fathers, the God of Abraham, Isaac and Jacob, has appeared to me, saying, "I am indeed concerned about you and what has been done to you in Egypt.

17 "So I said, I will bring you up out of the affliction of Egypt to the land of the Canaanite and the Hittite and the Amorite and the Perizzite and the Hivite and the Jebusite, to a land flowing with milk and honey."'

18 "They will pay heed to what you say; and you with the elders of Israel will come to the king of Egypt and you will say to him, 'The LORD, the God of the Hebrews, has met with us. So now, please, let us go a three days' journey into the wilderness, that we may sacrifice to the LORD our God.'

19 "But I know that the king of Egypt will not permit you to go, except under compulsion.

20 "So I will stretch out My hand and strike Egypt with all My miracles which I shall do in the midst of it; and after that he will let you go.

21 "I will grant this people favor in the sight of the Egyptians; and it shall be that when you go, you will not go empty-handed.

22 "But every woman shall ask of her neighbor and the woman who lives in her house, articles of silver and articles of gold, and clothing; and you will put them on your sons and daughters. Thus you will plunder the Egyptians."

Exodus 4

1 Then Moses said, "What if they will not believe me or listen to what I say? For they may say, 'The LORD has not appeared to you.'"

✦

Then YHWH gave Moses magical powers, centered in a staff.

Moses complained that he was not an eloquent public speaker, and YHWH made Moses' brother, Aaron, his mouthpiece.

YHWH bade Moses return to Egypt. Moses loaded his wife and sons on a donkey, took the staff of God in his hand, and returned to the land of Egypt.

Back in Egypt, Moses asked Pharaoh to let the Hebrews go on a spiritual retreat to worship YHWH, but YHWH hardened Pharaoh's heart.

Aaron turned his staff into a serpent to impress Pharaoh. Some of Pharaoh's magicians performed the same trick, but Aaron's staff swallowed up their staff/serpents.

Pharaoh still refused, and increased the Hebrews' workload by requiring them to gather straw (for manufacturing mud bricks) that had previously been provided to them, without changing their production quota.

Moses asked that the Hebrews be freed ten times, and each time Pharaoh refused, and each refusal was followed with a plague.

In the first plague, the water of the Nile was turned to blood, but still Pharaoh refused to let the people go.

This was followed with plagues of Frogs, Flies, the death of the Egyptian cattle, Boils, Hail, Locusts, and Darkness over the land

The Hebrews then asked their neighbors for articles of silver and gold, and YHWH sent the final plague, the death of the first born of each household. The Hebrews protected themselves from this plague by sacrificing first-born lambs, and painting the blood on their doorposts and lintels.

Pharaoh finally relented and let the Hebrews go, but changed his mind and attacked them while they were crossing the Sea of Reeds. However, the sea swallowed Pharaoh's army, and the Hebrews escaped into the wilderness.

Once freed, the Hebrews rebelled against YHWH six times, and in punishment spent forty years wandering in the wilderness before they were allowed to find the Promised Land. Most of those forty years were spent camped beneath the sacred mountain on which YHWH appeared to Moses.

During these forty years, YHWH appeared as a column of cloud by day and a column of fire by night.

YHWH gave Moses the Ten Commandments, commanded

the building of the Ark of the Covenant and the Tabernacle to house the Ark, and moved from the mountain into the Ark. He also gave detailed instructions on the sanctification of priests, and rituals of worship.

✦

YHWH was consistently capricious, acting like a spoiled, frightened, and jealous child. He kept His "chosen people" in the wilderness until all those who had escaped from Egypt (and later disobeyed him) had died. At the end of the forty years, even his greatest servant, Moses, was not allowed into the Promised Land.

Deuteronomy 34

1 Now Moses went up from the plains of Moab to Mount Nebo, to the top of Pisgah, which is opposite Jericho. And the LORD showed him all the land, Gilead as far as Dan,

2 and all Naphtali and the land of Ephraim and Manasseh, and all the land of Judah as far as the western sea,

3 and the Negev and the plain in the valley of Jericho, the city of palm trees, as far as Zoar.

4 Then the LORD said to him, "This is the land which I swore to Abraham, Isaac, and Jacob, saying, 'I will give it to your descendants'; I have let you see it with your eyes, but you shall not go over there."

5 So Moses the servant of the LORD died there in the land of Moab, according to the word of the LORD.

6 And He buried him in the valley in the land of Moab, opposite Beth-peor; but no man knows his burial place to this day.

7 Although Moses was one hundred and twenty years old when he died, his eye was not dim, nor his vigor abated.

8 So the sons of Israel wept for Moses in the plains of Moab thirty days; then the days of weeping and mourning for Moses came to an end.

9 Now Joshua the son of Nun was filled with the spirit of wisdom, for Moses had laid his hands on him; and the sons of Israel listened to him and did as the LORD had commanded Moses.

10 Since that time no prophet has risen in Israel like Moses, whom the LORD knew face to face,

11 for all the signs and wonders which the LORD sent him to perform in the land of Egypt against Pharaoh, all his servants, and all his land,

12 and for all the mighty power and for all the great terror which Moses performed in the sight of all Israel.

The Instrument of Redemption

During the purification process, the persona instrument (mental, astral/emotional, and physical-etheric bodies) is transformed from the trap or coffin into the instrument of redemption and at-one-ment. This purified vehicle consists of the following: [3]

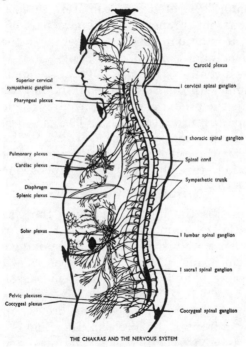

THE CHAKRAS AND THE NERVOUS SYSTEM

The Seven Major Chakras

The seven chakras[4] are organs of energy. Each of them is associated with a state of awareness, a ductless gland, a different way of experiencing or knowing, and (symbolically)

---

[3] Illustration from: *The Chakras*, by C.W. Leadbeater, The Theosophical Publishing House, Wheaton, IL, p. 40-b

[4] Quinn: Chakra is Sanskrit for wheel. They are also known as a node, plexus, center, or padma

with an animal and a planet. They are often depicted as flowers, particularly the water lily or lotus (in the East) or rose (in the West). Each of the seven has a different number of petals, with the highest having the most, while the lowest has the least. Beginning at the top, the centers are:

Crown, Head Center, or Thousand-Petaled Lotus
(Sanskrit - Sahasradala or Sahasrara chakra or padma)

This center is located approximately three inches above the head. It is not, properly speaking, a part of the persona instrument. It is actually the lowest center in the center system of the overshadowing Spiritual Soul.

The crown center is the place of transcendent awareness, or at-one-ment with the Spiritual Soul. Its physical-dense correspondent is the pineal gland or epithalmus. The center governs the upper brain and right eye. The chakra is sometimes symbolized by the unicorn or risen serpent, while the gland is symbolized by the pinecone and the pomegranate (both of which are said to resemble the gland in appearance).

Ajna or Brow Center

This center is the highest center in the persona instrument. It specializes in manipulating the higher frequencies of the mental plane, and is responsible for building and manipulating thought-forms. It also functions as a switchboard for the lower centers and states of consciousness, integrating them into a single, functioning whole.

The Ajna is located between the brows, approximately three inches in front of the forehead. Its gland is the pituitary or hypophysis, and hypothalamus. The pituitary sits on the wing-shaped sphenoid bone, inside the skull. The motion of the sphenoid circulates the brain and spinal fluid. The symbols of the Ajna include Pegasus, the winged horse.

Until this center is developed, the persona consciousness of most people functions rather like the human eye when gazing at a scene at the beach. One can either look out at the grand vista of the entire scene, or gaze closely at details such as individual grains of sand. One cannot do both simultaneously. The ajna center can. It integrates the mystical (the grand vista) and the intellectual (the minute details) into a single state of awareness. When the incarnate consciousness moves up into the Ajna, the Tree of Knowledge becomes the Tree of Wisdom.

Due to its location, the Ajna is often mistaken for the "Third Eye." The Third Eye is a mechanism of active sight or creative vision. This mechanism utilizes a number of energy organs, including the Crown, Cave, Alta Major, and Ajna Centers. The Third Eye functions like a projector, moving an idea downward in frequency and projecting it onto mental substance (creating thought-forms), onto astral substance (creating emotional forms), and onto physical-etheric and physical-dense substance (creating physical-dense forms of appearance).

Throat Center
(Visuddhi-chakra)[5]

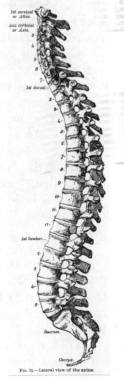

The center of the concrete rational mind, intellect, or conscious creativity. It specializes in manipulating the substance of the three lower sub-planes of the mental plane. The throat center is very good at perceiving details, but very poor at relationships. As a result, the intellect cannot know God. Its proper function is to organize abstract thought-forms into a sequence of activities or a plan of action.

The throat center is located in the spine, between vertebrae C6 and C7 (at the base of the neck). Its glands are the thyroid and parathyroids, and it governs the bronchial and vocal apparatus, lungs, and alimentary canal.

If we compare the Ajna to an Architect who creates the blueprint of a building, then the Throat Center is the Building Contractor who organizes the construction process. The symbols of the throat center include the cock or rooster.

Fig. 22.—Lateral view of the spine.

---

[5] Illustration from: The Classic Collector's Edition of "Gray's Anatomy".

The Heart Center
(Anahata-chakra or Hritpadma)

The organ of mystical union or at-one-ment, it processes the higher energies of the astral plane. This center is very good at perceiving relationships, but very poor at details. It is located in the spine, between vertebrae T5 and T6 (between the shoulder blades). Its gland is the thymus, and it governs the heart, blood, vagus nerve, and circulatory system. The symbols of the heart center include the lion and the dove.

The Solar Plexus Center
(Manipura chakra or padma, or Nabhipadma-chakra)

This dual center has two vortexes, both of which specialize in processing a portion of the lower energies of the astral plane. The lower of the two is the primary organ of separative desires and passions. The higher is the organ of personal aspiration. This center automatically splits all lower astral energies into two opposing poles:

- The persona automatically identifies with one polar energy, and perceives the related forms as "good."
- The persona simultaneously polarizes against the other energy, and perceives the related forms (to the extent that they appear different) as "bad."

Thus, the dual nature of this center creates the perception of so-called "good" and "bad". So long as the incarnate consciousness is dominated by this center, the dark "lunar" pillar of the etheric body functions as the Tree of Knowledge of Good and Evil.

The desires of the solar plexus are insatiable. They can be temporarily satisfied, but never quenched. It is presently the dominant center in most human beings, in whom it rules both the Throat and Sacral centers. As long as this center dominates the instrument, the incarnate consciousness is its victim.

The proper function of the Solar Plexus center is to quietly await impression from the Ajna, and then gather and channel the tremendous force of the astral-emotional body. It is an essential part of the process of moving a thought-form downward into appearance in the world of affairs. Thus, those who suppress this center, in a misplaced-attempt to control their emotions, are preventing themselves from being effective in the world.

The solar plexus is located between vertebrae T5 and T6. Its gland is the pancreas, and it governs the stomach, liver, gall bladder and nervous system. The symbols of the solar plexus center include the ram.

The Sacral Center
(Svadhisthana-chakra)

The organ of instinctual procreation, its function will eventually be lifted up to the throat center. This center naturally functions on annual and lunar cycles. However, in humans it has been dominated by the insatiable Solar Plexus for so long that its own cycle has been lost. As a result, most adult human beings are constantly "turned on" sexually. This condition will not change until the incarnate consciousness of humanity moves into the Ajna, draws the reproductive activity out of the solar plexus up into the throat center, and moves their emotional activity out of the solar plexus into the heart center.

Modern birth control methods are early expressions of this movement from the Sacral to the Throat. However, most of humanity has yet to develop the Ajna Center, leaving the insatiable Solar Plexus still in control of both the desire nature and the Sacral Center.

The Throat Center attempts to compensate by controlling reproduction through suppression (of both the desire nature and the mechanism of reproduction). The resulting physical technology (whether barrier based, spermicidal, or "ovicidal") are all expressions of this suppression.

This will change when humanity moves its primary place of residence in the body up into the Ajna Center, and integrates and takes conscious control of the other persona centers. Reproduction will then become a fully conscious process, with conception requiring an act of focused will by both prospective parents. In other words, human beings will not become parents unless they decide to become parents, and take the necessary inner and outer steps.

From this perspective, this choice is not a matter of "good" or "bad", but one of moving through the chaos created as an outmoded mechanism begins to be replaced by a new one. The solution is to turn the attention away from both poles and toward achieving the next step in our spiritual growth and development.

In the context of the present work, we may see all such polarizations, including Matriarchy and Patriarchy, as expressions of a dominant, out-of-control Solar Plexus. The solution to this, and any other such polarization, is to raise the place of residence of the incarnate consciousness out of the Solar Plexus and into the Ajna Center. Only then can the two poles be seen as two united sides of One Life.

The sacral center is located between vertebrae L4 and L5.

The symbols of the sacral center include fish and all creatures of the sea.

The Base or Kundalini center
(Muladhara chakra)

This center is located between the sacrum and the tip of the coccyx. Its glands are the adrenals and the coccygeal or Luschkas gland. The areas governed include the spinal column and kidneys. Very little is known about this center, and (although it has become popular in some circles) it can be very dangerous to mess with its energies. The symbols of the base center include the elephant, bull, and ox.

There are many lesser nadis, forming the underlying structure or framework of the mental, astral, and physical-etheric bodies. These lesser nadis often converge, producing lesser centers. There are twenty-one "minor" centers and a large number of "minute" centers. The entire system is connected upwards to the light body of the overshadowing Spiritual Soul, downwards with the earth itself, and horizontally with the subtle environment in which it functions.

How Many Depends on How You Count

The term "centers" is frequently confused and used interchangeably with "chakras". This is rather like using "mouth" for "speech" or "eating". While these terms refer to parts of the same activity, they do not mean the same thing.

A center is the "jewel" or point of consciousness at the heart of a chakra. At that point, the spark of consciousness sounds the creative note which forms a geometric shape or "jewel" (sometimes associated with the Platonic Solids).

The vibration of this etheric jewel stirs the surrounding etheric substance, creating a double vortex of etheric force, which moves energy into, through, and out of the center. Thus, "center" refers to the point of consciousness, the creative note, and the location of that point within the bodies.

As the waves of vibration (created by the sound of the soul) reach the top of the vortex, they form a geometric pattern. This pattern or mandala is similar in appearance to a lotus flower or a turning wheel (chakra means wheel in Sanskrit). Thus, "chakra" refers to the vortex, including the geometric shape or lotus at its top.

"Padma" or lotus, on the other hand, could be said to symbolize both the central jewel and the vortex.

While it is generally understood that there are 7 major centers, 21 minor, and a number of minute ones, the number of major chakras varies depending on who is counting them, and how and what they are counting. The number depends, in part, on how you define "major" and "chakra".

- Some count the input vortex at the back of the spine, and the output vortex at the front of the body (the positive and negative poles of the spinal chakras) as a single chakra, and state that there are 7.
- Some consider only one side of the spine, and also conclude that there are 7.
- Other systems count the poles (input and output vortexes) as separate chakras, which gives 9 spinal chakras and from 2 to 4 head chakras.
- One system counts the kundalini center as 1; Sacral, Solar Plexus, Spleen, Heart, and Throat as 2 each; Ajna, Brow, Alta and Crown as 1 each, making 15 major centers.
- Most systems include only major chakras that are on

or between the coccyx and the top of the head, and minor chakras between the soles of the feet and the top of the head. However, a few schools also include the "Soul Star" (located above the crown center) and the "Earth Star" (located about six inches below the feet).

The center count is also affected by the following:

- The systems that are based on older information (reflecting earlier stages in human growth and development) tend to include the spleen in the major centers, and leave out the solar plexus or throat.

- Systems based on more recent observation tend to place the spleen among the minor centers and include the solar plexus and throat among the major.

- The systems that focus on the substance of the centers are more likely to count the input and output vortexes as separate chakras.

- Systems that focus on the state of consciousness at the heart of the center tend to acknowledge that the notes of the soul create the vortexes, and count the input and output vortexes as expressions of one center.

It should be kept in mind that none of these systems is necessarily more or less correct than the others. Most of them are merely viewing the same structure from different perspectives.

The Cave Center
(The heart in the head, or Cave of Initiation)

This unique center is located in the third ventricle, in the center of the head, in the region of the pineal gland (it has no precise location). Symbolically, this is the place where "land, air, and water meet". It is the place of union or at-one-ment of the overshadowing Spiritual Soul and the incarnate human soul and animal soul (or group, individual, and species identities). When this at-one-ment is achieved, the initiate becomes a Conscious Soul Incarnate, one who lives in the world but is not of the world, a magician according to Divine Law.

The Cave is not part of either the persona or the Soul center system, but relates and merges the two. It has to be built consciously, following the activation of the Ajna and Crown centers. As an activity of Consciousness, rather than of Substance, it does not go into and out of incarnation with the form, but remains behind when a person discarnates. When they incarnate again, the Spiritual Soul Incarnate has to rebuild the Ajna and Crown, but merely moves back into the Cave.

Its gland is the pineal (taking over the control of that gland from the crown), and its symbols include the crystal cave, the pinecone and the pomegranate.

The Place of Residence

Back in the Foreword we asked you to point to the place where you —the conscious, thinking "I"— dwell in your body. When asked this question for the first time, most people point to their abdomen, chest, throat, or head. As the above indicates, each of these locations suggests something about the state of awareness of the incarnate consciousness.

- Those who point to their abdomen are indicating that they dwell in their lower emotions.
- Those who point to their solar plexus or chest are indicating that they dwell in their higher emotions.
- Those who point to their throat or forehead are indicating that they dwell in their mind.
- Those who point to the top of their head are indicating that they are identified with and as their Spiritual Soul.
- Those who point to the center of their head are indicating that they dwell in the place of magic, where the incarnate soul and Spiritual Soul become one.

This may be a bit abstract for those with a concrete mental perspective. For those who dwell in the rational mind, the centers can be best explained in engineering terms.

The Human Transformer

This entire nadi/chakra system is an energy transformer.[6] This transformer looks and works much like an electrical transformer, and the symbols are quite similar. As already seen, the human transformer is symbolized by a central column or rod surrounded by two twining snakes. As shown at left, the standard symbol of an electric transformer is two vertical lines enclosed by two twining lines.

If we combine the elements of the electric transformer symbol, we get the symbol below.

This symbol is remarkably similar to a caduceus. In fact, the basic principles are identical.

There is a standard formula for determining if an electrical transformer is a step up or a step down (in frequency) transformer. The results of applying this electrical formula to the human energy system are quite suggestive. If we presume that Pingala (the nadi of the Sun) is the input or primary windings, and Ida (the nadi of the Moon), is the output or secondary windings, then we can apply the standard formula for transformers to the human energy centers.

The basic formula is to divide the number of secondary or output windings (Ida) by the number of primary or input windings (Pingala).

Starting from the Soul Star and moving downward we encounter the following centers, and number of input or primary

---

[6] "Transformers are either step-up or step-down transformers, determined by the turns ratio between the primary and secondary windings. The primary winding is the input winding and the secondary winding is the output winding. While textbooks differ on determining the turns ratio between the primary and secondary windings, a widely accepted method is to divide the number of secondary turns by the number of primary turns. If the result is more than one, the transformer is a step-up transformer. If the result is less than one, the transformer is a step-down transformer."
Experiments for Electricity and Electronics, 2nd Edition, by Nelson W. Fuller/Rex Miller, Ed.D.

windings:

    Crown = 1

    Ajna = 2

    Throat = 3

    Heart = 4

    Solar Plexus = 5

    Sacral = 6

    Kundalini = 7

Moving back up from the Earth Star, below the Kundalini chakra, we encounter the following centers and number of output or secondary windings.

    Kundalini = 1

    Sacral = 2

    Solar Plexus = 3

    Heart = 4

    Throat = 5

    Ajna = 6

    Crown = 7

We can then complete the calculations by dividing the number of input windings by the number of output windings, keeping in mind that anything more than "1" is a "transform up" transformer while anything less is a "transform down" transformer.

The Transformer

Crown Center	=	$7 \div 1$ =	7
Ajna Center	=	$6 \div 2$ =	3
Throat Center	=	$5 \div 3$ =	1.666
Heart Center	=	$4 \div 4$ =	1
Solar Plexus Center	=	$3 \div 5$ =	0.6
Sacral Center	=	$2 \div 6$ =	0.333
Kundalini Center	=	$1 \div 7$ =	0.142857

Thus, the human energy system is capable of functioning as an energy transformer over a broad range of frequencies, including those of the mental, astral, and physical-etheric planes.

Which level it is actually functioning on depends on the placement of the incarnate consciousness. If that consciousness is identified with and as its lower emotions, then the Solar Plexus Center is dominant and the instrument is a step-down transformer.

If the incarnate consciousness dwells in the higher mind, then the Ajna Center is dominant and the instrument is a step-up transformer.

When the incarnate consciousness inhabits the Heart Center, however, its frequency is the same as its environment. The consciousness then experiences mystical unity or at-one-ment with that environment.

This is remarkable supporting evidence, suggesting that our assessment of the chakras or centers is fundamentally correct.

It is also highly suggestive of the way the Magic of Consciousness works, a subject we will explore in detail in a later work.

Addendum to Lesson 12

The Five Stages of Initiation

At each of these five stages, the Soul begins or initiates a new motion of consciousness, and thereby gradually moves from individual self awareness to union with the One Life. These five initiations are universal, experienced by every individual and group on the Path. In Christian terms, those five stages include:

1. Birth (aka the "Birth of the Christ in the Heart"): In terms of center or chakra development, this represents the first motion of the incarnate consciousness into the heart center. Like all such changes of residence, the transition from the solar plexus center into the heart center takes some time, and there is a great deal of motion back and forth during the transition. However, during the initial move into the heart center consciousness, one experiences a burst of mystical union with the One Life.

This blissful union triggers a transformation of the identity and sense of self. As these periodic mystical experiences continue, the initiate becomes aware that they are a Soul, rather than a persona. One then slowly begins to seek further experience of and as the Soul, thus entering into the path of conscious spiritual growth and development.

This stage symbolizes the beginning of the movement of the emotional life from the lower emotions of the Solar Plexus, up into the higher emotions and energies of the Heart Center. It should be emphasized that this is the beginning of a process of growth. As the gospels put it:

John 3: 3 "Except a man be born again, he cannot see the kingdom of God."

This is the rebirth of the Soul in the body, and, as with any rebirth, it requires a great deal of maturation before it can bear fruit.

In this stage, the physical-etheric bodies of the Divine

Daughter and Divine Son merge and unify, effectively becoming a single body.

During this stage, one learns of a teaching of truth, is inspired by and seeks to follow that teaching.

2. The Baptism by the Holy Spirit: In terms of center or chakra development, this represents the blossoming or complete activation of the heart center.

This stage symbolizes the purification of the persona instrument. It began with the immersion in the River Jordan. As mentioned above, water symbolizes the astral-emotional plane, and thus the immersion in these waters symbolizes the immersion in and trials of the astral-emotional plane, and the purification thereby. This process removes the crystallized forms (glamours) from the emotional body, leaving it a clean, clear pool of astral force, ready to respond to the focused will of the Soul. When this initiation is complete, the transformed astral-emotional body is an instrument of the self or Soul.

In this stage, the astral-emotional bodies of the Divine Daughter and Divine Son merge and unify, effectively becoming a single body.

During this stage, one is inspired by a vision of truth which one seeks to follow.

3. The Temptation on the Mount: In terms of center or chakra development, this represents the motion of the incarnate consciousness into the ajna center.

In this stage, the mental bodies of the Divine Daughter and Divine Son merge and unify, becoming a single body.

During this stage, one begins to embody the vision of truth and becomes a source of inspiration to others. One is inspiring.

4. The Crucifixion: In terms of center or chakra development, this represents the development of the cave center, the place of magic.

In this stage, the Divine Daughter and Divine Son merge and unify, becoming again a single identity. If and when they incarnate again, it will be in one persona, with a single mental, astral, and physical-etheric body.

At this stage, one completes the embodiment of truth and becomes a source of inspiration to groups.

5.   The Resurrection and Ascension: This stage so completely transcends the human level of growth and development that very little can be said about it.

At this stage, one achieves union with the Father–Mother, break the Wheel of Rebirth, and ascend to at-one-ment with the One Life.

Addendum to Lesson 13

The Magic of Consciousness

As outlined earlier, the creative process is a cycle with two basic stages, the downward movement of the One as it is differentiated into the Many, and the upward movement of the Many as it is re-united with the One. This grand creative cycle is reflected, in smaller scale, in every part or expression of the One Life, including humanity as a whole and every human being as an individual.

Humanity as a kingdom has reached a point in its growth where the majority of us are as differentiated or separate as we need to be, and are moving toward re-union with the greater life of which we are a part. This re-union is an ongoing process, a cycle within the greater cycle. However, in order to aid our understanding, we may divide it into a series of steps or stages:

Integrating the Persona

Before this step can begin, the three portions of the persona —the mental, astral/emotional, and physical-etheric bodies— must be built and reflected into the physical-dense world of affairs. The individualized Soul —having spent many incarnations living within and identified with each of these bodies— is now ready to begin unifying them into a single, coordinated instrument.

The process of persona integration begins when the three basic elements of the persona are all present and functioning, but before they are all complete. One could say that the process of integration completes the construction process.

Prior to persona integration, the three portions of the instrument function separately, and often at cross-purposes to each other and to themselves. For instance, the mind may will to do one thing, while the emotions desire something else, and the emotions may themselves desire two or more contradictory things. This internal conflict divides the person's economy (their mental energy, astral force, and physical-etheric substance), debilitating and weakening them.

Eventually, the conflict between the divided portions of the persona becomes so acute that they must be pacified. This proceeds through three basic stages:

- First, the fully-developed emotions dominate the budding intellect. The person rationalizes, but does not truly "think." This produces irrational behavior or thoughtless actions whose consequences eventually force the person to learn the error of this way.

- As the intellect develops further, it learns to suppress and dominate the emotions. However, while the individual is then able to use their concrete rational mind to process thought, they are unable to relate with the world around them, for perceiving horizontal relationships is a function of the suppressed emotions. This inability to relate produces mis-relationships, which gradually strengthen until they become so powerful that they force the person to learn how to relate with others.

- Thus, the person begins to integrate or unify their mental, emotional, and physical-etheric bodies into a single, coherent instrument in order to escape pain. The conflict between the various portions of the persona drive them to it.

At some point in this process, usually during the later stage, the consciousness or self in the persona becomes aware of the process (dimly at first, but with growing vision) and begins to actively cooperate with that process. The self then begins a conscious program of self-improvement, aimed at developing and improving their mind, emotions, and body, in aspiration to some dimly perceived goal.

When they persona reaches a sufficient degree of functionality and integration (the bodies are fully developed and capable of working together) the person is ready to contact their Higher Self or Overshadowing Spiritual Soul.

Integrating the Soul

Contacting the Spiritual Soul is the first step in another cycle of at-one-ment. The process of developing the persona has, by this time, made the self that had identified with and as that persona aware that it is not that persona. How could it be when, despite all the changes which the self has gone through, which the self brought about by its actions, the self "yet remains"?

Thus, the self becomes aware that it is a self that dwells within a persona but is not that persona. At this point, the process of persona improvement is transformed into a one of self-discovery as it attempts to become aware of what the self is.

At this point, one eventually discovers that the persona (body, emotions, and mind) can be used by the incarnate self to contact the Higher Self or Spiritual Soul. This contact is achieved via an internal ritual technique sometimes called the Ascent.

Ascent

In the Ascent process, the incarnate self uses the integrated persona to raise the frequency of its awareness up to that of the Spiritual Soul. This is accomplished in three basic steps:

- Identify as the incarnate self, and relax the physical-dense and physical-etheric bodies
- Calm and clarifying the astral-emotional body, and aspire to the Spiritual Soul
- Focus the mind on the idea of the Spiritual Soul

Remain quiet and attentive, receptive to any impression that may occur.

For best results, this technique must be practiced at least once a day, every day, from New Moon to Full Moon, during every lunar cycle.

The Ascent Technique is actually the first half of a magical process that, via contact with, receptivity to, and manifestation of the Soul, eventually brings about the union or at-one-ment of the Soul.

Descent

The second half the technique of Self integration is practiced (or, more properly emphasized, as all four stages of the technique are included in each performance) from Full Moon to New Moon, during every lunar cycle. This half is sometimes called the Descent or Manifestation technique.

During the Descent, one remains focused on the Idea of Truth contacted during the height of the Ascent, when one at-oned with the Soul. Then:

- Lower the frequency of your awareness to the mind, and silently sound the note of that idea within the mental plane. The mental body then attracts resonant mental energy and formulates it into a thought-form,
- Lower the frequency of your awareness to the astral, and silently sound the note of the idea within the astral plane. The astral body attracts the astral force that motivates the thought-forms,
- Lower the frequency of your awareness to the physical-etheric, and silently sound the note of the idea within the physical-etheric plane, and release the astral force, which then drives the thought-form into appearance in physical-etheric substance, and
- Reflect the physical-etheric form into the physical-dense world of affairs.

Thus, the individual's entire economy is united in a single, cycle of creation.

The Complete Meditation Cycle

The complete internal ritual can be briefly outlined as follows:

Ascent (relaxing the physical body, calming the emotions, and focusing the mind on the Idea of the Soul), from New Moon to Full Moon. This is the Divine Daughter, relating the lower to the higher.

First Interlude (emphasis on at-one-ing with and receptivity to the Idea of Truth radiated by the Soul), during the three days of the Full Moon. This is the marriage or union of the Daughter with the Father.

Descent (translating the Idea of Truth into mental energy, appropriating astral force, and projecting the mental energy into appearance as a physical-etheric form), from Full Moon to New Moon. This is the Divine Son, relating the higher to the lower.

Second Interlude (emphasis on projecting the physical-etheric appearance into the physical-dense world of affairs) during the three days of the New Moon. This is the marriage or union of the Son with the Mother.

Via the regular practice of this ritual technique, from day to day, moon to moon, and year to year, the incarnate self is gradually raised toward union with the Higher Self, while the Higher Self is reflected into the lower, until the Two become One. At that point, the united self becomes a Spiritual Soul Incarnate, a spiritual being who dwells in the world, and yet is aware and acts as her/his Self or Soul.

However, one can only go so far in this process on one's own. At some point in the practice of this technique, one discovers or becomes aware of the horizontal polarity of the Soul, the Divine Daughter and the Divine Son. One then realizes that in order to complete the process of at-one-ing the Soul, one must re-unite the Daughter and the Son within one's Self.

Re-uniting the Twin Soul

As mentioned above, in order to incarnate, the Spiritual Soul must (as do its divine parents) work through a positive and negative polarity. In this case, that polarity is the polarity of the self or Soul, the Divine Child born of the relationship between the Divine Mother and Father.

Thus, every Soul in incarnation, in order to be in incarnation, has two poles —a negative and a positive, or a Divine Daughter and a Divine Son. These poles will be in incarnation simultaneously, with mental, astral, physical-etheric, and physical-dense bodies that are polar reflections of each other. That is, each will have the same mental thought-forms, astral force, and physical-etheric substance as the other, but embodied in an instrument of the opposite polarity. In the physical-dense world of affairs, this polarity takes the form of two people with nearly identical personal characteristics, but opposite genders. A woman and a man with One Soul.

A great deal has been written about ideal relationships in which a couple are or become one soul (often called "Soul Mates"). Most such writings are written from a persona perspective, and thus have little if any relationship to our current discussion. Please keep this in mind as we proceed, for, as we shall see, all persona-based assumptions must be abandoned if one is to actually discover and unite with one's Self.

There is insufficient space here to cover the subject of Soul Mates in detail, but we can explore the basics, beginning with the purpose of the Re-union of the Soul.

Again, it is humanity's purpose to bring about the re-union of the Divine Parents. Re-uniting the Polarity of our Soul is a part of that process. It is really quite simple:

- The Positive Pole of the Soul, or Divine Son, relates the Purpose, Power, and Will of the Father to the Divine Mother.
- The Negative Pole of the Soul, or Divine Daughter, relates the Intelligent Activity of the Mother to the Divine Father.

The "Laws of Electromagnetics" are just as applicable (as an analogy) to the polarity of the Soul as they are to that of Divinity. Thus, if you have one pole you must have two poles, for one pole cannot exist without the other. The two poles must be equal in strength, and the strength of the two poles is determined by their *nearness to each other*.

In other words, so long as the Daughter and Son are apart, they do not have the strength, the magnetic energy and force, to bring together the Divine Mother and Father! In order to help re-unite the Two Poles of Divinity, one must first unify the two poles of one's Self.

Thus, in order to help re-unify the Divine Parents, you have to find and at-one with your Soul Mate.

Please keep in mind that this does not mean or imply an ideal romantic relationship. Quite the contrary, for before one can recognize and at-one with one's Soul Mate, one must:

- Relax the physical body, removing those crystallized physical-etheric forms which hold the self trapped within the etheric body (including the appetite for physical sensation for pleasure's sake).

If one does not transform those appetites, then they will influence, even control, the type of person you look for and see. Suppose, for instance, that the physical-instrument of one's Soul Mate is not "appetizing" according to the forms programmed into your physical-dense brain and physical-etheric body by our modern culture. You would overlook them because their body was "unappealing".

If you have some doubts about this, then please consider the physical body in which you presently find yourself. Are there features that you find "unappetizing"? Because of the polar relationship between you and your Soul Mate, their body may well have equally "unappetizing" features.

- Calm the emotions, removing those crystallized astral forms which hold the self trapped within the astral body, including desires (such as that for an ideal mate).

If one does not transform those desires, then they will influence, even control, the type of person you attract and to whom you are attracted. Suppose, for instance, that the emotions of one's Soul Mate are not "attractive" according to the ideal programmed into your astral-emotional body. You could be repelled by your Soul Mate because you found their emotions "unattractive".

Do you have any feelings, desires, ambitions, or other emotional patterns that you find "unattractive"? Because of the polar relationship between you and your Soul Mate, their astral-emotional body may well include the same "unattractive" feelings.

- Focus the mind, removing those crystallized thought-forms which hold the self trapped within the mental body (including the thought-form of an ideal mate).

If one does not transform those thought-forms, then they will influence, even control, your idea of what a Soul Mate is. Any preconceived thought-form of who your Soul Mate is, what or how they should think, feel, or act, will inevitably be wrong. Thus, that thought-form of your "Soul Mate" will interfere with your ability to recognize them.

Do you have any thoughts, or habits of thinking that you find distasteful? Because of the polar relationship between you and your Soul Mate, their astral-emotional body may well include the same distasteful thoughts and habits.

Do you like everything about your persona? Of course not!

Do you have features, feelings, thoughts that you dislike? Of course you do! None of us is Perfect, and we know that. Due to the polar relationship between us, the fact that we and our Soul Mate are One Soul incarnate in two personas, all of the characteristics that we dislike in our persona will be present in our Soul Mate's persona!

Thus, before one can find and at-one with one's Soul Mate, one has to, in effect, free one's self from the appetite, desire, and thought for a Soul Mate.

We do not mean to suggest by this that romantic relationships have no role in the path, for they do. The female-male relationships that precede Soul Re-union are a necessary precursor to that union, for they are a means by which the female-male polarity learns how to relate. Thus, they are the foundation for that which comes later.

However, having learned the basics of inter-personal relationships, and then removed the persona blocks that stand in the way of recognizing one's Soul Mate, one is still not capable of Re-uniting the Soul. One step yet remains.

- At-one with the Overshadowing Spiritual Soul.

Since your Soul Mate is you, your self or Soul incarnate in another person, in order to find and recognize your Soul Mate you must first find and know your Higher Self or Spiritual Soul. This is accomplished through regular practice of the ritual of Union with the Soul. Having achieved that union to some degree (at least while practicing the ritual itself), one then sounds an inner call to one's Self, and await the appearance of one's Self.

The true Soul Mate will appear when and only when you, "both" of you, are ready to begin the next step in the process of at-one-ment, the Re-union of the Soul Polarity.

Once Soul Mates find each other they *may* begin to practice the rite of union which, in ancient times was sometimes known as the Hieros Gamos, the ritual union of the Two Poles of Divinity. At this point in their development, it will be for the union of their Soul, via its instrument of incarnation (their mental, astral, physical-etheric, and physical-dense bodies).

This rite should never be practiced for pleasure or for personal power. Performing the rite for either reason is very, very dangerous. In fact, the whole practice is so open to abuse that we hesitate to provide a complete outline here, as there is insufficient room for the necessary instructions and precautions.[1]

We will say that the ancient practices hinted at by historical and anthropological references to the Hieros Gamos are incomplete and inaccurate reflections of the actual rite. In order for the rite to be effective, the partners must first realize union or at-one-ment within themselves. Otherwise, they cannot help bring it about within the Divine. For instance:

- If the couple achieves physical union only, then they will only be able to unify the will and substance of the physical-dense and physical-etheric planes.
- If the couple achieves astral union, then they will be able to unify the will and substance of the astral plane.
- If the couple achieves mental union, then they will be able to unify the will and substance of the mental plane.
- If the couple achieves union of their physical, astral, and mental, and ascends to at-one-ment with their Spiritual Soul, then they have achieved Re-union of the Soul, and will be able to reflect that union down into the mental, astral, physical-etheric and physical-dense world of affairs. At that point, and only at that point, is the re-united Soul ready to help re-unite the Divine Mother and Father.

The Re-union of Spirit and Substance

At some point in the process of the Re-union of the Soul, one moves the emphasis or focus of intent from Re-union of one's Soul to Re-union of that greater life of which the Soul is a part. This period of transition is quite lengthy and includes a number of stages within it (which we will examine in the next chapter).

---

[1] Quinn: I may, if conditions demand it, write a complete, detailed description of the process of Re-uniting the Soul Polarity.

However, it is this stage or level of at-one-ment, the Re-union of Spirit and Substance, or the Divine Father and Mother, that is specifically symbolized in the Kaballistic Myth of the Matronit. That Myth not only presents the idea that the Two Poles of Divinity have been split, but that it is humanity's task to re-unite them. But how, then, do we do that?

As we have seen, the overall path of re-union includes:

- Persona development and integration (the positive and negative poles of the persona or form of an incarnate human being are developed and integrated into a single unified instrument)
- Mate Relationships (the positive and negative poles, as manifest in two individuals, are integrated and unified into a single instrument)
- At-one-ment with the Spiritual Soul (the positive and negative poles of the Soul, the Overshadowing Spiritual Soul and the incarnate self, are integrated and unified into a single identity or Spiritual Soul Incarnate)
- Re-uniting the Soul Polarity (the horizontal poles of the Soul, the Divine Daughter and the Divine Son, are integrated and unified into a single identity or Soul Mate)

Each of the above has a single factor in common. They are the result of that motion of consciousness which produces an expanded identity. In other words, that inner ritual process which expands and integrates the persona and Soul is the Magic of Consciousness.

This type of magic does not depend on ritual words, gestures, furniture, or furnishings, but on the magical motion of the Soul, the movement of "I"dentity. As such, it is effective on every level of being on, in, and with which one can identify. For instance:

- When one is identified with and as one's persona, one is limited, in the creative ritual, by the inability of the identity to move beyond the persona with which it is identified. One can ascend to the height of one's mind, and descend to the physical-dense brain, but cannot move beyond the limits of the persona identity.

However, there is actually no such thing as "your" Soul, "his" Soul, "her" Soul, or "my" Soul. It is all One Soul, the magnetic field of the One Life, a portion of the Divine Daughter–Son that has projected itself into incarnation and identified as an individual being. As such, you have the capacity. The entire direction of your evolution as a Soul (having achieved individual awareness) is back up, in broader and broader spiralic motions, into ever wider states of identity. And it is as one moves into a higher point on the spiral, and broader awareness of self or identity, that one gains the ability to work the Magic of Consciousness on that level.

- Thus, when one is identified with and as the Soul, one is able to ascend to the Overshadowing Spiritual Soul, at-one with it, descend through the mind, emotions, and etheric to the physical-dense, relate the Positive-Pole Soul to the Negative Pole Substance, and then ascend again.

However, at this stage of growth the "high point" of one's identity or motion is the Daughter–Son or Soul. It may function as the "positive pole" in this working, but that is only because of the limited motion of one's identity. The use of the True Positive Pole waits yet another expansion of the identity.

That next step is the recognition of and identification with the Spirit, that fragment of the Divine Father which overshadows, and can be contacted by, the Spiritual Soul.

Identification as and union with the Spirit can only be achieved by the Spiritual Soul that has re-united with its incarnate self and with its polarities (the Daughter–Son). Having achieved such contact, the Son can then relate the Purpose, Power, and Will of the Father to the Mother, while the Daughter relates the Intelligent Activity of the Mother to the Father, slowly re-uniting the Two Aspects of Divinity.

This is, of course, only a bare outline of the process. A more detailed explanation will have to await *The Magic of Consciousness* series.

Addendum to Lesson 14

The Temple of Solomon

The Temple was located on the crest of Mount Moriah, a hill neighboring Jerusalem, the City of David.[1] A wall with three gates (to the west, east, and south) surrounded the Temple.[2] Inside the wall was a broad courtyard. The Temple sat in the north side of the courtyard, and faced the south gate. Two large ritual objects sat in the courtyard, in front of the Temple. The object slightly to the west was the Brazen Sea,[3] a very large ritual bowl. The one slightly to the east was the sacrificial altar, also of brass. Surrounding the temple itself were a number of raised metal bowls, which the priests used for cleansing sacrifices and themselves.

The Temple floor was raised above the level of the courtyard, and twelve steps led up to its porch or entrance (sometimes called the outer chamber). To either side of the entrance sat a large brazen pillar. Inside, in the middle chamber, a winding stair led to the upper rooms. Ahead, a doorway led to the inner chamber, the Holy of Holies where the Ark of the Covenant was kept.

---

[1] Quinn: 2 Chronicles 3:1 "Then Solomon began to build the house of the LORD in Jerusalem on Mount Mori'ah, where the LORD had appeared to David his father, at the place that David had appointed, on the threshing floor of Ornan the Jeb'usite"

[2] Quinn: There is disagreement about the orientation of the Temple and the location of the gates. The Temple Legend and the explanation above use the Biblical description (with the Temple in the north and the entrance facing south). This version has Hiram Abiff fleeing from the south gate to the west and then to the east, or clockwise. The meditations place the Temple in the east, and have the candidate walking toward the light of the rising sun.

[3] Quinn: Although "brass" is mentioned a number of times in the Old Testament, it is unlikely that it refers to the alloy of zinc and copper presently identified by that name, as zinc was not "discovered" until the late Middle Ages. It is likely that bronze or copper was meant.

The features that are important to us at this point include the location, gates, twelve steps, two columns, winding stair, three chambers, Ark of the Covenant, and the three Temples.

The Three Temples

A deep examination of the actions and penalties of the workers reveals that the Freemasonic degree system represents three overlapping stages of spiritual growth. Those stages are:

- Personal improvement
- Soul (the consciousness or true self)
- Spirit

The candidate to Freemasonic initiation may be passing through any of these stages of growth. Thus, their experience of the order's initiations will depend, in large part, on where they are. For instance, if they are focused in and identified as their persona instrument, then that focus will direct the effects of the initiations to that instrument. This produces what are, in effect, three very different layers of potential experience within and of a single system. One way of illustrating this is to suggest that there are three allegorical temples rather than one:

- If we approach the initiations as the persona (body, emotions, and mind) we see the Tabernacle. The three initiations then represent the spiritual progress of the persona, or body, emotions, and mind.
- If we approach as the Soul, we see the Temple of Solomon. The three initiations then represent the spiritual progress of the Soul.
- If we approach as the Spirit, we see the Temple of Ezekiel. The three initiations then represent the progress of the Spirit.

The Tabernacle

This represents the persona instrument, including the mental, astral, physical-etheric, and physical-dense bodies.[4]

---

[4] Quinn: The Tabernacle or Tent of Appointment was the original House of The Lord, built by the Hebrews during the forty years they wandered in the wilderness. Some scholars believe the Tent of Appointment was a

The allegorical Tent of Appointment was built along the same general design as the Temple of Solomon, but on a smaller scale and from impermanent materials.[5] Thus, the Tabernacle was a temporary house of God, used while the people wandered from place to place, lost in the wilderness and waiting for a generation to pass away.

This is a good allegory of the human condition: The Soul, incarnate in the world of form, is lost to its true identity and wanders aimlessly, bereft of its spiritual purpose or higher direction.

Possible predecessors of the Tabernacle include the tent of Sarah in the sacred terebinth grove in Mamre, and successors include the tent of Asherah (woven by the women in the Temple of Solomon). These sacred tents suggest a relationship between the Tabernacle and the Divine Mother or Substance.

Thus, we have an allegory of the human condition and a sacred enclosure that represents Substance. The Tabernacle represents the human form, the house or temple of the soul when it is incarnate in the world of appearances.

The Three Chambers

Represent the Three Aspects of Divinity, as expressed in the instruments of the incarnate soul (the persona), the Overshadowing Spiritual Soul, and the Spirit.

The Courtyard

The Tabernacle was surrounded by a courtyard, enclosed by a series of poles, supporting a fabric curtain or wall. This wall obscured the Tabernacle from view and was the face or mask it showed the world. This courtyard represented the physical-dense body of the human being, the body of matter that contains the other bodies and through which they find expression in the world of affairs.

---

separate structure, set aside for Moses, but for our purposes, they are symbolically identical. See: Exodus 25.1 - 27.19, 35.1 - 40.33

[5] Quinn: Most would put their architectural relationship the other way around, but for reasons which I will explain shortly, the preceding is correct.

The Entrance or Outer Chamber

The Outer Chamber of the Tabernacle was the entrance to the middle chamber. It was framed by two poles or pillars and faced the courtyard. The Outer Chamber represents the energy body, technically known as the physical-etheric. The physical-etheric body consists of substance that vibrates more rapidly than physical-dense, but less rapidly than the substance of the emotional body. The physical-etheric is shaped roughly like the physical-dense body, and although it interpenetrates the other bodies, it extends beyond the physical-dense body three or more inches.

The Middle Chamber

The Middle Chamber is the place where the priests of YHWH normally gathered to worship. It represents the emotional body, when that body is clear of polluting emotions and receptive to higher impression.

The Inner Chamber

The Inner Chamber or "Holy of Holies" was almost entirely empty. It contained the Ark of the Covenant —the sacred receptacle of the Ten Commandments— by means of which the High Priest communed with God.

The Inner Chamber represents the mental body, focused on and receptive to the Overshadowing Spiritual Soul. The mental body consists of substance that vibrates more rapidly than emotional substance, but less rapidly than the substance of the Soul Body.

This brings us to the furnishings of the Tabernacle, which include the Ark of the Covenant, and the two pillars at the porch or entrance.

The Two Pillars

These are a symbolic remnant from the Age of Gemini (approx. 6900 BC - 4700 BC). As such, they represent the Sacred Twins—the Divine Son and Daughter, or the outward and downward, and inward and upward motions of Divinity.

These Twin Attributes of the Second Aspect would, of course, be expressed somewhat differently depending on the degree of completion of a particular temple (Tabernacle, Temple of Solomon, or Temple of Ezekiel).

The Pillars

We have already discussed the twin columns, of fire and cloud, at the entrance of the tabernacle that represent Pingala and Ida, the nadis of the sun and the moon. Their higher correspondents in the Temple of Solomon are the twin pillars, Jachin and Boaz. They represent an equivalent system associated with the Light Body of the Soul. However, as part of the Light Body of the Soul, in the Temple of Solomon the pillars have a somewhat different meaning.

If Hiram Abiff represents the Soul, lost to awareness of self when it was born in form, then the Pillars at the Porch or Entrance represent the portal through which the Soul must pass, both in order to be born into the world (when exiting the temple) and in order to return to its Self (when returning to the temple after the long journey in the world). If this is the case, then the pillars must symbolize a mechanism by which the Soul both "dies" and is "reborn".

This mechanism is found in the *Antahkarana*, a Sanskrit term for the silver cord or rainbow bridge between the persona and soul.

The Antahkarana

In the Temple Legend, the Antahkarana is represented by the three rods or staffs in the inner chamber of the Temple. These rods include the two poles on either side of the Ark, and the Rod of Aaron kept inside the Ark.

The two carrying rods are normally used to move the state of consciousness, and the third rod is used to perform magic (or to impress intent on form). These three are related to the "principal supports" of freemasonry: Wisdom, Strength, and Beauty. They are also related to the spinal nadis, but are temporarily separate from them.

In most of humanity, the spinal nadis (Pingala, Ida, and Susumna) function separately from the Antahkarana. However, this is a temporary condition due to a break in the Antahkarana on the mental plane. This break is restored during the process of spiritual growth and development, and the three spinal nadis then merge with the Antahkarana.

This mental break separates the lower, concrete rational mind or intellect from the higher aspects of mind (including the Light Body of the Soul). In some systems this gap is referred to as the Antahkarana, while the portion of the silver cord above it is given another name. However, we will here refer to the entire length of the silver cord as the Antahkarana, and use other names for its various components.

The Antahkarana consists of three, intertwined "threads", which move downward from the Causal Body and are anchored at different points in the persona instrument.

The Life Thread or *sutratma*[6] is the nadi that transmits the life or Father Aspect from the Spirit, through the Soul to the persona instrument. Its upper end is anchored in the Temple of Ezekiel, and its lower end is anchored in the heart (in the sino-atrial node or pulse point). This makes the heart a seat of the One Life or Father Aspect.

The Life Thread connects to the heart during the fetal stage of development, setting the heart beating. At that point, the fetus has begun the process of becoming an independent living organism. When the Soul sounds the note of return, and withdraws the Life Thread, the heart stops beating and cannot be revived.

The Consciousness Thread is the nadi that transmits the Consciousness Aspect from the Soul to the persona instrument. Its upper end is connected to the Spiritual Soul, and its lower end is anchored in the middle of the brain, near the pituitary gland. This makes the brain the seat of consciousness or the Divine Daughter/Son.

The Consciousness Thread anchors over a period of time, completing the process around age two. Its anchoring produces the exploration of self sometimes known as "the terrible twos".

---

[6] Quinn: Various systems interchange the meanings of "Sutratma" and "Antahkarana", assigning one to the entire silver cord and the other to a portion of it. This is entirely arbitrary and neither usage is more correct than the other.

The Creativity Thread is the nadi that transmits the energy of the Substance Aspect from the persona instrument to the Soul. This makes the persona the seat of the Mother Aspect.

The Creativity Thread was misused during the decline of Atlantis, when human beings were natural magicians and created for selfish purposes. The resulting destruction was stopped by an emergency "overload" of humanity's Antahkarana. This overload broke the Antahkarana (producing the gap on the mental plane) and shattered the Creativity Thread.

The gap in the Antahkarana is functionally equivalent to cutting a phone line. The incarnate soul finds itself unable to communicate with its True Self, the overshadowing Spiritual Soul. Thus cut-off, the incarnate soul is unable to identify with its Self, and instead identifies with, and loses its identity in, its persona instrument. As it takes on the identity of the form, it also takes on the limits and rhythms of the form, including the cycles of birth, maturity, decline and death. Thus, the Soul "dies" as it incarnates in form.

This cycle of substance is seen in all forms, and was typically portrayed as the three-fold goddess (virgin, mother, and crone), or the three attributes of the Great Goddess, the Mother Aspect.

The form-identified Soul is trapped in the normal and natural motion of substance, also known as the "Wheel of Rebirth". The Soul remains trapped until it is "reborn".

The symbolic rebirth or resurrection occurs as the broken Antahkarana is rebuilt, restoring communication and enabling the incarnate Soul to merge with the Spiritual Soul and step off the Wheel of Rebirth. However, the rebuilt silver cord is not restored, it is not the same as it was before it was broken.

In Atlantean times, the Antahkarana was used, and misused, by humanity as a whole. It is now being rebuilt, and used, by individuals and groups. The Creativity Thread (Aaron's Rod) is rebuilt through a synthesis and extension of the remaining threads.

The first sub-thread of the Creativity Thread passes from the heart, through the spleen to the etheric body. It unites the physical-dense and the etheric bodies, and unites with the force from the will petals of the egoic lotus.

The second sub-thread of the Creativity Thread is built from the solar plexus to the heart, and then to the astral body. It unites the etheric and the astral bodies, connects with the energy of the first sub-thread, and unites it with the force of the love petals of the egoic lotus.

The third sub-thread flows from the ajna and head centers to the mental body, uniting the astral and mental vehicles, and unites the force of the will and love petals with that of the knowledge petals.

During Atlantean times, the Human Kingdom was creative, but individuals were not. However, as the Creativity Thread is rebuilt, those individuals and groups who accomplish it become themselves creative.

The Globes Atop the Pillars

Jachin and Boaz are frequently represented with globes at their very top, said to represent the heavens and the earth. This identification has led to dismissals of the globes as a recent addition, on the grounds that the ancients thought the earth was flat. However, the "flat earth" is a modern myth, produced in the nineteenth century in an effort to discredit religion. A careful study of the "flat earth" myth proves it to be baseless. Educated members of ancient and medieval society were well aware that the earth was round. Thus, it would have been entirely appropriate for the ancient mysteries to represent the earth with a globe.[7]

Building the Light Body

The Temple Legend portrays the death of the Soul in Form as the process of building the Light Body of the Soul. When the Temple is nearly complete, the forces of matter attack the consciousness, in an attempt to retain the consciousness and its power. The Soul enters the final struggle, and (when it succeeds) is reborn as its true self.

The Pillars represent part of the mechanism of this rebirth,

---

[7] See: *Inventing the Flat Earth*, by Jeffrey Burton Russell, Greenwood Publishing Group, 1997

but there are other parts.

The Builders

The "builders" are the workers who construct the Temple. These workers are usually presumed to be human beings, either Judeans or citizens of Tyre. However, since the Temple constructed "without the sound of tools" is the House of the Soul, the builders cannot be human.

As explained above, building a form on any of the planes involves gathering and shaping the substance of that plane. In order to gather and shape the substance of a plane, one needs a body made of the material of that plane. An incarnate human being is a Soul that has and is dwelling in a persona (consisting of mental, emotional, physical-etheric, and physical-dense bodies). Gathering and shaping the substance of those bodies is not the task of either the Soul (which acts as the supervisor of the work) or of the Spirit (the architect who provides the plan for the work).

If the builders are neither Soul nor Spirit, but must have bodies of substance, what is left? At this point we return to the simple analogy of the bar magnet. If the Spirit is the positive pole, and the Soul is the magnetic field, what is left is the negative pole or Substance itself. Thus, the builders are intelligent beings of substance.

But what are these beings of substance?

They appear in a variety of spiritual traditions under a number of different terms, including: cherubim, devas (a Sanskrit term meaning "being of light"), angels, and builders. These various traditions examine these beings from different perspectives.

- Cherubim were guardian spirits, throughout ancient Canaan and Mesopotamia. Depicted as winged sphinxes, they kept watch over city gates as well as sacred sites. In the Temple, they were the cloud that carried YHWH, the creatures that drew his chariot, or the glory through which he appeared.
- Devas are (in popular modern terminology) intelligent beings of physical-etheric, astral/emotional, or mental substance.

- Angels are intermediaries or messengers between YHWH and man.
- Builders are intelligent non-human workers who, in response to the plan of the Master Mason, create the form and structure of the Temple.

While all of the above are correct, none of them is a complete description of these beings of substance. Having already examined the nature of the Temple, we can discover a great deal about the builders by looking at the characteristics necessary to those beings that build those structures. The first such characteristic is the division of the workers into builders of impermanent and permanent structures.

Builders of Impermanent Forms

The Temporary House of the Soul or Tabernacle is the Temple in which the Soul or self resides during incarnation in the three lower worlds. The builders of the Tabernacle construct the "impermanent" forms of the mental, astral, physical-etheric, and physical-dense bodies. These builders are symbolically portrayed in the legend by workers in impermanent materials. Those workers include:

- The Herdsmen: These workers nurture and gather the substance from which the fabric of the Tabernacle is built.
- The Weavers: These craftswomen clean, card, spin, dye, and weave the gathered substance into the fabric of the Tabernacle.
- The Woodsmen: These workers nurture and gather the substance from which the supporting frame of the Tabernacle is built.
- The Carpenters: These craftsmen hew, join, and finish the supporting frame and wooden furnishings of the Tabernacle.

Thus, the builders of the Tabernacle can be divided into those who:

- Gather the substance, and
- Shape the substance.

of the structure and form of the temporary house or three-fold persona.

Builders of Permanent Forms

The Temple of Solomon is the Permanent House of the Soul in which the Soul or self resides. The builders of the Temple construct the "permanent" forms (ideas or archetypes) of the Buddhic Plane. These builders are symbolically portrayed in the legend by workers in permanent materials. Builders include:

- The Quarrymen: These relatively unskilled workers gather the substance from which the fabric of the Temple is built.
- The Stone Masons: These skilled craftsmen shape and smooth the gathered substance, and place it into the fabric of the Temple.
- The Miners: These workers gather the substance from which the tools of the work are built.
- The Smiths: These skilled craftsmen fire, cast, and pound the gathered substance into the tools of the Great Work.

Thus, the builders of the Temple can also be divided into those who:

- Gather the substance, and
- Shape the substance.

of the structure and form of the permanent house or light body of the Soul.

Gathering and shaping the substance of the temples is the task of those intelligent beings of substance who in their myriads constitute the body of the Great Mother, the Queen of Heaven.

These beings of substance respond to the intent conveyed to them by the supervisor, by gathering and shaping substance into forms. Each builder works in their own place, on their own plane, in accordance with their position and function in the greater life of which they are a part.

Together they constitute the Hosts of Heaven. However, while those Hosts have been generically referred to as "angels" that is not really a proper term in this case. In the Bible, the world "angel" refers to those beings of substance who act as intermediaries between God and humanity. In modern mythology, these messengers are often portrayed as deceased humans, but this is not correct.

These beings of pure substance are not and never were human. Where a human being is an evolving consciousness, the devas or builders are a parallel evolution of substance. Unlike saints, they do not *have* halos. They actually *are* the halo or body of light. These bodies of light do not have edges or surfaces, and thus have no humanoid or other shape.

There are a number of levels to this evolution, and a variety of types or functions within it. They may be thought of as cells in the body of the Great Mother, each having its place in the whole and together constituting the substance of the One Life.

Those commonly called "angels" are messengers between the Divine and humanity, and might be thought of as the nervous system of the Divine Mother.

Those portrayed as "builders" are the creative intelligences who construct the shape and form of everything that exists.

The building process generally proceeds as follows:

- The Architect presents the Plan to the Supervisor of the Work.
- The Supervisor of the Work conveys that Plan to the appropriate Builders of Permanent Structures.
- The Builders of Permanent Structures gather the appropriate buddhic substance, and shape it into an idea or archetype.
- The Supervisor or Soul then conveys the idea to the appropriate builders of the mental plane.
- The builders of the mental plane gather the appropriate mental substance, shape it into a thought-form, and organize that thought-form into a plan of action.
- The Supervisor then instructs the builders of the astral plane to gather the appropriate astral/emotional energy, and hold it in readiness.
- The Supervisor conveys the plan of action to the appropriate builders of the physical-etheric plane.
- The builders of the physical-etheric plane gather the appropriate physical-etheric substance and shape it into a physical-etheric form.

- The Supervisor then focuses the astral/emotional energy on the physical-etheric form, and releases it. The resulting torrent of force drives the physical-etheric form downward into appearance in the physical-dense world of affairs.

This is a basic outline of the process by which all forms are created. At each step: the Architect provides the plan, the Supervisor conveys the plan to the builders, and the builders give shape and form to the plan.

Thus, the builders are the substance which, by its intelligent activity, creates all form.

What is the Lost Word?

The identity of the "Lost Word" is one of the great mysteries of Freemasonry. Initiates of the highest Freemasonic degree are sworn to search for it, in the understanding that the mysteries cannot be fully restored until the Lost Word is found. But what is the Lost Word?

As mentioned in an earlier lesson, there are four basic elements:

- Esoteric Sound or Air
- Esoteric Color or Fire
- Esoteric Vibration or Water
- Esoteric Light or Earth

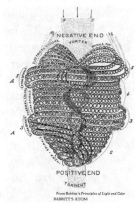

NEGATIVE END

POSITIVE END

From Babbitt's *Principles of Light and Color*
BABBITT'S ATOM

Esoteric Sound includes three primal motions. In *Babbitt's Atom* these are depicted as:

- The Straight Line (between the "Vortex" and the "Torrent")
- The Spiral
- Rotation—of the 'Atom' on its axis

Each of these three primal motions is also associated with one of the Three Aspects of Divinity:

- Spirit —Divine Will— moves in a straight line.
- Consciousness moves in a spiral.
- Substance moves in a circle.

One of these three primal motions predominates in each of the three elements:

- Straight motion predominates in Esoteric Color.
- Spiral motion predominates in Esoteric Vibration.
- Circular Motion predominates in Esoteric Light.

Each of these three primal motions or elements also predominates on one of the three lower worlds:

- Esoteric Color or Fire predominates on the mental plane.
- Esoteric Vibration or Water predominates on the astral/emotional plane.
- Esoteric Light or Earth predominates on the physical-etheric plane.

Esoteric Sound or Air predominates on the buddhic plane (the realm of the Soul, above the mental plane).

When we put all this together, it strongly suggests that the Word really did come first:

- The Three Aspects of Divinity emanate from the One God who spoke the First Word.
- Color, Vibration, and Light flow out of Sound (just as all the visible colors grow out of white light).

At this point, we have stretched the Father – Mother – Child analogy about as far as we can. It is time to return to the symbol of the magnet, and recognize that all three aspects exist simultaneously, in balanced relationship.

There is, in actuality, only one creative Divine Word. The appearance of a different word, motion, or element for each Aspect is a product of our perception or perspective. It would be more correct to say:

- The One Word has attributes of all Three Aspects within it, and at different points in its sounding different Aspects appear to predominate.
- Esoteric Sound has the attributes of all four elements within it, and on different planes, different elements or motions predominate.

So long as we are living in and identified with our persona (mind, emotions, or body), we are subject to Substance, including both its rotary motion and its differentiation of intent into forms. The results include a tendency to perceive differences rather than relationships.

The Magic of Consciousness

The Two Kings

Before the builders can create a new form, they must receive a new intent or purpose. That purpose originates in King Solomon, the Father Aspect of Divinity. Thus, the creative process consists of:

- Purpose or Intent, formulated by King Solomon.
- Intelligent Activity or form, provided by King Hiram.
- The coordinated relationship of Intent and Activity, provided by Hiram Abiff.

The work of King Solomon has no direct relationship to our experience in the three lower worlds. His intent or commands exist so far above the life and affairs of the lesser builders that neither they nor we can even perceive it (so long as we are identified as the persona). Thus, Grand Master Hiram Abiff, who can know Solomon's Purpose, interprets that Intent into Thought and organizes that thought on the tracing board in the Temple. With Purpose translated into a plan of action (at a level and in a manner in which they can recognize it), the builders respond with intelligent activity.

This creative process works only so long as all Three Aspects are able to carry out their proper function. In order to function properly:

- King Solomon and King Hiram must be equals. Since they are two poles of a One Life, lessening one automatically lessens the other.
- Hiram Abiff must relate—the Divine Purpose of King Solomon to the builders of King Hiram, and the Intelligent Activity of the builders back up to King Solomon.

If King Solomon and King Hiram are out of balance, then neither will be able to express themselves properly.

The Father Aspect either:

- Disappears from sight,
- Fragments into multiple expressions,
- or is weakened into a lesser being such as a minor deity, king, prince, or lord.

The Mother Aspect either:
- Disappears from sight,
- Fragments into multiple expressions,
- or is weakened into a lesser being such as a queen, princess, or lady.

If Hiram Abiff is unable to properly relate the Father and Mother Aspects, then:
- The Father Aspect may be overemphasized, producing a strong, selfish Father and a weak submissive Mother.
- The Mother Aspect may be overemphasized, producing a strong manipulative Mother and a weak subservient Father.

In any of the above, the resulting expressions of the Three Aspects will be immature, and limited to the persona (mind, emotions, and body).

Bibliography

The following works were among the many resources used in writing *Raising the Queen of Heaven*.

Adam, Eve, and the Serpent, Elaine Pagels, Vintage Books, New York, 1989

A Dictionary of Angels, Including the Fallen Angels, by Gustav Davidson, The Free Press, New York, 1967

A Dictionary of Egyptian Gods And Goddesses, by George Hart, Routledge, NY, 1986 (2000 edition)

Applied Wisdom, by Lucille Cedercrans, Wisdom Impressions Publishers, Whittier, CA, (2005)

A Treatise On Cosmic Fire, Alice A. Bailey, Lucis Publishing Company, New York, 1925

Alone Of All Her Sex, The Myth And Cult Of The Virgin Mary, by Marina Warner, Vintage Books, 1983

Becoming Osiris, The Ancient Egyptian Death Experience, by Ruth Schumann Antelme & Stephane Rossini, Inner Traditions International, Rochester, Vermont, 1998

Bible Unearthed, The, by Israel Finkelstein and Neil Asher Silberman, The Free Press, NY, 2001

Blessed Virgin Mary, Her Life And Mission, by Corinne Heline, New Age Bible and Philosophy Center, Santa Monica, CA 1971

Body Of Light, The, by John Mann and Lar Short, Globe Press Books, New York, 1990

Causal Body and the Ego, The, Arthur E. Powell, Stellar Books, Manila, Philippines, 1928 (1992 edition)

Chakras And The Human Energy Fields, The, Shafica Karagulla, M.D., and Dora van Gelder Kunz, Quest Books – The Theosophical Publishing House, Wheaton, IL, 1989

Chakras, The, by C. W. Leadbeater, Quest Books – The Theosophical Publishing House, Wheaton, IL, 1927

Chalice & The Blade, The, by Riane Eisler, Harper & Row, San Francisco, CA, 1987

Clairvoyant Investigations, by Geoffrey Hodson, Quest – The Theosophical Publishing House, Wheaton, IL, 1984

Creative Thinking, by Lucille Cedercrans, Wisdom Impressions Publishers, Whittier, CA, 2001

Dictionary of All Scriptures And Myths, by G.A. Gaskell, The Julian Press, New York, 1960

Dictionary of Classical Mythology, by J. E. Zimmerman, Bantam Books, New York, 1964 (1971 edition)

Dictionary of Classical Mythology, The, by Pierre Grimal, Blackwell Publishers, Malden, Mass, 1986

Disciple and Economy, The, by Lucille Cedercrans, Wisdom Impressions Publishers, Whittier, CA, 2002

Drawing Down the Moon, Margot Adler, The Viking Press, New York, 1979

Epic of Gilgamesh, A New Translation, Andrew George, Penguin Books, New York, 1999

Etheric Double, The, by A. E. Powell, Quest Books – The Theosophical Publishing House, Wheaton, IL, 1969

From Bethlehem to Calvary, by Alice A. Bailey, Lucis Publishing Company, New York, 1937 (1974 edition)

Goddesses & Heroines, by Patricia Monaghan, Llewellyn Publications, St. Paul, MN, 2000

Gods, Demons And Symbols Of Ancient Mesopotamia, An Illustrated Dictionary, by Jeremy Black and Anthony Green, University of Texas Press, Austin, TX, 1992

Golden Bough, The, by Sir James George Frazer, The MacMillan Company, 1922 (1942 edition)

Gospel of Mary Magdalene, The, by Jean-Yves Leloup, Inner Traditions, Rochester, VT, 2002

Harlot by the Side of the Road, The, Forbidden Tales of the Bible, Jonathan Kirsch, Ballantine, New York, 1997

Hebrew Goddess, The, Third Enlarged Edition, by Raphael Patai, Wayne State University Press, Detroit, Michigan, 1990

Hero With A Thousand Faces, The, by Joseph Campbell, Princeton University Press, Princeton, NJ, 1949 (1973 edition)

Hiram Key, The, by Christopher Knight & Robert Lomas, Element Books, Rockport, MA, 1997

Homeric Hymn to Demeter, The, Helene P. Foley, Ed., Princeton University Press, Princeton, NJ, 1994

Inanna, Lady of Largest Heart, by Betty De Shong Meador, University of Texas Press, Austin, TX, 2000

Bibliography

Interpreter's Bible, The, A Commentary in Twelve Volumes, Abingdon Press, Nashville, TN

Isis In The Ancient World, by R. E. Witt, The Johns Hopkins University Press, Boston, MA, 1971

Mary Magdalene, Beyond the Myth, by Esther de Boer, Trinity Press International, Harrisburg, PA, 1996

Moses, From the Mysteries of Egypt to the Judges of Israel, by Emil Bock, Inner Traditions International, Ltd., Rochester, VT., 1986

Mysteries of Isis, The, Her Worship and Magick, by DeTraci Regula, Llewellyn Publications, St. Paul, Minnesota, 1999

Nature Of The Soul, The, by Lucille Cedercrans, Wisdom Impressions Publishers, Whittier, CA, 1993

New Book of Goddesses and Heroines, The, by Patricia Monaghan, Llewellyn Publications, Chicago, 2000

Number Words and Number Symbols, A Cultural History of Numbers, by Karl Menninger, Dover Publications, NY, 1992

Orpheus and Greek Religion, W.K.C. Guthrie, Princeton University Press, Princeton, NJ, 1952 (1993 edition)

Rosicrucian Cosmo-Conception, The, by Max Heindel, The Rosicrucian Fellowship, Oceanside California, 1977 edition

Sarah The Priestess, The First Matriarch Of Genesis, by Savina J. Teubal, Ohio University Press, Athens, Ohio, 1984

Schocken Bible, Volume 1, The Five Books of Moses, by Everett Fox, Schocken Books, 1983

Sirius, M. Temple Richmond, Source Publications, Mariposa, CA, 1997

Sirius Mystery, The, by Robert Temple, Destiny Books, Rochester, Vermont, 1998

Song Of Songs, by Ariel Bloch and Chana Bloch, University of California Press, Berkeley, CA, 1998

Sumerian Mythology, A Study of Spiritual and Literary Achievement in the Third Millennium B.C., Samuel Noah Kramer, University of Pennsylvania Press, Philadelphia, 1961

Theories Of The Chakras: Bridge to Higher Consciousness, by Hiroshi Motoyama, Quest Books – The Theosophical Publishing House, Wheaton, IL, 1981

Thought-Forms, by Annie Besant & C.W. Leadbeater, Quest Books – The Theosophical Publishing House, Wheaton, IL, 1925

White Goddess, The, by Robert Graves, Farrar, Straus, and Giroux, New York, 1948 (1980 edition)

Woman's Encyclopedia Of Myths And Secrets, by Barbara G. Walker, Harper and Row, San Francisco, 1983

Zohar, The, Harry Sperling and Maurice Simon, Translators, The Soncino Press, New York, 1984

Zohar, The Book of Splendor, Basic Readings from the Kabbalah, Gershom Scholem, Editor, Schocken Books, New York, 1949